John Connor left his job as a barrister to write full time. During the fifteen years of his legal career, he prosecuted numerous homicide cases in West Yorkshire and London. He advised the police in numerous drugs cases and organised-crime operations, many involving covert activity. He now lives in Brussels with his family.

The Vanishing

John Connor

An Orion paperback

First published in Great Britain in 2013
by Orion Books
This paperback published in 2014
by Orion Books,
an imprint of The Orion Publishing Group Ltd,
Orion House, 5 Upper St Martin's Lane,
London WC2H 9EA

An Hachette UK company

1 3 5 7 9 10 8 6 4 2

A CIP catalogue record for this book
is available from the British Library.

ISBN 978-1-4091-3614-9

Typeset by Deltatype Ltd, Birkenhead, Merseyside

Printed and bound in Great Britain
by Clays Ltd, St Ives, plc

The Orion Publishing Group's policy is to use papers that
are natural, renewable and recyclable products and
made from wood grown in sustainable forests. The logging
and manufacturing processes are expected to conform to
the environmental regulations of the country of origin.

www.orionbooks.co.uk

For Anna, Tom and Sara.

With thanks to Lovisa

1

Ile des Singes Noirs, Seychelles, 1990

It was over now. From the room beyond the bolted double doors Arisha could hear Liz shrieking and wailing. She turned away in fright, biting her lip and wiping the tears that came to her eyes. She walked shakily through the cool, wood-lined passage with its rattling, antiquated air-conditioning unit, along to the gloomy, intricately carved staircase, then down to the hall and out. Through the open front doors and into the smothering heat. She needed time to think, but on the wide veranda the raw sunlight made her stagger. She leaned on the balustrade and took deep breaths of the insufferable, humid air, heavy with the stench of rotting fruit. There were parrots screeching from the treeline – or was it the monkeys, the filthy black monkeys that gave the place its name? She could still hear the screaming in the room above, so she put her hands over her ears and stared out towards the dock and the shimmering sea – a picture-postcard image of tropical paradise.

She hated it. She had hated it from the first day they had been forced to come here – it was too hot, too muggy, everything rotting and riddled with mould. The sea looked inviting, but it was full of tiny stinging jellyfish, the beach hid bugs that burrowed into your skin and laid eggs, the jungle

I

was alive with frogs so toxic you would choke just from touching their skin. There was nowhere here that you could be comfortable. She spent the day drenched in sweat, with a permanent headache. But now they would have to leave. The child was dead. This place had killed it.

When the howling stopped, Liz was going to shout for her, she knew that. She was going to get the blame. It wasn't her fault, but Liz Wellbeck would need to blame someone else – that was the way it always was with her. Arisha walked carefully down the six, creaking steps on to the compacted red earth of the clearing in front of the house, then kept going, towards the dock, shading her eyes from the sun. She had left her sunglasses by her bed, but her room was right next to the one Liz was in, so she wasn't going back for them. She had a wide-brimmed straw hat on, but only a tight pair of white shorts, a T-shirt and sandals. She could feel the sun burning her skin as soon as she stepped into it.

She needed Maxim. She needed him to reassure her. A sob caught in her throat. She had treated the baby as her own, whispered in its ear that it would be safe, that she loved it. A baby girl – a bright, alert, thirteen-month-old. Arisha had fallen for her the moment Maxim had first placed her into her arms. She had held her to her chest and smiled at her and felt her tiny heart beating through their bodies. She had marvelled at the luxurious, thick, jet-black, curly hair – so clean and wonderful that she had pushed her nose into it and smelled it. The little girl's eyes had been a startling deep blue and she had looked at her with a wide-open, innocent interest that at first, because of what they were doing, had made Arisha want to cry. So trusting, so helpless, so dependent. She hadn't a clue what was happening to her. Until Arisha had her in her arms and was holding her miniature fingers, looking into her eyes and talking softly, until she had experienced that sudden swelling feeling in her heart as the baby grinned at her and she saw her four, delicate milk teeth – until right then, Arisha had no idea just how much she loved babies, no idea at all.

The girl could walk a little – a few hesitant steps before she fell back on to all fours. She could mutter or shout a few unintelligible words, things her own mother would have immediately understood, perhaps. But mainly she had been reliant on Arisha to get her to where she wanted to go, to place into her hands the objects that interested her. And Arisha had slipped into the role effortlessly. The journey on the plane had worked so well – Arisha completely focused on the baby's needs and responses. It seemed like a dream now.

Children had short memories. Maxim said they could flourish like weeds, adapting, moving on, taking whatever they needed from wherever they could get it, just as he had. And it was true. Arisha had felt a pang of loss – even though it was what they wanted to happen – because the child had warmed to Liz almost immediately. As if able to sense that really Arisha counted for nothing, could guarantee nothing. She was just the delivery girl. It was Liz the baby needed to bond with, Liz who would provide.

And Liz had been surprisingly affectionate. Elizabeth Wellbeck-Eaton liked to say that she was half Russian, with a Russian mother's instincts. Her own mother had been an émigrée, something aristocratic and titled, from the Tsarist *époque*, but that counted for nothing in modern Russia – she spoke Russian, sure, but she understood nothing of what it meant to be from that shithole. The reality was that she was an American, and had lived her entire thirty years in the lap of absolute excess. Despite that, until this moment Arisha had thought there was something emotionally broken in her. In the year she had been working for Liz she had never seen her cry, rarely seen her laugh. Liz was fastidious to an extreme, control obsessed, a difficult person to please or work for. In private she spoke derisively of her friends, had a fraught relationship with her father and brother, viewed her husband – Freddie Eaton – with undisguised contempt. She spent over an hour each morning dressing and decorating herself, with the assistance of two or three staff – in the Paris house, at least, not here, because the staff had been left behind when they came here, along with everything else, in order to keep this whole thing secret. Arisha had assumed Liz would be useless with a child, that she wouldn't have a clue. But she had behaved immediately like the baby really was hers, holding her close, rocking her, talking quietly, taking over everything Arisha had been doing, even the changing. The baby had brought Liz to life. Against all odds, it had worked.

Arisha had watched with astonishment. And for a while she had really believed that the baby would be safe, that the monstrous thing she and Maxim had done together – *stolen a baby* – could actually, in the end, have been a *good* thing. They had given a desperate woman a child, and the child would be happy. After all, her new mother was one of the richest women on the planet. What could go wrong?

They had been here a week when the symptoms started. Some standard flu the parrots caught and survived each year – that's what the doctor had said – 'nothing to worry about'. But it had lingered and got worse, overwhelming the child's immature immune system, filling her lungs with bright green, infected mucus. Today she had gone from a cough and a runny nose to blue lips and breathing difficulties in less than four hours. They had sent someone in the seaplane to get the doctor again, but it was a three-and-a-half-hour flight to the big island, and now it was too late.

The place was only fit for the monkeys, the precious,

stinking monkeys Liz was in love with, trying to save them from extinction or whatever – her little pet project, prior to the baby. That would change now, Arisha guessed. Liz could shift loyalties as she could change clothing. Everything Arisha had been taught as a child was true, even the crude communist slogans – rich people were degenerate, self-serving, immoral, they had no allegiance to anything but themselves.

As she reached the slope down to the dock she saw with relief that Maxim was already running towards her, coming from the boat. He too had a pair of shorts on, though longer than her own and baggy with pockets, no doubt stuffed with ammunition and cigarettes. His legs, chest, head and feet were bare – but he had tanned within days of getting here. No matter how careful she was, that didn't happen to her skin. She was too pale, too freckly, her hair naturally a light red. It had been long, beautiful – almost down to her waist – but she had cut it and dyed it an ugly brown the day they got to Paris with the baby, because Maxim had told her to, because that was part of his plan – so that now it wasn't even long enough to shade her neck from the sun. His blond hair – growing longer now he was out of the military – had bleached almost white, because he swam and stood in the sun every day, despite the jellyfish and bugs and the danger of heatstroke. He was loving every minute of this place. He thought it was paradise.

She started to run towards him and had a fleeting fantasy that they would both just turn around, get in the boat and sail away from it all. He stopped when he saw her and shouted something, but she couldn't hear for the birds and monkeys. The parrots were very near her, off to her right. She could hear their wings thrashing the air as they took off in alarm. Maxim glanced at them, distracted. 'What's happening?' he yelled, and she heard this time. He had the gun in his hands. While they were here he was in charge of security for the Wellbeck-Eatons, which meant he was never without some gun or other. There was a constant danger of kidnap, he said. She waved her arms at him, slowed down, then suddenly started to really cry. As she got to him he grabbed her by the shoulder with one hand, his face intense with concentration and worry. 'What's happened, Arisha? Tell me what's going on.' He spoke Russian with her, as they always did when alone. She leaned her head against his chest, smelling his sweat, feeling it damp against her cheek, catching her breath and telling him at the same time, 'The baby died … I think the baby died …'

'Jesus Christ.' She could feel him tightening up. 'Are you sure?'

She could hear the fear in his voice. She wanted him to put his arms around her, to hug her, but he was on edge now.

'I thought it might be someone attacking Liz,' he muttered. 'She's screaming like an animal …'

'The little girl, Max … the little girl …'

He pulled her into him now, ran a hand across her hair. 'We have to be calm,' he said, trying to control his voice, to be gentle with her. 'It's a terrible thing. But it wasn't your fault. If we had a child we would never bring her to a place like this. That was *her* decision. Not ours. If it had been her own natural child she would never have brought it to this place. She's not fit to have children. She's a fucking idiot …'

'The child hurt nobody … she was only thirteen months old …'

He tilted her head up, so that she was looking at him. 'The child is safe,' he said quietly. 'Wherever she is now, she's safe. No more pain.' He frowned at her. 'We have to think of *us* now, not the child. We have to be very careful. Remember where we are, remember what we've done. Don't think about the child. You need to get back up there and be there for *her*. She's shouting for you.'

'I can't stand this, Max. I can't take any more of it …'

'Don't be stupid. You want to go back to Russia? You want that life again?' He lifted her chin so that she was looking into his eyes. He was twenty-one, a year older than her, but over a foot taller, with a lean body, stripped of fat during his recent spell in Afghanistan. He was about to say something else, maybe something kinder, but then something caught his attention from behind her. 'Christ,' he said. 'She's coming down here …'

Arisha turned and looked. Liz Wellbeck was on the path, stumbling towards them, weeping uncontrollably, shouting Arisha's name. She was in a shabby, soiled dressing gown, her hair matted and stuck across her face, her eyes black pools of smudged mascara that had run down her cheeks like clown paint. There was something in her arms, a bundle.

'She's got the little girl with her,' Maxim hissed. 'Are you sure she's dead? Are you sure?'

She wasn't sure of anything, but she couldn't do anything but go to her now. They both began to run back up the path, pretending they had only just realised what was happening. As they reached Liz she fell forward so that Maxim had to catch her by the arms and brace her against himself. Arisha gasped. Liz was holding the baby in a silk blanket. She could see its tiny white hands, the curly black hair, the little closed eyes, the skin grey and loose, all its features fixed and wax-like – as if it were a bizarre, macabre doll, a replica of a dead baby. It didn't look like the child she remembered from the plane journey. She started to tremble, holding her hands to her mouth.

'Get off me!' Liz spat at Maxim. 'Get your hands off me.' She pushed herself away. She was on one knee, shielding the bundle from him. 'You did this,' she hissed, in Russian. 'You killed her …' Her eyes were fierce, but they quickly dimmed as she collapsed on to the path. She started to rock the dead baby, the tears streaming from her eyes, her mouth twisted in an awful grimace of anguish. 'My baby's dead,' she screamed. 'My little baby is dead ...'

2

Even from fifty feet back in the queue, Tom Lomax could see that the security presence was unusual. There were at least six guys on the gate and they weren't doing anything but looking at the people going through. They were all wearing sunglasses and smart, dark suits, standing like people who were carrying guns, hands hanging loose and ready, jackets open. He smiled to himself. It was part of the circus, he assumed – the celebrity spectacular that had brought them all here.

He was holding his son's hand, waiting to get into the place which presently served as the football ground for Hatton FC, a struggling county league club that probably gated about five hundred supporters on a good day. As far as he could see, the ground consisted of a row of scrappy fields bordering the south-eastern tip of Heathrow Airport. The planes came over low and loud every fifty seconds. But today would be a bumper day for the club. Over a wire fence to his right he could see a couple of thousand people already inside, groups of kids running around while they waited for the event to get under way.

It was too warm for the leather jacket he was wearing. 'You can take your fleece off,' he said to Jamie. 'I'll hang on to it for you.' But right then a jumbo came in, drowning everything.

9

Jamie, seven years old, put his hands over his ears. From where Tom was standing there was a row of houses blocking his view of the south runway, but from the height of the jet it couldn't have been more than a few hundred yards away.

He checked his watch again. Almost one o'clock. He had to have Jamie back with his mother by three. Half-term was just ending, but Sally had got Jamie an extra week and booked a holiday in Spain for them in the only week she could get off from work. She and Jamie were flying out at six that evening. But Alex – Tom's closest friend – had told Jamie about this 'unmissable' event, and so here they were, rushing to fit it in. Both Alex and his son – Garth – were meant to be with them, but Garth had pulled a muscle in his ankle the evening before and couldn't walk, so now Tom and Jamie were going alone.

They were here not to watch Hatton play, but because a premiership striker was doing an appearance, proceeds to some charity. Someone called Dimitri Barsukov had apparently set up and paid for the striker's visit, because Barsukov had some connection to the club, either owned it, or wanted to own it – most likely in order to buy the land from under them, according to Alex (and Alex would know about such things). Hence the muscle – to protect the celeb striker. Or so Tom imagined until he heard them speak. As he went past them, through the gates and into the ground – begrudgingly handing over his twenty on the way – he noticed they were speaking some Eastern Bloc language – possibly Russian – which meant they were probably here for Barsukov, not for the striker – the striker was from Merseyside. Tom's hand went to the stiff envelope in his inside jacket pocket and his mind turned over the little sequence of events that had brought him here. He began to worry.

He was meant to serve the envelope on the Russian, on Barsukov. Alex had persuaded him to do it. There was some kind of legal document inside, a writ, most probably. Tom hadn't looked. The only info he'd been given was that Barsukov was careful and other methods had failed. He had no idea who was behind it, who needed it served. Over the last six months there had been seven or eight of these jobs, all simple enough. Alex worked for Glynn Powell, a 'west London businessman', as he put it, one that Tom had first come across during his seven years in the Met, under a less benign description. Back then he wouldn't have taken Glynn Powell's hand to spit on it. But that world had been turned on its head three years ago. These days he took what he could get.

'Just a straightforward service job,' Alex had said. 'Just walk up to Barsukov and give him the envelope. He'll be there with his kid. Just like you.' For which Tom would get the usual fee. 'Jamie won't even see what you're doing, mate,' Alex had added. 'He'll be watching his hero – the great striker. Come on. I'd do it myself if Garth weren't crippled.'

Alex had given him a photo of Barsukov – cut out of a gossip magazine – and told him to expect a guy standing inconspicuously with the other fathers, waiting for an autograph. Now that he was here, Tom thought the reality was that it seemed unlikely he would even be able to get near Barsukov.

The star attraction was late, so Tom led Jamie slowly towards the pitch, where the striker was scheduled to give a lesson of some sort to some hand-picked kids from a school in Bedfont. Perhaps a lesson in speaking unintelligible Scouse. Tom wasn't much into football, never had been. He suspected Jamie was only interested because of Garth. Most times Jamie tried to play he ended up with a fat lip, in tears. He was better at more thoughtful things – drawing, reading, maths. Tom was thinking that he was going to end up disappointed today, because it was unlikely, given the absence of tiered seating, that they would even get a glimpse of the striker. He picked Jamie up and sat him on his shoulders, and just at that point caught sight of Barsukov.

He was a short, squat man, with a big, flat nose, bald. In his mid-fifties, perhaps. Easy to recognise from the photo. He didn't have a kid with him, but was walking casually around the back of the crowd gathered at the pitch, talking to a fat guy in a tracksuit. The nearest of his minders was a good ten feet behind, talking into his earpiece mic. All very relaxed. He was about thirty feet from Tom and Jamie, coming towards them.

As Tom watched, a couple of kids ran up to the Russian, holding out pieces of paper and pens. They were after his autograph. The patron saint of Hatton FC. The minder didn't react. Barsukov stooped to the kids' level and spoke to them, smiling. Then he signed their brochures as if to the manner born.

It all looked too easy. So why not try? Tom started to walk towards him, Jamie still on his shoulders. As he drew near the guard was still way behind, still occupied. All safe. He told Jamie to hang on and took the envelope and a pen from his pocket. He held the envelope and the pen towards Barsukov. The man smiled up at Jamie, then said, 'I'm not him, you know.' Meaning the striker. His accent was obvious. 'He's a bit taller than me,' he added. It was a joke, so Jamie laughed politely.

'You're Dimitri Barsukov, right?' Tom asked, just to check. By now Barsukov had taken the envelope and was reaching for the pen.

'I am,' he said, still smiling. The man at his side, in the tracksuit, was smiling too. Everyone was smiling. Tom put the pen back in his pocket. 'Sorry,' he said. He pointed at the envelope. 'That's court papers, Mr Barsukov. You're served.' He turned to leave as Barsukov's face dropped.

The blow came out of the blue, from behind him, knocking him forwards so that he started to fall with Jamie hanging on to his hair. As he went down, he felt Jamie coming off him and tried to get his hands up to catch him, but by then Barsukov was right in front of him, swinging at his face. He had looked solid, Tom recalled, as the first blow landed. Damn right. He had a punch like a sledgehammer. Tom took two of them and hit the ground, sprawled on his side, little pinpoints of light swirling through his eyes. He heard Jamie shouting something, but as he turned to get up someone else stamped on his head, very hard, knocking him down again and momentarily blacking out his vision. He shielded his head and managed to get into a sitting position, then on to his knees. There was shouting all around him now, men running to intervene. He could see a face peering down at him, mouthing words. One of the security guards. Then Barsukov's voice telling everyone to get off him, to leave him alone, speaking in English. A huge shadow appeared in the sky, moving rapidly. Another 747, but for an instant Tom couldn't even hear it.

He got to his feet and saw Jamie being held by one of the guards. He was staring in complete panic at his dad, a hand extended towards him, shouting something. Tom's hearing returned. He moved towards Jamie as Barsukov shouted some instruction and the guard released him. Tom got to him and put his arms around him. He could hear Barsukov trying to calm things, shouting that everything was a mistake.

'Are you all right, Jamie?' Tom asked, his ears ringing. Jamie began to shake and cry. Tom started to check him, but then someone was pulling at his shoulder. He turned to find Barsukov leaning towards him, breath reeking of garlic, pushing the envelope back into his pocket, a big smile on his face. 'A mistake. A mistake,' he was saying, for the benefit of the crowd that had gathered. 'I'm sorry.' His face came very close to Tom. 'If I ever see you again,' he hissed, 'I'll break your kid's neck.'

3

Forty minutes later Tom was standing on Sally's doorstep listening to a tirade of criticism. He took it in silence, with his head down. He was average height at five nine; Sally was two years younger than him and short, five inches shorter, in fact. But she had a fearless temper. Since she'd become 'a single mum' she'd gone through a bit of a Sarah Connor phase, running, doing weights, putting muscle on and wearing clothes that would show it. Terminator mum. Right now she looked like she might take a swing at him. It wouldn't be the first time, and he was sore enough already, so he kept well back, hung his head and waited.

Jamie stood behind his mum – where she'd pushed him to shield him from his father. He had cried all the way back in the car. Not because they were peremptorily ejected from the grounds and he didn't get to see the striker, but because he had thought his dad was going to be hurt. 'I thought they were going to kill you, Dad,' he snivelled into Tom's shoulder, once they got back to the car. 'I was really scared they were going to kill you.' He was shaking like a leaf.

Tom hadn't known what to say. He hugged Jamie and apologised over and over again. It was pure luck he was unhurt. Barsukov hadn't given a shit that he had a kid on his shoulders. But then, Tom hadn't shown much concern himself when he'd walked up to him with Jamie sitting there.

What had he been thinking of? He hadn't been thinking at all.

'You're a fuckhead,' Sally yelled up at him, with classic eloquence. 'Pure and simple. You're a complete and utter fuck.' It was true. He didn't deserve time with Jamie. Etc. Etc. Everything she was saying was correct.

Once she was done and the door slammed in his face Tom walked miserably back to the car. The kick to the head had broken a tooth. He'd felt it in his mouth, but hadn't spat it out, so thought he might have swallowed it. The gap wasn't sore yet, just jagged against his tongue. As he was using the rear-view mirror to look at the steadily growing bruise across the left side of his face, his mobile rang.

He ignored it, instead getting out the envelope Barsukov had stuffed back in his pocket. He hadn't even bothered to open it. Alex had some explaining to do. Tom would return the envelope and demand an explanation. He tore it across and pulled out a single folded sheet of thick paper. His phone beeped to indicate a text had come in. He got it up with one hand and used the other to unfold the sheet of paper. It was blank. He turned it over. There was a single sentence written in the middle of the page: '*Introducing Tom Lomax, as requested.*'

He was totally thrown. Some scheme between Glynn Powell and Barsukov? Some stupid joke? At any rate something had gone wrong. Had Alex screwed up the communications, telling him it was court papers? Instead, for some reason, he was meant to have met Barsukov? But what was *that* about?

He threw the paper on to the passenger seat and looked at his phone. There was a text from someone signing off as David Simmons. He said he was outside Tom's house, waiting for him, wanting to talk urgently. Tom had never heard of him, but was irritated he was outside his house. He had hired a six-by-six box in Hounslow precisely so that there would be some separation between his home address, also in Hounslow, and the working world. The working world was full of middle-tier criminals wanting information on rivals, Glynn Powell included. David Simmons was probably another. He didn't want that shit at home.

Fifteen minutes later, as he pulled the car on to the driveway of his semi, he saw that the man was actually waiting on his doorstep, right on his doorstep, sitting there. That was annoying, but as Tom got out and Simmons came over, Tom saw that he had to be about sixty, if not older. The anger started to dissipate. Simmons was harmless, stooped and thin, wearing a tailored grey suit, with a shirt and tie, his face clean-shaven. He had a smart briefcase and polished black brogues. He didn't look like the usual client. 'David Simmons,' he said, introducing himself. 'I'm a solicitor. You're Tom Lomax?'

'Yes,' Tom said, heart sinking, thinking now that it had to be some new maintenance demand from Sally. 'How did you find my home address?'

'We called someone and asked them for the information.' He said it as if to say, 'obviously'. 'You are Tom Lomax, the detective constable? DC Lomax, of the Metropolitan Police?' he asked.

'Not any more,' Tom said, curious now. 'I quit that.'

Simmons considered this for a moment. Definitely not sent by Sally, then. Tom watched the grey eyes take in the bruise on his face, the blood on his T-shirt and jacket.

'It's been a bit of a hard day,' Tom said. That would have to be explanation enough. 'I'm no longer a policeman,' he repeated. 'Does that change things, or is there something I can help you with – since you're here, standing on my driveway?'

'Is there somewhere we can talk?'

'Not in my house.'

'How about your car, then?' Simmons asked, as if he were cracking a joke.

'I usually speak to people at the office. That's what it's for.'

'I haven't time for that.' Simmons lowered his voice and started to mutter something about his 'principal'.

'Your principal?' Tom asked.

'Yes. I'm here on her behalf. Her name is Sara Eaton. Have you heard of her?'

Tom shook his head. His face was beginning to throb now. He needed painkillers.

'Have you heard of Elizabeth Wellbeck? Or Freddie Eaton?'

'Should I have?'

Simmons started telling him about the Wellbeck-Eaton family. Sara Eaton was part of it, Freddie was her father, Liz her mother. Simmons made it sound like a dynasty. They were big in this and that, had a lot of cash and so on. He phrased it all very delicately, but Tom got the idea. 'I'm here on behalf of Sara Eaton,' he said. 'She wants to meet you.'

'You mean she wants some work done?'

'She wants to talk to you, at least. I can take you to her now.'

'It's the weekend. She can come to the office on Monday.'

'That might be difficult. She's actually in the Seychelles.'

'The Seychelles? As in ... in the Indian Ocean?'

'That's right. I have a private jet waiting at an airfield just outside Luton. We can be there in about eighteen hours, if we leave now.'

Tom stared at him with his mouth open. 'Are you being serious? This is one of Alex's little jokes, right?'

'Alex?'

'You're being paid by someone, right? You're filming me?'

18

Simmons didn't find that funny. He started to walk past Tom. 'I'll wait in my car,' he said. 'I'm instructed to offer you five thousand pounds for your time – to fly out to Miss Eaton, meet her and speak to her, spend perhaps two nights maximum at her location in guaranteed comfort, then you will return here by private jet.' He was on the pavement now. 'You can think about it for a few minutes then let me know.'

4

Seven miles away, in her house in Fulham, Rachel Gower lay curled on her bed with all the curtains drawn and the lights off. Today was the anniversary. Twenty-two years ago, to the day. Outside it was sunny, and the garden was full of flowers and colour, but she didn't want to see that. She didn't want to see anything. She wanted to be a blank space, empty of thought, without consciousness. She wanted to dissolve into the bed, become part of it, sink into oblivion until the day was past and gone.

But there was no chance of that. No matter what she did there was no chance of that. So she kept her eyes closed, listened to her heart racing and stammering, felt the panic rising.

She couldn't stop herself. The memories were there even if she managed to ignore them. They were there constantly, every day of her life, a movie reel that played endlessly in her head, just behind the surface illusion of rationality she wore like a set of clothes. But all the time they were insisting, probing, trying to find a way through. She had to fight it with all her strength, because if they got through they would kill her.

April 14 1990. The anguish was still a raw wound. If she allowed her mind to go there, each trivial memory could trigger a mental collapse that would require hospitalisation, literally.

It had happened ten times in the last twenty-two years. On three occasions, in the early years, she had been so desperate that she had self-harmed. In 1998 a kind of cold-blooded insanity had found her plunging her arm into a fire, trying to drive back the endless terrifying scenarios with overwhelming physical pain. She had wanted to push her face into the flames, but that would have killed her, and that was the one thing she was absolutely forbidden. She had to live, survive, be here. Because the event had left her a responsibility, a splinter of hope that bored daily into her sanity – the possibility that Lauren would return. And if that happened – and it *could* – she had to be alive, she had to be ready.

She had been alone the morning it happened. Roger had worked the night at Barts, so was asleep in the spare room when they got up. She had dressed and fed Lauren herself, without waking him, then Lauren had played on the floor of the bedroom while Rachel herself washed and dressed, turning many times to speak to her. Nothing significant, though she could remember every word. Just normal chatter, a mother to her baby.

They managed to leave the house just after eight. It was a sunny, warm day, hints of spring in the air. The sunlight had picked Rachel's spirits up, made her feel lighter as they left. That was why she didn't want to see it now. She had stopped to show Lauren a clump of daffodils growing by the gate. Lauren had reached her hand out, touched the petals and smiled, kicking her legs in excitement as she had when she was only a few months old. So Rachel had picked one and given it to her. The moment, so simple and beautiful in itself – her holding out the flower and Lauren's hand taking it – was burned into her brain like an image of horror. Over the years it had come to stand for everything. She couldn't look at a daffodil now without the distress rising in her throat like a physical lump, suffocating her.

After that they got into the car and drove to Belgravia. At the time they were renting an apartment in Clapham and she had driven with Lauren in the baby chair, on the back seat of their Golf, passenger side, so she could turn round and see her, or even reach a hand across if she cried. But Lauren rarely cried. At precisely thirteen months and six days old she was a model baby. Everybody had said it about her. She had thick curly black hair and beautiful blue eyes, a face that wasn't flabby, unlike many babies of that age that Rachel saw. She looked like her mum, people said. Roger had very light brown hair, brown eyes, but Rachel's eyes were light blue, and back then her hair had been as dark as Lauren's. Lauren had only just started walking, hesitantly, but with great enthusiasm. She was intensely interested in exploring her world, and had sussed already that walking would allow her to move more quickly, if she could only get the balance right. She would stumble towards an object – anything was interesting, but animals, especially the neighbour's pet cat, would make her literally squeal with curiosity – and when she reached it, usually reverting to all fours still, she would look back at Rachel with a massive, proud grin, showing her four perfect, tiny front teeth.

They got into work at just after five past nine and Rachel had carried Lauren straight to the crèche, in a hurry. In January she had started as a junior doctor at the Wellbeck Clinic, in Belgravia, a small but very well-appointed private clinic that specialised in oncology, and particularly in inheritable forms of cancer. It was private medicine – exclusive medicine, actually – which wasn't what she had ever intended to do, but the years of study had left them with considerable debts, so while Roger was doing the right thing at Barts, Rachel had agreed, for a short time, to take what Elizabeth Wellbeck's foundation had to offer, which was roughly three times what Roger was earning. The hours were sensible too, with Rachel starting on half-time until Lauren reached eighteen months old. The crèche was within the clinic itself.

Two full-time nursery assistants looked after eleven children belonging to doctors who worked there. Lauren had quickly taken to one of them – a twenty-one-year-old called Lovisa Dahlbacka, who whispered in Swedish to Lauren – and that had made the mornings easy. There had never been any crying or hanging on to Rachel.

This morning had been the same – so that Rachel's last ever contact with her child had been unthinking, fleeting, void of the significance the moment was to later acquire. Rachel had simply passed Lauren to Lovisa, then bent forward and kissed her on the nose. Lauren, as usual, hadn't even appeared to notice that this was a transition. She was with Lovisa now. She would see her mummy later. Then Rachel was rushing off, because her first appointment was for nine, and would be waiting.

At three minutes to ten the entire clinic suffered a power cut which lasted nearly fifteen minutes, an event which caused a measure of quiet panic since most of the systems had only limited back-up power. Rachel had just finished her first consultation and for a time she stood in the windowless, darkened corridor outside her cubicle, listening to the running footsteps and voices. Then she decided to go down to the crèche and check on Lauren. There was no real reason to, and by the time she got there the lights were back on.

She entered the crèche at thirteen minutes past ten, according to the wall clock with Mickey Mouse hands, which she looked at as she came in. She found Lovisa absent, but Millie – the other assistant – was fussing over a very young baby, who was crying. She looked for Lauren among the other kids playing on the floor and it took about ten seconds, she calculated, to realise that the reason she couldn't see her wasn't because she wasn't looking properly, but because Lauren wasn't there.

The sudden, shocking perception of her child's absence had come to her once previously, when Lauren had crawled off into some shrubs in a friend's garden, so she knew not to give into it immediately, not to let loose and yell with panic. But that came pretty quickly once she discovered that Millie wasn't even aware that Lauren was gone.

All the predictable stages of reaction had followed. She could recall them less well now, because they had dragged into months of police enquiries and useless activity and all become blurred together in her (often drugged) recollection. The immediate responses were significant enough – the frantic combing of the corridors near by, then the hospital, then the street outside, before some kind of worse realisation began to set in – but oddly, they weren't the moments that had stuck clearly in her head. Not like bending down and showing Lauren the daffodil.

She had been living with the truth ever since. Lauren had been snatched. Someone had come in and deliberately removed her from Rachel's world – possibly arranging the power cut to facilitate this, the police had said, waiting until Millie had run out of the room leaving the kids *for just a few seconds*' unprotected. It had taken months to realise, to fully sink in, but around ten minutes past ten on 14 April 1990 Lauren Gower had vanished.

Twenty-two years ago. If alive, Lauren would be twenty-three years old now. *If.*

They had told her that time alone could heal her, that she would get used to the livid absence at the heart of her life, that the need to live and move on would finally dull the agonising mental trauma. But they had lied. Nothing had changed. Only her limited ability to control her focus, to turn away from it. There was no living with it, and never would be, no accommodation with the horror. All she could do was avert her concentration and hang on. Fill her head with other things. By a sheer effort of will she had to trick herself that she was just like everyone else around her. The normal people. She had to pretend she was one of them.

5

Ile des Singes Noirs, Sunday, 15 April 2012, 4.20 p.m.

Sara Eaton sat on the very end of the wooden dock, the letter in her hand, waiting. In front of her, shimmering in the intense afternoon sunlight, stretched the vast, translucent blue of the Indian Ocean, framed in the near distance by the twin horseshoe promontories of the island. The wide bays to either side of her – formed on the inside of the horseshoe – were rimmed with a thin edge of golden beach fringed by the palms and mangoes cascading out of the jungle interior. The view was stunning, and though she had sat here and gazed at it almost every day she had been here, it never failed to inspire, to lift her spirits, to leave her mentally gasping at whatever it was such perfect natural views revealed – something *beyond* the image, she thought, without being able to articulate it better than that.

Today the sea was extraordinarily calm, the surface utterly unruffled by wind or waves – like a huge azure mirror, reflecting perfectly the rare clumps of high white cumulus. The humidity was uncharacteristically low, making the naked sunlight seem stronger, enough to send the monkeys and parrots into the shade, producing an almost unreal level of silence. Below her, the smaller white motor launch made the only sound she could hear as it moved rhythmically on the imperceptible swell, gently butting against the jetty piers where it was fastened, causing the lines up to the short mast to jingle slightly in their loops.

She wore a yellow, long-sleeved cotton shirt, very loose white trousers and a broad-brimmed white sunhat. The only part of her left exposed was between her trousers, which ended at her knees, and the canvas deck shoes, and she had heavily coated the bare skin with total block. She had learned the hard way what the midday heat could do. Two years ago, just before her nineteenth birthday, she had burned badly, got sunstroke and had to be flown out to the hospital in Victoria, on Mahe, in the Seychelles. Ile des Singes Noirs wasn't strictly a part of the Seychelles chain, but the facilities on Mahe were the nearest thing to civilisation.

She was waiting for the seaplane to appear. The island was short on modern means of communication – there were no fixed phone lines to the nearest, larger island (which would be Remogos, approximately two hours away, via the launch), no antennas for mobile phones and no signal even if there were one. There was a single satellite phone installation, with an intermittent connection, powered by solar energy, at the farthest end of the island, on a hill. You could drive there on the heavily rutted road in about two hours, using one of the jeeps. She had done that earlier and had called to check the schedule. The plane was on time and on its way, but she was still having to estimate when it would arrive. Transport didn't work like clockwork out here. She had been on the jetty for an hour now, reading her magazine, or rereading the letter or just sitting staring at the sea.

She turned her attention back to the letter. It troubled her. They sent the seaplane to bring provisions and mail once a week and this had come back with it on Tuesday. It was from her old nanny, Felice Cotte, sent from Paris, where Felice lived, and redirected by the staff in Sara's London flat. So by the time it got to her it was over two weeks out of date. She read the relevant parts again. Felice had received a letter – an actual written letter, not an email – from Sara's mother, Liz Wellbeck. This was unusual. For almost two years Liz had been living in a bespoke clinic she had established for herself in Brussels. She was a virtual recluse. Felice had heard nothing from her in over three years when this letter arrived out of the blue.

The letter had reached Felice fourteen days ago, on the first of the month. It was short and written in Liz Wellbeck's distinctive, near-illegible scrawl – Felice had sent it on to Sara, with a covering letter explaining its origins and indicating that she had subsequently tried to contact Liz at the clinic, without success. Sara read the note again now.

My Dearest Felice. What I did is unforgivable, unspeakable – I can live no longer with the burden of it. I feel a filthy disgust in my heart. I cannot put things right, but I must try to help those I have inflicted with suffering and loss, before it's all too late. I cannot leave this wretched place, so it is up to Sara now. She needs to contact a man called Tom Lomax, in the Metropolitan Police, in London. He will tell her why. He knows it all. Elizabeth Wellbeck-Eaton.

That was it. Sara had no idea what it meant, what it referred to, or why her mother had not contacted her directly, and while her mother's mental condition often gave rise to quixotic behaviour, the note had a disturbing tone. She had tried to contact her mother, taking Thursday to fly out to their house in Victoria to use the more reliable communications there, but that had, as usual, drawn a blank. One of her mother's specialities was an aversion to telephone contact. There would be phone lines into her clinic, no doubt, but Sara didn't know the numbers. They were secret. She had two mobile numbers for her mum – including an 'emergency' number – but on Thursday, at least, they had both been switched off.

Sara hadn't liked it. But nearly all communications with her mother were odd. It had been that way for half her life, and she had got used to it. She could contact her father, of course, but she knew from past experience what his reaction would be. He would dismiss the note as gibberish, more of her mother's nonsense. So she decided, in the interim, to locate and speak to this Tom Lomax, whoever he was, before attempting to go to Brussels herself. Perhaps he would be able to explain what her mother had meant. It took only money and staff to arrange a meeting, and she was short of neither of those resources, even here. It would be far easier than flying to Brussels to be told that her mother couldn't even recall writing the note.

She heard footsteps on the planking behind her and turned to see Janine Mailot walking towards her, carrying two tall glasses. 'I thought you might need to cool down,' Janine said in French. She was from Mahe, and spoke the local Creole, plus French and English, but she had been to university in Paris, so usually used French when speaking to Sara. Sara had completed the last four years of her secondary education in Paris and had spent much of her childhood there, so her French was fluent. Janine was five years older than Sara, but Sara's closest friend nevertheless. It had been that way all her life – she had never been able to get on comfortably with people her own age, even as a child. She had met Janine through the project here, just over a year ago – Janine was a research scientist, here to do the blood analysis on the monkeys – but they had very quickly formed a bond.

'Perfect.' Sara smiled at her. 'Sit down with me. What is it?'

'Fresh lemonade. Arthur just made it.' Arthur was local too, Janine's uncle. Sara used him as a caretaker for the old house when she wasn't here, as a chef when she was.

Janine was about to sit, but right then they heard the faint drone of the seaplane's twin engines. 'That's it now,' Janine said, squinting into the distance. Sara stood beside her, taking the glass of lemonade and sipping it appreciatively. They watched as the speck in the distance grew larger, the engines shattering the silence. Life was so slow and leisurely on the island that the coming and going of the seaplane – their main link to the world outside – was always an event, even if it wasn't bringing in a complete stranger, as it was now.

The pilot set it down easily and taxied almost right into the dock. He cut the throttles, jumped out on to the float and attached lines to two fixed buoys, at the other side of the plane. Then he crossed to the near float, shouted a greeting to Sara and threw her a line. She caught it and tied it to a block, while the pilot threw the second line to Janine, to secure the tail. Sara then let herself down a ladder, got into a little rubber dinghy and used a large rod to push the boat across to the nearest float, rowing the last few yards. She tied the dinghy to the float and stood up, balancing carefully but easily. The pilot greeted her again – he was a Senegalese who had been flying for her for nearly a year now – and they exchanged pleasantries about the trip as the passenger struggled to get himself out of the cabin and on to the float.

He looked tired, ruffled, uncomfortable. One side of his face was discoloured by a livid bruise, beneath his left eye. He was badly dressed for the island – in a thick, striped dress shirt already soaked with sweat, a tie (untidily loosened), suit trousers and black brogues, a crumpled jacket in his hands. He looked like a thug, Sara thought. But an attractive one? Maybe. Hard to tell with the bruise. Automatically she glanced back towards the dock and the treeline. There was a watchtower in the trees there, built especially to give a clear field of fire across the dock. She could see a figure moving on the high platform, see the sights of the sniper rifle trained on them. The figure – Jean-Marc, she guessed – saw her looking and waved briefly, to let her know she was covered. Jean-Marc was local too, the man she trusted with what little security she allowed when here. He had a team of three who patrolled the island.

'You didn't get that bruise during the trip, did you?' she asked. The man was standing unsteadily on the seaplane's float.

'No. Am I meant to get into that thing?' He was pointing at the dinghy. His eyes caught hers and she had to stop herself from reacting. He had intense, dark eyes. They were beautiful. For a second too long she couldn't get her gaze away from them. 'Yes. Just step across,' she said. 'Don't worry. If you slip the water's only waist deep here.'

He grinned. 'Maybe I should just dive in. It's been like a sauna in that cabin.'

The pilot explained quickly. 'AC down again. Sorry. I'll get it checked tomorrow.'

'How unfortunate,' Sara said, holding a hand out to steady the visitor. 'I'll get you a change of clothes.'

'A cold beer would be good too.'

'Of course. I'll check if we have any.'

He got himself into the dinghy. 'Tom Lomax,' he said, extending his hand to her. 'I must stink. Have I time for a shower before I meet the client?'

'The client?' She frowned at him, then shook his hand. 'I'm not sure what you mean,' she said. 'But I'm Sara Eaton. Thanks so much for coming.'

6

What had he expected? Someone very much older – older than he was, certainly – but she looked like she was about twenty. He hadn't dared ask. She was a fraction taller than him, with very short, very blonde hair and the lightly tanned, smooth, perfect skin that only the very wealthy or the very young could have. He had sat beside her in the dinghy feeling dirty and old, her laughing eyes taking him in. Green eyes – a child's eyes, in a child's curious face, but she didn't have the shyness of a child. She moved and acted like she was used to being in control. It made her seem older than she looked. In the enclosed space, her long legs had rested against his until they got to the dock, apparently without any self-consciousness. She spoke to him like she was five years older than him.

He took the shower and the beer she offered, not wanting to refuse now. She had given him a room on the top floor of a big, old, colonial house, built from a dense black wood. There were carved panels all over the staircase, colonial images of hundreds of naked savages, running amok, slaughtering, killing. The ceiling of his room was covered with them too – racist imaginings from another age and world. They made him wince, but from the window there were incredible views of the bay. Everything was comfortable, especially the air conditioning, but he showered quickly, drank the beer only because he was uncertain if he should drink the tap water and he was very thirsty.

This journey had sounded like something promising, when proposed to him by the flunkey solicitor in London. He had slept for the first half, letting the swelling over his cheek settle down, the confusion in his brain dissipate. After that some excitement had crept into his head – at the very least he had been plucked out of all that London shit – the shit that was his present life; the grinding warfare with Sally, trenches dug in front of her twin desires that he should pay more and at the same time see Jamie less, the miserable daily business of trying to claw in enough cash from reluctant clients, in order to service his own debts. That was the real fight, and even with Alex's help he was losing it. The next big, desperate decision would be to get rid of the house and car, downgrade. Or jack it in and try something entirely different. But what? There was a faint chance that this thing with Sara Eaton – whoever she was – would deliver better options than working for criminals.

After the refuelling stop in Dubai there had been dramatic turbulence, then a very rushed change in Victoria, on Mahe, in the Seychelles, with barely enough time for him to get to the waiting seaplane. There had followed a miserable, cramped, bumpy and parched three-hour trip here. That had dampened his enthusiasm. By the time the pilot was pointing out the island to him – a very indistinct green speck on an endless blue horizon – he was feeling so sick he didn't care.

Here was called Ile des Singes Noirs. Black Monkey Island. He had no idea where it was. Nor had he seen any monkeys yet, black or otherwise. But he had seen plenty of men with guns. By the dock there had been a watchtower and a guard with a sniper rifle trained directly on him. Looking out of his window he had seen another two, walking around with automatic weapons. All of which made him nervous. So he drank the freezing beer (flinching as it passed across the broken tooth), dressed in the clean, light clothing they had left out for him in the room, took more of the painkillers he had brought along and went out to meet her, as she had suggested, in a large, open summerhouse, to the side of the main building. She was already in there, waiting for him.

The summerhouse was a spacious circular structure, on short stilts, with a rush roof and open sides, bare boarding on the floor. It looked like it had been built in a hurry and patched periodically to keep it upright. Maybe that was the fashion with these things, for these people. There was a table in the middle with several chairs. She sat at one side, with the other, older woman he'd seen at the dock opposite her. The jungle started a few feet past the shelter and the bigger trees were leaning over it. He could see movement in the higher fronds, and a chattering noise, but couldn't make out what was making it. Looking back in the direction of the dock, he was startled to see that the sun had become a huge, crimson orb, very low in the sky. The entire horizon was stained a deep red, the colour running into the sea. Above him it was already shading into darkness. He stopped as he took the two steps into the summerhouse, looking across at the view with his mouth open.

'Beautiful, isn't it,' she said.

'Sudden,' he said. 'It was still daylight when I was in the shower.'

'It takes about half an hour,' she said. 'Day to night in half an hour. It's because we're near the equator. You live in London, right?'

'Yes.' He stepped inside.

'Sit down,' she said. 'Would you like a drink? Another beer? We found a full crate in the fridge, and luckily the electricity is OK today. This is Janine Mailot. She does blood analysis as part of a project we have here. We're trying to work out why the black mandrills are dying out, trying to stop the decline. She's also a great friend.'

She'd already been introduced to him, though not like that. He smiled at her, sat down on the same side as her, one chair removed, so that he could look across at Sara Eaton. He said he would like a glass of water.

She turned to the wall behind her – where there was another entrance – and said something in French. A tall man emerged from the shadows by the steps there, very black, with a gun slung over his shoulder. He looked hard at Tom, then walked off.

'You'll have to forgive the weapons, Mr Lomax,' she said. 'It's always like that.'

'Like what?'

'Wherever I am there's some type of security. It's been like that all my life. Worse recently. Pirates, kidnappers, et cetera. It's part of the fabric – you learn to ignore it. He'll bring you some water. And some lemonade we made this afternoon. It's very refreshing. Better than water. We can eat whenever you like. Would you like to eat here or inside?'

He shrugged. He would have preferred her to just tell him what she wanted, but it was her call, and she was paying nicely, so if chit-chat about dinner and lemonade was what it took he could oblige. 'Anywhere is good, Miss Eaton,' he said.

'You can call me Sara,' she said. 'In fact you must. Everything is first names on this island. Can I call you Tom?'

'Of course.'

'You live in London, Tom,' she continued, barely pausing for breath. 'You have a child, aged eight, and you're divorced. You work for the Metropolitan Police as a detective. That's the sum of what I know about you.'

That took him by surprise. Now he had to think quickly. He'd been assuming he was here because he was a private investigator, because she wanted some work done. The question of why someone like Sara Eaton would select someone like him for anything was a pressing issue, but he was assuming that that was nevertheless what had to have happened. Only now he realised, the same as the flunkey in London, she didn't even know that he had left the police. So why was he here? 'How did you find all that out?' he asked, stalling, trying to work it out.

'We paid. An agency provided a report.'

He was interested in which 'agency', and how much she'd paid, but didn't ask. 'They didn't give you very good value for money,' he said. 'Five pieces of information and two are wrong. My boy's seven, not eight, and I quit the police three years ago. I told your man in London that.' He waited for a reaction, but there was none he could read. 'Which leaves me a bit confused,' he continued. 'Now I'm even more puzzled as to why you've brought me here.'

'Of course you are,' she said. 'I'm sorry.' She turned to the other woman, who had been quietly watching. 'Could you excuse us, Janine? Please? We have to discuss some matters in private.'

The 'great friend' stood at once – presumably she had been warned this would happen. She went round the table and kissed Sara quickly on one cheek, said something quietly in French, then nodded politely at Tom.

'So you're no longer a policeman,' Sara said, once they were alone. 'What do you do now?'

'Private enquiries.' He almost cringed as he said it.

'A private investigator?' She gave a little ironic smile, kept her eyes on his. 'We've used a few in the US – the family, I mean. I didn't think they existed in the UK.'

'Maybe I'm the only one.'

She laughed. 'And you thought I brought you out here to hire you. I understand now.'

'But you didn't?'

'No. Sorry. Though you will be remunerated, of course.' She kept staring at him, the smile lingering. He found it uncomfortable. She was beautiful, he thought, though not perfect, because there was something about the positioning of her eyes and the expression on her face which made it look like she was always about to laugh at you – and maybe she was. But the inner confidence came straight at you. It was rare that you met people who were completely comfortable with themselves. She had that. It gave her a certain presence. He wondered if she was aware of it.

'So why *am* I here?' he asked.

She opened her mouth to reply just as the guard reappeared, bearing a jug in each hand. He set them on the table with too loud a noise – not part of his job description, perhaps – raising a frown from his employer. A pretty young girl followed him – short, with long, tightly curled jet-black hair and coal-black skin. She put a tray and glasses on the table, then started to pour them both lemonade and set out little bowls of some kind of snack. The man stood to one side. Sara waited – clearly not keen to speak while they were there.

Something like an awkward silence developed. 'This is an amazing place,' he said to fill it. 'Do you actually live here?' The island had looked small from the air, and mainly jungle – the sort of place it might be OK to visit for a two-week holiday.

'We're here for the project,' Sara said. 'Though I did grow up here. I don't usually stay all year now – the island is tiny, after all. It takes only a couple of hours to get to the other end in a jeep. We keep eight permanent staff here, though. They're here all year round.'

'"We"?'

She shrugged. 'I just meant the organisation here.' She waved a hand at the girl, as an example.

'The monkey project?'

'Yes.'

'That's what you do?'

'At the moment. Yes.'

He caught the defensive tone. No doubt what she 'did' was actually nothing.

'You're a scientist, then?' he asked. 'Like Janine?'

'I don't have a qualification,' she said, frowning. 'Is that what you mean? I dropped out of uni last year. I'm only twenty, though very nearly twenty-one. Too young to be an expert on anything.' She switched to that queer smile again, those intense green eyes coming back to his. He made himself stare back this time, but it didn't work. It felt like he was being aggressive, when all she was doing was looking at him. She was several years younger than him, he reminded himself, and rich. Maybe she wasn't used to dealing with ordinary people, didn't know it was considered rude to stare.

He pointed to the bruise under his eye – perhaps that was what she was looking at. 'I got that yesterday afternoon, at a football match with my son.' It wasn't quite a lie.

'I hope it's OK,' she said. 'It looks painful. If you need a doctor...'

'It's fine.'

'... I was going to say – the nearest one is several hours away and we can't get you there until morning...'

The girl finally stepped away. The man had already vanished into the shadows. Tom took a sip of the lemonade. It was delicious – cold, sharp and sweet. Just the ticket. He held the glass up to her, waiting for her to start, to tell him what it was about, but saw that she was just sitting there, still doing it, staring. 'What?' he asked. 'Why are you looking at me like that?'

'Your eyes,' she said, very quietly. 'Your eyes are incredible. Do people tell you that all the time?'

He swallowed, embarrassed. She was looking at his eyes – not looking at *him*. Like they were a flower or a butterfly out in the forest. As far as he was aware there was nothing particularly special or unusual about his eyes.

'Is *that* why you brought me here?' he asked. 'Because you heard about my eyes?'

She laughed again, then turned serious without warning. 'I asked you to come because you know my mother.'

That caught him. He frowned at her. 'Your mother? I don't think so.'

'Elizabeth Wellbeck.'

He shook his head, tried quickly to get away from the small talk. 'Elizabeth Wellbeck? That rings no bells. I mean, I came across a lot of people when I was in the job, obviously. Maybe I met her then. Maybe she was burgled and I took a statement off her, for example, but if so I don't recall. Why do you say I know her?'

She pulled something from her trouser pocket, a sheet of paper, unfolded it and passed it to him. 'That's a letter my mother wrote to a friend,' she said. 'That's why I asked you out here. Please read it.'

He pulled it over and tried to read it. 'I can't,' he said. 'Is it in English?'

She laughed. 'Sorry. That's her handwriting. Yes. It's in English.' She read it to him: '*My Dearest Felice. What I did is unforgivable, unspeakable – I can live no longer with the burden of it. I feel a filthy disgust in my heart. I cannot put things right,*

39

but I must try to help those I have inflicted with suffering and loss, before it's all too late. I cannot leave this wretched place, so it is up to Sara now. She needs to contact a man called Tom Lomax, in the Metropolitan Police, in London. He will tell her why. He knows it all. Elizabeth Wellbeck-Eaton.'

He knew immediately what had happened, of course. Tom Lomax/John Lomax. His father was John Lomax. Easy mistake to make. Plus, his father's middle name was Tom and at work people had called him that. So somebody had screwed up – it was his father they were after, not him. His father had been a detective superintendent on Major Inquiries, a senior investigating officer – much more likely to have had something to do with someone super-rich, like this girl's mother. If Elizabeth Wellbeck-Eaton had had some trouble it wouldn't have come to a DC like Tom. He had a sinking feeling in his heart as he realised the error. He shook his head. 'I'm sorry,' he said. 'But that makes no sense at all to me.'

She thought about that in silence for a while, then folded the letter and put it back in her pocket. 'OK,' she said. 'Let's eat. We can come back to business later.' She smiled that smile again. 'Shall we open a bottle of wine?'

7

Seven and a half hours later. Just after two in the morning, but it might as well have been noon. The sky was cloudless and everything was bathed in its blue light. Maxim sat on the jetty, back to the sea, facing inland – on a wooden crate full of coiled rope they must have used to secure the boats.

He was trying to keep his mind off the whimpering noise the girl was making, but without much success. He knew exactly what she was going through. He'd been there. He could *feel* it. If he looked down at her there was a good chance he would start crying, shaking, because he remembered what it was like, because he would pity her.

It had happened before. He knew how his heart could take over. Watching people afraid, suffering – he couldn't control his emotions any more. Not easily. He couldn't stop the pity, couldn't stop putting himself in their place – or imagining it was Arisha, God forbid. If he looked at the girl his mind would start it all – picturing it was Arisha down there. Was the girl any different to Arisha? Maybe now, yes – because Arisha had never been through anything like this. In a weird way, this girl was closer to him than Arisha could ever be. She knew the value of those breaths she was taking, heard the beats of her heart as something fragile, the contractions of a mere muscle that could be stopped at any minute. Arisha had

41

never felt that terror. Now this girl knew what he knew. She was like a sister.

He shook his head. Mad thoughts. He couldn't let himself think like that. What would happen if he lost it? He had to keep his face straight in front of all these fucking Somali savages. He had to pretend he was in control. He tried to concentrate on the problem, the purely tactical problem. There was too much light from the moon. In the open he would be fully visible. His past was littered with the memories of what a full moon could do. A full moon brought fear, something instinctive gnawing at his gut, no matter what the circumstances. Ninety-eight per cent of the time darkness protected you – the darker it was, the more comfortable he was. But maybe all that didn't much matter. Not here, not now. This wasn't Grozny. There wasn't a *real* threat here. Nothing he couldn't deal with, if he kept his head, kept himself hard, unmoved. But the girl kept making that pathetic noise. It kept dragging him back. He needed her to shut up.

The jetty he was on was about forty feet long, and wider than he remembered it. He was about one hundred and twenty yards from a one-storey, whitewashed building that he knew housed the servants – 'staff', they called them. This building had not existed when he had last been here, twenty-two years ago. Back then there had been only the big old house at the end of the pathway up from the dock. The new building straddled the pathway at the exact spot Liz Wellbeck had collapsed to the ground in front of him, a dead baby in her arms. He had been a different man then – not a man, even – a twenty-one-year-old child. He hadn't felt much about that baby dying, but it had come back to haunt him since, worming into his conscience as he had got older, as he had learned.

The old house was still there. He could see its black shape rising behind the servants' quarters, all the windows shuttered or curtained, no lights showing. A little to the side of it there was another new building, long and low, with a flat roof and skylights – the lab – and adjoining it the area where they kept the animals they were working on, a fenced area with mesh pens. Right now, he knew, the pens were all empty.

He had learned nearly everything from one of the security staff. There were four of them, and he had been warned that their boss – Jean-Marc Forestier – would not be so easy to buy, so he hadn't tried. The other three had proved willing, though. He had left Steiner with them. Steiner – a corrupt policeman from Mahe, who personally knew the security staff – was the only one of the present crew he could half trust, and so he was using him as a deputy. He would have to deal with Forestier himself, as a priority. He wasn't looking forward to that. According to the information, Forestier had a room in the main house. It faced the path into the jungle, at the side, obscured from view now by the servants' quarters. But Maxim knew there was a light on there, and that Forestier wasn't yet asleep, so he had one of the Somalis up in the treeline watching it, waiting for the light to be switched off. Forestier had a variety of weapons, so would have to be handled carefully, preferably when he was asleep. Maxim could wait another couple of hours for that to happen.

In the main house there was only Forestier, the Eaton girl, a woman called Mailot, who worked in the lab. All the rest were in the building right in front of him now, except the pretty little black servant girl who had inexplicably come out half an hour ago, the one whining down below him. She was in the boat, with another of the Somalis holding a gun to her head. Maxim risked a quick glance over the side of the jetty, and could see her panting in the bottom of the boat, her staring, white, animal eyes on the gun. He screwed his face up, hating it. He had used coils of rope from the crate he was now

43

sitting on to tie her, then her own shirt to gag her, so that her chest was exposed. He could see her breasts rising and falling as she struggled to breathe. She was terrified, and had wet herself. The Somali was sitting in the stern just staring at her, like she was a specimen.

Her appearance in the middle of the night had been an upsetting complication, reminding him that he had promised the Somalis they could do what they liked with the women here. That had been a lie. He didn't want them acting like animals. He wanted to do what he had come here to do then get out. If possible, he wanted no deaths at all. He loathed all of it with a visceral feeling, right in the pit of his stomach. He couldn't handle it any more.

Ten years ago his life had been turned on its head in the classroom of a burned-out school on the outskirts of Grozny. Age thirty-three, he had rejoined the 466th Infantry as a volunteer, on a contract, starting at sergeant – and he had walked into the Second Chechen War with eyes wide open, having already been there for the first conflict, five years earlier. But preparation was nothing. A stupid set of errors had resulted in him being wounded and captured, along with half his section.

They had been kept in the basement of a hospital first – five of them – then moved to a wrecked school. The school was closer to the front line – within hearing of the Russian troops – so at night the mutilations had started. Before this he had only heard about it – one of those rumours of brutality which were attributed to both sides, and which he had never quite believed.

But that night Maxim had watched the Chechens cut off fingers, ears, noses, lips, taking turns to do the hacking while four or five held the victim down. They did it in an abandoned classroom, where Chechen kids had once sat at desks and learned about the solar system (there was a torn wall chart showing the stars and planets). All the windows were smashed out by shelling, so that the screams carried clearly across the open ground to where the Russians were sleeping. There was a purpose to it, Maxim realised – to frighten the enemy – but that couldn't account for the laughter. The Chechens were a mix of ages, but they shared a common sense of humour. They laughed genuinely, loudly, as if watching slapstick on TV. Eighteen-year-old Russian kids writhed in terror on the floor, blood welling from their hacked joints, and the Chechens stood and pointed and laughed until there were tears in their eyes. At some point one of them brought in a dog and it started to eat something they had cut off a scrawny little kid called Sergei, who had only been in Maxim's section seven days. Sergei had cried and convulsed on the floor, the knowledge of his death etched into his gaping, innocent, little-boy eyes, while the dog had eaten his severed fingers. One of the older Chechens had to actually crouch down, doubled up – he was laughing so much it gave him a stitch.

They moved on to castration afterwards, two holding the legs apart by sitting on them, cutting crudely with their bayonets, throwing the parts to the dogs, now that the idea had caught on. And they still giggled and laughed, or sat in a corner and smoked and watched. Maxim thought he had seen everything, thought he could not be taught, but that classroom had given him his final lesson. Before they even got to him he was permanently changed. Now usually, when he was alone, thinking, even when his eyes were dry and he looked normal, it felt like he was crying all the time, inside – secretly, silently crying.

When it came to his turn he kicked and screamed and struggled as they tore his trousers off and held his legs apart. He made as much noise as he could, ignoring the laughter, ignoring the idiotic idea that he should try to bear it in silence, to deprive them of the point. The shells started landing right then, while they were in the middle of doing him. The whistle, the crump, the world shattering, the clouds of dust and debris, the blinding flash of the blast. Then there was the usual chaos. The same every time artillery struck.

His own side were mortaring the school. They'd had enough – some officer had decided sleep was more important than shelling his own men. The attack killed three out of the five prisoners, but maybe they would have bled to death anyway. Maxim hadn't complained. It was an unintended consequence that the mortars saved his life. All the Chechens fled, leaving Maxim and his corporal bleeding on the floor, slipping in and out of consciousness as the world came down on them. That's how they were found the next morning, when the advance started again and the school was retaken. They were pulled out of the rubble half dead, mutilated, their war over.

He pulled his eyes away from the terrified black girl and picked up the magazine he had found lying on the end of the jetty. *Intelligent Life*. Was this what Sara Eaton read to amuse herself? He flicked through it, trying to read it, to get his mind off the black girl's panic. It was full of glossy adverts for expensive watches and pens. It confirmed everything he thought about the wealthy. They let life slip through their hands, they had no idea what it meant to be alive.

He heard footsteps on the jetty and looked up, throwing the magazine aside. Time to concentrate. Self-consciously, he wiped a hand across his eyes, just to check. They were dry. The man he had put on the house was walking towards him. Maxim stood to meet him. 'Something wrong with your radio?' he asked, once the man was near enough. He felt contempt staring at the man's flat, ignorant, animal face. He was no better than the rest. Maxim had provided all five of the Somalis with very sophisticated radios, to speed up communications, but for some reason they wouldn't use them. 'Is there something wrong with your fucking radio?' he asked again. He spoke in English. He'd been assured they all understood English.

'The light has gone off,' the man said, ignoring the question.

Maxim nodded. It had been like this throughout his dealings with them. He had picked them because they were for hire and they matched the cover perfectly. Pirates. That's what everyone would think. But he wished now he'd thought of something else. Arisha would tell him he was being racist, but how could he help it? All they wanted to do was rape, kill and steal. He looked down at the one in the boat, who had stood now. He would have to stay here, guarding the girl. 'You stay with her,' he said to the man. 'No messing around. You understand?' The man looked blankly at him, licked his lips, looked up to the other one. Had he understood anything? The girl had seen Max, of course, seen him telling the others what to do, so she was a problem. The cover story wouldn't last long once she started talking. And she could identify him, if things really went wrong. He could threaten her, threaten her family – would that solve it? He really didn't want to kill her. But he couldn't think about it now. Right now he had to forget about her, get his mind on what was about to happen. 'Let's go,' he said to the one beside him. 'Time to start.'

no faster than the radio. Maxim had provided all five of the Somalia library sections, refused also, to spend no more transmitions, but I knew no reason they wouldn't use them. Is there something wrong with your fucking radio? he asked again. He spoke in English. Hed hammered the fall understood. Enississ.

the light had gone off. He push said. Ignoring the question.

Maxim nodded. If hadn't seen like this almost about his obvi-

8

Tom woke into blackness, unsure where he was, fireworks going off somewhere in the distance. It took him a while to place himself. Then he remembered in quick succession the plane journey out, the meeting with Sara Eaton, the food, the drink. Too much drink. His head was sore. He needed water. He had no watch, so no idea what time it was, and since there was no mobile cover out here he'd switched his phone off.

He lay for a few seconds in the pitch darkness trying to recall the entire evening, most of it spent in the summerhouse with his new client. Except she had never been a client, he recalled, and wouldn't ever be, now. That had been the disappointing conclusion to the evening. Not being able to help her with the business side she had already arranged for him to fly back to the UK in two days' time. But she'd kept him that long. That was interesting – that she had wanted him to stay two days with her, for no apparent purpose. She had not been what he would have expected from the super-wealthy. But then, she was the only person he had ever met who fitted that description. Maybe she was typical. He didn't have a clue.

Another noise from outside made him remember that he had woken to the sound of fireworks. At least, that was his impression as his eyes had opened. Could that be right? Or had he dreamed it? He tried to place the sound he had just heard, but couldn't. Something breaking? He rolled in the big bed and found the water bottle she had given him on the floor. He took a drink, clumsily in the darkness, then got his feet on to the floor. The room was so dark because he had pulled big wooden shutters over the windows, he recalled. Outside it had been clear, bright moonlight as they had sat drinking and chatting, swatting the mosquitoes. He groaned, still feeling half asleep. How much had he told her about himself? Considering her age, she had been surprisingly good at getting him to talk. And all that stuff about his eyes. He smiled to himself. Had she been flirting? Incredible. He wondered whether that would continue over the next couple of days.

Again a noise interrupted his thoughts. Fireworks again? He could hear shouting now. Why would there be fireworks? Some private celebration among the staff? Some pagan ritual, maybe. God knows what went on out here after dark. He was in the middle of nowhere. Sara had seemed oddly normal, but at the end of the day the world she lived in was incomprehensible to him. He wouldn't be surprised by anything.

A loud shrieking started. It got louder before he realised it wasn't a monkey. Immediately he was on his feet. Was it a woman? His body went into panic mode, his heart suddenly thumping furiously. A short stream of crackling explosions split the air, like firecrackers. He recognised the sound at once. He was listening to an automatic weapon, maybe more than one. What had woken him was gunfire, not fireworks. And a woman screaming in distress.

He thought to pull his clothes on quickly and found the light switch by the bed. It didn't work. The electricity was down. Of course. That was why he could hear everything. That was why he was sweating so much. The rattling air-conditioning unit was off. He stumbled to the window and pushed the shutters wide open. The moonlight streamed in, blinding him. He shielded his eyes and saw figures running, down by the dock and nearer, then another scream, from somewhere in front of him, not from the house.

He stepped back, now very frightened. Something was going on. He saw he already had all his clothes on, his wallet, mobile and passport in his trouser pockets. Even his shoes were on. He must have collapsed like that into the bed, a little drunk, exhausted by the heat. But now he had to get out of here. He had to find out what was happening, hide if necessary, but not stay in here, waiting for it to come to him.

He pulled the door open too quickly, too carelessly, then shut it again. There could be people out there, waiting to shoot at him. There were guns involved. He had to think before he acted. His brain was going into overdrive, running through the information. What *could* be going on?

It was like a burglary, maybe. But they were on an inaccessible island in the Indian Ocean. Did that happen? Could burglaries happen out here? He moved cautiously back to the window and looked out again. This time he could see nothing at all – no running figures, no muzzle flashes. Had he really heard guns being fired down there? He had a dizzying sensation of confusion. Everything was silent now, totally silent. Was he dreaming it all, right now?

He heard a man's voice, shouting something, high-pitched, full of fear. There was nothing dreamlike about it. He went back to the door. He was on the top floor, Sara had a huge room on the floor below him. He'd been given a tour and seen where it was. He should go there. That was the only thing he could do. He edged the door open a fraction and squinted into the gloomy passageway beyond. There was no one there. But from below he could hear running feet, doors slamming, definitely in this house. There was a palpable atmosphere of danger and panic. He realised he could smell smoke, something burning. He moved out into the passage and ran to the stairway. There was movement somewhere farther down. He looked over the edge but it was too dark to see.

He took the stairs as quickly and quietly as possible, on tiptoe, but running. On the floor below he turned towards where her room was and immediately saw something lying in the shadows, halfway along the passage. He crept to it, his muscles tense. Before he was anywhere near he realised it was a person, lying flat on their stomach, arms spread. He took in the blood, in a dark, glistening patch on the bare boarding, the clothing pulled up around the head as after a struggle and violence. It was a man, he thought. There was no movement at all. No breathing. Was it the man called Arthur, the chef? He inched forward, intending to check for vital signs, but immediately heard Sara speaking. At the same time there were three more shots from outside, but closer. The shots drowned out her voice, so he couldn't make out the words, but he could hear the fear in them. She was speaking very quickly, like she was pleading, breathless. He stood and moved quickly along the gloomy passage, towards the point where there were three chairs placed against the wall. Past them were the double doors to her room. They were wide open.

He came round the chairs with his pulse racing, instinctively in a crouch. He was sure she was speaking to someone, that something was happening inside her room. He had no time to think about it, but all his police experience was screaming that there must be some kind of robbery under way. As he passed the last chair he picked it up and held it in front of him, as a shield, then stuck his head round the door.

His brain registered the images like a series of snapshots, in a split second, everything racing. There was a tall man directly in front of him, back to the door, blocking his view, about two metres inside the room. The room was lit by moonlight streaming in through a long, wide window. The man was armed – a long weapon, a rifle. He was black, short hair, very muscular, very tall. He was pointing the gun at Sara. She was on the floor, on her knees, hands on top of her head. As Tom's head came into view the man started to turn, towards him, following Sara's glance. Her eyes had flicked to Tom immediately, giving him away.

There were only two choices – move back behind the wall, drop the chair and run, or go for the man. But he was already in view. There was no turning back now, so he stepped in and threw the chair.

The gun went off as the man was still twisting towards him, firing off to the left, smashing something. The chair hit the man's arm, raised to ward it off. The man staggered backwards, not falling, but going down on to one knee, off balance. As he went down Tom was running forward, all his attention on the gun. He was right behind the chair as it clattered to the floor. He needed to close the man down, get him to the floor, pin him. Or at least hit him, kick him. All he could see was the gun, swinging round towards him. It looked massive, double-barrelled – a shotgun, not a rifle. He had to get his hands on it. But the chair was in his way now, between himself and the man. He was stumbling over it already. Behind them, out of the corner of his eye, he could see Sara diving towards her bed, getting clear.

He knew before he got over the chair that the gun would be pointed at him before he could get to it. So he dived low, trying to get under the barrels, going for the man's legs. It went off again, right above his head, deafening him. But he was already into the man's thighs, pushing him backwards and down to the floor in a clumsy rugby tackle. Something hit his shoulder and the man started to yell. Tom got his head up and started to thrash out with his fists, not feeling anything as they connected, his brain flooded with adrenalin, everything a chaotic blur of movement. He was on the floor, on top of the guy, so close he could smell the sweat on him. He struggled against the sheer weight of his body – trying desperately to get up by pushing off him, feeling only slightly the blows from the guy's free hand – but then the butt of the weapon caught his head. He reeled backwards, falling against the chair, lights spinning through his vision. But he was up almost immediately, coming right back at the man, striking out at him again. As he got to his knees he saw the guy was again trying to get the barrels on to him, but it was point-blank range now – there wasn't even enough room to aim. If he pulled the trigger it would blow Tom's legs off. In a blind panic, Tom kicked out at him, catching his face, then the gun. Surprisingly, it spun out of the man's hands and slid across the floor. Tom rolled away and started scrambling towards it. He got into a crouch, took two steps then heard a loud, percussive crack. He spun round to see Sara leaning across the bed, pointing something. The man was flat out on his back, blood spreading rapidly over his shirt, chest heaving. He opened his mouth to gasp for air and blood ran out in a thick stream. He started to convulse, back arching, fingers clawing at the floor, eyes still open. The blood was already puddling around him, spreading quickly across the boards.

Tom started to shake uncontrollably. He put the shotgun down. Sara was clutching something that must have been a hunting rifle. Something very large calibre. There were telescopic sights, but she was staring past them, watching the man, her eyes wide, her face trembling with shock. Tom pushed himself into a standing position. He could hear shouting from outside. Her eyes came off the man. She looked at Tom and he stared back at her. 'We have to get out of here,' she said. 'Right now.'

9

'It's kidnappers,' Sara said, her voice breaking. She was over by a small window, opening it. 'Jean-Marc got me on the intercom. They were coming for him ...' She turned back to him and her eyes crossed the body on the floor. She flinched, then started to cry. 'It's finally happening,' she said, wiping her eyes. 'I've had this fear all my life. Now it's happening. They've come for me. We have to get out of here. I think they killed Jean-Marc. There are more of them. They will be coming. They'll kill you, kidnap me. We have to get out.'

Tom looked back at the body. It was trembling, like there was still life there. He should walk over to it, check it, do first aid, he thought. He was standing in the middle of the room uselessly, in a daze. But if the man were alive, what could be done? She had shot him through the chest. He could see the hole where the round had entered. If they got him to a good casualty unit within minutes he might live. But the exit wound would be a mess, too big to patch up with any facilities they might find here, if they had time. And the nearest hospital was hours away.

Was the man what they called a pirate? He looked like one. He looked like all the Somali pirates Tom had ever seen on TV, the same height, the same distinctive facial features.

'I think I killed him,' Sara said, very faintly.

'He might not be dead ...' Tom had seen dead people

before, seen violence, but never anything like this, never anything so close up. All his muscles were tight with the shock of it. He didn't know what he should do. Then, from the stairwell beyond her door, he thought he could hear voices, raised, getting nearer. He wrenched his eyes from the body. 'How do we get out?' he asked, his voice betraying his panic.

'Down here,' she said, her voice rushed. She was pointing at the open window. 'There's a ladder. It's a fire escape.'

He moved quickly to the window. Outside he could see a ladder on to a roof section. 'Is this the only way?'

She nodded. 'They're in the house, below us. I can hear. We can't go down the stairs.'

'OK. You go first,' he said. 'Give me the gun. I'll cover us.'

'Do you know how to shoot it?'

'Point it, pull the trigger.'

'It's not that simple. You go first. I'll cover you.'

She was right, of course. She'd already proved that. 'Just go,' he said. 'Go now. Hurry. I don't know where I'm meant to be going. I'll follow you.'

She slung the rifle over her shoulder and went straight over the sill. He was immediately behind her, over the short wooden sill and down on to the metal-runged ladder fixed to the wall of the house. He went down expecting a shot to hit him, or that he would fall off, clatter across the roof, give them away. But he made it down despite his sweaty palms, then stood panting in the warm darkness, on the short sloping first-floor roof, beside her. She was listening into the silence. 'We jump down from here,' she whispered. 'Jump down and run over there, to the lab block.' Like she had a plan. There wasn't time to ask her about that, but to get over to the lab block made sense. There was plenty of shadow, bushes against the wall. They could crouch down and hide, think about it.

She went a second before him, jumping with the gun in her

hands. The drop was a bit more than her height. He landed easily and started immediately to sprint across the short open space to the lab block. But halfway across he realised she hadn't followed. He doubled back into the shadow at the base of the house wall. She was leaning against it, vomiting. He put a hand on her shoulder and asked her if she was OK, at the same time glancing back across the open space behind the house, watching for movement. She was sobbing between retches, sobbing and gasping for breath. 'I killed him,' she hissed. 'I shot him.'

He kept his head moving, watching. They were too exposed. He turned her face up towards his. 'Look. You had no choice,' he said, not looking at her, watching instead the gap over by the summerhouse. They would come from there, he thought. Any minute now. 'He would have killed us both,' he said. 'He was armed . . .'

'I killed him . . .'

'You did. But now's not the time to fucking worry about it. We have to get into cover.' He pulled her away from the wall and dragged her into the open. They ran together across the space between the house and the lab. He still had hold of her arm. He took her round the back of the building. The jungle was right there, breathing on them. He thought they should bolt into it, keep running, get some distance between themselves and the house. Then he could talk to her, find out how they could get off the island, or where the emergency button was, or whatever it was they must have had planned for this kind of thing. But she pulled him back as he stepped towards the bushes. 'I can't,' she said.

'Can't what?'

'I can't just run.'

'If you don't they'll kill you.'

'I don't think so. I'm valuable alive. You should run,

though. You should get away from me …' She stopped. He saw in her eyes that she was terrified he would actually leave her. 'Get away from me,' she said again, her lips twisting. 'You'll get killed if you're with me. Leave me.'

'No fucking way,' he said. 'I haven't a clue where I am. And we both need to run. I can't just leave you. It doesn't work like that.'

'I have to help Janine,' she said. 'She's my friend.'

He caught himself. Friendship was one thing, but this was extremity. It was everyone for themselves now. Besides, Janine had probably already been caught. God knew what had happened to her if this really was some kind of pirate attack. He held his tongue, went down into a crouch, listening intently to see if anyone was following. Still no noise. 'OK,' he said, gritting his teeth. 'Where is she?'

'In the house. Where we've come from. Ground floor.'

'We can't go back in there. There were …' He stopped abruptly. They had both heard something. Footsteps coming from the area between the house and the lab. 'Down here,' she hissed. Before he could stop her she was flat on her belly and crawling fast through the undergrowth, back towards the lab wall. He went down but kept completely still, too nervous to move. Within seconds she was ahead of him, up by the concrete lab wall. He couldn't see her but she was making too much noise. He wanted to shout at her to shut up, keep still. If someone came round the side now they would hear her at once. Then all they would have to do was fire at the noise. He could hear more shouting now, but from much farther away.

Then a shot. It sounded close. He flinched, covering his head with his hands. He held his breath, waiting. He was in shadow and half covered by the undergrowth. He kept his eyes screwed tightly shut, in a kind of instinctive flinch, certain there was someone standing there, at the very end of the lab block, looking down the line of the building, staring right at him, about to shoot. He started to count.

Nothing happened. He kept counting, reached eighty and exhaled slowly. He held his breath again, all his concentration on his ears. He waited some more. Still nothing. Then he could hear her whispering to him from the shadows, telling him to come, urgently. He opened his eyes and looked. There was no one there.

He began to inch forward, into the thicker bushes growing against the wall of the building, following her obvious trail, where she had flattened everything down. When he got through to the wall he realised she was underneath the building itself. It didn't look like it was raised off the ground, but it must have been, because she had pulled away a section of fine mesh grilling, about two foot high, revealing some kind of space beneath. She had managed to wriggle underneath the actual building.

He followed her reluctantly into a tight, claustrophobic space like a coffin. He was crawling on compacted mud, into the total darkness. He got past her, his hands feeling the dirt ahead, his head pressed against the floor above, then waited while she pulled the mesh back into place and crept up beside him. 'We have a drill,' she whispered into his ear. 'We go through problems and what to do ... Jean-Marc made me do it every month. One plan was to hide here.'

'And then what?' he hissed. 'What's the rest of the plan?'

'No more. I don't have any more ideas.'

'So why the fuck are we here?'

'I don't know. I'm terrified. Sorry. I'm completely terrified. We can crawl ahead, towards the light ...' His eyes must have been adjusting. He could see she was pointing now, see that there was light coming in from other sections of mesh, right over at the other side of the building. 'We'll be able to see the area behind the house,' she said. 'See what they're doing . . .'

'What good will that do?' he hissed. 'We should get out of here. Run.'

'Not without Janine. And anyway, there's nowhere to run to. The best we can do is hide until they leave . . .'

'Not under here, then. Somewhere where we can breathe . . . until we can get help . . .'

'How will we get help?'

'There's no emergency line . . . or anything like that?'

'No. There's a satellite phone facility at the other end of the island. About four hours away, on foot, by daylight . . .'

'That's it, then. We should get to it.'

'We need to get to Janine first.' She started to crawl ahead. He rested his head on the mud and tried to control the leaping panic in his gut. Then, very carefully, very slowly, he followed her. She had stopped about three feet back from another section of metal mesh, this one at the other side of the building, he guessed. He came up beside her and she pointed in silence. He looked through the holes and could see the area outside the big house, the flattened, cleared area between the lab block, the house and the summerhouse, beautifully lit by the bright full moon. There were shapes lying there, right in the middle. As he tried to make out what they were he saw two men emerge from a rear door to the house. They were carrying a body. A lifeless body. They dumped it with effort on top of the other shapes. 'They're all bodies,' she spluttered. 'They're all bodies.' She started to sob again, very quietly.

He felt very cold, frozen, like his blood had stopped flowing. He had never felt fear like this in his life. Not even close. It was completely numbing. He put his head down on the hard surface and started to shiver. For a minute or more he couldn't do anything else. Beside him he could see her face – about twenty inches away from his. She was crying silently.

'What do we do?' she started to say. 'What do we do?' She kept whispering it, like she was going to really start kicking and shrieking. He took a big breath and reached a hand out to her. She jumped when he touched her, banging her head off the roof. Her eyes turned to him like those of some animal, totally overcome with fear.

'Shut up,' he whispered. He put a finger on her lips. 'Shut the fuck up. Now.'

There was movement above them, inside the actual lab block, over their heads. He heard a door swing open, then there was a man right in front of them, legs moving in front of the grille. He was walking across the space in front of the lab. His legs stopped in front of the grille and Tom heard the crackle of static from a radio set, then words: 'Max? You there?'

Another crackle, then: *'Yes.'*

The man was standing not four feet from them. 'We can't find her,' he said quietly, in broken English. What was the accent? German? 'They fucked it up. Went fucking crazy, shooting everything. Can you get over here?'

A short break, then a crackle and click. *'Yes. I'm done.'*

'Any problems?'

'No problems. He didn't get far. It was a diversion, I think. But he wouldn't let me near. He was armed. He got one of the Somalis. You clear at that end?'

'You could say that. They shot everything that fucking moved. One left only. The woman – Mailot.' A pause, then the man added: 'One down here too. The target shot him.'

There was a longer gap before they heard the voice on the radio again. *'Clarify. They missed the target and the other woman?'*

'No. Just the target. Mailot is here. I have her.'

'Fuck ...' More words followed, but in a completely

different language. Russian? Whatever it was, the anger was very clear.

'Suggest we just sit tight and wait,' the one in front of them said. 'We've got it all covered. The target will have to eat and drink. There's nowhere to go.'

'We can't wait. It has to be sorted quickly. We have five days maximum. That's the deal. And she could lie low for much longer than that. Or there could be interruptions before then – it's likely there will be. It's her birthday in five days, so anyone could arrive – people like this use helicopters like they're taxis. They can get here quickly. She could have invited a cruise ship full of people. We have to find her now ...'

The voice was silenced by the man in front of them cutting in. 'But we can't cover the whole island.'

Another pause.

'I agree. But maybe the other girl can help. Wait for me. I'll ask her.'

10

She scrambled too quickly back to the first mesh, making too much noise. Tom followed, grabbing at her legs, trying to slow her. She'd flipped, he thought. Something had snapped inside her. She was going to give them away, get them both shot.

But at the other side, back in the open, she stood immediately and moved straight into the jungle. She clearly knew where she was going, and he had trouble keeping up with her. She ran through the fronds with the gun in both hands, head down to stop the branches lashing her eyes. They were deep into the trees before he could catch up, grab her and spin her to face him. 'What are you doing? What the fuck are you doing?'

'They're going to do something to Janine,' she panted. 'You heard. I have to stop them ...'

'For Christ's sake! You can't stop them. There's four of them. Maybe more. All armed ...'

But already she was off again, heading downhill into deeper layers of fern that rose well above her height. He cursed and followed into the damp darkness. As the ground levelled out she pushed through to a narrow trail, with less vegetation around her legs, then started running along it in the half-light.

He had to stop her. Precisely what they wanted was to get her to break cover. If they were covering this trail then it was already too late. He kept pulling at her shoulder, trying to halt her, but she shook him off, kept going. She was much stronger than he had imagined. And determined. The trail was getting wider, moving uphill, the trees farther apart at each side, letting in more light through the gaps in the canopy. If they were up ahead, waiting for her, then she would be perfectly visible. 'Sara, please stop,' he cried, trying to whisper and shout at the same time. 'Please stop...' He was out of breath but managed to hold on to one of her arms and swing her sideways. She stopped and raised the gun. He thought she was going to hit him with the stock, but right then, from off to the left, they heard a woman starting to scream. Sara's face twisted in pain and she started to run at full speed along the trail, completely careless. 'It's Janine,' she shouted back at him. 'It's Janine.'

For a moment the options went through his brain. She was going to get killed, or captured. He was sure of it. So he didn't have to follow her. She was no longer being rational, she was dangerous. The kidnappers' plan was working. Get her friend screaming, get Sara out into the open. But he didn't have to follow. He kept saying it to himself. He didn't have to follow. He felt something scratching his arm and looked down to see three black ants – each as big as his thumb – walking across his bare flesh. He brushed them off, then glanced around at the hanging vegetation, the trailing creepers and darker areas above. There were wet, rotting plants all around him, soft beneath his feet, their smell thick in his nostrils. Already he had no idea where he was. Already his options were closing down.

One more try, he told himself. One more. He started after her again.

By the time he caught up she was at some kind of structure, hidden away in the trees, tall poles fastened together into a narrow platform, with a ladder going up. He couldn't see the top clearly, but she was already pulling herself up the ladder. Was it one of the watchtowers? It looked less solid than the one he had seen from the dock, which had been a metal frame structure. He started up after her, the wooden ladder creaking with their joint weight. He wanted to shout again, to try to get her to talk to him, but he was frightened more than anything that the kidnappers were already right here, all around them.

As he got to the top of the ladder he realised it was some kind of observation tower, built to watch the monkeys, maybe. The floor was rough boards, the jungle hanging right there over the low railing. She was flat on her stomach already as he got off the ladder, the gun out in front of her, eye on the scope, like some kind of big-game hunter. He crouched down beside her but she reached out an arm and pulled him lower. 'They're there,' she hissed. 'Straight ahead. Get down.'

He lay flat, so that he was pressed up against her side, staring through a slit in a kind of rush fence that fronted the platform. He thought they must be about thirty feet off the ground. He could feel the platform swaying slightly. 'What the fuck are you doing, Sara?' He whispered the words into her ear, so close her hair was in his eyes. 'Are you fucking mad?' She was aiming the gun, ignoring him. He inched forward to see better through the slits and saw that she must have intended to find this place all along. She hadn't been just running madly. The angle gave her a clear view into the area they had been watching from beneath the lab block, the area just behind the big house, though now from the reverse angle, from up behind the summerhouse. And now she had a clear field of fire. He could see figures moving around down there. The distance was about one hundred yards.

'I'm going to stop them,' she said. 'I have to.'

'If you shoot that thing they'll know we're here. They'll fire at us ...'

'It's a hunting rifle. It has a suppressor fitted …'

'They'll see the flash.'

'The muzzle flash is suppressed too. They won't see so clearly. They'll hear something, but won't know where it came from …'

'If they look *now* they can see us, without you fucking advertising it. We're *already* too close. Please listen to me. I've worked with these kinds of people. I have experience you don't have. They will just start shooting blind. If you want to get us killed then fire that thing. Please stop and think …'

'That's Janine,' she said. She started to shake. She had to bring her eyes off the sight. 'Look at her. Look what they've done …'

He stared through the slit. He didn't need the scope. They were close enough to see. There was a woman kneeling on the ground, next to the pile of bodies. The woman he had met last night, perhaps – Janine Mailot. But she looked different now. She was naked, he thought, blood streaked across her skin. She was crying hysterically. Just kneeling there, hands behind her back, crying. In the thick of the nightmare. He gritted his teeth. He could guess what they had done to her. 'Christ,' he whispered. 'Christ Jesus …' There was a white guy in view, standing behind her. He had a gun, though it wasn't pointed at her. Was he holding her hair in one of his hands? Another guy – also white – was walking around the edges of the area, saying something. Nearer to the big house two black men were leaning against the wall, one squatting, smoking, both armed, both just watching the woman, as though something perfectly normal was going on.

'There's nothing we can do, Sara,' Tom said. 'The only thing we can do is get down from here, get to that phone and try to get help …'

'They'll kill her …'

'No. They're using her ...'

Even as he spoke he heard a loud shout. Not the man standing beside Janine, but the other, who was out of sight now. What had he said?

'SARA EATON!'

They both heard it clearly this time. He was shouting her name.

'SARA EATON. I HAVE YOUR FRIEND, JANINE MAILOT. I HAVE HER HERE. IF YOU COME TO ME THEN SHE WILL NOT BE HURT. YOU TOO WILL NOT BE HURT. THAT IS MY PROMISE. I WILL GIVE YOU TEN MINUTES. TEN MINUTES, THEN I KILL HER.'

There was a heavy accent to the voice. Tom took his eyes from the scene and moved closer to Sara, so his face was almost touching hers. 'Let's go,' he said urgently. 'It's a trick. We have to get away from here.' But she had her eyes on the scope again. 'Don't touch me,' she said. 'Don't move.' He heard her take a breath, then hold it. He reached a hand to pull the gun away from her. His fingers were less than an inch from the stock when she squeezed the trigger.

Suppressed or not, the report was deafening, the recoil kicking back into her so hard the entire platform moved. His jaw dropped, but his eyes were still focused on the scene ahead. He saw the man behind Janine punched backwards, on to his knees, then over on to his face. She'd hit him. She'd actually aimed the thing, fired and hit him. Tom was dumbstruck. He couldn't believe it. She had just squeezed and fired while he was lying there uselessly, right beside her.

While he was still getting his head round it she fired a second round, making him jump again. He had imagined she would have to do something with the bolt first – maybe she had, but so quickly he'd missed it.

The black guys began to run now. 'Stop. For God's sake stop,' he hissed. But it was too late. Someone started firing an automatic weapon. One of the black guys stumbled, then brought up a gun and started shooting towards them. Suddenly, there was tracer whipping through the air above them. He could hear the singing crack as bullets went over his head and thwacked into the tree trunks. He cowered down, pressing his chin into the boards, but Sara was still going, pulling a magazine from the gun, slotting in another, working the action. He kept his eyes open, squinting through the slit. He wanted to move, to get up and leap backwards, run. But his limbs were frozen with fright. All he could do was watch. The tracers came in short bursts, arcing upwards and zipping away to the left of them.

The man she'd shot was crawling towards Janine, reaching a hand out to grab her. Janine was still kneeling there, in the middle of it all, howling and trembling. Sara got the gun down and fired once more. The man on the ground jerked back again, pulled his hand away, then started plucking at his clothing. She had hit him twice now. As Tom watched he managed to get something out of his clothing, then rolled on to his back. It was a pistol of some sort. It looked small, but the man could hardly hold it steady. There was blood all over him. He started shouting something at the top of his voice, pointing the gun at Janine. Tom saw it recoil, then heard the crack. Janine went over on to her face. He had shot her, brought the gun up and shot her.

Tom was frozen, his heart thundering, his eyes fixed on the body, unable to move or speak or react. *The girl had been shot.* It had happened, in real life, right there, less than one hundred yards away.

Sara snapped him back to life. She fired again, three times in quick succession, though all the men were now out of sight.

Even the one on the ground was now behind Janine's body. The tracer was still streaking above them, though. He felt the platform shudder and forced himself backwards to where the ladder was. He thought someone might have found them already and be climbing up. But there was no one there. He turned back to Sara. She'd dropped the gun and was flat out on the boards, arms splayed. He crawled to her, asking her if she was hit. He asked four times, finally almost shouting it. Her face was pressed into the wood and she was shaking her head violently. He couldn't see any blood on her. 'Let's go,' he shouted, abandoning caution. The shooting stopped, then started again. He could hear the men shouting things, see the tracer probing lazily into the trees about twenty feet to their right. They were firing wildly. She had been right – they couldn't place their location. Not yet.

'They killed her,' Sara moaned. 'They killed her ...'

'Let's go. Now.' He shook her roughly, but still she wouldn't move.

'I fucked it up,' she wailed. 'I hit him twice and he still killed her. I fucked it up ...'

He felt like there was a block of ice in his stomach. He slapped the side of her face, very hard, then shouted at her; 'Get up. Let's go. Now.'

She frowned and stared at him, as if not even aware he was there. He was on his knees now, acutely conscious that the position placed his head too high, above the level of the fencing.

'She's dead, we're alive,' he said urgently. 'I don't want to die. You have to help me.'

11

In London, John Lomax was still up, in his Hammersmith apartment with his mobile phone pressed to his ear, Rachel Gower talking to him in the unsteady, nervous voice he had come to associate with this time of year. He was in the room he called his office, sitting at the wooden desk there in the pool of light cast by two anglepoise lamps that had belonged to his father, with the paperwork from Folder 328 spread out on the desk in front of him, though he wasn't going to mention any of that to Rachel. He had been staring uselessly at it all when she called, half an hour ago. His eyes were tired and dry, but that didn't mean he was ready for bed. These days it wasn't unusual if he got to sleep after four and slept until ten or eleven in the morning. At fifty-two he was regressing to his teenage habits.

'It's Easter coming up,' she said. 'Next week, right? You doing anything? What about Tom? Will you see Tom? Or Eric? Tell me your plans. Talk to me.'

He frowned and waited for her to finish. Easter had been last Sunday. He'd spent it with her. They'd had roast lamb. 'I have no idea where Tom is,' he said, sighing. 'Eric is in the States. He'll be with his mother. I don't expect to hear from any of them.' Rachel knew all this too – he'd told her it all most recently about five hours ago – but her head was filled with other things right now. He knew the routine. She was talking for the sake of it, to keep the thoughts at bay.

Eric was his eldest lad – thirty-three, married with two kids. He worked for a software company based in California, and lived there. He'd always been his mother's boy, and since Jane and John had split up – eighteen years ago – they had only grown farther apart. Relations were cordial, but face-to-face meetings were very infrequent. Eric visited the UK often enough, but not to see his dad.

More depressing, something had also gone wrong with Tom, his youngest. When Tom was little they had been very close. He had grown into a good kid, rock solid, had even followed John into the police, though that had never been John's desire for him. Then suddenly there had been all the trouble, three years ago, ending with Tom being sacked from the Met. John blamed himself, because the tosser who had brought it all on Tom had been there throughout Tom's childhood, hanging around the edges, just waiting to do the damage. A 'friend' Tom should never have had. John should have seen that more clearly, he knew, done something to separate them earlier. But he hadn't; instead he had thought Tom would grow out of it, ditch the 'friendship' at the very latest when they all left school. But Tom was nothing if not loyal, though maybe he also blamed his father for that, because it seemed now like he hated him. Since he'd lost the job there had been barely any contact between them.

'I'm leaving here in about ten minutes, Rachel,' he said. 'I'll be at yours within an hour. Is that OK? Will you be OK till then?'

'Yes. Of course. Good. I'm glad you're coming, John. I'll put something on. Cook for us. What do you want? You want to go out and eat? Or shall I put something on?'

John looked at his wristwatch. It was ten past one in the morning. 'It's a bit late to go out,' he said gently. There was

a long silence. He waited a bit, thinking she might be checking the time, then started to worry. 'OK. Put something on,'
he said. 'I'm hungry. Cook something. Good idea. We don't
want to go out ...'

'No. Maybe not ...'

'Too warm to go out. We can sit on your terrace instead.
Drink some wine ...' In the middle of the night, he thought.
But so what? Go along with it. At least until he got over there.
It was a mistake to suggest a drink, though. She couldn't
drink anything, of course. She needed all her wits about her.
Wine would relax her, and then she would start thinking
about it all. This happened every year for a couple of days,
around the anniversary date. Only a few days, and it usually
vanished as quickly as it came, like a switch in her personality.
'*Can* you cook something for us?' he asked. He tried to think
of something complicated. 'Do you know how to do Beef
Wellington?'

'Beef Wellington?'

'Yes. Beef in pastry ...'

'I don't have any beef ...'

'Can you do pastry? Puff pastry, I think?' Or was it some
other kind? He didn't really know. It didn't matter. She could
look it up. That was something else to do, something else to
occupy her thoughts.

'Yes. But I don't have beef ...'

'I'll bring the beef. Look it up in a recipe book. I'll get some
beef out of the freezer and bring it, you do the pastry now.
Can you do that?'

'Yes. I'll try.'

'I'll be an hour. I promise. I'll leave now. I look forward to
it.'

'OK. Thanks, John. Thanks. I really appreciate this.'

He said goodbye then rang off and rubbed his face. Would

72

she really start to make pastry at one in the morning? And were they really going to make a Beef Wellington, then eat it at four, just before bed? 'What a fucking mess,' he said, out loud. 'What a miserable fucking mess.'

In front of him – from the back of Folder 328 – was a photo of Rachel as a twenty-eight-year-old, as she had been when he had first met her. Well, not quite. Because in her arms was her daughter, Lauren. Lauren had gone missing twenty-two years ago, when she was just thirteen months old. She was the reason Rachel and John Lomax had met, because John Lomax, a thirty-year-old detective inspector at the time, had been appointed Deputy Senior Investigating Officer on Operation Grenser, the inquiry into Lauren's disappearance. The Rachel Gower he had met back then, though very different to the fifty-year-old woman he knew so well now, was already something different to the woman in this photo. In this photo – taken about three weeks before Lauren vanished – Rachel was happy, her world intact.

Their friendship – was that what it should be called? – had started about two years after Lauren's disappearance. At first he had regarded it as part of his job that he should spend at least part of the anniversary with Rachel, counselling her, comforting her, bringing her up to date with what they were doing. Rachel and Roger, in fact, because her husband had been there also in the earlier years. But Roger had left her in 1993. For all the obvious reasons their relationship hadn't stood a chance. And Roger had pretty quickly decided that his daughter was dead. They had divorced, but Rachel had kept his name, because that was Lauren's name. For Rachel, Lauren would never be dead unless they found a body. But they had found nothing. And John's yearly visits had continued, and turned gradually into something else. Very gradually.

Now – twenty-two years on – he saw her once or twice a

week, and they were clearly having some kind of odd relationship, that neither truly understood. Since his retirement it had been building up to something, he thought. The new thing was the physicality. There was enough of it – of the sort that couldn't be written off as what friends or siblings might share – to make things frequently charged between them. But so far it had all led nowhere. They hadn't spoken about it, and he guessed neither of them knew what was going on, or what they wanted. It was going to end in some kind of crisis, he assumed – without having a clue why – but that wouldn't happen today. Today was too close to the dread date, the anniversary. For the last few days she had been like a completely different person. One who needed every ounce of energy focused on avoiding the memories and suppressing the images, both real and imaginary.

The original Grenser Senior Investigating Officer had retired in 1995, and died of a heart attack a year after that. Which had left John as the most senior officer who had worked the case for the two years it had been really active. He had been made SIO in due course, and had carried out frequent reviews, including the grand reopening during 2003, with a full squad and ambitious forensic strategies centred on new possibilities in DNA technology. But nothing had come of it all. He had been left with it – the case that wouldn't go away. It had become his obsession, no longer a secret obsession since the reopening in 2003, because he had gone public with his hopes then, and colleagues had immediately realised that it wasn't just another job for him.

Not surprisingly. As Deputy SIO he had practically run the hunt for Lauren back in 1990 and 1991 – it had been his entire life for over two years, exactly as it had been Rachel's entire life ever since then. He had lived and breathed every detail of the inquiry. Indeed, as the material had mounted to nearly a hundred thousand pages he was the only person on the team who had actual knowledge of every single item. Statement readers and detective sergeants running the various teams, HOLMES compilers and his own deputies had all come and gone over the years. He was the only point of continuity. He had known everything there was to know about the case, and still did, though it was harder now to remember details.

On shelves around his study he had all his policy books, plus hard copies of nearly half the material gathered. And even now, two years after he had retired, they were only too happy to allow him to borrow box after box from the store. No one else was looking at it, no one else cared. He was a cheap review facility. All they had to pay for was the photocopying.

He did it because he was haunted by a single idea and a single image. The image was a simple photo of Lauren, taken by her mother on 13 April 1990 – Friday the thirteenth, unlucky Friday – the day before she was snatched. In it Lauren's beautiful, wide open, unsuspecting blue eyes looked directly at the camera and she was smiling, her head a mass of gorgeous black curls, just like her mother's. John couldn't look at the image without a lump catching in his throat. Because he knew the reality of these cases, he knew what had probably happened; he knew what Lauren – the harmless, helpless child in that image – must have been put through in the hours following her disappearance. And that was his fault, because he had been charged with finding her, and he had failed.

The idea was more rational, and more persuasive: they had spent more than three years at Grenser, full time, with over fifty dedicated detectives working to trace Lauren, they had gathered nearly a hundred thousand pages of statements and information. It was more than enough. John was convinced that *somewhere* in all of that material, the answer was *already* found. It *had* to be.

And he had missed it.

So for the last year he had been going through it all again, box by box.

12

They crouched knee-deep in decaying vegetation, squeezed under the rotting, broken trunk of a fallen tree, with their backs against an outcrop of slippery, moss-covered rock. The spot was in darkness, in a dense, boggy part of the jungle, infested with flies that bit at will, unchecked. He could barely see her face beside him. All around them there was a high-pitched shrilling. He couldn't locate the insect that was making it, but there must have been thousands of them. At some point the noise was so loud it sounded like they were next to a racing track. Where his feet were buried in the leaf mould or mud – or whatever it was – he could sometimes feel things wriggling or crawling against his shins. When he moved his feet the mud sucked at them, then gave off bubbles of gas that smelled like bad eggs and would probably poison them, if they breathed enough of it. He was trying to keep focus. Survival was all that mattered, which right now meant getting under cover. This stinking swamp was cover. Above them, through the trees, they could still hear intermittent gunfire.

'Is it dangerous here?' he asked, keeping his voice low. He wanted to know the extent of the threat. Maybe there would be some species of deadly wildlife he had no idea about.

She didn't answer him. She was right beside him, pressed up against him, the gun across her knees so that the stock was half on his also. He could see her outline, see her shoulders trembling. She had her head down. She was struggling with her own images and thoughts, trying to keep the lid on them. They had run for maybe thirty minutes through the jungle, keeping off the trails, going straight through anything in their way, so that their faces, hands, arms and legs were scratched and bleeding. They were still catching their breath. Tom thought they might have put about one thousand five hundred yards between themselves and the compound. It seemed a long way, in relative darkness, but come daylight it would be only a short walk. 'It's not far enough,' he said to her. 'We have to keep going. What's making that noise?' Whatever it was had got suddenly louder, becoming so raucous he could no longer whisper.

'It's a tree frog,' she said. 'It's harmless, tiny. There are thousands of them. We're at the edge of a mangrove swamp. In six hours this place will be flooded.'

The guns started up again – short bursts of automatic fire, quite far off, though. 'They brought plenty of ammo,' he said. 'But they'll start running low. Those things must fire off a whole clip in a few seconds.'

She shook her head. 'I don't know. I don't know anything about those guns.'

'I thought you must be an expert.' She was going to break down again, he thought. He needed her to keep her brain working, not give in to it. She was the only one who might know where they were and how to get to the phone. 'You do a lot of hunting? Is that how you know how to shoot?' It seemed like the thing someone with her background might go for.

'Hunting?' Her face turned towards him. He could just see the whites of her eyes. 'We're here on a project to save animals, not kill them.'

78

'But you know how to shoot. Did your father teach you?' Keep her talking. Keep her mind off it.

'My father? That's a nice idea. I hardly know my father. Jean-Marc trained me, for protection. I've been shooting this one gun – and a few pistols – for about two years. That's it. We don't shoot animals. Just targets. For self-defence. In case something like this happened. It's not actually a hunting rifle. It's a sniper rifle, an AIAW. The same kind the British army uses.'

OK – for hunting *people*, then, not animals. 'He taught you well.'

She nodded, then started to sob out loud as she remembered what had just happened to Jean-Marc. Jean-Marc was dead, he assumed, one of the pile of people they had tossed out the back. 'Let's not assume anything,' he said, and right then the frog noise stopped suddenly, all of them together, as if on cue, leaving a silence so deafening it sounded like he had shouted. He reverted to whispering. 'Let's not imagine things. We need to get help. That's the priority.'

'He's dead,' she said, also whispering. 'The one on the radio was talking about him. Jean-Marc told me he was going to make a run for the south trail. I spoke to him on the two-way before they got to my room. It was one of the drills we did – he runs that way to try to draw them off, while I get out to the north. He did it to protect me ...'

'He might have got away, then.'

'That's not what they said.'

'No.' She was right, but he didn't want her dwelling on it. 'They knew about your birthday. Did you hear that? Were they right? Is it your birthday in five days?'

She nodded miserably. 'I'll be twenty-one.' She groaned. 'I think I recognised the one who was near us – later, when he was behind Janine, when ...'

When you shot him. Twice. 'Recognised him? Who is he?' Who *was* he?

'I think he's a policeman from Mahe.'

'Fuck. Are you sure?'

She shook her head. 'Not sure, but there was a German on Mahe, working for the CID. We had a burglary at one of the houses there. I think he interviewed me. About two months ago. Maybe.'

'And that's how he knows about your birthday? But did you understand what they meant about it?'

'No. None of it. I don't know what's going on.'

'If it was a simple kidnap, or robbery, why would your birthday matter?'

'Because he thinks there'll be people coming here, like he said – to celebrate it.'

'And are there? Are there people coming that we can wait for?'

'There's no one coming. I don't give a shit about my birthday. And I don't have friends like that. I hardly have any friends at all. Janine was my single friend. You don't know what it's like being me, having all this fucking money.' She'd said something like that last night, over the wine, while they were getting pleasantly drunk, getting to know each other. It seemed a world away now.

He swatted the flies off his bare arm, then shuffled closer to her. He put an arm around her shoulders, pushing it between the slimy rock and her shirt. 'It's OK, Sara,' he said, his voice weak, as though he was far from convinced. 'It's OK. We're OK here. They won't come for us here.' Was it true? It didn't matter. He had to get her calm, then get moving again. He had a splitting headache – through the heat, the wine, the dead guy whacking him with the shotgun stock, the Russian guy stamping on him yesterday. He needed water, painkillers, an

X-ray, maybe – but anyway, they couldn't just lie here. They had to get to the phone. 'They will go now, if we're lucky,' he added. 'What they were trying hasn't worked. I doubt they have a plan B. Besides, they'll never find us in this jungle. They must know that. So we're OK.'

'I'm not worried about us,' she said. She pushed her head into his shoulder. 'They killed Janine.' She started to take big gulps of air. 'They had her stripped ... kneeling there ... Janine ... poor Janine ... she never hurt anybody ... she was terrified. I could see it. She's dead because she was here, because of me ... they're all dead because of me ... my mother was right ... it's too dangerous here ... I should never have come ... I was too reckless, too selfish ... I've killed them all ...'

He tightened his arm, pulling her closer. 'Listen to me,' he said, very gently. He stroked his hand across her shoulder. 'Listen to me, Sara. This had nothing to do with you. This is crime. Those people up there made the choices, *they* decided to kidnap you. You were just living your life. You're not to blame for any of this. Trust me. I know this.'

'They came for *me*. Because I am here ...'

'But you didn't do anything wrong. *They* did the killing. *They* made those decisions. Not you.'

She wasn't convinced. He held her while she shook and sobbed. After a few minutes she moved her head to the side and started to dry-retch. 'I'm so frightened,' she said, between gasps. 'I'm so frightened. I think we're going to die ...' She sounded like she was choking.

'Listen to me,' he said, louder this time. 'I'm frightened too. I've never been in anything like this. But we've got to fight it. We've got to keep ourselves working, thinking, moving. If we don't then they win. This is a big enough island. Big enough to get lost in. They can't find us. We can work our way round to the phone – you know how to get to it, right?'

She didn't respond. She was still retching.

'Do you know how to get to the phone, Sara?'

'I can't do it. I can't …'

He used his hand to move her face so he could see her eyes. 'You have to think of your family. There are people who need you, who love you … people you want to see again …'

She shook her head, then made an effort to wipe her eyes. 'I'm sorry,' she said. 'I sound pathetic. But my family aren't like an ordinary family. If I were kidnapped and a ransom were demanded they wouldn't pay. It's a family policy – like a state might have a policy of not dealing with terrorists. There's so much fucking money they have to have policies for it – so they don't lose it by making silly decisions, so *feelings* don't get in the way.'

'That's what they say – that's the information they put out. But it will be different now it's happening. Believe me. Your mother will care.'

'My mother isn't even sane … you haven't met her, you don't know …'

'Your father, then …?'

She shook her head. 'Don't even think about him. The only people who ever really cared about me were people we have paid to care. That's the truth.'

'Well, I care …'

'I paid you.'

'Not yet you didn't.'

'I'm sorry.' She wiped her eyes again, took deeper, more controlled breaths. 'I'm really sorry. I must sound pathetic. You saved my life up there. If you hadn't come in …'

'Ditto. You shot the fucker. Just in time, because I'm no fighter, and guns scare me shitless. We're doing well. We're working together. So let's keep it up. OK?'

She was silent, but at least calming down a bit.

'There'll be time enough to think about all of this,' he said carefully. 'But not right now. Right now we have to think about getting to that phone and getting help. OK?'

He thought he saw her nod. 'OK,' she murmured. 'And thank you.' He felt her hand get hold of his and hang on to it. 'Thank you for not leaving me back there, when I said you should.'

There'll be time enough to think about all of this, he said carefully, but not right now. Right now we have to think about getting to that phone and perhaps help. OK?

He thought he saw her nod. OK, she murmured. You do that again? He felt her hand let hold of his and jump on to it. Thank you for not leaving, back there, when I said you should.

13

For hours Maxim was strung out on adrenalin, too emotional to act sensibly. He could hardly believe things had gone so wrong. In the darkness he sat in a huddle, trying to control his breathing, trying to get the killing out of his head. As the sun started to rise his heart finally began to slow. Then he could think about it, work out what to do.

He took one of the Land Rovers parked behind the generator shed and drove very slowly over a heavily rutted road, the only one on the island. He got to the hill at the other end by eight, two hours later. By then he was beginning to feel more solid. He would be ahead of her – he was certain of that, because she wouldn't dare use the road, and he'd been told she knew the island well, so she would know not to risk moving too far through the jungle in darkness. He remembered all too well, from twenty-two years ago, just how difficult it was to move through the jungle, even by day. There were multiple hazards, including some type of poisonous frog a previous inhabitant had introduced from the Amazon. He had once seen one of the servants step on one and nearly choke to death.

He drove the Land Rover into a dip by the end of the road and made some effort to cover it with broken branches. She would find it if she walked that way, or looked hard enough, but that didn't matter. The keys were on a bulky ring, which would make noise, so he placed them on top of the nearside wheel. That would do. At the end of the day she was a spoilt little rich kid who was desperate and alone. He hoped – with a feeling of some bitterness now, because when things went as wrong as this it was hard not to take it personally – that the night had brought her a little dose of reality. That would make her careful, but she didn't have any options that would make her unpredictable. She had to try to get to this phone – the one at the hill summit – because it was the only communication facility she had. So even if she found the Land Rover and suspected he was here ahead of her, she would still have to make her way up the hill eventually. And when that happened, he would be waiting. He had water, he had food, he had patience. He would get her.

Nevertheless, he took the single, stony path up the slope slowly, the machine pistol ready, just in case he was wrong and she'd somehow beaten him to it.

By 8.30 it was already getting hot. The hill wasn't high, no more than a hundred and fifty feet, but stood out because most of the island was flat, and because the slopes were suddenly rocky, relatively clear of vegetation. It was possible to get to the summit, he remembered, without using the path, but difficult. You would need rock-climbing skills, and he doubted she had those.

On the other hand, she had already surprised him enough to fuck things up this badly. His original plan had been to send in only the Somalis – keeping a low profile himself – get them to take the girl alive and then get off the island without bloodshed. He had wanted the staff left alive to report the event – to report the descriptions of the Somalis, in particular. That was his cover plan – the pirate raid fiction.

But everything had fucked up. First Forestier, the security guy, running off armed, trying to lure him away. He had got one of the Somalis while they were chasing him through the jungle, a clean head shot from twenty feet back, while moving. That had been a warning to Max – after that it had been a question of self-preservation. So Forestier was dead. And then Sara Eaton had a gun, it seemed – from the damage it inflicted he was guessing it was a hunting rifle – and knew how to use it. She had managed to kill the man he had sent in to take her, and later, more irritatingly, she had taken out his one connection to this place – Steiner. She had hit Steiner twice, though not before he had shot her friend, for no good reason at all. They had both died at Maxim's feet, with Maxim trying desperately to stem the bleeding, while the three stupid Somalis that were left had gone into a senseless, fear-driven shooting frenzy, killing everything in sight, including the security staff that Maxim had already bought off, who might now have been useful, and including the poor girl at the boat.

Maxim had sent them off in the second boat. They were a waste of space once the pirate story wasn't going to run – there was no one still alive to spread it – and they'd used up all their ammo. Plus, they were a liability. So there was only himself left now.

It was a risk coming here, he knew. It left no one covering the house and the dock, and while the seaplane was useless – the Somalis had killed the pilot – it was just possible that if the girl put her mind to it she might find the first boat, hidden off the beach at the top of the southern promontory. But then she would have to know how to navigate to the nearest island – Remogos – and he didn't think she would have a clue where to start with that. She had people to do that for her. All her life she'd had people doing things for her.

He thought about that on the way up and had a moment of doubt. Was he underestimating her? Steiner was dead because he'd underestimated her ability to shoot. Max should have guessed someone from that background would know how to use a hunting rifle. They spent half their time killing animals for pleasure – foxes, boars, bears, deer – they shot them all, so why not humans? He felt a begrudging, bitter admiration for her – she had surprised him, matched him, beaten him. He would need to be careful not to compound the errors.

He got to the top of the hill and made his way to the small concrete blockhouse they'd erected there, housing the satellite phone – the dish prominent on the roof – plus the solar panels and battery that powered it. It was the same building that had been here twenty-two years ago, maybe even the same dated technology. At first he was just going to pull the dish down and break it, but then he thought she might see that from a distance, so instead he got his knife out and simply cut the cabling connecting it to the rest of the installation. That done, he quickly scouted the summit and the fields of fire across the boulder-strewn slopes that led down to the cliffs, then picked a spot under a growth of ferns, lay down and tried to get himself comfortable. He was on the edge of a low cliff that fell off towards the road, and if he turned his head he could see where he'd hidden the Land Rover. That was about three hundred and fifty yards distant – too far for anything but a lucky hit with the little machine pistol – but then he had no intention of trying to kill her. Sara Eaton was worth a fortune – he needed her alive.

14

It was nearing midday by the time they got to within sight of the hill, and by then Sara was beginning to worry about Tom Lomax. He said nothing to her, was continuously out of breath and drenched in sweat, and was beginning to stagger, rather than walk, tripping frequently. Once they had to stop for half an hour as he struggled to stop himself vomiting. He was dehydrated, obviously, but was he concussed as well? She didn't know what they could do about it if he was. He had a very angry bruise over his left temple, to match the swelling over his right cheek – she had not seen it but the man he had tackled in her bedroom had struck him there with the stock of his weapon, he said.

She led them slowly through dense vegetation – so thick she would normally have used a machete to get through – up a small rise, from the top of which she knew they would be able to observe the southern slopes of the hill. Tom had insisted they not walk straight up. 'They know about your birthday,' he had said, 'so they will probably know about this phone.'

The temperatures were high and they'd had no liquid for many hours, and even then only the juice from fruits that had been far from ripe. There had been two streams on the way, but she had stopped him from drinking; drinking any water on the island without sterilisation could result in a form of dysentery, the onset of which was rapid and exhausting. It wouldn't do any good if he drank his fill only to be reduced within hours to an invalid, shivering feverishly between bouts of bloody diarrhoea. Eating the unripe fruit ran lesser risks – stomach cramps, perhaps, but usually not the fever.

She knew the area around the hill very well, knew the entire island better than anyone else, but especially the area around the hill, because this was where the black mandrills had had their largest colony about a year ago. They'd moved on now, but she had spent a lot of the previous year in this area, with Janine.

Thinking about that time brought on intense sensations of panic and disorientation. She had to pause, crouch, screw her eyes shut, concentrate. It was light now, and the events of the previous night were already absurdly obscure. They were night memories, clouded by the effects of adrenalin and desperation. Nothing she could recall seemed real. Yet she knew it had all happened, knew it was still going on, knew Janine and Jean-Marc and possibly all the others were dead. When she gave in to it, and just sat down and cried and trembled, *then* everything seemed real. But if she succeeded in doing what he repeatedly told her to do – refusing to think about Janine or dwell on anything that was happening – then she had a bewildering, terrifying sense of the ground being pulled from beneath her, like she was falling through some void, with no way out. 'We just need to concentrate on one task,' he had told her. 'And that's to get to that phone safely. Everything else will get us killed.' So she crouched low and tried to blot out the thoughts and images. She was like that for about five minutes, just below the brow of the rise.

Getting here safely had gone more slowly than expected. They had waited until light because the jungle was full of potentially fatal hazards. They hadn't dared use the road either, so she had led them a very long route, right around

89

her beloved, picturesque East Bay – now reduced in her eyes to nothing but a series of irritating obstacles and exposed areas – before cutting inland. This meant they had also had to pass very close to the area that was infested with the golden dart frogs. A major part of their programme to save the black mandrills involved an effort to wipe out this non-indigenous population. They had calculated that about forty per cent of the mandrill decline was due to contact with the frogs, and Sara knew exactly how unpleasant it could be to come into contact with their skin. The effect was far from fatal – they lacked the toxins their native Amazonian cousins could produce – but it was enough to incapacitate.

When she could breathe normally, she went down on to her belly and inched forward to the crest. She was pushing through the last fronds and getting the gun into position before she realised Tom was no longer with her. Nevertheless, she spent a few minutes looking through the powerful scope. The satellite dish was clearly visible, a few hundred yards distant – along with the shed there, the relatively bare hilltop, the stony path up that they had only recently resurfaced with rubble. Her heart started to beat faster, her spirits picking up. For a fleeting second she was almost hopeful. There was no one in sight, no one there. So they could get up there quickly, call for help. They could do it. For the first time since all this had started she felt that she might actually be able to get out of it.

She edged away and then picked her way back down the treacherous incline. She found him at the bottom, gulping greedily from a tiny spring he had found. 'I'm sorry,' he said, looking at her strangely. 'But I can't function unless I drink some water … no choice …' He was shivering like he already had a fever.

'It will make you ill,' she said quietly.

'Not right away,' he said. 'And maybe not at all. It's a calculated risk.' He straightened up with difficulty and tried to smile at her. 'I was going to pass out. It's the lesser of two evils.'

She shook her head. 'It's not. I've had dysentery twice. It can kill you.' She went over and looked at the source he was drinking from. It came straight out of the rocks in a tiny trickle. It looked pure, beautiful, tempting. But that didn't guarantee much. 'You should have listened to me,' she said, feeling a little angry. What was she going to do when he collapsed? He shrugged, said sorry again, but seemed distracted.

'I've seen the hill,' she said, getting her mind off it. 'It's clear.' She almost smiled at him. Her heart jumped inside her as she told him.

But he just frowned. 'Let *me* look,' he said.

That annoyed her as well – the lack of trust he'd shown all morning, despite this being *her* island, despite him not having a clue – but she led him back up the slope.

They both lay flat in the grasses and ferns, side by side. He took the gun off her and spent ten minutes staring through the scope, moving it around. He was breathing in short little breaths and looked like he was struggling to keep his eyes open. Finally he laid it aside and asked her to look. 'Down by the bend in the road. I think it's a car.'

She put the scope to her eyes, suddenly frightened again, and focused it where he directed. She saw it at once. She couldn't understand how she had missed it first time. It was a Land Rover, one of hers. 'It could be one of the security staff,' she said. 'It must be.' They'd talked about the security staff a few hours ago. He had thought that they'd been bought off, probably by the man who she knew as a policeman from Mahe. The second one she'd shot. He couldn't see how people could have come ashore otherwise. But she hadn't liked that idea.

'They knew I would come here,' she suggested now. 'They're covering it for me.'

'The car is certainly covered,' he said. 'Covered in leaves and branches, so we can't see it. Would they do that?'

He took the gun again, spent another few minutes staring ahead, at the hill this time. 'The dish is there,' he said, as if wondering whether she could be right. 'If it was the Somalis they'd have trashed that, maybe. Just to be sure.'

But she already knew he was right. Her security people wouldn't camouflage the car. They were all former police officers from the islands, which meant they were of limited intelligence. The truth was they wouldn't even come here. If they were nowhere to be seen it was more likely they had taken her boat and fled at the first sign of trouble. She started to get emotional again, and took the gun off him quickly. The fear was like something physical, rising up in her throat. She put the crosshairs on the dish and examined it carefully. It looked intact. She moved to the shed, the windows, the door lock. Everything looked normal. She slid it up to the twin solar panels, then followed the cabling running away from them. Nothing to see. A couple of degrees higher were the cables coming out of the dish. She stared at them. She put the gun down, feeling it flooding over her. She started to cry.

'What?' he whispered, nervous now. 'What is it?'

'The wires from the dish,' she spluttered. 'They've all been hacked through.'

He checked. Then they both lay there, in silence, breathing too fast.

'They're already here,' she said. 'They're watching us. They know we're here.'

He pulled her back, away from the exposed edge. 'OK,' he said, squinting his eyes against the sunlight. 'Plan B. We can't call for help. But we must be able to find a boat.'

'All the boats are back by the house,' she said, trying to think about it. 'At the dock. But they must have boats too. So even if we could get into one of ours without them seeing, they could follow us out …'

She watched him chewing his lip, thinking furiously. 'And you're sure the pilot was one of those bodies?' he demanded.

She nodded. They had carried Philippe out of the house, tossed him on to the ground.

'So they killed him,' he said. 'So we can't use the fucking plane …'

'I can fly the plane,' she told him.

He looked startled. 'You know how to fly?'

'Yes. If we can get to it. Flying it isn't the problem …'

'You know how to fly and navigate?' It looked like he didn't believe her.

'Yes. Of course.' She had taken a course, two years ago. She had a full private licence, though hadn't kept her hours up. 'That's not unusual …' she started, then stopped. Not unusual in her world, she thought.

'So why didn't you say you could fly when we were back at the other end of the island, where the fucking plane is?'

'What good would that have done? They were trying to kill us, remember? They were all over the dock, all over the house.'

He sighed. 'Well, we've no option now. We have to get to it. We have to try.' He looked back towards the brow of the hill. 'We take the Land Rover,' he said quickly. 'Drive back to the dock. That way we leave at least some of them here. They will be waiting in a spot that covers the hill, not the car – that's why they've put the branches on it, because they're not covering it. So we can get to the car and get away, leave them here, on foot. That will be enough of a head start.'

'You think they were stupid enough to leave the keys in the ignition?'

'I can start it without keys. It's an old Land Rover, right? No security systems?'

'Yes.'

'I can handle that. You cover me, from here. I work my way down. I start the car, drive it to the road right below where you are. You run down. We drive off.'

'What do I do if I see someone?'

'Shoot them.'

'Kill them? You want me to kill them?'

'If they're coming at me and they're armed. Fuck, yes. Kill them.'

He was gone before she could object, stumbling quickly to the base of the slope, movements filled with a sudden urgency. She didn't understand it at all. They had just spent hours laboriously toiling through the thickets just so as to avoid the road, in case it was covered. Yet now he wanted to take a car and drive along it. What had changed? Too much heat, not enough food and water?

She went after him a couple of steps, hissing at him to stop. He turned back and waved at her, telling her to get going to the top again. He was in a half-crouch, face lathered with sweat. For a moment she wondered whether to chase him, or trust that he knew what he was doing, but he was already cutting left, skirting the thicker bushes to put him on a level with the Land Rover. She would have to shout to slow him, and she didn't dare do that. In a few seconds he would be past the shoulder of the slope they were on and fully exposed to view. When that happened she had to have the rifle ready, she had to be able to cover him. She started to move quickly back up the slope.

15

Rachel could feel it passing. It was leaving her. Same thing every year, the same process she had to go through. The frantic fear – all her nightmare scenarios about what might be happening to Lauren – giving way to a numb desperation. She was in her garden now, standing barefoot, in her pyjamas, at three in the afternoon, staring fixedly at the clematis which completely covered the crumbling brick wall between her property and the next, though without really seeing it. The sun was hot on the back of her head, she had a pounding headache. A bright, clear sky, too warm for the time of year, like it was summer already.

Behind her John was in the house, still sleeping in her bed. They had gone to bed at eight o'clock this morning. She couldn't think about that now, couldn't think about what she was to make of her relationship with him. That would count as dealing with normal life, or what passed for normal these days. John had kept her going through it this year, as he had last year and the year before. Close to her, but not too close. Were they moving into something more intimate? Was that what was happening? She couldn't even contemplate it. She shook her head to get rid of the thought.

She remembered that she had stood out here like this twenty-two years ago, two days after Lauren had vanished, and the weather had been the same. Same garden, same sunlight.

Same lost hours between. But it was Roger who had been inside the house then. Dealing with things, on the phone, with the police, the press. She had collapsed inside herself, stopped functioning. There had been no sleep at all between the disappearance and some point about seven days later, when she had literally collapsed and been taken into hospital. But before that she had stood out here, as she was now, and as she had every year since, silently staring at nothing, numb. She was caught in an endless behavioural loop. It would never be over. Not until Lauren came back. Or until she accepted it. Accepted what everyone else was convinced was true.

That day – the first time – twenty-two years ago, it had been worse, of course. Everything had been horrifically overpowering, pushing her under, suffocating her. She hadn't slept, hadn't eaten. Her digestive system wouldn't let her eat. She had tried – because Roger had told her that she would need strength – but it had been futile.

It was the day of the interview, the famous TV interview. The police were behind it, thinking it could only help – to get as much publicity as possible, as quickly as possible. And the only way to really get widespread coverage was TV. So Roger had persuaded her. But before they had all arrived, invading their house (*their* house – it had still been Lauren's house then too) with their lights and their cameras and microphones and false concern, before all that she had been out here, sitting on this lawn in her pyjamas, shivering.

She couldn't remember all that she had been thinking, fifty-five hours into the nightmare. Not exactly. It was a blur now, the continuous knife edge, waiting and waiting and waiting for news that never came – the impossible, compressing mental tension. She had come out here with the thought that she would smash her head on the tree at the bottom of the garden – she recalled that. The tree had been cut down now, but she hadn't reached it anyway. She had collapsed in the middle of the lawn. Roger had come out and found her, to tell her the TV producers were here already, and she had stood up very unsteadily, looking at him, but hardly seeing him.

'We have to go in,' he said. 'We have to get ready for them. It's important.' Then he had screwed his face up and looked strangely at her. 'Christ above, Rachel,' he had said. 'What have you done?'

She had realised only gradually what he was talking about. She had soiled herself. She had sat there on this grass and it had just come out, without her knowing. 'I'm sorry,' she had mumbled. 'I didn't know. I didn't notice.'

He had leaned into her and hugged her, tried to comfort her. She had thought, at first, that he was going to shout at her or get angry. But he didn't. He had just put his arms around her, not caring. Had they cried for a while, standing here, on the lawn, with the TV producers waiting in the living room? Probably.

The nightmare had been everywhere, including inside her guts. They were living within it. A lifetime of overwhelming emotion expended in a few hours, then on and on and on, with no end. There was nothing left for afterwards, for the rest of their lives. It had sterilised them. That was how she thought of it now. Everything afterwards was seen from a perspective that trivialised the ordinary details of life. Because nothing could match the absence of Lauren.

She was tired of it. Exhausted. If it could be got rid of, somehow, now, she would do it. But she didn't know how. Still, twenty-two years later, she didn't have a clue.

16

Tom was functioning on adrenalin. His head was on fire, the headache like a drumbeat behind his eyes, his heart too fast and too loud. He was shaking like he had a fever, sweating, clumsy on his feet. But he had stared through the scope and seen the car. He had spotted it. So his eyes were OK, his brain was still working. He was doing what he had to. They were trapped here. The phone was cut, covered. So there wasn't another option to consider. If he hung around in the sunlight any longer, without water, waiting for them to find them, he would crack. So he had to act.

As he came round the slope and started running unsteadily down towards the road all he could think about was that he was running into somebody's crosshairs. He tripped twice, the second time going down and rolling messily. But as he came up there was still no shot, no movement from the hill in front of him, nothing between himself and the road except a short flat stretch of long grass. He could see where the Land Rover would be. He kept going, gasping for air. He was so unfit. If he got out of this he was going to start training again. For definite. He promised it to himself.

The grass was stiff and hard, whipping against his face so that he had to flail his arms in front, like he was fighting off some invisible force. Just before the road there was a ditch that he missed. He went down again, jarring his chin on the ground. But still no shooting.

He was halfway across the road, head down, before he heard the muffled crack of her gun. Or thought he did. He froze, stupidly, skidding to a stop and staring wildly behind him to try to see. Then he saw movement up on the bigger hill, a shape running.

He started to sprint for the Land Rover again. He could see it now, not twenty paces in front, down a small dip, into bushes. He leapt over the rim of the dip, into the undergrowth, just as a crackle sounded off to his left. A machine pistol. Or something like that – something small. He saw no bullets striking anywhere, heard no whining as they passed close, so kept going. He almost ran into the back of the Land Rover. He pushed through the branches around it, going for the driver's door. The crackle came again, somewhere behind and above him. This time he heard something snapping through the air, saw the back window of the Land Rover shatter. He hit the ground, flat out, crawled under the car and lay still.

But it took him only a split second to realise that like that he was certainly going to die. He had to move. To get the car going was their only chance. He pulled himself out and crouched by the front wheel, waiting to see if the bullets started again. Someone had been shooting at him, trying to kill him. He tried to get a proper grip on that thought. His eyes passed across a metallic cluster on top of the wheel. He came back to it and, despite everything, couldn't stop himself smirking. He wasn't going to have to mess around with the wiring while some fucker took potshots. He'd found the keys. There were six or seven on a big ring. He moved quickly sideways and yanked the driver's door open. He was up to his head in long reeds, but still he heard the burst of fire. This time nothing broke. It sounded different. Were they shooting at Sara instead? He climbed quickly inside, chest tight, checked the keys, found the one that looked the best match, held his breath, put his foot on the clutch and tried it. The engine spluttered into life first time.

Sara heard the engine, but couldn't look in that direction. She had her eye fixed to the scope and was concentrating all her attention on keeping the weapon steady. Right in the crosshairs was the man's head. She had the cross right over his temple. She took a long slow breath and listened for her heart, as Jean-Marc had taught her. The man was tall, with long blond hair, pushed back from his face. He was white. Tanned skin, hard face. She could see him very clearly because the scope was first class and very powerful. He had a distinctive, V-shaped scar below his right temple, extending into his cheek. She had seen it yesterday too – though not as clearly – and thought then that she had seen it somewhere before, that she had seen this man before, somewhere. But if she had, then she didn't know him. He certainly wasn't Somali. He wasn't a pirate from East Africa.

He was crouched behind a boulder with bushes growing near to it. Some of the bushes obscured his body. But not his head. He had run from near to the shed first, then took aim towards the Land Rover and let off a quick burst with some short, stubby weapon. It had jerked all over as he fired and she had thought then – even with her limited knowledge – that he would be lucky to hit Tom. Very lucky. The distance was over three hundred yards. What he was firing with had to be worse than a handgun, in terms of accuracy.

Nevertheless, she had panicked and her first shot at him had gone so wide she was sure he hadn't even heard it. But now he had fired again, paused, and as he had taken aim and crouched she had fired another shot. Still clumsy, but it had hit the rock near his body and he had seen it, she thought, or felt it. Immediately he had gone low. But not low enough. He had no idea where she was. She was firing a bespoke Accuracy International Arctic Warfare sniper rifle, with integral suppressor, and she had brought three magazines with her. The magazines were custom-made – five shots instead of ten, to reduce their weight. She was on the last now, and the last two rounds. She had to make them count. She had to remember everything Jean-Marc had taught her. She had hit targets at triple this distance. But she had never been panicking like this. The man wasn't looking for Tom now, he was looking for her. She heard the Land Rover engine revving. If she was accurate she would kill him now. She knew she could do it.

The difficulty – shooting alone – was knowing whether you had hit, and if not, how close you'd got, because you couldn't keep the scope and your eyes motionless through the discharge, so you normally missed seeing the exact location of the hit, especially at short range. Jean-Marc had spent hours on end practising this with her, getting the blind spot down to a minimum. In the army, he'd told her, snipers always had someone else to spot for them. Sometimes he had spotted for her with a special ranged sight. But now she was alone. She settled the crosshairs over the head, about an inch from the neck.

But suddenly she felt sick with it. She didn't want to kill this man. She didn't want to kill anybody. She moved the crosshairs down and placed them over his gun instead. It was resting against the rock he was leaning against. She squeezed the trigger. Blinked through the recoil. Took a breath. Quick adjustment, then eyes back to the scope, as fast as she could. As her eyes refocused she saw the man was staggering backwards, the gun out of his hands, out of sight. Had she hit it?

She thought she must have. Jean-Marc would have leapt up from beside her and slapped her on the back.

She could hear the Land Rover moving now, revving too high. She slipped her eyes off the scope and looked right, in time to see Tom spin it round in a cloud of dust, already on the road, then start to accelerate towards her position. She put her eye to the scope again. It took a second, but she could see the man crawling for safety. She placed the crosshairs about two foot from his head and fired a shot into the ground there. Her last round. When she got her eye back on target she could see him motionless, trying to pull his head in. He definitely knew what was going on now. There was blood on his hands – from where she had hit the gun, she assumed. Or maybe she'd hit his arm. She got to her feet, pushed the rifle away and started to run down the slope in front of her, waving towards Tom.

He was at the base of the slope ahead of her, the truck stopped. He was leaning over, opening the passenger door, the engine going full blast. She dived in and yelled something at him, then he was revving the motor and zigzagging crazily across the road. She pulled the door shut behind her and got her head down. 'Go! Go! Go!' she was yelling.

He drove with his head low and deliberately moved the truck from one side of the road to the other. She was waiting for something to happen, waiting for bullets to start hitting them, or the car to turn over. After a few seconds she risked putting her head up and looked back through the smashed rear window. The road behind them twisted off into the trees. There was no one there. She couldn't see the hill any more. They'd done it. She started to laugh hysterically. He slowed down and held an unsteady hand up to her, for a high five, a big, crooked grin on his bruised face. She slapped his palm, then leaned over and hugged his arm.

But the feeling of euphoria didn't last. When she was certain they were not being followed she made him stop. 'I saw only one guy,' she said. 'It was the other white guy, the one with the scar.'

'The scar?'

'He has a V-shaped scar on his cheek. The other one didn't have that.'

'Did you get him?'

'I hit him, I think. I'm not sure. But there was only one. That means the rest could be anywhere.'

He leaned his head on the wheel, but then snapped it up and stared out at the wall of trees. 'Fuck,' he whispered, automatically. 'What was the plan again?'

17

The TV interview had taken place in her living room. But it hadn't looked like her living room. That was the first thing that had thrown her. She recognised nothing. It was like passing through a door into another building, into a sea of staring faces. So many unknown faces she had barely been able to get in. To squeeze them in – she found out later – all her furniture had been moved out to the garage, except her beige sofa and a couple of chairs. Everything else was gone – the pictures on the wall, the rug from the floor, the plant pots and ornaments. The room had been stripped and filled with technicians and reporters and their electronic equipment. She was so confused by it that as she went through the door and looked at them all she stopped dead, frowning, thinking there had been some kind of absurd mistake.

Then Roger had taken over. He held her arm and walked just in front of her, pushing past them all, gently pulling her in after him. They had all been talking – she realised that was the noise she could hear coming down the stairs – but as soon as she appeared there was silence, voices trailing abruptly off, leaving an atmosphere full of body odour, heat and discomfort – not just because there must have been between twenty and thirty people filling the space in front of her sofa and around it, but also from the lights they'd put up. Too bright to look at, they were shining on to huge reflectors that were angled to point down at the sofa, making it almost white with light. Like a stage set. Not *like* it, in fact – because that's exactly what her home had become – a theatre for a vast, ugly reality show that was only just getting into gear. Worse was to come in the following weeks and months.

She felt the sweat start pouring off her as she sat down. Roger was fussing around her, asking things in a hushed, professional voice, like she was one of his patients. She squinted at the reflectors and asked him to move them, told him they were too bright. But they wouldn't do that. Someone from the TV company was whispering things in her ear – the same person who had spent forty minutes applying a thick, uncomfortable coating of make-up to her face, neck and hands, and had then sorted through her wardrobe for 'something suitable', as if *she* owned it and Rachel was merely a visitor. The police liaison officer had been there as well. Not John. She hadn't even met John yet. At that stage someone else was in charge. The liaison woman was a hard-faced blonde who looked at her with dispassionate eyes and tried to sound concerned. Everyone was trying to ape concern, but she knew that wasn't why all these people were there, staring at her like she was something about to explode. They were here because this was grim entertainment. For the world out there, this was better than fiction.

The man running the inquiry sat with them on the sofa. The interviewer sat on a chair in front of the sofa. There were cameras all over – hand-held, on tripods, video cameras, big TV-type cameras. And microphones on stands, sticking out above her, across the ceiling, pointing down at her from all directions. The interviewer was a young girl with short, black hair and a Scottish accent – Alison something. She had a professional manner, no room for any sympathy, though she did slot some in, perfunctorily, like saying 'have a nice day' to a customer. Rachel just nodded through it all as she explained the procedure, not hearing enough of it for anything to subsequently make sense.

She didn't know how long it went on for. They were probably over two-thirds of the way through before she realised they had already started. Nearly all the questions were handled by Roger or the policeman. She just sat there, eyes on the interviewer, but in fact not seeing her at all. Because her head was still choked with her fears and scenarios, still on Lauren, one hundred per cent of the time. So much so that when she was finally asked a few questions Roger had to nudge her and the questions had to be repeated more than once.

She had seen the broadcast version a couple of times, cringing as she watched it – many years afterwards. About twenty seconds went out to the world, though someone had told her they might have been in there for twenty minutes or more, to get those trimmed and dressed moments of real-life TV drama. Ten seconds were given to the policeman, nearly all the rest to Roger. There was a single clip of her speaking. She could remember, she thought, the moment she spoke the words. She could see herself doing it. She had no idea what the question was, but what she said – and what the world heard – was: *This is all a waste of time. Lauren's OK. She'll come back. There's no need for all this.* In the room there had been a moment's stunned pause after that, the interviewer clearly wrong-footed. Then she had asked another question, something like: 'Are you saying you think she's safe – that she hasn't been kidnapped?' The question was never broadcast. Nor her reply: *Of course not. She's fine.*

From inside herself, from within her patchy memory of the day and her recollection of those words, she could see only a confused and desperate woman who didn't really have a clue what was going on, who dearly wished that her daughter hadn't been kidnapped. When she looked down at herself saying the words she saw big, glazed eyes and a fixed, shocked stare. Classic, clinical symptoms. But she had seen the broadcast version, seen herself as the cameras saw her, as the world saw her. And the wonder was that the woman speaking hadn't looked confused or shocked at all, not on TV. She had looked as hard as nails. Done up so that you couldn't even see the red eyes and blotchy face, the lank, greasy hair. Sitting there looking for all the world that she really resented the intrusion. When she spoke it wasn't in a soft, frightened voice. She spoke clearly, almost aggressively. As if telling the interviewer to shut up.

They had gone off her then, she thought, the Great British Public. Right then. They had watched her and failed to find a mother that fitted their expectations. So they had in turn got confused, then decided she was some rich, stuck-up, upper-class bitch (to some newspapers, it seemed, all doctors were somehow 'upper class'). This response – absurd as it was, not a detail of it being true – had somehow filtered through the media, and within days they were running stories about the hard-nosed mother who hadn't shed a tear, who looked immaculate though her daughter was missing, who was only concerned about her appearance, who was vain and selfish and heartless, who was getting on with her life as if nothing had happened. Some foreign rag had picked it up and speculated that she might even have killed her daughter. And it had all taken off from there. Until they got tired of it, half a year later. Speculation, supposition, prejudice and pure malice.

But thinking about it now, and thinking about all the additional grief it had caused her, none of it seemed to matter much. It had all been publicity, after all. Lauren's photo had gone out with every story. And nothing had made any difference, in the end. What struck her as really, truly awful now, twenty-two years on, was that the woman who had sat there answering questions hadn't a clue just how bad it was going to be. If she had been asked – 'where do you think you will be in twenty-two years' time?' – she would probably have said something stupidly positive. Because she would never have imagined that she would be *here*, in exactly the same position as then, in the very same garden, still knowing nothing about Lauren's whereabouts, still aching for her touch.

18

The water was working on him. There was more of it in the back of the Land Rover, plus some kind of gun that Sara found. She took over the driving and he tried to figure out how to work the gun. Without pulling the trigger to test-fire it, though, that was impossible. And they didn't want to start shooting. The truck was loud enough. His head was clearing, though – he had that to be grateful for.

They were making very slow progress. They had left the main road after about four miles, taking a turn on to a dry mud trail that would get them to the beaches at the southern promontory, eventually, but she didn't think they would be able to drive far. The trail was narrowing, the jungle closing in. Soon there wouldn't be room for a truck. Then they would have to walk.

They had decided they couldn't just drive back to the docks. They had no idea how many men might be there, waiting. Instead they would cross to the seaplane from the other side of the bay. If they got there within a few hours the tide would be low, she thought, and they could wade across. But even with the tide right in the water would still be fairly shallow – only a small stretch above the height of their heads. They could swim that if they had to. Once it started to recede, though, it would uncover a large sandflat. When that happened the seaplane would be grounded. So they were up against the clock.

As it turned out they had to abandon the truck much sooner than expected, because a tree had fallen across the trail. To save time they took a forest path she knew which led them back to a point much nearer the dock than they had intended. They came out of the treeline quite suddenly, on to a perfect white beach, saw how close the dock was and retreated quickly to observe. It was just after three, the sun was blinding, the tide not quite high. The seaplane was still there, bobbing lazily on the swell. There was no sign of life, anywhere. If there was someone in the watchtower they had to be lying flat out on the boards, asleep.

The distance from where they were across to the jetty was about one hundred yards.

'Right now, it's shallow all the way over,' she told him. 'Chest height at most.'

'So what do we do?'

'We should just go for it. We can't wait. The man we left will be headed back here.'

'Just walk across?'

'Keep the gun out of the water. If anything happens then use it.' She had looked at it, worked out how to fire it, she thought, and given him instructions.

'You take the gun,' he said. 'You can shoot.'

'Not with that. And I need to start the plane. You go to the jetty, loosen the lines. I'll do the start sequence while you're doing that. The first danger will be when the engine fires.'

He stared at her. It was absurd. He couldn't believe they were even discussing it. As they walked across the bay they would be totally exposed. He saw the expression in her eyes change and she took hold of his hand. 'What else can we do?' she asked.

'Wait until darkness.'

'I can't fly in darkness.'

'Not at all?'

'I can fly and navigate, but I can't land safely. Not in darkness, on water. I haven't done that.'

They went through other options, but she had made her mind up. They were going in the plane, right now. 'Do we do this or not?' she demanded. 'There's no other way.'

He nodded, staring all the time at the flat, open stretch of water. 'If we have to,' he said. 'OK.'

They walked quickly, carefully, but didn't run. From leaving the trees they were in full view of the watchtower and the dock. He kept his finger over the trigger, kept his eyes on the building at the end of the path up from the dock – the low building where the servants had lived. Behind it he could see the house. Everything looked exactly as it had the day before. No clue at all as to what had happened here during the night.

The water quickly came up to his waist. It was warm. He held the gun above his head, the barrel pointed roughly towards the jetty. 'Keep going,' he heard her whisper back to him. 'Just keep going. Even if they come out keep going. There's nothing else we can do.'

He thought they were making a lot of noise. He thought they were super-visible. He thought it took about an hour to wade through a hundred yards of water, his breathing fast, his vision constricted and his eyes twitching with fear. But suddenly he was there. He was standing up to his chest in water and the jetty ladder was right in front of him. She was saying something to him, but he couldn't hear her now. The blood was pounding in his ears. She was climbing on to the nearest float, opening the plane door. He pulled himself up the ladder and lay in a flat wet pool on the jetty, the sun hot on his back and head, facing the buildings, looking.

No movement. Nothing. He forced himself into a crouch, then shuffled backwards and started to find the ropes mooring the plane. It took a while to figure out how to loosen them. He had to actually put the gun down and heave at the rope securing the plane to create some slack. While he was doing that he had his back to the buildings, the skin on his neck crawling. As he got the last rope loose he heard the engines starting to turn, saw the props spinning. His stomach lurched. Now it was going to happen. Now they would rush out. He turned back, picked up the gun and waited. But the jetty was empty, and moments later she was shouting at him to get in.

He went down the ladder quickly, still carrying the gun. As he dropped into the water he miscalculated and the gun went under. He cursed, threw it away and started to wade as fast as he could towards the seaplane. He hardly had the door closed before she was pulling back the throttles and the thing was moving. 'This isn't the way you're meant to do this,' she shouted, above the roar. 'I hope the engines are good,' she added. 'If they don't pack up we have enough fuel to get us to Victoria in two and a half hours.' He looked out of the window, ducking instinctively, still expecting shots to streak towards them. But nothing came.

When it took off, smoothly, as if this was some kind of normal trip, she started to cry and he had to pull his eyes from the receding sea and the view back to the jetty and the buildings, lean over and stroke the side of her face. 'It's OK,' he yelled. 'It's OK, Sara. You're fucking brilliant. We're alive. You got us off it. You did it.' She took one hand from the flight controller and crossed it over her other arm to grab his hand. The plane wobbled in the air, but she didn't bat an eyelid at that.

19

Just over three hours later Maxim stood panting at the end of the jetty, staring at the place where the seaplane had been. He could hardly believe it. The pilot was dead, which meant the man she had with her could fly. He had fucked up badly. No one had told him about the man. He had just appeared out of the blue, by the Land Rover. Maxim had no idea who it was.

He walked slowly back along the jetty, waiting for his heart and lungs to recover. He had run all the way from the far end of the island, and while he could run well, his usual pace was much slower, and not in this heat. He felt dizzy, confused, angry. He had lost her. Everything that could have gone wrong had gone wrong. He still couldn't work out why.

Behind the house he stepped over the bodies with care, with an increasing feeling of vertigo. The Somalis had gone completely crazy. He tried not to look at the upturned, gaping faces. He went into the staff building and went through it, looking for some clue. Even in here the stench was already like something coating his nostrils.

The man who had protected her had either lived here or up in the house. Who was he? The security guards could have told him, but they were all needlessly dead. He started shouting at the top of his voice, cursing the Somalis. But there was no one to hear.

At the main house he went through each room methodically,

looking for clues. All wasn't lost. His boat was intact. He could be back on the big boat within an hour. He could take it from there, use the helicopter to get to Victoria, make contact with Arisha in London, move on, start again, find her. There was still time. There *had* to be time. This was his last chance with Arisha, his last hope for bringing her back to him. Because he wasn't stupid, he knew what Arisha was, what she had become. She hated where she was now – he was certain of that – but that didn't mean she would come back to *him*, erase the last twenty years. The money would have to be there too. She wouldn't go anywhere without money. Not now. But this plan, *her* plan, would deliver both – Arisha and the money. So it had to work.

He found nothing downstairs. There were papers in a set of drawers in her room, which he didn't have time to go through, and a computer, though he wasn't sure how useful it would be as there was no internet connection here. In the room directly above Sara Eaton's he found a crumpled jacket and went through the pockets. He opened a tattered envelope from the inside pocket and found a bill from an electricity company in the UK, for someone called Tom Lomax, with an address in Hounslow. The name rang bells – something he'd seen downstairs.

He walked back down to the kitchen, sat down at the big wooden table there – the very same one that had been here twenty-two years ago. His hand was throbbing painfully, his pulse still too fast. She had shot the weapon out of his hands. He was still trying to accept how lucky he had been. She would have been aiming for his head, no doubt. But she had hit the weapon, destroying it and wrenching his hand and arm, possibly breaking a finger of his right hand. He hadn't had time to bind it up yet. A piece of the gun stock had shattered and spun off into his left arm, gashing him. It had bled a lot as he was running.

He put his head in his hands and gave in to the trembling for a good five minutes. He could feel the scar to the side of his right eye swelling up. Ten years ago a piece of shrapnel had gashed him there when he was lying on the floor of the schoolroom, bleeding to death. It had been the least of his injuries back then, but it was the most obvious and public now. It began to ache when he got stressed, or exhausted, then turned an angry red. He massaged it gently with his fingers, at the same time picking up the letter he had found on the table when he had first searched here. It was from Liz Wellbeck. It mentioned Tom Lomax, a policeman from London. So it was a good bet that Tom Lomax was the man who was with her. Which was good, because he had his address now.

20

Arisha was in the back of a chauffeur-driven car, on her way to Wentworth, where Dima Barsukov lived. She sat with her muscles tight, her lips compressed, trying to keep her feelings down. As the car eased through the big gates and started on the short avenue up to the familiar cluster of buildings, she pulled down the mirror in the partition dividing her from the driver and inspected again her face, her hair, her clothing. 'Precociously and exceptionally beautiful' – that was what Dimitri Barsukov had said to her, the first time they spoke. But she wasn't that smooth eighteen-year-old any more. That had been in 1988, at a theatre production her mother had forced her to attend – some boring political crap that her mother's friends were staging in a boarded-over ice arena in Konkovo. Dima Barsukov had noticed her from the other side of the arena and sought her out during the interval. She had been sitting in the reserved rows of seating, chain-smoking. A very unhappy eighteen-year-old, regardless of how striking her appearance was.

Though only thirty-one, Dima had been the guest of honour. He had some post in Gorbachev's regime, a junior role in a ministry that controlled the state-owned land and buildings used for sporting clubs in the Moscow area. Later, under Yeltsin, this position had enabled his acquisition – his private acquisition – of some choice real estate. But when she had first met him the lies were still in place. He was an ordinary worker, just like her.

Back then, there were no differences in wealth in the Soviet Union, just differences in proximity to power. If you had something to do with the state and influence over how real estate was allocated, for example, you could get a two-floor, eight-bedroom central Moscow apartment like the one Dima lived in. When Yeltsin changed the rules you could then buy this for next to nothing. They had nearly all done it – all those close enough to the centre to get a slice. But at this point – in the summer of 1988 – with everything in flux and the changes only just beginning, what Dima Barsukov's activities on the fringes of his official post made him was something closer to a mobster. She had accepted his invitation to dinner because it had made her mother jealous, not because she had seen anything attractive in him.

He had taken her to one of the new restaurants, this one serving French-style cuisine. You couldn't get in if you weren't something in the Party, or on someone's list. Dima had led her straight past a queue and they had been given a huge table in a room that looked like something out of an old film demonstrating Tsarist excesses – everything decorated in gold and silver, huge oil portraits on the walls, a palatial staircase, chandeliers. There had been exceptional food, and drink – champagne (her first time) – but she couldn't recall much of that. For the entire evening Dima had sat right next to her, holding her hand like he would never let go. His face was dreadful, the nose broken flat in some childhood gang fight that had also cost him a bullet wound that made him limp, the head bald, the chin jutting out too far. He was short, he spoke roughly. She found out later that he had a politics degree from Moscow State University, but you wouldn't have guessed that by looking at him. From a distance he looked like a black-marketeer. But close up he was different: the intense attention he paid to her, the way he could speak as if uttering one long, rambling poem, peculiar but melodic (so that at first she had been inclined to laugh, until she saw that was just how he spoke, always) – all of this had her almost mesmerised within the first hour. She had never experienced anything like it. For the first time in her life she was in the presence of someone who made her feel like she was the only person who mattered on the planet.

A relationship had followed, but not the relationship she expected. From the beginning he had treated her as if she were a daughter, or perhaps a sister, but never a lover. 'I sleep with prostitutes, tarts,' he had explained that night. 'You will meet them. Don't be fooled by manners. Some of them have money and connections, but they're all sluts. I cannot even imagine you being part of that side of me.' She had laughed, but then saw he was serious. 'If you become my friend,' he had said, with a touching, naive turn of phrase that reminded her of the way kids would speak about these things, 'then I will look after you and love you – as a family member, or a friend, closely, with all my heart.' She didn't understand it, had thought he was lying, in fact, that it was a chat-up line, a ruse to put her at ease. But it wasn't. From that day to this, nothing sexual had happened between them. She had gone along with all his proposals, starting with her moving into his apartment right then, that first night. And everything else that had brought her to here – to this point of no return – had followed from that.

She saw him now coming down the big steps at the main entrance as the car came to a stop in the gravel semicircle. The house behind him, the midday sun bright on the white paintwork, was a restored seventeenth-century manor, a beautiful place. Even with everything she had now – even if she managed to pull this off – she would never be able to live in such a house, never be able to afford anything similar. She bent down and kissed Sasha's head, whispered that she loved him. Sasha was four years old. She couldn't even imagine treating him as her mother had treated her. It was for Sasha that she was doing all this, so that he wouldn't have to live as she had. When she looked back on her life, mostly she saw it as one long prostitution.

Dima was at the bottom of the steps, a big smile cracking his ugly face. There were two bodyguards a little behind him, keeping a discreet distance. She got out without waiting for the driver to come round and open her door. For a moment she felt like running towards Dima, putting her head on his shoulder, letting go. But Sasha held her back, hanging on to her leg. She crouched down and hugged him, asked him what was wrong. Was he shy of Dima?

She whispered in his ear as Dima came closer. 'Don't be afraid, Sasha. This man is your uncle. It's Dimka. He's a friend.' Sasha could speak exceptionally well, in Russian, in English, even a little French, but he said nothing now, his eyes fixed on Dima. 'You've been here before,' she said. 'Don't you remember?'

She stood up and hugged Dima, the urge to cry gone already. She trusted children's instincts absolutely. She thought they were like dogs – they had pre-conscious capacities to judge that you lost as you got older. She needed to know what was bothering Sasha.

'Any developments?' Dima asked, face very serious now.

She shook her head. 'Nothing yet.' They spoke Russian, as always.

'I knew it would fuck up. I shouldn't have let you persuade

me.' He winked at her, reached a hand out and stroked her cheek. She felt Sasha's little hand tighten on her leg. 'But how could I refuse?' he said. He glanced back at the house, at the big clock mounted on the tower there. 'We'll give it a few hours more, I think, then it all stops. It's silly to take these risks...'

'It can still work,' she said quickly. What would she do if it didn't work? That thought was too awful. 'Max will do it. I trust him.'

'Maybe. Maybe not. I'll decide. You can come inside and tell me the details.' He looked down at Sasha and put a hand out, to ruffle his hair, or touch his head, but Sasha pulled back, slipped behind his mother's legs. 'He's feeling shy,' Arisha said.

'So I see.' Dima squatted suddenly, right in front of Sasha. 'Come here, Alexandre,' he said, too sternly. 'Let me see you.'

But Sasha wouldn't move. Dima looked puzzled. It didn't happen often that he was disobeyed.

'He'll come out of it,' Arisha said. Sasha was pulling at her leg, trying to get her to bend down, so he could whisper to her.

Dima stood up, his smile fading. 'How very unfortunate,' he muttered. 'He looks more than ever like his father.'

21

Tom was just beyond the barriers fronting the arrivals gate at Brussels airport, with crowds of people around him, most staring past him at the doorway he had just come through, waiting for family, or friends, or business connections to walk out. Some held signs in the air with names written on them. He read the time on an arrivals monitor – just after 11.00 a.m., but the place was like a rush-hour train station. Behind the crowd of static faces people flowed back and forth in the main concourse. The ceiling was low and the noise level high, the air stuffy. The images became a blur and he rubbed his eyes.

He felt scruffy, exhausted, bewildered. He'd never been in the position he was in now. He looked at Sara, standing at his side, head down and on her mobile, trying to call someone to arrange a 'ride'. She had kept her phone clear of the water en route to the seaplane. His hadn't done so well. His had been in his pocket, with his wallet and passport, as he had waded to the dock. He had managed to buy a new phone at the airport in Victoria, and had put his old SIM card in it, but still with no effect. The passport also was probably now unusable, but no one had bothered to ask for it between the Seychelles and here. On landing Sara had led him to an area reserved for private jet passengers. There hadn't even been staff on the gate. It seemed in her world you didn't really need a passport.

'Let's go over there,' she said quietly, pointing to an open bar area that didn't look too full. She had spent most of the flight from Mahe huddled into a corner seat, staring into space. She didn't look quite so young now, or fresh and full of life. Her face was blotchy, her eyes red-rimmed, her short hair unkempt because she had been running her hands through it all morning, compulsively.

'We need to decide what to do now,' she said. 'We can talk over there.'

He followed her over, watching the faces in front of him, the eyes passing over them without reaction. The worst of it was inside their heads – images and memories that no one else had access to. They had both taken showers on the plane, done their best to look normal. There had been clean clothes to wear – in his case a spare set belonging to the pilot; jeans, and another T-shirt. Sleep should have been possible – the flight had been comfortable – but it hadn't happened, for either of them. He thought he might have dozed for an hour, maximum. It wasn't enough to support his slender grip on what was real and what wasn't.

'So what do we do now?' she whispered, standing very close to him at the bar, while waiting for the waiter to pay attention. She sounded desperate.

'We do what we agreed,' he said.

'So you're going to leave me?'

At some time yesterday he had said he would go with her as far as Brussels. As he had seen it, the crucial thing – for both of them – had been to get away from the Seychelles as quickly as possible. He had no trust in the police, not even the police from relatively controlled, ethical forces like the one that had sacked him. And as far as he was concerned the Seychelles was a banana republic. He had absolutely no idea what their police force was like. Maybe it was a beacon of tropical rectitude, but Tom wasn't taking any risks with his personal liberty, and had made that very clear to her while they were still on the way to Mahe. All the guards she had entrusted with her security were ex-police from the Seychelles, and he was certain that the only reason they hadn't repaid that trust was because someone had paid them a higher fee, or they were in on the kidnap plan. Plus, she had probably killed someone who was a police officer from Victoria, so her idea of landing at Mahe and reporting what had happened to the forces of law and order was a non-starter.

She also had come round to that view shortly after putting the plane down. She had navigated effortlessly to a private, highly secluded bay owned by her family and, in the fading evening light, brought the plane into a dock about two miles from a massive mansion she referred to as the 'beach house'. In a hot tropical twilight, they had made their way on foot along a winding path until the building was in view. Then she had started to get frightened. The house was in complete darkness, no sign of life. Only a few days before she had left the place with three permanent staff looking after it, but now, at seven o'clock in the evening, they were nowhere to be seen.

They had agreed right then that it would be stupid to just walk up to the place, that it was stupid to be standing where they were, fully exposed, that it had been naive to land the plane at so obvious a location. They had no real idea what had happened on the Ile des Singes Noirs. There had been people who looked like kidnappers, yes, but also two white guys who had looked more like mercenaries, one probably a policeman from here. If they had got to her out there then they could have this building covered too.

Because the pilot of her personal flight – the plane that had brought Tom from Luton – was employed by her mother, and had nothing to do with the Seychelles, and because risking contact with him was preferable to trying to get on a public flight, she had used her mobile to call him and arrange transport to the airport in Victoria. All too easy, and they were in the air again by midnight.

By then she was as wary as Tom and had decided that what she needed to do, above all else, was get to her mother. Her mother was here, in Brussels. So Tom had come along, not only because it was his quickest route out, but also because he felt some responsibility for her, because right now, until it was sorted, they were in this together. 'I think what you decided yesterday was right,' he said, reluctantly, in a very low whisper, after the barman had taken an order for two coffees. 'Get to your mother. Get her help. I think that's what you should do. Don't go to the police here either. Not until you've spoken to your mother. Or someone else with some clout. Your father, perhaps. I don't trust the police. Not here, not anywhere. If you have access to them, then big lawyers and big money are what you need, just to make sure everybody does their duty properly.'

What he felt like telling her was that she should never ever admit anything, even if she thought she was completely innocent. Especially not that she had put the crosshairs of a high-powered military rifle over someone's head and pulled the trigger. But he had already gone over all this with her during the flight.

Financially, it seemed to him, she undoubtedly had enough resources to get the legal help she would need, without having to go anywhere near her parents. She had told him she was on a 'modest' allowance until her twenty-first birthday – now only three days away – when she *might* get more funds of her own. She didn't seem to know whether that would definitely happen or not, didn't seem to care. Money wasn't something that had much reality for her. He had been too tired to smile at what her idea of a 'modest allowance' might be, given everything he had seen so far of her lifestyle. But he understood very well that she felt out of her depth and wanted someone with her who would know what to do in this kind of circumstance. That wasn't him. So she had to get family help. Her father was out of the question, she said – she actually seemed afraid of him, in a surprisingly childish way – and anyway, he was in the States. So that left her mother, mentally unstable or not.

'You should come with me,' she muttered now. She took the coffee and walked to a table. He followed. They sat down and she stared miserably at her coffee. 'You could help me explain it all to her. You're a witness. And you can tell it better. I don't know if I can say all this to my mother.'

'She's your mother. It'll be OK. Don't worry.'

'It's not as simple as that. She's my mother, yes, but I haven't seen much of her recently.' She pulled a face. 'In fact, I haven't really seen much of her since I was ten years old … I'm not sure she will want anything to do with all this …'

He smiled gently at her. All these de luxe toys, all this money, yet she was too scared to go to her parents when she most needed them. 'I'm sure that's not true,' he said.

'I'm sure it is. You wouldn't believe what my childhood was like. I thought it was normal, that everything was happy and normal, that everyone had a childhood like that. That's what you're like as a child, right? – you just adapt and get on with it. It was only when I went off to uni and I started meeting ordinary people – I mean people without all that money – that I began to realise just how weird it all was. My mother got ill, you see, when I was about ten. Before that – when we were living on the island – everything was wonderful. Mummy and I. There was only me and her – no sisters or brothers, so we were very close. I can remember it. But then she had to go into a clinic. I was left with my father, and he's never had much time for me. He's like a stranger, in a way. And I think he always wanted a son, not a weak little girl.' She bit her lip. 'Truth is, I don't know him at all. Money replaces everything, you see. When there's so much of it washing around, it has to be serviced, continually. It doesn't leave time for much else. So you buy help for your kids, buy people to love them.' She looked up at him. 'I'm not moaning about it. Just telling you why it might be better if you came with me, if you told her what happened. She won't believe me. But you're not family. You're someone I paid. So she might take it all from you. She might understand. I can ... it can be ...' She paused, thinking again. 'I can extend your contract, increase it ...'

'My contract?'

'You know what I mean.'

He sighed, then put a hand across the table and held hers. 'What do you want me to do, Sara? Whatever it is, you don't need to buy it. We've survived something together, something appalling. So there's something different between us now. Not money. Not a contract.'

Her lip trembled and she looked around nervously. 'I just want you to stay with me until I get to my mother. That's all. I'm sorry. But I feel so scared. I've never been so frightened before. I just want you to stick with me. There's no one else I can ask. No one else I can trust.'

'OK,' he said. 'I'll come with you ...' He saw her relax a fraction and held up a hand to stop her. 'But there's something you should know first. Just so we're all straight about who we are, now that money isn't in the equation.' He took a mental breath, then told her the truth about getting kicked out of the Met, accused of corruption. He told her he thought her mother had perhaps confused him with his dad.

She didn't react much. 'Is he also Tom Lomax?' she asked.

'No. He's John Thomas Lomax. But it wouldn't be the first time people got the wrong Lomax. It happens.'

'I couldn't get anyone to get us,' she said, meaning the 'ride'. He thought his revelation might have gone in one ear and out the other. 'No one is answering. So we'll have to get a taxi from here. But I've no money.'

'I've got pounds in my wallet. Slightly damp pounds. We can change them. Don't worry.'

'You'll take me there? All the way there? You'll stay with me until we get there?'

'I'll be stuck to you. OK?' He dragged a half-smile up. It was meant to reassure.

She almost smiled back, but not quite. 'What did you do?' she asked, switching abruptly back to his revelation. 'Why were you sacked?'

'Long story,' he said, feeling a twinge of shame. 'Short version is I tried to help a friend when I should have known better.'

22

They took a taxi across Brussels and he thought about it all the way. His great mistake. It was over three years ago now. A turning point in his life, no doubt, but a petty, mundane story nevertheless. It galled him that he featured in it, his role so predictable that he really ought to have known better. He had made a phone call to Alex and warned him about an arrest warrant. That was the crime, the big secret, the thing he was meant to be so ashamed about.

The job behind it had been significant, but Alex's part in it had been peripheral. He had been seen with someone who was connected to someone who featured in the target's phone logs. But the policy was to pull everyone in, to pile pressure on the target. The intermediary had been Glynn Powell. Powell *was* connected to the target, and Powell *was* eventually arrested (later than intended, because Alex warned him after Tom warned Alex). Tom had known all along that Alex was one of Powell's foot soldiers, but he had been convinced, back then, that Alex was unaware of the depth of Powell's involve-ment. He wasn't so certain about that now, but hindsight was a great thing. If Alex had been directly implicated, if he had been suspected of violence or something serious, then maybe Tom would have thought differently about it at the time. But Alex was nothing. The SIO admitted Alex was nothing, admitted that they merely wanted to use him to get at Powell.

And Alex was Tom's oldest friend, his best friend. He had other friends through the job, of course, but Alex was the only friend he had who went right back to childhood. For no reason that Tom had ever been able to work out Alex had stepped in and protected him when he'd been on the receiving end of some childhood bullying. Trivial stuff. They had all been eight years old. 'Minor' was how the teachers had referred to it – how could it be anything else when everyone involved was no more than eight or nine years old? But Tom hadn't known it was 'minor' at the time. It had felt major to him, made his life a complete and utter misery. He could still recall his fear – pinned against a wall by a group of seven or eight kids, as they went through his pockets, night after night on the walk home. The same kids every night. It had gone on for weeks, gradually getting more violent. Just kiddie violence, of course, nothing to cry about.

But cry he had. Bloody noses, bruises, a black eye. His dad had seen it all and asked, been down to the school, sat him down and tried to get it out of him. But he hadn't been able to tell his dad a thing. For as long as he could recall all he had wanted to do when he grew up was what his dad did – be a policeman. And his dad had drummed it into him many times that the most important thing was to 'keep his nose clean, keep out of trouble'. Being picked on, somehow, went against that – as if it were his fault. So he had said nothing, come up with stupid explanations, felt ashamed and guilty, put up with it. He couldn't understand it, especially now he had a kid of his own.

It had stopped when Alex had intervened. Tom had hardly spoken to Alex before that. Alex had owed him nothing. Yet Tom could still recall Alex wading into the kids, knocking them down, kicking them, pulling their hair, sending them running. Even at eight he had had been a brutal little fighter, no holding back. It had been magnificent, a key moment in Tom's childhood, a memory that would never leave him. The beauty of violence and strength. He could feel now the leaping joy he had experienced as the ringleader ran off screaming, nose pouring with blood.

And afterwards – very surprisingly – Alex had wanted to be friends. He had asked Tom, because that was the way eight-year-olds did it – no beating around the bush – *Do you wanna be mates?* And that friendship – awkward and odd from the beginning – had improbably continued right through school and beyond. It had survived everything, even his dad's efforts to stamp it out. His dad wanted it to stop because Alex's dad was some kind of crook, because he suspected Alex was fleecing Tom, somehow, conning him. But he didn't know Alex. Alex had stood by Tom through a further eight or nine years of school and pulled him out of tough spots many, many times. And never – not even once – had he ever asked for anything in return.

Now they met once a week, had a drink and chatted the same way they always had – with no connection between their worlds. Parallel conversations. Alex went on about bodybuilding, his house, his kids, football. He bragged about all the women he shagged behind his wife's back, letched and leered at women he didn't know, told crude, sexist jokes, drank gallons of lager. Tom talked about other things, was altogether more moderate. They were totally different, always had been. But it took all sorts. It was possible to have as your closest friend someone who shared none of your world views, and with whom you could barely have an interesting conversation. Tom had learned that. Because Alex had been there through thick and thin for nearly eighteen years by the time his name cropped up in the paperwork of Tom's drug job. So Tom made the call. No hesitation about it.

A miserable little DC on some squad set up to root out corruption had, by chance, come across a record of the call while doing a random audit. Not the detail, just the time and number. That had been enough, though – hours of uncomfortable interviews later, that had been enough. There had been no criminal charges, but he'd had to resign to avoid them. Did he regret his carelessness? He had made the call from his personal mobile, judging that no one would have an interest that would extend beyond a random check on his work phones. All the consequences could have been avoided if he'd been only a little more careful and used a phone work had no record of – so, yes, he regretted that. He'd been stupid. Did he regret making the call, though? No. Absolutely, no. They were two different things. So when he told Sara he should have known better he had actually told her a lie. As far as he was concerned he'd done the right thing.

The clinic her mother was living in was on a wide, four-lane boulevard with heavy traffic. Avenue Louise. Tom had never been to Brussels before, so had no idea where they were. He paid the driver and they walked very quickly to a set of double glass doors, then waited for someone to answer the buzzer.

'This is a hospital?' Tom asked. It didn't look like one. It looked like a dirty-fronted nine-storey art deco building sandwiched between two ugly fifteen-storey modern office blocks.

'It's her clinic,' Sara said, finger still on the buzzer. 'I mean it's hers only. She had the building converted. She's the only patient.'

'With her own doctors?'

'Yes. Her own consultant. Monsieur Hulpe. I hate the fucker.'

Someone answered – a woman's voice – and she snapped

an introduction into the grille, in French. Some argument seemed to follow. Tom's school French was nowhere near keeping up with it. It ended with Sara shouting her name at the woman. That seemed to work. The door clicked open and they went in.

'Was that your mother?' Tom asked as they stood by a set of lifts in a narrow, wood-panelled hallway.

'Of course not. Some assistant. She must be new. I don't understand what's going on here.' She moved her head to indicate the large, empty atrium. 'Where's the security?' she asked. 'There's normally people here. And outside.'

'People?'

'Armed guards. Here. On the roof, out the back. She keeps a team of them. She's one of the wealthiest women in Europe. The risk to her is even greater than the risk to me. But like this anyone can walk in. I don't get it.'

She frowned about this all the way up to the ninth floor. There, they emerged into a room that looked like a waiting room, also conspicuously devoid of security. The assistant was waiting for them right by the lift, a twenty-year-old with dark hair and glasses, a smart grey suit, a panicky look on her face. Her hands were up to bar their way. 'Monsieur Hulpe is not here,' she said, then said it again, this time in English.

Sara made to go past her. 'I'm not here to see Hulpe. I'm here to see my mother. Are you here alone? Where's the security?'

The woman took a step back and moved so that she was in front of Sara, blocking her. 'Your mother?' That seemed to cause alarm. 'You are here for your mother?'

'Yes. I'm Sara Eaton. That's what I just told you. I'm her daughter ...'

'I see. I see.' Her hands were still up. Sara made to go past, but she kept them up. 'You cannot go through,' she said quickly. 'This is a private clinic. I will call the doctor. He will speak to you.'

That started a heated discussion. Tom watched it for a moment or two, and saw that the receptionist – if that's what she was – wasn't going to give in. She was getting increasingly nervous. Behind her – at the far end of the room – he could see a set of heavy, opaque sliding doors. Next to them was the semicircular desk this woman presumably occupied. It looked like it had been built specially – to curve out of the wall and end near the doors – and very recently. It was only half painted and there were still holes in the wall near it and a sheet laid out on the floor with plaster dust scattered across it. Nearer to them there was a suite of easy chairs and a set of coffee tables bearing pot plants. He assumed this was where Liz Wellbeck's visitors waited to see the great woman. She was some kind of control and health freak, Sara had said – so undoubtedly the doors would be barred, or locked. He put a hand out and touched Sara's arm. 'Maybe we should just wait,' he suggested. The last thing they wanted was for this woman to decide to call the police. Sara looked back at him and he tried to communicate that in his look. She got it, he thought, and gave in. 'Tell Hulpe to be quick,' she snapped.

'Of course. Please take a seat.'

They sat on the chairs. The woman went back to the desk, then the doors opened and she slipped through.

'I thought this was the routine?' Tom said.

'Hardly. I'm her daughter.' Sara looked round her for the first time. 'All this is new,' she said. 'It looks like a dentist's waiting room. There used to be a big metal detector here, and an explosives scanner. It's all been ripped out.'

'There wasn't a waiting room before?'

'Of course not. Just security. Always security. My mother

lives here. *Only* my mother. There *needs* to be security.' She looked worried about it.

'But you had to book an appointment before?'

'Yes. And speak to Hulpe.' She lowered her voice slightly and leaned over towards him. 'I think she might be seeing Hulpe – I mean having some kind of affair. You can't get near her without him having something to do with it. That's why she's here – in Brussels, I mean – because he's from here. It's ridiculous.'

Tom nodded. 'It's certainly not anything I've come across in my world.' She shot him a sharp glance, so he smiled. 'What illness does she have – if you don't mind me asking?' He assumed it was something trivial, perhaps imaginary.

'Cancer,' she said, matter-of-factly. 'A rare bone cancer that is one hundred per cent inheritable. They can almost predict at what age you will get it – if you let them do the tests. I haven't. But it's coming to me anyway. Some time.' She was looking round as she spoke, still fretting about the lack of guards. She didn't seem perturbed by what she had just told him. 'This is all new,' she repeated. It clearly bothered her more than the inheritable cancer. 'No guards, no cameras. I don't know what's going on. This is like … well … like *anyone* could live here. I mean, not my mother.'

'I'm sorry about the cancer,' he said. 'Is she very ill?'

'Not last time I saw her. But that was months ago. Not in her body, I mean. I worry about her mind more. Hulpe is being paid to deal with the cancer. He's a consultant on-cologist. The best for this particular thing. He's famous for it – famous among doctors, I mean. She had him when we lived in Paris, but he decided to return here, to his family or something. So she followed him. Bribed him with this place, so he would care only for her. How bizarre is that?' She was speaking too quickly, Tom thought, her eyes never still. 'She told me she's promised him this place when she dies.'

'The building?'

She nodded. 'So he can have his own clinic here.' She glanced around again. 'Looks like he's already started.'

Right then the doors opened and a man walked through, heading straight for them. Sara stood at once. The man stopped in front of her. He was tall and well fed, in a suit, no white coat, about fifty years old. He looked more like a politician than a doctor.

'Sara,' he said calmly. 'You're here. I did not expect you.'

'I'm not here to see you. I want to see my mother. Now. It's very urgent.'

He nodded, as if he felt sorry for her, then looked over at Tom, eyebrows raised. 'He's with me,' Sara said quickly. They were both speaking French.

'I see,' he said. 'You will have to come to my office. We can talk.'

Tom went with them, through the doors, down a short corridor and into a room that looked like a dining room. There was a big table down the middle, expansive floor-to-ceiling windows the length of one wall. Various lesser tables and expensive-looking chairs. No paperwork anywhere, no computers. No trace of anything vaguely medical, in fact. They were offered chairs at the big table. Hulpe sat down one seat removed from Sara and turned his chair to face her. Tom sat behind her, so that he had to lean out a bit to see Hulpe. Sara started talking immediately, but Hulpe held a hand up to silence her, leaned in close and spoke very quietly. 'Please listen to what I have to say,' he said, in English. He took a deep breath. 'I'm really very, very sorry. I don't know how this has happened. A misunderstanding.' He paused, frowning hard. Guessing something bad was coming, Tom shifted his chair and quickly closed his fingers round Sara's right hand, where it was resting on the table. She didn't react. 'How what has happened?' she asked mechanically, eyes on Hulpe.

'I don't know how you are here, now, like this. Has your father not spoken to you?'

'About what?'

Another awful pause.

'Your mother has gone, Sara,' he said finally.

'Gone where?'

'I'm so sorry, but she passed away a week ago. She died.'

23

She didn't react as Tom expected she would. He had thought, as Hulpe said the words, that it would crack her, right there and then. But everyone reacted differently. He had ample experience of it, from his years in the Met. She blanched immediately, then slumped back in the chair. For what seemed like ages she was just sitting there, her lips pressed tightly together, staring off to one side. Hulpe looked at the floor. Tom held on to her hand, no one said anything. But then she cleared her throat and her eyes narrowed. She pushed herself to the edge of the chair, stood up. She started demanding cold, rational explanations. That seemed to take Hulpe by surprise. Tom was still holding her hand, but he wasn't sure she even knew he was touching her, and the position was now uncomfortable, so he tried to move his hand. But she wouldn't let him. She was acting as if in control, but her grip on his fingers suggested she was hanging on for dear life.

It went on for over ten minutes – quickfire questions delivered with a voice full of suspicion. At one point she even told Hulpe she didn't believe him. Then they had to go and see the room where it had happened. And other rooms. She insisted on having a tour of the place, all the time snapping out the questions, all the time hanging on to Tom's hand – so that he had to walk right by her side – as if they were together, a couple. More than once he saw Hulpe looking at their joined hands and could see that he was thinking just that.

The huge room where her mother had apparently died was a major source of confusion to her, and she got very angry looking at it. 'Where's the bed?' she demanded. 'Where's my mother's bed?' She was almost shouting. The room looked like a sort of rest room, with sets of low, easy chairs pulled up to the window to catch the sun, a big, flashy flatscreen on the wall, coffee tables, magazines, a drink dispenser.

'We moved it,' Hulpe said. 'Our plans for this room are different now. Your mother knew all about them. And approved, of course. We planned all this together. This will be a social space for the patients ...'

'Your plans? This isn't your property. You shouldn't be changing anything. You've altered the area by the lifts ...'

'That will be the reception area ...'

'How long have you had all this planned?'

He held his arms up helplessly. 'Your mother was a part of all these plans,' he said again.

'Has she already given you this place?'

'No. But it's in her will. It was part of our contract. As you know, the will is to be read on Friday, in London. It's a formality, so we thought ...'

'I don't know anything about her will. Nothing is a formality.' She was getting very frustrated.

'Who certified death?' Tom asked quietly. They both looked at him.

'I did,' Hulpe said. 'And a colleague.'

'Was there a post-mortem?'

'Of course not. She died peacefully, of an illness she contracted over ten years ago ...'

'Was there a coroner involved?' He had no idea why he was asking the questions. It felt like he was on autopilot, from five years ago. There was nothing to make him really suspicious, given how weird these people were. What was normal here was off the rails in the world outside.

'No,' Hulpe said. 'No *coroner*, as you call it. We are in Belgium. The requirements are perhaps different to your own country. But all the legal formalities were, naturally, complied with.'

'Where is she?' Sara asked. '*Where* is my mother?'

'I'm sorry, Sara,' Hulpe said. He looked at the ground. 'But she really has gone. I'm sorry.'

'So where is her body? Is it here? What have you done with her, if she's dead?'

'The funeral was on Saturday.' He paused because Sara had gasped. 'I'm sorry. But your mother had planned well. She was aware of what was coming. Her body was flown to Paris and buried there. Those were her wishes. I don't know why your father hasn't told you any of this ... I assumed you would know ... that there was a reason you weren't there ...'

There was a long silence. Tom watched her struggling with the facts, trying to get on top of them. Finally, she found her voice again. 'You're lying. My father isn't even in the UK right now. He's in New York.'

Hulpe looked acutely embarrassed. He said nothing.

'Did *you* go to the funeral?' she asked.

'Of course. Your father was there too, I assure you. On Saturday. A small gathering in Paris. Very private. But it was in the newspapers, of course. It was reported ...'

A sob slipped from her lips. She put her head down. Now it was beginning to build up, he thought. No fucking wonder. Bizarre wasn't the word for it. And coming on top of everything else. 'Let's get out of here, Sara,' Tom said to her. Clearly she had many questions, but he was sure the next step – in the light of *all* their present problems – wasn't to irritate Hulpe, but to contact her father. She nodded.

Hulpe walked them in silence to the lifts. The reception-ist had vanished. At the lifts Sara turned back to him. 'Was anybody with her, when it happened?' she asked.

Hulpe seemed to hesitate, then shook his head. 'I was at home. I came within fifteen minutes …'

'She was here alone? She died alone?'

'Not alone, no. Monsieur Meyer was here, of course. He has rooms on the ground floor and the monitors were all linked in, twenty-four-hour surveillance …'

'Meyer?' she interrupted. 'Who is he?'

'One of her nurses. Stefan Meyer. You know him, Sara. He's my nephew, a trusted family member. He has cared for her for nearly a year now.'

'So where was Alison Spencer?'

'Not here,' he said. 'Elizabeth was too ill. In the end she was too ill to need Miss Spencer …'

'Too ill? I was here two months ago. She was fine then. She was walking around, talking …'

'I'm sorry. It's often like that. The final progression can be sudden …'

'Why wasn't I called? If she became ill why didn't you contact me?'

'That's not for me to decide. We immediately informed your father of everyone she asked to see.'

'*Did* she ask to see me?'

He was silent, clearly very uncomfortable now.

'Tell me if she asked to see me.'

'You should speak to your father about that. I'm sorry. Again. I'm so sorry.'

Sara took a breath, then stared at him, waiting until he looked up. 'You're lying,' she said again. 'You're lying to me.'

He nodded. He didn't look surprised that she should ac-cuse him. 'I'm sorry, Sara,' he repeated.

'You will be,' she said, just as the lift doors were closing.

Outside, they stood on the pavement like they were lost. She still didn't cry, but it was going to come. He kept an arm round her, feeling desperately sorry for her. He had been intending to leave her at this point, but that was out of the question now. 'We should call your father, I think,' he suggested cautiously. Hulpe was right.

She shook her head. 'She died alone,' she muttered, then put a hand up to her mouth. 'Meyer isn't family. Not *my* family. I don't have a clue who he is. And that man was at her funeral ... and I was not even told about it ... it's beyond belief...'

'I don't know what's going on,' he said. 'But I think your father might be the one to speak to.'

She shook her head again, more vigorously this time. 'No. My father lives in another world. He's a fool. How could he do that? How?'

He assumed she meant not telling her. He had no answer.

'We need to get to Alison,' she said. 'Alison has more sense.'

'Alison?'

'Yes. Alison Spencer. She was my mother's principal PA. She will know what has gone on. I don't trust that fucker as far as I could throw him.' Hulpe, or her father? 'Alison was the only friend my mother trusted,' she continued. 'She handled everything. We need to speak to her first. Then I'll deal with Daddy.'

'Your father might ...'

'My father is a ...' She stopped herself. 'I don't know what my father is doing. I don't know where he is. I already tried calling him, this morning. He didn't answer.' A sob caught in her throat again, but she held it back. She looked dazed, punch-drunk. He wasn't sure she was taking any of it in properly. 'Why didn't he tell me?' she gasped. 'Why?'

'You could try him again. Ask *him* that.'

'We'll try when we've spoken to Alison,' she said. 'I need to know more first.'

He could see he wasn't going to get her out of the idea. He sighed. Now wasn't the time to remind her that, in actual fact, they had far worse problems to deal with than the death of her mother. He had an image of the pile of dead bodies, lying there in the open on the island, where they had left them. They would be there, rotting, until they told someone about it all. 'Where does she live?' he asked. 'Where does Alison live?'

'In the suburbs. Woluwe St Pierre. It's only ten minutes away. Will you come with me?' He realised she was still holding his hand. She hadn't let go since they were in the office with Hulpe.

24

Stefan Meyer was in the ground-floor bathroom of Alison Spencer's place, in the quiet, affluent suburbs at the eastern edge of Brussels. He was on his knees, crouched over an open toilet, vomiting violently, his arms and legs shaking.

Through in the main room of the same floor Alison Spencer herself was flat on her stomach, her body twitching, a thin trickle of vomit coming from between her lips, her eyes closed. Her heart was still beating, but Stefan didn't know that, because he had been unable to go anywhere near her from the moment she had clutched at her chest and rolled off her sofa on to the floor, gasping like she was choking. He had watched in horror as she had implored him to help in a feeble, cracking voice, a hand stretched out to him. Then she had grasped the truth as he sat there immobile, refusing to go to her. She had accused him with a look of hatred, spitting out the words with rasping breaths, then keeled over on to her front and lay panting. He had only been able to move when she had stopped trying to speak, when her chest was no longer heaving, and though he knew then that he should have bent down and tested her vital signs, assured himself that she definitely was dead, he couldn't do it. He had run in here instead. If he hadn't run in here he would have spewed all over the floor.

It hadn't been like it was with Liz Wellbeck at all. Liz had already been asleep when the drug had started to work, and he had been downstairs, out of the way. On the monitor showing her bed he had watched as her body jerked around. She had started to shout, crying out her daughter's name, over and over again, but he had switched the sound off, then switched the TV screen off too. He hadn't wanted to watch. Instead he kept his eyes on the heart-rate monitor and waited until it was a still, flat line. Only then had he gone up to the room.

This wasn't what he was meant to be doing. None of it. All his life he had looked after people, never harmed them. He put both his hands in his hair and yanked on it, pulling until the roots started to give. He started to scream with the pain, but it wasn't enough. He pushed himself off the toilet and banged his head off the mirror above the sink, reeling back then headbutting it again with all his force. The mirror cracked and some pieces clattered into the sink. A few shards stuck in his skin. He stood trembling in front of the distorted image, watching the blood seep down his forehead. He shouldn't have done that, he realised. He was leaving his traces here, his DNA. How was he going to explain that if they asked him?

But they wouldn't ask him. His uncle – Monsieur Hulpe – had assured him. They would assume it was a burglary gone wrong, that the woman had suffered a heart attack with the shock. The drug he had given her was almost impossible to detect, unless you were specifically testing for it, and they didn't do that. They hadn't tested Liz for it and her body was in the ground now.

Still, leaving blood was reckless. He had to clean it up. He took deep breaths, pulling his mind from the pain and trying desperately to think. He took a towel and pressed it against his forehead. What else had his uncle told him? There were things he had to do, things to remember. The security system. There were cameras at the front gates and doors, recording. The recordings would be somewhere in the house. He had to find them. And the envelope, the letter from Liz Wellbeck. He had to find that too. That was why he was here. Because Liz had told this woman something, maybe told her everything, everything she knew or suspected. She'd got a letter out to Alison Spencer, just three weeks ago. She'd used the woman who brought the food from the basement kitchens. So maybe Liz had known what was going on, known that his uncle had stopped the treatments – the chemo, the radiation therapy. They were letting her die and had been doing it for nearly three months.

But she hadn't gone quickly enough. So then his uncle had told him to put the chemical into her drip. It was his idea, his fault. Bernard Hulpe. Everything was his fault. He hated his uncle, hated the way he spoke to him like he was a retarded six-year-old. He bent his head and started to cry about it, uncontrollably. This woman – Alison Spencer – had done nothing. Absolutely nothing. He'd given her the drug because his uncle had told him to. Because once you started you couldn't stop, you had to follow through. They'd got rid of Liz then found out this woman had the letter, that she knew something. So that had to be dealt with. His uncle had stood over him, shouting at him, blaming him because she'd got the letter out.

But Alison Spencer had let him in today like he was an old friend – so whatever it was she knew his uncle must have lied to him, because she hadn't looked at him like he was a killer. What was it she knew? He had to search this place, find everything Liz had sent her recently. There wasn't time to cry over her. If this all went wrong then the police would come for him. Who then would care for Lancelot and Guinevere?

He was the only person who loved them. The dogs were his life. His real life. They would be taken away, destroyed. He couldn't stand that. He would not be able to live with himself if that happened.

And Liz Wellbeck had only herself to blame. That bitch. He had been making her food, changing her bed, fetching and carrying for her for over a year. Servicing her insane ideas about infection and sterilisation. She had been a lunatic long before she was dying of the cancer – everything had to be spotless, sanitised, disinfected. She had money enough to employ a whole army of nurses and cleaners, but during the last six months had in fact sacked everyone else. She wanted just Stefan. She wanted him to do everything, night and day. Foolishly, he had imagined this implied some kind of trust. Now, he knew, it was just control. The fewer servants she had, the more effectively she could control them.

He had spent his entire day cleaning. The whole floor she lived on had stunk of disinfectant. It was the only smell she could bear. She had to have different shoes for each different part of the place, special baths of disinfectant to wash her hands and feet. She couldn't touch anything without washing her hands or wearing rubber gloves. They had got through three thousand rubber gloves and disposable slippers a month. He'd had no life away from her. Nine hours a day he had put up with it, living that life, cleaning and scrubbing and sterilising her world. In the last months he had even wiped her arse, bathed her, cleaned the spittle off her chin, spoon-fed her. She would have died anyway. Anyone could see that. You didn't need to be a doctor. At the end she couldn't even walk. The treatment halted, she had slipped into decay suddenly, over a space of no more than two weeks. Her brain was scrambled. There was cancer all over her, his uncle said, she was riddled with it.

But ten days ago she had stared at him as he changed her pillows and started to cackle like a witch. 'You'll get nothing,' she'd shouted suddenly in that coarse American accent. 'Nothing. You and that quack. You'll be out on the fucking street.'

He had tried to soothe her, thinking it was the illness, but she had pushed him away, lashed out at him. She had never been like that before. 'Your dogs will die,' she'd said. 'They'll shoot them. They'll hang you and shoot your fucking dogs.' He had stood gasping, stunned, not sure how to deal with it. She had sunk back into herself then, and he had waited until he thought she was asleep then tried to arrange the pillows, but as soon as he stepped near her hand had caught his arm and held on to it with a grip like a claw. 'You think I like you?' she hissed. 'You think I don't know what you two are doing? I fucking hate you. I hate you both. You'll get nothing off me, nothing.'

He had reported it all to his uncle, who had made some enquiries, probably with her husband. Her husband – Sir Frederick Eaton – was an English gentleman, always polite, always supportive. Though never there. A very busy man. That was when they had discovered it was true. Everything she had told him was true. She had made a will and left them nothing. Every promise she had made them she had broken.

That hadn't bothered him as it had his uncle. His uncle had been screaming and shouting about it. Stefan hadn't been able to get over her ingratitude. He had cared for this odd woman like she was his own dying mother, but she hated him. How could that be? He didn't understand, but it had made it easier to give her the drug. That and the idea she was going to die anyway.

But this woman – Alison Spencer – was different. She

hadn't hated him, she'd done nothing against him. He would rot in hell for this, for what he had done to her. He started to feel sick all over again, his head spinning. *Don't think about it*, his uncle had said. *Just do it.* But he couldn't keep his thoughts off her. He had slipped it into her drink and sat there with her, trying to seem normal, chatting, waiting for it to work. He was worse than the Nazi doctors they showed those documentaries about on Télé Deux.

He pulled his mobile phone from his trouser pocket and realised it had been ringing for some time. He could see from the number it was his uncle. He switched it off. He was meant to have come here and done this abominable thing several days ago, but hadn't had the courage. He didn't dare tell his uncle that. He wished now he had stayed at home today. This was all a mistake.

He started to tidy the blood, quickly. Then thought better of it. Time was against him. Two people – a couple – lived and worked here, besides the dead woman, though they occupied the smaller building at the gates that he hadn't even been in. Her housekeepers. Right now they were enjoying a vacation somewhere that his uncle had somehow arranged. So there was little chance of interruption from them. But there was always a chance that Alison Spencer had other staff that they didn't know about. He couldn't hang around. And he had to get back to the dogs, give them their lunch. They would be going crazy, barking and scratching. He couldn't leave them too long. They would need a walk as well. They depended on him. They were like his children. His beautiful little dogs.

He stood at the sink and itemised again what he needed to do. The priority was to find the letter from Liz Wellbeck. That was all that really mattered.

He started to open the drawers in front of him, pulling

them right out and tipping the contents on to the floor. He would have to do this with the whole house. Turn it upside down, search everywhere. It would take hours.

drawn I guess and ripping the contents out on the floor. It
we'd have to do this with the whole house. Turn it upside
down, search how you here. It would take hours.

25

Sixteen minutes later, Tom was standing on the pavement
right outside Alison Spencer's house, Sara beside him.

In a street full of spacious properties, each set back from
the road in its own grounds, screened by mature trees, this
particular one looked significant. Tom put it at roughly ten
bedrooms. Certainly big enough to be a small hotel. There
were eight-foot wrought-iron gates with security cameras,
and then a double-winged building, about twice the size of
the semi Tom had grown up in, but that appeared to be only
a gatehouse. About one hundred feet behind it was the main
event, a squat, three-storey, French-style miniature chateau,
complete with towers and decorated archways, three sides
partially enclosing a courtyard. Past it Tom could see the
beginnings of neat, ornamental hedges and closely cut lawns,
stretching back to a wooded area about two hundred yards
past the main building. 'This belongs to your mother's PA?'
he asked, slightly incredulous.

'No. She just lives here,' Sara said. 'This belongs to the family. She's looking after it, I suppose.'

'So this will be yours one day?'

She looked at him and he turned red. 'Sorry,' he said. Her
mother was dead, the will was being read on Friday. It was
possible this would belong to her before the end of the week.

'I don't know,' she said quietly. 'I have no idea. I don't care.'

'No. Of course not. I'm sorry. That was insensitive.'

But she wasn't listening. 'The gates are open,' she said. 'I wonder if that means anything?' She stepped up to the inter-com panel set in one of the big granite pillars, pressed the button to speak and waited. Nothing happened. She pressed again. No one answered.

'She's not in,' Tom said. 'Shall we try your father now?'

'Alison. It's me – Sara,' she said, speaking with her mouth close to the microphone. 'Are you there? I need to speak to you. It's urgent. Please answer if you're there.'

Silence. She had Alison Spencer's phone numbers, and had tried them all in the taxi over, to no avail. She tried the inter-com again. 'Alison. I need to talk to you about my mother. Please, Alison …' She stopped suddenly and wiped a sleeve across her eyes. 'Please, Alison. I need your help. Please.'

'She's not there,' Tom said gently. 'I think we should make contact with your father now.'

'I think we should go in,' she said, already stepping through the gap between the two gates. 'I don't know why she's left the gates open.'

They walked in silence past the gatehouse on a light gravel surface. There was no sign of life in the windows ahead. He asked her if she knew the place. She'd been a lot, she said, a few years back, before Alison Spencer had the place. The skies were heavy above them, the air close. As they reached the house a few drops of rain picked at his skin.

There was another intercom by a door round the side of the place. She said it was the service entrance, but it had been the one they usually used. She spoke again into the microphone, again got no response. She pushed the door tentatively and it opened immediately. That stopped her. 'This door is open as well,' she said. She looked around her suspiciously.

'Maybe she's in the garden,' Tom said. 'Or gone to get a packet of cigarettes from the corner shop ...'

'She has people to do that for her.'

'Of course. Maybe *they* left it open?'

She pushed it fully open, standing warily at the threshold, peering inside. There was a corridor, leading to steps and other doorways, an interior that looked spotless, painted in clean colours, mainly white. She shouted feebly. 'Alison! Are you in?'

It was too big a place for that to be effective, he thought. She turned back to him and looked frightened.

'What's the matter?' he asked.

'It's all wide open. No security. It's the same thing everywhere. All the security has been removed. Will you come in with me? I don't want to go in alone.'

He shrugged, then stepped past her and shouted, very loud: 'Alison Spencer! Are you here?'

He thought he heard some movement somewhere. But there was no reply. The noise was too far away to be distinct. He turned back to her. 'I really don't think she's in.'

'Let's check. Please.' She edged past him.

'I don't think there's anything to be afraid of,' he said. Then started to think about it. It didn't take him long to come up with a couple of improbable, but frightening, scenarios. 'Do you know where we go?' he asked, dropping his voice.

'Straight through,' she whispered. 'Up those stairs, then down the next set. That brings us to the reception hall ...' She stopped, listening to some sound. He too had heard a banging noise. 'Did you hear that?' she hissed. He nodded, then tried to smile at her. 'Maybe she *is* in,' he said.

'She would have answered the intercom if she was here.'

'Well, I think *someone's* in. You want to go and speak to them, or not?'

'You don't think it's dangerous?'

He frowned at her. 'Why should it be? Someone tried to kidnap you, but that was several thousand miles away. No one could know you were coming here.'

'They could have followed us from my mother's.'

'That didn't happen. If they'd followed us they'd be behind us, not in front.'

'You think I'm being silly?'

'It's understandable, but I don't think what has happened half a world away should make you feel cautious *here*.'

'But they're trying to convince me my mother is dead. What about that?'

He didn't know how to reply to that. Not by insisting her mother *was* dead. He spoke very gently to her. 'OK. Let's go in and look,' he said. 'I'll be right with you. OK?'

She wanted to creep down the corridor, so he held her hand, then started walking at a normal pace. He tried to speak to her in a normal voice, at normal volume, asking about the paintings on the walls, the age of the building, but she wouldn't reply. She was too focused on listening.

They came down a flight of steps, turned a corner and were in the reception room. A big set of double doors gave directly on to the courtyard. They were wide open. Outside he could see big drops of rain starting to fall, bouncing off the flagstones. The room was big, with a high ceiling decorated with a massive abstract pattern. There were gilt mirrors down the walls. 'Nice place,' he said.

'Ssh,' she said. 'I don't like this. All the doors are open. Anyone could walk in.'

'Like we just have. Where do we go now?'

She pointed to a door, slightly ajar. 'That's the main ground-floor room.'

He walked over with her hanging on to his arm again,

pushed the door open and stopped dead. 'Christ. Oh, Christ,' she said, beside him, her voice full of panic. The place had been turned over. There were bookcases pulled down, drawers yanked out, tables on their side, papers and objects all over the floor.

'She's been burgled,' he said, feeling his heart picking up, but right then Sara let out a stifled scream, one hand over her mouth, the other pointing frantically to a corner of the room. There was a body on the floor, stretched out towards the wall next to an overturned table. 'Not again ... not again ... this can't be happening ...' she sobbed, shaking her head and struggling to get the words out. 'It's Alison ... they've killed Alison ...'

'Wait there,' he said, loud enough to get through to her. 'Wait there.' He walked over to the body on autopilot, without thinking it through, stooped quickly and felt for a pulse at the neck. Behind him Sara was making a faint, terrified wailing noise.

'She's still alive,' he said. It was a woman, lying on her stomach, head turned sideways. She had brown hair in a bun, ashen skin. Her eyes were closed and she was covered in sweat. There was a small pool of vomit around her mouth. Her breathing was so shallow you could hardly see her chest moving, but the pulse was there. She looked like she might be about fifty years old. 'Is this her?' he asked. Sara was right at his side now, crouching with him.

'It's Alison,' she said. 'Something terrible is going on. They've killed her ...'

He started to speak to the woman, quietly, but insistently, seeing if he could get her back to consciousness. 'Alison! Can you hear me? My name's Tom Lomax. I'm here with Sara Eaton. We're here to help you. Can you hear me, Alison? You're going to be all right. We'll call an ambulance. You'll be OK. Nod if you can hear what I'm saying …' As he spoke he started checking her body for any obvious injuries, all the while his ears focusing on the room around him. He kept glancing back over his shoulder at the door they had come through. There was another opposite. Whoever had been here might still be here. 'Does she understand English?' he asked. Sara mumbled that she *was* English. He couldn't see any injuries, but couldn't check beneath her. He didn't want to move her. She might have a spinal injury. There was no blood anywhere. 'Maybe she had a heart attack,' he said. 'I can't find any injuries.' There was no bruising on her head. 'You're OK, Alison,' he said again. He told Sara to use her mobile, call the emergency services. He didn't know the number. She managed to get her phone out. He didn't think it through – consider what they would tell the police or doctors – because all the planning was redundant now. They had to react to this immediately.

Sara was starting to press the buttons, her hands jagging all over, when he saw movement out of the corner of his eye. He spun quickly and stood, his heart racing. Beside him Sara shrieked at the top of her voice. There was a man in the other doorway, staring at them. He was tall, overweight, with hair that was sticking up on his head, blood streaked across his face. He had on a suit that was crumpled, with something spilled all over the jacket and down the front of the trousers. He moved his hand from his side, revealing what he was holding – a kitchen knife. The blade was about twelve inches long. He stepped forward, his eyes moving from Sara to Tom. She screamed again, so loud it hurt Tom's ears. Tom was frozen to the spot, trying to work out what to do. The man was heavy, bigger than him, but he looked worried. He didn't look like a burglar. More like one of Alison Spencer's staff. Tom let out a breath. That could be it. Maybe he thought *they* were the burglars. He opened his mouth to speak but then Sara screamed for the third time. The look in the man's eyes changed suddenly. His eyes went to the body on the floor, then back up to Tom. Instantly, Tom saw the truth: the man wasn't staff, he wasn't meant to be here at all. Tom took a step forward, towards him. That was enough. Something shifted between them and the expression on the man's face switched to fear. Suddenly he turned and started to run, back the way he had come.

Tom got hold of Sara. She looked terrified. He had time to ask if she was OK, time to tell her again to call the ambulance and police, then he too turned and started running. 'I'm going after him,' he shouted. 'Wait here. Don't leave this room.' He could hear her yelling at him to stop, but he was already through the door, already sprinting.

26

The man may have looked clumsy and fat, but he was fast enough. Already, through in the next room, he was out of sight. But there was only one door swinging wide open and Tom could hear his footsteps clattering across the wooden floors beyond. He went straight after him, into another room, then down a short corridor on the other side of that. That brought him to the foot of a winding stairwell. He took the steps two at a time, taking deep breaths and listening up ahead to make sure the man hadn't stopped and turned to face him. At the first landing he came out into a circular room with desks and chairs. There were papers in heaps, drawers pulled out, books from a bookshelf all over the floor. He stumbled over them and took the next flight more slowly. They had to be ascending one of the towers he had seen. So it was going to be a dead end. The man couldn't go anywhere. He would have to turn and either fight, or give in. From the look Tom had read in his eyes, and from the desperate speed of his flight, Tom guessed the latter. But the man was armed, so best to assess the options carefully, keep an escape route open.

He shouted up after him, in English, telling him he was police. He repeated the word 'police' several times, hoping the lie would have some effect, but he could still hear the guy panting up above. He ran up to the next room, a smaller place with boxes piled in storage. He went straight to the stairs but stopped because he saw now that there were two doors off. He could hear nothing up the stairs, so he backed into the room and approached the other door more cautiously. It led into a long loft space, with the sloping roof down one side, strung with cobwebs and dust, and more crates and stacked furniture at the other. The door right opposite him – forty feet distant – was swinging open. He swore and started to sprint again. He could hear the rain clattering heavily off the roof tiles, inches from his head.

The farther door opened on to another long loft coming off at right angles, but this time the door at the far end was closed. About halfway along, a set of wooden, four-paned windows were hanging open. Over the din from the rainfall, he could hear a scraping, fumbling noise from out on the roof. Tom guessed the door ahead was locked so he'd gone out the window.

He put his head out very cautiously. Staring through the now driving rain, he saw that the man was already quite a distance along a narrow ledge that ran the length of the roof, just above the guttering. He was running in a crouch, arms out to steady himself, the knife still there. Tom shouted at him and saw him flinch, like something had been thrown. But he didn't pause, didn't look back. It looked like he knew where he was going.

Tom hauled himself out on to the ledge, balanced with care, then began to trot after him, still shouting at him to stop. He even put it into bad French. The rain was so heavy it would be hard to hear anything, though. The water was already coursing off the tiles, and the ledge was treacherous, worse in those places where the flashing cut into it in strips of slippery zinc. He wasn't good with heights anyway, so had to stop himself from looking at the drop. It took all his concentration to keep his footwork safe. They were three floors up, and though the floors weren't high, it was enough to break something even if you landed well.

Twice he saw the man falter and wobble. Tom was going slowly, but he was gaining. He slipped himself when he was only twenty feet from him, a foot going over the edge before he could recover. He went down and grabbed the edge of a wet tile, but it came away in his hand. He dropped to one knee, brought the other leg up, took a breath and got his stance back, then stood to find that the man had for the first time paused to look at him, perhaps hearing that he had stumbled. He shouted something incomprehensible to Tom then turned to continue. He looked very frightened. Tom stood, changed the tile to his left hand, switching his grip so that he had some purchase on it. His hand moved back to throw it. He was less than twenty feet away and the tile was about as heavy as a half-brick. If it hit his head it would seriously injure him. He took a breath, paused, and right then heard the man shout out. He looked up and saw him flailing at the air, his balance gone. Tom stepped forward, yelling at him, telling him to get his hands down. But already the man was going over. Tom was too far away to stop it. He watched as the man managed to catch hold of the guttering. He was poised like that for a split second, shouting something, dangling in mid-air. Tom started to run towards him. He was only feet from him when the gutter broke.

Tom went into a crouch, putting a hand out to steady himself. He heard a muffled thump from below, then silence. He looked over, hoping to see the guy sitting there with a broken ankle maybe – he had dropped in the best possible way, feet first with his fall slowed by his hold on the guttering. But the guy was lying in a crumpled pile, face up.

'Fuck,' Tom whispered. 'Fucking shit.'

*

He found his way down via the fire escape the man had probably been aiming for. He moved quickly, cursing himself. He had no idea who the man was, no idea if he was the actual burglar. Why had he been chasing him? And besides, what did any of this really have to do with him, with Tom Lomax? He was a fucking idiot.

The man was in exactly the same position when Tom got to him. He was completely still, a pool of blood spreading out beneath his head. He had gone feet first, but clearly he hadn't landed like that. The head was crushed at the back where it had hit the flagstones, the neck bent at an impossible angle. The eyes were open, staring at him, but there was no sight there. Tom felt a whack in his chest, his heart tripping as he realised what he was seeing. The guy was dead. He bent down and tried to breathe properly. He couldn't accept it, couldn't understand that this had happened. He searched with trembling fingers, looking desperately for a pulse, but finding nothing. He listened for a heartbeat, felt for a pulse again, held his ear over the gaping mouth to see if there was breath or warmth. But it was all stupid. The man's eyes were wide open, rain dropping into them without even a reflex response. Two minutes ago, whoever he was, he had been running, speaking, breathing. But he was gone now. Completely gone.

The rain was coming straight down now, in massive drops, like something tropical. Tom's clothing was drenched. He gazed up at the broken guttering. It wasn't even that high. On a good day you could jump from there, roll like a parachutist and walk off.

He remembered Sara, and the other person. He pushed himself unsteadily to his feet to walk back to her, then, on impulse, he stooped again and very gently went through the pockets of the man's jacket. He found a big brown envelope, a wallet and an ID card. The envelope was soaking wet. It had someone's name on, but it was smudged with the rain and he couldn't read it. The ID card was plastic-covered and belonged to Stefan Marc Meyer. He frowned, put the ID card in his pocket to show Sara. Stefan Meyer? Was that the name of the nurse who had been looking after her mother? He swore again.

His eyes scanned the surrounding gardens. There were big trees and dense hedges obscuring the views to other properties, but it was possible someone had seen something. It was possible someone was going to come along and say he had murdered this man, burglar or not. And how could he be a burglar if he was Elizabeth Wellbeck's nurse?

He turned in a kind of stupor to get back into the house, but saw that Sara was already standing there, only ten feet away from him, the rain streaming over her. Just standing there watching him. He looked away from her, feeling the shame rushing at him. She shouted something, but he couldn't hear it. He ran a hand over his face, wiping away the rain. He was breathing heavily, and not just because he'd run all the way down.

She came up to him while he was still standing like that, unable to move. He felt her take his hand and he looked at her, his face quivering. There was a strange, wild look in her eyes.

'He fell,' he told her. 'He's fucking dead.'

'So what? He killed Alison,' she said. She was gritting her teeth, forcing the words out. 'She died while I was talking to her. He killed her.'

He frowned at her. 'What do you mean?'

'It's Stefan Meyer,' she said. 'I recognised him. Alison said he poisoned her. She told me ...'

'She spoke to you?'

'She whispered to me. She was whispering, so I had to bend down to hear. She said it was him …'

'He poisoned her?'

She nodded. 'She told me that.'

'Is she alive still? Did you call the police or …'

She shook her head. Then started to cry, softly.

'Let's go in,' he said. 'I need to check her …'

'She died right then.' She screwed her eyes up. 'She died while I was stroking her hair. She was trying to tell me things. She started convulsing. I couldn't stop it …'

They went back in and he did it all again, checking for signs of life, going through the motions. When he was finished he stood up and walked back to the doorway, where Sara was standing, head down, still crying.

'She spoke to you?' he forced himself to ask, again. 'Are you sure?'

'Of course I'm fucking sure.'

'What did she say – about the poison, I mean?' He was trying to get to grips with it, thinking that if the Belgian police arrived any minute now it would make a massive difference to everything if the man out there really had killed this woman. He looked around the floor for anything that might have been used to poison her – a syringe, perhaps – but couldn't see anything beyond the mess. 'Did she say anything else about the poison?' he asked again. How did Alison Spencer know she had been poisoned? There must be a clue. Or maybe the guy told her that. Or she felt the effects. But what would he use to poison her?

He was being cold-blooded, he thought. But there wasn't time for sympathy and consolation. Not right now. He was in a perilous situation. Or was he? In actual fact he had done nothing wrong at all. The man had slipped and fallen. 'Sara,' he said. 'Can you tell me, please? What did she say – all of it?' He put a hand on her arm. She looked up at him, her face a mask of twisted grief and shock. 'She didn't say anything about how he did it,' she muttered, the words coming out indistinctly. 'But she told me something else.'

27

John Lomax was in his kitchen, just finishing the preparations on a cod and bacon dish he'd first found in a Jamie Oliver book. Only now he hadn't been able to find the cookbook, so he was going from memory. He was beginning to think he'd forgotten something important. It was meant to be a quick meal for himself and Rachel. She was on lunch break from a shift at New Charing Cross Hospital – only a five-minute walk from his riverside flat, so she wasn't desperately pressed, but he didn't want to spend the whole time in the kitchen. Her visit was the high point of today – the only bit he had been looking forward to. He wasn't rushed at all, of course, because since he'd retired he had nothing to do. Not really. A year and a half ago he'd been looking forward to doing nothing, but now it was driving him mad. He was filling the time with going through the old Grenser files, but there was something desperate about that. And messing around with food wasn't going to keep him sane.

The cookbook had promised, he recalled, that the meal would be ready – from start to finish – in thirty minutes, but he'd already spent fifteen minutes trying to tie little pieces of string round the cod and bacon bundles. Also, he couldn't remember whether the parcels were meant to be wrapped in foil or not. Surely something like that, otherwise the white wine would just cook off and wouldn't steam the fish. Or was the white wine from another recipe that he was muddling with this one? Maybe the string too. He was getting annoyed with it. He had arthritis in the joints of his little fingers – not a new thing, this had started over ten years ago – which made fiddly stuff like this a bit difficult, and anyway, it was all a waste of time, trivia. What did it matter what they ate?

The kitchen was open-plan with the rest of the downstairs space and from where he was standing, at the dividing bar, he could see the television screen in the opposite corner of the room. Rachel was lounged on the sofa in front of it, watching the midday news, drinking a coffee. She still had her white coat on, the stethoscope and hospital ID tag hanging around her neck. She looked relaxed, the coat unbuttoned – showing the open-necked blouse beneath, the bare skin at her throat. She had her long legs up on the couch, half tucked under her, but he could still see a lot of them. There was something illicit about it, in his head. *Still*, after all these years, and even though he was retired. Because she had been a victim in one of his cases. *One of his cases* – that was a laugh. As if Grenser could be ranked level with anything else he'd done. If only.

It was illicit, but what was he to do? She was a victim, yes, she was saddled with that burden, it was always there, between them. She lived with the crushing weight of it, it was the element she lived within. But life went on within it. That was the brutal, absurd truth, for her, for him, for all survivors. She still had her life to live, and was living it. And she was still a woman. For him, an extremely attractive woman. Too thin for most, he was aware, but he had always gone for women like that. He hated fat, and most women over forty got fatter in certain areas. It was a natural process. But not Rachel. She did too much worrying to put on weight. She was tall too – his own height, just under six foot. Of course, that her hair was bone-white – it had turned that way in the first year after Lauren's disappearance – shouldn't really be something positive. To him it made her look like some tall, leggy, Scandinavian blonde. His imaginary take on her – because white wasn't blonde, and her hair had been dark. Her body was fit and lean because she had started an obsessive exercise regime about fifteen years ago – originally a therapy to help get her past the downers – so even that was something loaded with the shadow of the past. And you could see twenty-two years of acute anxiety etched into her face and lurking behind her eyes. It was there even when she laughed. But she was still attractive. Despite it all. Attractive both as she was and as he recalled her – because she had been stunning when younger, and the traces of that were still there. He couldn't get away from that. No use pretending to himself that it was otherwise.

So was that what was going on between them? he wondered Something that simple? Something *sexual*? Why not?

He finally got the tray of cod into the oven and went over to the sofa, sitting down beside her. She didn't notice. She was focused on a news item about healthcare funding. The big anniversary was past and she was suddenly back to normal, the memories of Lauren, the corrosive imaginings, pushed back to wherever it was she kept them bolted down, controlled. The change in her mood was schizo – as it always was – unsettling for him, though he was relieved. Yesterday she had still been under it, today she was almost normal. Maybe twenty-two years of practice did that. He listened with half an ear to the news item, his eyes on her face.

What did *she* think was going on with them? he wondered. When she came round in the evenings they usually just watched the TV, or sat out on his balcony, looking at the river, chatting. His apartment was directly opposite the Harrods Furniture Depository – as it had been before they converted it into yet more luxury flats – with a view up to

Hammersmith Bridge – a beautiful aspect, even on an overcast, miserable day. It was enough to sit there with her, he thought, holding hands, sipping wine, staring at the sunset, or the bridge, or the boats on the river.

But he wanted more. There was something unhinged about their relationship. That was what made it interesting and infuriating. She had a vein of insanity, of course. It wasn't the usual sort of madness, as with bipolar sufferers, or depressives, or alcoholics. But her moods and thoughts were all sudden like that. She took him by surprise.

This time of year aside, she was rarely low. More often she had an excess of energy. She wasn't what people assumed she would be – crippled by the past, humourless, always about to drop into an emotional abyss. Mostly she wasn't like that at all, on the surface. But there was always that edge to her. There must be something twisted about him too, he thought, for him to want to be with her. Brothers and sisters didn't sit and hold hands – not at his age, anyway. That wasn't what they were. Nor did friends – not as much as they did. And friends certainly didn't sleep together, but they did that frequently now, clinging to each other like frightened lovers, yet never going farther.

The news item changed to something about a pirate incident, somewhere too far away to worry about. He saw her focus ease and she turned to look at him. He smiled at her and opened his mouth to tell her she looked beautiful – something else friends didn't do – but then something the presenter said caught his attention. The name of the place. *Ile des Singes Noirs.* He frowned and listened.

A new and sinister activity; Somali pirates had kidnapped someone – they were saying – but not from a boat, or from Kenya, instead from a remote island. At least that was what was assumed. Sara Eaton. A twenty-year-old heiress to an immeasurable fortune. Her mother had only just died, he gathered, but he had missed her name while he was staring at Rachel. There was a picture of Sara Eaton on a boat somewhere, looking tanned and young, just like an heiress should. All her staff had been killed – at least eight people. She was missing.

'Poor girl,' Rachel said.

He looked at her. 'Ile des Singes Noirs,' he said. 'Sara Eaton? That ring any bells?'

She shook her head. He stood up and told her he wouldn't be a minute. 'Just have to check something,' he said. He could feel her eyes on him as he walked over to the stairs to the second floor.

He didn't close the door to his study – though he didn't want her seeing the paperwork in there – because she would have heard that from downstairs. Instead he walked quietly over to the desk and thought about the name. Ile des Singes Noirs. Wasn't that the name of Elizabeth Wellbeck's private island in the Indian Ocean? It had come up in the inquiry. He was sure of it. And did that mean Elizabeth Wellbeck was the mother of this kidnapped girl, the mother who had just died? He sat down, switched on the anglepoise and pulled out a pile of policy books from the shelving behind him. Maybe he had the name wrong. French wasn't his forte. Or any language.

He started leafing through the book covering the second month of the inquiry. He had a vague feeling about it, plus he was sure he could remember where exactly on the page a reference might appear. He turned the pages quickly, looking only at that spot – the middle of the left-hand page. He found it within half a minute.

Ile des Singes Noirs. He was right. It was an island that back then, at least, they had been told belonged to Elizabeth Wellbeck. In the weeks following the incident her staff had reported that that was where she was, where she lived. She had some eccentric wildlife project going there, spent most of the year on the island. That was where she had been on 14 April 1990, the day Lauren had been taken. On that day Elizabeth Wellbeck – the founder, chief benefactor and director of the Wellbeck Foundation, the organisation that owned and ran the Wellbeck Clinic from which Lauren Gower had been snatched – on that day Elizabeth Wellbeck had been several thousand miles away. Hence the inquiry had no need to speak to her, except as a kind of formality, very low down on the list of priorities. It had been three weeks before they had finally got round to meeting her. By then she had already publicly announced a three-million-dollar reward for information about the disappearance. Not that that had helped. He supposed it was still available, technically, sitting in some forgotten bank account somewhere.

He found the interview now, in his copy of Box 221, and skimmed through the sheets. A short interview, conducted by DI Pearce, not himself, since Elizabeth Wellbeck wasn't a suspect. Nothing of interest revealed. There was some time taken up at the end with how soon she could make available one of her PAs – a young Russian woman who might or might not have been at the clinic that day – and who, at the time of this interview, had still not been spoken to. On that date the PA – Arina Vostrikova – had still been on this paradise island Wellbeck owned – Ile des Singes Noirs. Not so tempting a place now, he thought. Now that the kidnappers had found it.

What about Sara Eaton? A quick search through the indexing material revealed that Elizabeth Wellbeck was married to Sir Freddie Eaton. How had he forgotten that? So he assumed the girl taken, or killed, today was their child. The news item had given her age as twenty. She was born, therefore, two years after the kidnap of Lauren. Maybe she'd been mentioned in the 2003 inquiry, when they'd reopened it all, but not in the original material, of course.

He started to search for a mention of her. He was standing behind the desk with one of the boxes open and was getting out the sheets of paper when he became aware that Rachel was leaning against the open study door, watching him. He stopped, closed the box, turned red with embarrassment. He felt like he'd been caught out doing something forbidden.

'What are you doing?' she asked, but he could see from her look that she already knew. She stepped in and looked down at the paperwork scattered across the desk. She bit her lip, stared at him.

'I've been reviewing the inquiry,' he said quietly. He sat down and sighed. He thought she might start crying now, then it would get worse. The whole day would be ruined, perhaps the whole week. It would knock her back.

But she didn't cry. Instead, she walked round to his side of the desk and put a hand on his head. She stroked his hair. He looked up at her. She was staring out of the window, a strange look on her face. Her skin was flushed red, like she'd just sprinted from somewhere, but her breathing was slow. He put a hand up and held her arm. He wanted to say sorry, but wasn't sure what for. When their eyes met she smiled, as if with sympathy. Without warning, she bent down and kissed him on the cheek, then held her face against his, cheek to cheek. She stayed like that for a long time. He didn't dare move. He had the feeling her eyes were closed.

'She's dead,' she said eventually, very softly. 'I know she's dead.'

He swallowed hard, shocked. It was the first time he had heard her say anything like that. Immediately, he wanted to contradict her. But he didn't. That wasn't his right. And anyway, she was probably correct.

'I wish I knew where she was, and what happened,' she said. 'I wish someone would tell me where she is. But I don't think she's alive any more. I thought you should know that.'

He waited for her to straighten up, then took a breath. He stood up and put his arms round her, pulling her close. Absurdly, he thought she was going to turn her head into him, start kissing him. Her hands were round his neck like that would happen. He couldn't work out what was going on with her, what she was thinking, or feeling. 'Your food is going to burn,' she murmured. Her face was right in front of his. He didn't move. He waited for her to come forward to him. There was a long, awkward silence while they stood like that, too close for misinterpretation, yet nothing happening. He thought the moment would pass as suddenly as it had arrived. That was what always happened. But then she pressed her mouth against his and started to kiss him.

28

Sara stood right in the corner of the wide, glass-panelled room, the phone pressed to her ear, listening anxiously to the sound of her father's voice. Only half of what he was saying was registering. Her attention was all over the place; she was exhausted and distracted, unable to focus clearly for more than a few seconds at a time. Tom was only a few steps behind her, also listening – watching to make sure she followed his advice. He had told her – again and again – not to mention anything she had personally done with her gun. They were in the entrance lobby of the Eurostar terminal, part of a large, dirty, teeming station called the Gare du Midi, in Brussels. Out on the main concourse she had suffered a new kind of panic, surrounded by too many people, all far too close to her, intruding into her personal space. She didn't like big public places, wasn't used to them. But this disgust with humanity had taken her by surprise. It was more like something Liz would have experienced, one of the reasons she'd fled to the clinic.

Inside the Eurostar lounge it was a bit quieter than out in the station proper. They were about fifty feet from the entry gates they were going to go through when she had finished making this call. The train would board in about fifteen minutes. Another couple of hours after that and they'd be in London.

'Christ Almighty ...' her father said, his voice low, tense, almost a whisper. 'I don't know how you're managing to speak about it. Christ Almighty ...' Usually when he spoke to her – no matter what it was about – he managed to convey an impression of indifference, as if she were interrupting something important, or her concerns weren't terribly interesting. But not now. She had given him the whole terrifying sequence of events – how she had watched her best friend shot dead, seen piles of bodies in the dirt, a man shot at point-blank range (without saying who had shot him), the desperate flight across the island, the plane out, all of it – how a woman he had once known well had died in her arms, how she had discovered her mother was dead and buried, with her not even told, or invited to the funeral. She had got it all out without her voice cracking. It had taken a tremendous effort of will to keep talking, to keep telling him it all. And yet, at the end of the account there was a massive, terrifying gap. A crucial absence of information. She had left out the very last thing that Alison Spencer had told her. She had kept that from him, kept it from Tom too. Because it was information she couldn't deal with right now, couldn't bring herself to even consider. It was sitting inside her, worming away, burning her up, while she tried desperately not to even look at it, not to acknowledge it had even been said. Because if she went there, if she let herself think about *that*, she thought she might crack down the middle, crack and collapse.

At the end there had been silence from her father, his shock palpable. She had to ask him if he were still there before he could get himself to speak. 'I'll need to speak to you about your mother,' he said now. 'Properly. We're all devastated, Sara. There are reasons for everything that's happened. But now is not the time. Now we have to deal with all this ...'

She scanned the faces in the room, most people either

sitting down waiting, or standing under the monitors watching the TV news. All either businessmen or tourists, she thought. All looking pretty comfortable. Not the mad mix out in the station. Beggars and drunks. She had felt threatened out there, clung on to Tom until they got in here. She was overreacting, of course. She knew that. Spoilt little rich brat. But it hardly mattered. She felt nauseous, dizzy. It was the simple fact that she was standing here, alive, still functioning. That was what was doing it. *Nothing had changed.* It was preposterous, completely unreal. The complete nightmare of the last seventy-two hours. It was playing now in the back of her head – all the images and sounds – playing like a continuous reel of gut-wrenching horror, right there behind her eyes. But no one knew. *No one saw it except her.* Everything out here was the same as it ever was.

'Daddy,' she said, interrupting the voice. 'Listen to what I'm telling you, Daddy. Please.' She spoke in low, urgent tones. 'We are about to board a Eurostar train. We will be in London in a couple of hours. I need to see you right then. I need you to get someone to pick us up. OK? This is more important than anything else. I'm in very serious difficulties here ...'

'It's sorted already, Sara. Try to stay calm. Everything will be taken care of. Security will be there. They will bring you and your friend directly to me ...'

'You must not forget to arrange it, Daddy ...'

'It's already arranged ...' His tone of voice cut her short. 'They know what I want. Arisha has arranged it already.' She heard him say something to someone else – probably his principal PA – Arina Vostrikova, 'Arisha', as they had always called her. Sara knew her well, got on with her well enough. There were rumours about Arisha and her father, of course. Probably true. But so what? Arisha had been listening in, Sara assumed. That was what she should have assumed, at any rate, because that was what nearly always happened. Silly to forget that. Her father did nothing in private.

'Security will be there to meet you,' he said again. 'It's arranged. Please don't worry ...'

'I need you to tell me why this has happened, Daddy. Why you didn't contact me ...'

'Not now, darling. There are reasons. Things are going on that I need to tell you about. But not now, not over a public phone system. Trust me. I'll explain everything when we meet. Everything.'

'I can't understand it ... I can't get my head around why you would do that to me ...' She paused, breathing hard. She had to get the lump out of her throat. 'I can't believe she's dead, Daddy, because I haven't seen her. If she'd died you would have told me ...' She could hear herself sobbing as she said it, then Tom's hand holding her free hand, squeezing it.

'How really, bloody awful for you,' her father said. 'I'm so sorry, darling. So sorry. But please don't think about it now. I will explain everything. I promise. But now is not the time.'

She remembered again what Alison had told her. The last thing. It kept squirming into her consciousness, she couldn't stop it. Her heart started to pound, in overdrive. She leaned back against the wall, put her head back, screwed her eyes closed. *That* was what she should be asking her father about. She let the arm holding the phone fall to her side. Then Tom was speaking to her, trying to get her to look at him. She opened her eyes. People were looking over at her, alarm on their faces.

'Shut up, Sara,' Tom was hissing. 'Please shut up.' He was pulling her out of the room, back on to the station concourse.

'Where are we ... what are you doing ...?

'Walk normally,' he said, leaning close to her. 'Look normal.'

She remembered the phone and brought it up to cut the connection, but saw her father had already done that. 'Why are we coming out here?' she asked him. 'I don't want to be out here again ...' Her voice sounded far away.

'There was something on the TV in there,' he whispered. They were out past the sliding doors now, the people flooding around her again, the smell of them in her nose. 'Something about you,' he said. 'There was a picture of you on the screen. It was about you being kidnapped, about the island.' He stopped walking and stood very close to her. 'They're looking for you,' he said. 'I think they think you've been kidnapped. So if we want to get to your father before you start speaking to the police then we can't just get on the Eurostar. We need to find another way across the Channel.'

29

They took an ordinary train to the Belgian coast. It seemed to stop at a station every five minutes. They sat in a shabby, rattling carriage that was virtually empty, opposite each other across a stained, pull-down table, in window seats that were almost threadbare, with lewd, pictorial graffiti on the walls. The train smelled of cigarette smoke and wet overcoats, though outside the rain had stopped and the sun was breaking through bruised clouds in dramatic shafts of light. It was almost enough to make the scenery interesting. They stared at the uniform Flanders countryside with its dull modern housing and monotonous, flat fields and they said nothing to each other – not a single word – for the entire two-hour journey.

Tom kept bringing his eyes back to her, trying to catch her attention, to work out what she was thinking. But she was avoiding his gaze. She wouldn't look at him. It was suddenly different, and getting worse by the hour – like she'd gone cold and didn't want him there. He wished dearly that he wasn't there, but at least until they got back to the UK he couldn't see a way to get out of this without her. He was hoping her father was going to come up with some kind of answer. Some resources, at least. They were going to have to get the police involved, but he wanted lawyers there when that happened. He wanted them to know what they were doing and to have expert advice and influence available. The kind her father could buy and he couldn't.

He'd got himself into this position because of her, so couldn't understand why she was giving him the cold shoulder. The change had started when she had refused to tell him what Alison Spencer had told her – the secret information. Like suddenly she had started to suspect him of something. There had been a bond of trust between them, but then suddenly it was gone. He couldn't work it out. Back in Brussels – before the thing with Alison – she had been unable to let go of his hand. She'd been leaning on his shoulder, crying, hugging him. Now she didn't want him anywhere near her – unless she was inexplicably frightened, as she had been back at the station. That was how it seemed, anyway. The abrupt change was un-nerving. He didn't know how to manage it, didn't know what she was going to do next. And right now he needed her to be predictable.

They were going to some place on the coast where there was a posh marina and an ex-boyfriend. Roland Lastenouse. She'd already called him, made him promise secrecy. He had 'boats'. That was how she had put it. He would get them across the Channel without anyone knowing. That was all Tom had been able to get out of her. He wasn't happy with it, as a plan. Because all it would take to get them stranded in this country was for the ex to turn his back on her, make a call to the local police. But it had been the best she could come up with, and it was way better than any ideas he had. So they were trying it.

At the terminus they took a bus along the coast, again in virtual silence. The road ran through mile after mile of soulless development – concrete apartment blocks for cheap coastal holidays. It was like the Costa del Sol, but without the *sol*. Past the drab flats and tower blocks he could see a strip of beach dotted with the parasols and deckchairs of those who were making the most of it. Beyond them, the depressing, freezing grey of the English Channel ran into a sky of the same colour. He thought it would probably start raining again soon.

They took a cab after the bus, and ended up in a marina flanked by heavy-duty dock cranes. She walked ahead of him, too quickly, through a series of jetties, past scores of beautiful yachts and powerboats. At one point, he thought she might turn and shout at him to get a move on. But she didn't. She didn't say anything. She was making a beeline, he guessed, for the biggest thing in the harbour – a very conspicuous luxury yacht done out in blue and white diagonal stripes. It wasn't a super-yacht – the kind he'd seen online, the kind the sheikhs and Russian oligarchs collected – it didn't have space for a helicopter, but it still dwarfed everything else in the harbour.

When they got to it she walked straight up a railed gangway and shouted for the ex. Tom stopped short, still on the jetty. A man appeared in a uniform and she followed him, not looking back to see if Tom was with her. He waited a bit, then walked up the gangway and sat down on a raised part of the deck, feeling decidedly surplus to requirements. The cold smell of seaweed and brine started to clear his head a little. He could feel the boat's motors thrumming gently beneath his body. Maybe they were already getting ready to go.

She had disappeared inside somewhere. He thought he could just get up and walk away and she probably wouldn't care now. But he wasn't going to do that. If the authorities were assuming she'd been kidnapped then they had probably spoken to the staff who had brought him to the Seychelles, so it wouldn't be long before they were looking for him too. He didn't want to end up in police custody in Belgium, or anywhere other than the UK. At least in the UK he would know the language.

He started thinking about Jamie. Jamie would be in

Spain, on some beach somewhere with his mum and her new boyfriend. Swimming in the sea, maybe, with the new bloke playing dad. Maybe. In fact he had no idea what was going on in Sally's private life. If there was a boyfriend she wouldn't necessarily take him with her. He had a pang of longing for his son. He wanted to feel his hand in his again. He didn't want to be chucked into a Belgian holding cell for a few months while they worked out who was to blame for all this shit, or charged him with the killing of Stefan Meyer. He took a deep breath, put his head in his hands.

After a good ten minutes he felt someone sit down next to him and looked up. It was Sara.

'We sail in half an hour,' she said, very quietly. 'Roland thinks it will take a couple of hours to complete the crossing – to get to where he wants to on the other side. The weather is good, though.'

'Right,' he said. 'Good.'

She was looking at him now, so he looked back, waiting to see if there was anything else. She looked predominantly sad, he thought. But she wasn't trembling like a leaf, incapacitated with shock. There was certainly a tough streak in her.

'I'm sorry,' she said.

He nodded. 'No need.'

'I'm trying to keep on top of my feelings ...'

'I understand.'

'So much ... so much is happening ... more than you know, more than I can tell you ... I don't know where I am. I really don't ... I'm sorry.'

'It's fine. Don't worry. You do what you have to ...'

'I couldn't have got here without you, Tom.'

He shrugged at that. 'I'm sure you could,' he said. 'But I'm not sure I could get back to the UK without you.'

She was looking at him still, her expression very serious.

She put a hand out and touched his arm, let her fingers stay there. She looked like she was unsure if she should do more. 'I need to spend some time with Roland,' she said, surprising him. 'I need to keep him sweet.'

'OK.' He wasn't sure how that might impact on him. Or what exactly she meant.

'He's very close to me,' she said. 'We used to be ... very close. I studied with him, about two years ago. The same university, I mean. He's French. He's fifteen years older than me, in fact. He was a guest lecturer on a poetry course. That's how we met.'

He nodded. 'I see. Good.' Fifteen-year difference. Guest lecherer, he thought.

She nodded as well, her eyes on her fingers, where they were still on his arm. She stroked it a little, with affection, he thought. She didn't seem like a twenty-year-old kid any more. Her expression was pensive. He was still waiting for her to go on. But after a while he realised there was nothing else. She wasn't going to say more. He cleared his throat. 'Is it his boat?' he asked. Polite conversation.

'Yes.'

'They really rate their intellectuals in France.'

She frowned. Didn't get the joke.

'I mean, they pay them well ...' he said. 'It's a joke.'

'He has family money,' she said, still frowning. She stood up with a sigh. 'They'll come and show you to your cabin.' She looked down at him. 'Thank you, Tom.' She didn't smile.

He watched her walk off. He wondered if she'd just said goodbye to him. He felt like calling out to her – *so you'll put the cheque in the post?* But he'd already cracked one joke too many.

30

In the end, by the time they got going, it was getting dark. He kept below – as instructed – as they manoeuvred out of the harbour. There seemed to be a crew of about five men. One of them had shown him to the cabin. It was very comfortably kitted out, but tiny. There was a window. He watched the dark, low shape of Belgium receding, then lay back on the bunk and felt the engines gaining power. He closed his eyes, but couldn't sleep.

After an hour he felt sick enough to have to go up on deck.

The air was fresh and freezing. The sea looked flat and calm, but the boat was going fast, the bow lifting and smashing down. He couldn't see anyone else on deck. In the stern – sheltered from the wind – he found what he imagined was a sun deck and sat there alone, in the growing darkness, leaning on the railings and waiting to vomit. It didn't happen, though. He'd eaten nothing for a long while – nothing since the meal he'd eaten with Sara, in fact. That was Sunday evening and it was Tuesday now. Coming up to forty-eight hours. If it weren't for the seasickness he guessed he would be famished. Or maybe it was *because* he needed food that he felt like this. He wondered if he could force something down – if he could find someone to give him something. Above and behind him there were two more decks, one of them the bridge – if that's what they called it on a boat this size. There would be crew up there that he could ask.

He turned to go up and saw that there was a man standing right behind him in the darkness, in the doorway he'd used to get out here. He was leaning against it, looking pretty casual in an Aran sailing sweater, staring at Tom. Tom stopped himself from reacting, opened his mouth to speak, but the man beat him to it. 'Lastenouse,' he said. 'Roland Lastenouse. You must be Lomax.' He held a hand out. Tom gripped the wire running round the stern to steady himself, then shook the hand quickly.

'Nice to meet you,' Tom said. 'Thanks for the …' He gestured at the deck. 'Thanks for the ride home.'

'I can see you're feeling seasick,' Lastenouse said. He had a very slight French accent. 'Come in and I'll fix you something.'

Tom followed him just inside the doorway, where there was a carpeted bar area, with easy chairs. Lastenouse switched some lights on, then opened a hatch and slipped behind the bar. 'A gin and tonic will settle you,' he said. Tom thought that unlikely, but didn't object. He sat heavily in one of the deep armchairs, next to an empty champagne bucket, just in case. Lastenouse started mixing drinks like they were lounging around in some country club. He was a short man – much shorter than Sara, anyway – dressed in baggy shorts and a sweater, with bare feet. He had skin that looked weathered – too dark and rough for it to pass for a fashionable tan. The face was craggy, with a big nose. He wasn't attractive, but he looked strong. He wasn't what Tom had imagined. *This is what she goes for*, he thought. Lastenouse looked more than fifteen years older.

He brought over a drink in a long glass. There was ice and lemon in it. Tom sipped it. Lastenouse leaned against the bar and smiled at him. He had a smaller tumbler of something, whisky, maybe. He hadn't touched it yet, waited for Tom to finish sipping, then held it aloft. 'Here's to you,' he said. 'We all owe you a great deal, it seems.' Then he drank.

'We?' Tom asked.

'Sara's friends.'

'Ah.'

'Sara has told me a lot about you. You saved her life.'

Tom shrugged. 'I was being paid to. And anyway, she saved mine. Right after.'

Lastenouse smiled again. 'You're what?' he asked. 'I wasn't clear on that detail. What is it you do?'

Tom took another gulp. 'This and that. How much did Sara tell you, I wonder?' He hoped not very much.

'Sara and I are very close. Never forget that.'

It felt like a warning – delivered with a hard stare. Tom looked at his feet, felt embarrassed.

'You understand what I'm saying?' Lastenouse asked quietly. There was certainly an edge to his tone. But maybe that was how he spoke to the crew, and Tom probably fell more into that category than any other the man could think of.

'I understand,' Tom said. 'Of course.' He was on his boat, after all.

'I care very deeply about her,' Lastenouse explained. 'I won't let her be hurt, tricked or conned. I will intervene in any way I have to in order to prevent that. Is that clear?'

'Very.' He raised his glass, took a sip. 'Here's to Sara, then. Is she OK?'

'Don't underestimate her. She is tougher than you think.'

'Very possibly.' He'd seen her shoot two men, kill them. He wondered what Lastenouse had witnessed. 'It's a nice boat,' he said, trying to get on to something easier. 'Do you live on it?'

Lastenouse laughed. 'Are you trying to be funny?'

Tom shook his head. 'Just trying to make polite conversation.'

'Ah. Well, in that case – no. I live elsewhere, naturally. On land.' He laughed again, as if Tom really had cracked a good joke. 'This is merely a ...' He searched for the word. '... a little hobby, perhaps.'

'You live in Belgium?'

'Sometimes. Sometimes elsewhere.' He waved his hand vaguely.

'I was just wondering if it was chance you were there when she called. That's all.'

'It was certainly good luck. Yes. We arrived one week ago and we sail again next week.'

Sara had made eight or nine calls before trying Lastenouse, Tom recalled. So he had been quite far down the list.

'I hope you will be very careful with her,' Lastenouse said. 'In fact, I am telling you to be very careful with her. It's a warning.'

Tom frowned. 'Sorry?'

'She is tough – I told you that – but she is in a very bad place right now. She can be hurt.'

'Not by me.'

That brought another little chuckle. 'Come, come, Lomax. You know what she feels about you.'

'I know she hired me to do a job.'

'She *feels* for you. Do you understand? I can see that. Anyone could see it. And she has told me so. So I feel a little ... forgive me ... a little *paternal* about it. She is so young. I don't want to see her hurt. You have been through so much together, perhaps, over the last few months. So maybe you don't realise how very much out of your depth you are ...'

'The last few months? I've known her less than seventy-two hours.'

That stumped him. He actually coloured a little, then drank from the glass and looked at the floor. 'I was not aware ...' he started. 'Or I assumed. Assumed because of what she has told me. Good God! She is so impulsive. I cannot believe it ...' He stopped suddenly and looked to his right. Sara was standing in the doorway, frowning at him. She was wearing a white towel dressing gown. Her hair was wet. 'Sara!' he said. 'Come and join us. We were just ...'

'Talking about me. I heard.' She walked in and came over to Tom. 'Leave us,' she said, over her shoulder, to Lastenouse. 'Tom and I have to talk.' She sat down in the chair next to him, leaned across and took his hand. Then just sat there like that, looking up at Lastenouse, as if daring him to say something. Tom could feel his face turning pink. So much for keeping him sweet, she thought. 'And stop being an idiot, Roland,' Sara added. 'I don't need another fucking father.'

31

Lastenouse left them, but they didn't stay there for long. Sara wanted privacy, she said. So she took him back to her cabin. Except it wasn't a cabin. At least, not like his. It seemed to take up an entire deck of the boat. 'This is more like it,' he said, as she closed the door behind them. 'A tad bigger than what I've got.'

'It's Roland's room – the stateroom,' she said, without interest. She stood in front of him, holding both his hands. The dressing gown she was wearing had come loose, but she didn't seem to notice. He kept his eyes high. He wasn't sure what she was wearing beneath. 'I'm so tired, Tom,' she said. She stepped towards him and rested her head against his chest. He was thrown, didn't know what to say. 'I need to sleep,' she said wearily. 'I need to put my head down and sleep. But every time I close my eyes I just see everything happening.'

He brought an arm round and hugged her. 'I'll lie down with you,' he said. 'If you want I'll lie down with you, until you sleep.'

She had her arms around him now. 'No. Not just until I go to sleep. I want you to stay with me. Can you do that? Can you stay?'

'Yes. Of course.' He started to stroke her hair. 'Of course. You're frightened. I understand.'

187

'That's not why I want you to stay,' she said. 'That's not it at all.'

He followed her to the bed. It was a huge round thing. She took the dressing gown off and got under the quilt without batting an eyelid. He had a glimpse of her body and felt an odd sort of unease. She wasn't wearing anything. He tried to keep the facts clear in his head, right in the forefront of his thinking. Everything that had happened to them. The condition she must be in. Lastenouse was right, maybe. Should he walk out, now? Would that be the *right* thing to do?

'Get in,' she said. The quilt was pulled up to her chin. There was a different look in her eyes. He thought briefly about taking his clothes off, but that was an absurd idea. He took his shoes off and started to crawl over the bed. She moved like she was going to pull the quilt away, so he could get in beside her. 'I'll lie on top,' he said quickly. She didn't object.

He lay down beside her, on top of the quilt, pulling a pillow under his head. He put an arm under her neck and she moved backwards, still beneath the quilt, until her back was pressed against him. He brought the other arm round her and rested his chin and his mouth against the nape of her neck, against the skin there that was hidden by her hair. He kissed her there, almost automatically. Then felt confused and somehow immoral. He did it again, trying to make it more obviously like a fatherly or brotherly thing, a little peck. She didn't react, or didn't react in any bad way. Her breathing was getting deeper already. She was relaxing. He was lying next to her, hugging her, and she was relaxing. Job done. A small bonus on top of his final fee? He didn't want to think like that. About her using him, switching it on and off to suit. But that was what she was doing, he thought. He closed his eyes and started to talk to her, telling her to go to sleep.

'I will,' she said sleepily. 'I will.'

He thought he might sleep himself. It was possible. He realised that something – maybe Lastenouse's G&T – had worked. He no longer felt sick, though he could still feel the steady, rhythmic thrumming of the boat, the movement unsettling his inner ear. The smell of her hair was incredible. He pulled her closer. Then, without even knowing why, without thinking about it, he started to whisper to her, telling her a story from his childhood, about his mother cuddling him in bed. He wasn't sure she was listening, but he kept going. His mother had been awful to sleep with, because she would never let him move. He told her about how he had longed to sleep with his mum, even when as old as eight or nine, to be hugged by her and fall asleep with her stroking his brow. He started to stroke her brow as his mother had stroked his. His mother had sung songs to him, from Ireland. She wasn't from Ireland, but her grandmother was, and the memory was still there in the songs. It all sounded very loving and warm, until he started telling her about his mother kicking him out because he was fidgeting so much. He stopped that story then, and started to sing the same Irish lullaby that he sang to Jamie. But then he felt unexpectedly guilty – because the song was something special between him and Jamie only. So he stopped that too, closed his eyes again and let his breathing slow. He thought she might already be asleep.

He woke because she was kissing him. He opened his eyes and saw that it was very dark, the boat still moving, the noise of the engines still coming through the decks. She was on top of him, moving against him, her mouth against his, her skin hot to the touch. He had no idea how long they had been like that – or how long they had been asleep. She started whispering things to him. For a moment he thought she might be asleep still, that she was doing it in her sleep. He got his hands up and held her head, very gently, looking into her eyes. She was crying. 'I want to feel something else,' she murmured. 'I want to feel normal. I don't just want these images going round and round behind my eyes ...'

'Stop, Sara,' he said quietly. 'Stop.'

She stopped at once.

'It's OK,' he said. 'I know how bad you feel. But that's not a good reason to do this ...'

She laughed softly, her face inches from his. 'Tom Lomax,' she said. 'You fucking idiot, Tom Lomax. Did you realise you were such a gentleman? Did you know that before you met me?'

'I'm not sure I ...' he started, but she put a finger over his lips.

'Just shut up,' she whispered. She wiped her eyes with her other hand. 'I'm not doing this because I feel bad. This would have happened anyway. It would have happened last night, if we hadn't been interrupted by someone else's horror story. This was going to happen from the very first time I set eyes on you, getting out of my seaplane with your eye all bruised. You know that. You know what's been going on. Or maybe you don't. But you've felt all these things I'm feeling for you. You've felt everything the same. I've seen it in your eyes. Tell me that's not true.'

He took a breath. 'I don't know ...'

'Don't pretend. Please don't pretend.'

He let the breath out, slowly. 'OK,' he said. 'You're right ...'

'So don't think about it,' she said. 'Just this once, don't think about it.'

'That's not ...'

'Ssh ...' The finger was on his lips again. 'SShh ...'

32

Maxim sat exhausted in the hired Toyota, illegally parked at the back of a cab rank between St Pancras and King's Cross stations, two cars behind the Merc that Freddie Eaton had sent to pick up Sara Eaton. He tried to stay awake by keeping an eye on the mirrors, just in case someone felt like ticketing him at 8.30 in the evening. The driver of the Merc didn't know he was here, didn't have a clue what was going on, in fact. Nor the security guy who had been sent with the driver, and who was now inside the station waiting for Eaton and Lomax to emerge from the Eurostar exit.

Two hours ago Maxim had walked in and scanned the lines of faces waiting for loved ones or family members or business colleagues. The name Arisha had given him for the security guy didn't ring bells, but Maxim had found him easily enough. He'd had plenty of time to do so. The information was that Sara Eaton would be aboard the 6.30 from Brussels. There had been three arrivals since then and she wasn't on any of them. The small waiting crowd had thus changed three times, except for Freddie Eaton's man, making him pretty conspicuous. That was good, because it made the man careless and unprofessional, which would be useful later on – if this plan ever got off the ground – when Maxim would probably have to point a gun at the man's face and issue threats. No doubt Arisha had already thought of all this.

When Eaton wasn't on the second train the man had come back to the Merc and phone calls had been made. Maxim had watched from the station and made his own calls at the same time. Apparently independently – but in fact as instructed by Arisha, handling Freddie Eaton's calls as usual – they had then all decided to wait for one more train. At Arisha's end, no one had a clue where Sara Eaton was, or what had happened. Arisha had sounded like she was panicking, her big escape plan slipping away from her. Barsukov had already wanted to call it off, she said. Max had tried to keep her calm.

It was a warm spring night in London, dry and clear. He could recall very clearly that it had been exactly the same twenty-three years ago, when he had first come here. That had been his first trip outside Russia, the stint in Afghanistan aside. He didn't like to remember the Afghan months, because they had ended in a kind of shame for him – pulled out of his unit and sent back to Moscow before he'd seen action. His father – a man Maxim had barely known before his death a year later in a drive-by shooting on the streets of Krasnodar – had got Dima Barsukov to pull some strings, to 'rescue' his son, at his mother's request. His father had been a 'gun runner' – that was how his mother described it – a criminal of the worst kind, because he had operated by supplying weaponry to the mujahedin, weaponry stolen from Russian forces. That had been a lucrative game back then, one that had got even bigger when the wars in Chechnya kicked off. Many men who were now respectable, prominent members of modern Russian society had started out by selling high-tech stolen weaponry to the country's enemies. Dima Barsukov had had a finger in that pot too, and owed his father something as a consequence. So Maxim – against his will – had ended up working for Barsukov's security team, being trained by an ex-sergeant called Rakachev, long since dead of his drunken carelessness.

That was how he had ended up in London, in May 1989, while the Wall was still up, but with the writing very clearly on it, at least for those – like Barsukov – who were on the inside track. They had been guests of Liz Wellbeck, and stayed at a place like a palace, somewhere out in the Surrey countryside. Wellbeck had seemed very American, but spoke Russian and apparently had blood connections to people who were part of the Yeltsin circle. Barsukov was part of that clique and had ended up in Surrey as some kind of messenger, sent at Wellbeck's request to consider future business possibilities, once the barriers fell – or so they had thought.

Maxim had been there as a bodyguard. The group had been Barsukov, Rakachev and one other security guy, plus Arisha – by that time one of Dima's many female 'assistants' – and an older woman who had been with Dima longer. Dima had been put up with the women, in lavish guest rooms. The three men had been lodged in a dingy cellar room and virtually ignored throughout the five days they were there. There hadn't been a need for security, because the Wellbecks had their own, and plenty of it.

Maxim hadn't dared look at Arisha back then, and doubted she had noticed him much. The start for them had come almost a year later, when they'd been picked – via Barsukov – to steal a child for Liz Wellbeck. But in 1989 Maxim was a nobody. Arisha – they said – was in bed with Dima, so was far above his level. She had been at the meetings with Liz Wellbeck, while Maxim and Rakachev had been confined to the basement. Later, much later, she had told him that Wellbeck had only been interested in some property claim her family had, an attempt to repossess estates they had held in Golovchino, in southern Russia, taken into state ownership after the revolution, as far back as 1921. The land was worth nothing, Arisha had said, but Wellbeck wanted it back on principle, and refused to discuss anything else until guarantees were given.

That trip had been an eye-opener for him. Until then the richest people he had ever come across hadn't really had any money at all, merely power – people like Barsukov. Liz Wellbeck had treated Barsukov politely enough, but nevertheless as if he were stupid – from another, dirtier planet. Which was true. For her, Barsukov was there to be instructed, not asked or consulted. It had been humiliating. Since then, the same thing had happened to the whole of Russia, as a nation. He was glad to be out of the place.

There had been some half-pleasant memories too, he supposed. On the fourth day Barsukov had let Rakachev and him travel by train into London itself. They had spent the day wandering around like dazed tourists, staring at everything. They'd had enough cash to buy a meal and a few drinks, but little else. He had wanted to buy Arisha something, stupidly, since he couldn't even speak to her, but everything had been too expensive, even the silly T-shirts. Perhaps just as well, since he wasn't sure now how she might have reacted to that kind of thing. Would it have been impertinent to give her a gift, back then?

The pleasant memories were hard to recover now, because he had spent most of the time in a secret and miserable state of obsession, eaten away by jealousy of Barsukov and what he was doing to Arisha, imagining all of it. A year later she had laughed at him when he had confessed all this to her. Barsukov hadn't been anywhere near her, she claimed. He still didn't know whether to believe that.

They had all come a long way since then. In so many respects. It was like thinking about something childish and naive when he saw them all sitting uncomfortably in Liz Wellbeck's chauffeur-driven cars, in their shoddy Soviet clothing, with their pale, poor complexions, startled by the West and its incredible excesses, mumbling their atrocious English on demand. Things had come full circle since then. Or would soon.

Or maybe not. He looked down at his bandaged hand – throbbing constantly now, clearly infected – and swore softly to himself. Nothing could be taken for granted.

He checked his watch as he saw the security guy leave the exit from St Pancras. Alone. No Sara Eaton. No Tom Lomax. But he'd expected that, by now.

He waited until the guy got into the Merc, waited another five minutes while they called Arisha for instructions. Then watched the Merc drive off. Arisha had said Barsukov was making his own enquiries to try to locate Sara Eaton via the connection to Lomax. Lomax, apparently, worked for a minor player called Glynn Powell. Barsukov had asked Powell to find Lomax for him. But Max wouldn't wait for that. He gently rubbed the thick scar tissue to the side of his right eye, then got the piece of paper with Lomax's address out of his pocket and looked at it. That would be his next stop.

33

It was still before midnight, but John Lomax was asleep when his mobile started to vibrate on the little bedside table. He was pressed tight against Rachel's naked back, one arm beneath her and completely numb. He had to move her forward to get it free, and expected her to wake, but she didn't. As he moved away from her he remembered with sudden bewilderment the progress of the evening, what had happened between them, how they had ended up like this. But that was as far as his reactions got. The phone was too loud. He got it into his other hand, pressed the button and put it to his ear. It took a while to recognise the voice speaking in a hushed tone. Ian Mercer, a good friend who was still in the job, a DI he had worked with on countless inquiries, including Grenser. He listened to a few sentences, let the initial information sink in, then asked Ian to wait a moment. He rolled carefully out of bed and walked out of the bedroom on tiptoe, closing the door behind him. He went into the study and stood behind his desk in the darkness, stark naked.

'Tell me about it,' he said.

'It's an APA. Came in two hours ago.'

APA. That was a piece of Interpol jargon – it meant an All Ports Alert. Some foreign police force wanted info sent out to every UK entry point alerting the authorities to detain an individual.

'And it's for Tom? My Tom? You're sure?' That's what Ian had told him a minute ago.

'Thomas Lomax. I'm looking at it now. I cross-checked the date of birth. Plus there's a photo. It's for Tom and one other. The request is from Belgium.'

'Belgium?' The Belgian police had never scored high on his respect meter. 'How long will it take to action it?'

'It's done. They go through automatically now. Been like that a year or more.'

'So there's already an active All Ports Alert for Tom.' He said it to himself, not as a question. He was trying to work out what it might mean.

'There's a bit of info on the demand,' Ian said. 'They suspect he's kidnapped someone. At least that's what they say in the summary.'

'Kidnapped? Who? A child?' He was thinking maybe Tom's ex-wife had moved to Belgium with Jamie, and Tom had gone over there to get him back.

'A kid?' Mercer sounded surprised. 'No. A twenty-year-old girl. She's the other they've got the alert for, so I don't really get it, to be honest. They're both down in the particulars as homicide suspects – an incident this afternoon in Brussels, but no more detail than that. But then the summary says Tom is suspected of kidnapping this girl. So it's a mess. A classic Belgian request. They don't have a clue ...'

'So who is the girl?' John interrupted him. 'The other one. You got her name?'

'Yes. And a photo too. There's an attached photo of both of them, clear as day, staring up at some CCTV camera in a station somewhere. She looks pretty ...'

'What's her name?'

'You're going to love this. That's why I took an interest. The name jumped out at me. The girl is Sara Eaton.'

John was so shocked he had to sit down. 'Sara Eaton? The daughter of Freddie Eaton and Liz Wellbeck?'

'Yes.'

He took a deep breath, the thoughts spinning through his head too fast. 'Does it mention that?' he asked. 'Does it mention whose daughter she is?'

'No. But the kidnap allegation relates to her. And that was all over the news earlier …'

'The island thing?'

'Ile des Singes Noirs. Exactly. I saw that this evening – about Wellbeck being dead and her daughter being kidnapped from there – so I had Grenser in my head already. Then this APA comes through with her name on it and a picture of your boy. So I called you. Hope you don't mind.'

'Christ above.' He was completely stumped. He had no idea what any of it could mean. 'What the fuck is going on?' he wondered, aloud.

'I have no idea. He kidnaps her and then they both do a murder? Doesn't really work. Obviously the Belgians are covering all the bases. That's the way they do it over there. I assume they haven't a clue what has gone on …'

'But it still went through? Two years ago we would have sent it back for clarification.'

'Not any more. Speed is the name of the game now.'

'And there's no more info on the homicide?'

'None at all.'

John paused, thinking furiously. 'He's definitely down as having kidnapped Eaton?'

'Suspected of involvement.'

'I don't get it. I don't understand any of it.'

'Me neither. But I thought you should know. What will you do?'

John sat in silence, letting the question stew. 'I don't know,' he said eventually. 'But I really appreciate the heads-up, Ian.'

'No problem.'

'You covered, if they audit it?'

That was exactly what had happened to Tom, of course. He had made a phone call, just like this, to a friend, giving a warning. Then someone had done an internal audit, found the number, made the enquiries. And that was the end of his police career. For no greater offence than Ian had just committed.

'I called you to check if you had recent contact,' Ian said. 'That's what I'll say.' But he hadn't asked that question at all. John waited for it, but it didn't come. Ian was the real thing, a straight-up, loyal friend. He knew his priorities. John thanked him again. They exchanged some vague ideas about meeting up, but John couldn't really get his head around that right now.

After the connection was cut he sat in the darkness, listening to his heart. What Tom had done wasn't that similar, he realised, because Ian Mercer was one of the best DIs he'd ever worked with, a solid, honest man. Tom, on the other hand, had made a call to warn a piece of criminal shit who he'd been inexplicably attached to since age eight, a species of bad company who John hadn't tried hard enough to discourage. There weren't many similarities there. Except that Ian Mercer had broken the rules too, technically – and had done it for the same reasons, out of friendship and loyalty. Assuming he was being truthful. Maybe the call had been official, maybe they had a connect on John's mobile, right now, set up, ready and waiting for him to make the warning call to Tom, so they could trace him. It seemed unlikely. Ian had done only what John would have done in the same circumstances. Only what his son had done too. John needed to acknowledge that. That Tom had been misguided, to say the least, in his choice of friends – or unlucky enough to be caught – didn't change the principle. Poor judgement was one thing, loyalty quite another. If Tom had a problem with excessive loyalty it was probably because his father had planted it in him.

John stood up and peered out of the window, into the darkness, across the river. Was he going to call Tom, warn him? Or ask him what was going on, at least? It was stunning – the connections lining up. *Tom involved in kidnapping someone with a link to Grenser.* It couldn't be a coincidence. But *kidnapping*? Had Tom slipped that far? It seemed absurd, but it was possible, he supposed. Tom's 'friend' – the one who had cost him his job, Alex Renton – could easily have a part in something like that. John knew all about Renton's connections. He had made it his business to know.

He walked quietly back to the bedroom and sat on the bed beside Rachel. He pulled open the drawer on the bedside table and took out his alternative mobile. It had been a standard part of his precautions, three years ago, to have an alternative mobile. This one was brand new. No one knew about it. He hadn't even set up the chip. Rachel was still asleep, turned away from him. He didn't know what to do, felt he didn't have enough information to think it through properly. But he wasn't going to get any more information. He wanted to wake Rachel up, ask her what he should do. But he resisted.

Instead, he tried to work out what his gut feeling was. It was what he had done throughout his career when things got stuck – he had gone with his instincts. Simple enough, and they had rarely been wrong.

He remembered suddenly the moment Tom had been born. John had been there, right there, with the best view in the house. For Tom's brother it had been different – there had been some work thing on, a double murder. He wished now he had ignored the double murder, been there for both births. But he'd been younger then, more stupid. So Eric had been born without him. But not Tom. He had even done the training for Tom, gone to the prenatal classes Jane had been so keen on, reminded her about her breathing when it was happening, massaged the base of her spine, and all the rest of it – watched dumbstruck as his second son had come out into the world. A tiny, grey, curled-up thing, completely still – he had looked dead, and John had actually suffered a moment thinking that ... that the baby was stillborn. But a few seconds later Tom had thrown his arms out and changed colour, coming to life as blood flooded through him. His face screwed up and he started screaming. John had felt his heart somersault with relief and joy. It had been the most incredible thing.

That was his son, the one he had loved most dearly, no doubt about that. Eric had only wanted his mother. But Tom had been his special lad. Could he have kidnapped someone, killed someone? Did having a dodgy friend mean that he could do that? It was stupid, impossible. *That* was his gut feeling. Choose between Belgian incompetence or Tom having turned into something unrecognisable. That was what the Americans called a 'no-brainer', surely?

34

The boat was quiet, moving gently beneath them. They sat on the bed in her stateroom, facing each other, but not touching. They were moored in some private harbour near Hayling Island. The cabin lights were off, but there was light coming through the row of windows, from the arc lights on the jetty they were nearest to. Until a moment ago they had been waiting for a car, which Lastenouse was organising, to take them to a private airfield near Portsmouth. From there a plane, also set up by Lastenouse, to another airstrip close to her father's place in Surrey. It was all very convenient. But then her father had called her mobile and she had stood whispering to him in the semi-darkness.

As she had just reported it to Tom, her father was panicking. She'd never heard him like that before. He had been expecting her off the Eurostar, and had sent people there to get her. Now he told her that there were security problems, that she shouldn't come to the Surrey place until he could get to her. He had asked her where she was, so that he could arrange something alternative, but she wouldn't tell him. 'Just somewhere,' she had said. 'Call me when you can, when we can come to you.' Tom had heard that very clearly. The call had ended abruptly after that.

'Why not tell him where we are?' Tom asked at once. 'We could use his help.'

She stared at him, frowning hard. 'I don't know,' she said, slowly. She seemed confused by her reactions, as if she'd done it without thinking.

'Call him now. Tell him.'

She shook her head. He frowned at her.

'Phones aren't secure,' she muttered. 'It's happened more than once that we've had problems – a newspaper did it one time – bugged all our phones. Daddy had to give evidence to an inquiry about it all …'

'That's why you wouldn't say?'

She shook her head again. 'I don't know …'

Something else was bothering her. 'Did he say *anything* about why we couldn't go to him?' he asked. 'Any clue about what he meant?'

'No. He sounded frightened. As if he wanted to say more, but couldn't. As if someone might be listening.'

'The newspapers, you mean?'

She shrugged. 'I don't know. I had a feeling about it …'

'So what now? We go somewhere else until he contacts you again?'

'Yes.'

She was frightened. And confused. He could see that. She had her phone out already and was trying to think of somewhere they could disappear to, someone she could call to arrange it. Wherever it was, they should get there under their own steam, Tom thought. He didn't like relying on Lastenouse. They needed to be less predictable. The present plan meant that Lastenouse and his staff knew every step of their itinerary.

He felt the phone in his pocket start to buzz. He took it out quickly, standing up from the bed. 'It's working,' he said, amazed. He'd tried to fire up the SIM card several times, without success. He pressed the button and put it to his ear.

To his complete surprise the voice he heard was his father's: 'Tom? Is that you?'

'Dad?' He felt a sudden mix of emotions.

'This will have to be quick, Tom. I've been trying this number for an hour ...'

'How did you get it? Did I give you it?'

'No. I spoke to Sally ...'

'But she's in Spain ...'

'They have phones in Spain ... listen ...'

'You called Sally in Spain ...?'

'Shut up, son. Listen. There's an All Ports Alert out for you. You get that?'

Tom closed his mouth.

'That's why I'm calling ...'

'Did you say anything to Sally about it?'

'Obviously not. I'm saying it to you and I don't want to be on this mobile any longer than I have to be. Just in case. Don't tell me where you are. Ring on some public landline if you want the detail. Got it?'

'Yes.'

'Good.' The line went dead.

He stood in the room, listening to his heart, then turned back to Sara. 'That was my father,' he said, feeling stunned.

'I thought you didn't speak?'

'He was warning me. There's an alert out for me.' He felt a little surge of pride, unexpectedly, that his father had actually done that, had actually broken the rules, warned him.

'An alert?'

'At UK entry points – ports, airports, et cetera.'

'To do what? Arrest you?'

'Yes. He didn't give me any detail other than that. He wanted me to call back on a public phone.'

'There won't be any checks here,' she said. 'Roland knows the people here. That's why he brought us this far.'

'Good. But it's a bigger problem than that, I think.'

'Is it? Why do they want you? I mean, why you, and not me?'

'I don't know without ringing him back.'

'So what do we do?'

He moved round the bed and sat down beside her. She immediately reached over and touched his hand. He remembered what they had just done. Suddenly it seemed very far away.

'I've got you into trouble,' she said. 'I'm sorry. You'll regret you ever set eyes on me.'

'I don't think so,' he said. He leaned into her and kissed her quickly, on the lips. 'What we did was just the start of something,' he whispered. 'OK? It's on hold, but we'll get back there.'

'Yes,' she said, putting a hand on his leg. 'It was a start.' She smiled half-heartedly.

He took a breath. 'I've been thinking about what's going on. Your mother died and no one told you. That meant you were on the island when the kidnap attempt went down. If they'd told you about her dying then you wouldn't have been there at all and it couldn't have happened.' She frowned. 'I'm just joining the dots,' he continued. 'I'm thinking that maybe your father tried to tell you, but something intervened. We've been acting like the two things are a coincidence. But maybe they're not. They were saying something about your birthday – the kidnappers. Remember?' She nodded. 'So maybe something more complex is going on,' he said. 'More complex than a bunch of armed men trying to kidnap you, then – *as it happens* – your mum being dead ...' He shrugged. 'I don't know, but I think we need to be more cautious than we have been.

Until we really can join the dots. I'm hoping your father will fill in the gaps. There must be a good reason for not telling you about the death – perhaps a security reason. Or maybe he knew something was going to happen, but got the detail wrong. Or – like I said – maybe he tried to tell you and someone interfered. He's your father, though – so there will be an explanation.' He paused, thinking through the options. 'At the end of the day I'm probably going to end up sitting in a police station talking to the police, hoping they'll believe me. It won't be the first time. But once you're with your father you have a world of resources at your disposal. You don't have to sit around and talk to anyone. Not if it doesn't look safe, or favourable.'

'You mean I can just leave you? That's out of the question. Certainly now, after what just happened. I hope you realise that.'

He nodded. *Depends on the stakes*, he thought. What they had just done had felt like the real thing, like a connection being made. It hadn't been like that often in his life. Once or twice only. So easy to think there was something special there, the beginning of something that could grow and deepen, if given the chance. Right now, all the time, sitting next to her, he could feel the thrill in his blood still, feel the overpowering need between them, the desire to be closer, to touch each other. But he shouldn't kid himself. The circumstances were unnatural, their sense of reality stretched to breaking point. They were bound to feel something from that, from what they had survived together. It might be nothing more than fear throwing them together, tricking them. And even if there were more, at the end of the day she lived in a completely different world. What could he *really* expect from her?

'I have a friend called Alex Renton,' he said. 'I've known

him since I was eight years old. I can trust him. I can call him and he will come and get us, or send someone. He can put us somewhere off radar until your father gets back to you.'

35

Two hours later they were in the back of someone's car driving through deserted country roads. Back in England. In a car Tom's friend had sent for them. Sara sat with her face against the window, her eyes on the dark hedges and silhouettes, her attention completely absorbed by her confusion. She felt Tom touching her arm and looked up. He was at the other side of the long back seat. She had wanted him to be closer as they had got in, had wanted to sit with her head on his shoulder, his arms around her, hugging her, but he had made some sign to her, mouthing something silently, so that the driver didn't get it, then sat far away from her, as if they weren't connected at all. Clearly, he didn't want the driver to know about them, about the link between them. She didn't know why.

'You'll be OK, Sara,' he said quietly now. 'It will all be OK.'

She frowned. 'Where are we?' The car was slowing, pulling over.

'I think this is where Alex will come for us.'

'But where is it?' She could see only darkness, some bushes and trees.

'I don't know. Somewhere on some minor road, on the way up to London. He should be here soon. It's all OK. This is what Alex arranged. Don't worry. We can trust him.'

The car stopped. Three years ago, she recalled, she had been at a party in Paris when there was some stupid, massive police raid and everyone ended up in cells on drugs charges, herself included. It was all so silly, but had seemed serious at the time. It was the worst trouble she had ever been in, prior to this. And what had happened? Liz had made some calls and pulled some strings. Within a few hours she was out of there and on her way to the UK. They even cleared the family helicopter to land on the roof of the gendarmerie. That's what she was used to. If things went wrong she made some calls and people were sent to pull her out. At once. Yet what was happening now was way beyond any previous difficulties and nothing was happening. *Nothing*.

'Why is my father not sending people to pull me out of this?' she said, aloud. 'Why didn't that happen back in Brussels, when I spoke to him?' She hadn't asked him to do that, of course. She'd told him she was about to get the train. But he could have stopped her. He hadn't even tried. And *why* hadn't she asked him – why the reluctance to trust him, if that's what it had been? The same caution had operated to stop her telling him where they were two hours ago. Didn't she trust her own father?

She ran her hands through her hair, staring out of the window as the driver got out and walked off into the darkness. What Alison Spencer had told her was twisting things in her head – *that* was what was going on. Why else would she keep her location from her father? It was absurd. Until that moment – when he had asked her where she was – their whole plan had been to get to him, rely on him. If she no longer wanted to do that then what was left? There was no one else who could solve this. She *had* to trust her own father.

She felt lost. The man beside her was the only person she felt sure of right now. But she had known him only a few days, so that was absurd. Nevertheless, she should tell him what Alison had said, she thought, tell him before this went any farther. If something went wrong – if something happened to her – then someone else ought to know what this was all about. And there was no one else she *could* tell right now. No one.

It was like she was someone else entirely, someone without money or connections. She was skulking in the darkness by a roadside, waiting for some nobody to help her. *Why?* 'Something is wrong with all this,' she muttered.

'That's an understatement,' Tom said.

'My father should have sent people to get me,' she repeated. 'Why hasn't he done that?'

'Maybe because you wouldn't tell him where you were,' he said. She caught the implied criticism in his tone. He pointed through the windscreen. 'Anyway, it looks like someone is coming now.' She saw headlights swing around the bend in the road, coming towards them. 'It will be Alex,' he said. 'I'll get out and speak to him. Explain things. You stay here. Is that OK?' A car pulled into the space in front of them, its headlights dazzling. 'It will only take a few minutes,' he said. 'Then I'll be back.'

'Wait,' she said. She grabbed his arm. 'I have to tell you something. I have to tell you now.'

He frowned at her. He wanted to get out, go to his friend. He already had the door open. 'Can't you tell me when ... ?' he started.

'No,' she said. 'It has to be now. I have to tell you what Alison Spencer told me.'

Outside the car the night was surprisingly warm. Tom stood in the glare of the headlights. He tried to work out what she had just told him might mean. It was more than another piece of information, clearly. More important. She should have told him earlier, he thought, so he could factor it into the decisions they were making. But too late now. Here they were. Here was Alex, walking towards him.

He felt relief as he saw him. Alex would know what to do. This was the world he was at home in – kidnapping, extortion, violence. He would handle it.

Alex was wearing a T-shirt and jeans. He was the same height as Tom, but built much bigger, the T-shirt tight across his biceps and chest. Ever since his teens he had put in about two hours each day working out, pushing weights, building strength. He never tired of trying to get Tom to join him. There was a fully kitted gym in Alex's basement, but he never used it, preferring a club in Hounslow instead. Attendance at the club, Tom knew, was like a rite of passage. If you were invited then you were in with a set that Tom had never wanted to get closer to – the people who populated Alex's 'working' world. And Glynn Powell, of course, who owned the place. It was an affront to Powell that Alex had repeatedly invited Tom and Tom had repeatedly declined.

Alex's car was a big American SUV, black with tinted windows. Past the dazzling headlights Tom could see there was at least one other person in there, in the back, plus a driver. Their own driver was already standing by the nearside rear door of Alex's car, by the window, speaking to whoever was in there.

'Who did you bring?' Tom asked. 'Who's in there?'

'Just back-up.' Alex smiled at him, then put a hand on his arm and led him between the cars. 'Just in case,' he added.

'Thanks for coming, Alex,' Tom said. 'I really appreciate it.'

'No problem. That's what friends are for – right? Tell me what it's about, mate. Come over here and brief me.'

They went between the cars, Alex keeping Tom between himself and where Sara was. Tom could see her looking out through the window. As they walked alongside the car her window started to slide down. 'Tell her to close the window,' Alex said. 'I don't want to see her …' Then he shouted. '*Keep the window closed.*' Tom was taken by surprise. The window stopped halfway. Tom raised a hand towards her, meant as reassurance, then they were past the car. 'I thought you were going to take us to your place?' Tom said. 'You'll see her there, so what's the problem seeing her now? I don't get it.'

'I don't want her to see me until I know what's going on,' Alex said, still calm. 'Just a standard precaution. Don't worry.' He flashed another smile. In the half-light Tom could barely see him, but he could sense something was off, not as it usually was between them. Alex was smiling, taking control, doing what he did. But something was wrong. They were well past the car now, walking along beside a hedge. 'Where the fuck are we?' Tom asked. All he could see in the darkness was fields.

'Middle of nowhere,' Alex said. 'A random lay-by on a minor road picked at random off the GPS. Safest that way.' But he seemed to be heading for a gap in the hedge, like he knew the place.

'We going into the field?' Tom asked. 'With the cows?'

'Just out of earshot. While you get me up to speed.'

Tom stepped across a ditch, then through long grass between two trees, following Alex.

'She's Sara Eaton,' Alex said suddenly, stopping in front of him. 'That's the name you gave me, right?'

'That's right.' Tom looked back, but the hedge was in the way now. He couldn't see the car. He could see the headlights of the other one still, through the leaves. He looked up into a sky filled with cloud. No stars, no moon. The atmosphere was warm and humid, like there might be a storm. There was a street light off to the left, shining across the hedge and into the field where they stood.

'She's worth a fucking fortune,' Alex said. 'Did you know that?'

'What do you mean, "worth"?' I know she's got money ...'

Alex laughed again. 'Got money. That's the understatement of the year. That kid ...' He pointed over Tom's shoulder in the direction of the car. 'That kid is one of the richest people on the fucking planet.'

'She's not a kid.'

He saw Alex open his mouth to say something, then stop, looking more closely at Tom's face. 'Wait a minute,' he said, dropping his voice to a whisper. 'You haven't fucked her, have you?' His face broke into a broad grin. 'Fucking amazing! You're at it with her, right? I see it in your face. You're fucking shagging her! Good boy, Tom. I'm proud of you, mate ...'

'Cut it out, Alex. Listen to what I have to say. This is serious, fucking serious. I need to tell you what's happened ...' He stopped. He had heard car doors closing, footsteps. He turned to look, then felt Alex's hand on his shoulder, turning him round. 'Other way around,' Alex said. 'You need to listen to me.'

Tom frowned, tried to shake the hand off, but Alex kept it there, gripping his shoulder too hard for comfort. 'This has bigger dimensions than you thought, mate,' he said, face grim. 'You understand?'

'What are you talking about?' Tom tried to turn, but Alex stopped him again.

'Whatever you think is going on between you and the little girl doesn't matter a toss. The little girl is a big deal. She's not your property. Get it? I'm telling you this as a friend.'

'No. I don't get it. Get your hand off my shoulder.'

'Listen to me. I don't have any choice in this. There are people that want her, see.'

'People that ...' Tom tried to turn again, more determined now.

'Yes. Big people. And our man has made a deal with them. They have been in contact with Glynn, and Glynn has made a deal. So she's going with them. Right now. That's all there is to it.'

Tom's mouth dropped open. He turned and looked at Alex, looked into his eyes, trying to read if he was messing around. Alex looked straight back at him, but there was nothing amused in his expression. Just a hard stare. 'Are you serious?' Tom asked. He couldn't believe it. 'Are you fucking serious? You told Glynn you were coming here? I asked you to keep it to yourself. I asked you ...' He felt dizzy. It was like some big black hole opening at his feet. He'd left her back there with them. He'd trusted Alex.

'I'm sorry, mate,' Alex said. He sounded sorry, but his eyes were hard, holding Tom's stare. 'Some things I have no control over. I'm chickenshit, a foot soldier. You know how it is. I was given instructions, orders. I'm here for Glynn, not you, and that's the way it has to be. I'm sorry. So just stand here and wait. Just let them take her. Or I'll have to put you down. Get it?'

'*Put me down?* Are you taking the piss, Alex? I'm your fucking friend ...'

'I know that. And that's why I'm here. That's why it's happening like this – *because* we're friends. What they wanted to do to you was worse. But I talked them out of it, told them I could persuade you. Look. They would have come with shooters, mate. They would have just plugged you. That's how big she is. I talked them out of it. No problem. But I gave my word. So you have to do this for me – get it? You have to just wait here and ...'

Tom ducked and turned, wrenching away from the arm

and dropping beneath it. He stumbled on the grass, but was scrabbling already back towards the hedge. He just got to his feet before Alex caught him and kicked his legs away, dropping him heavily into the grass. Tom opened his mouth and shouted as loud as he could, putting everything into it: '*SARA!! RUN!!! RUN, SARA!!!*' He heard Alex curse, right beside him, then there was a blow to the side of his head that sent him rolling across the ground. Alex had hit him. 'Leave me, Alex!' he shouted. 'Leave me ...' He got to his knees and started to stand.

'Don't do this, Tom,' he heard Alex pant. 'Don't make me hit you again. Do as you're fucking told. Stay there. Stay down.'

He was right in front of Tom, ready to kick out. Tom rolled sideways and shouted again towards the car. He could hear more doors now, voices. He got to his feet, about to run, but Alex had him by the T-shirt, yanking him backwards. 'Get off, Alex. You can't do this ...'

'Don't make me deck you, Tom. You're a fucking friend. Stay here. Shut up. Don't make me do it ...'

They started to struggle, everything speeding up, movements fast and increasingly vicious. Tom spun round, knocking Alex's arm away. But Alex got his legs across his and then they were both on the ground, Alex pinning Tom beneath him. '*Stay down. Or I'll fucking damage you. Stay down.*' He was hissing the words into Tom's ear.

Tom started to lash out at him with all his strength. Alex was on top of him, heavy, his knees digging into Tom's legs. Tom swung sideways, unbalanced him, then got his fists free enough to strike his head and face. Alex moved back instinctively, into a crouch, then punched straight through Tom's flailing arms, into his nose. Tom felt it crack, his head snapping backwards. He shouted out with sudden disbelief and pain. Now it was real, the awareness fully in his mind: *Alex was going to stop him getting to her.* He was going to kick and hit him and keep him down.

Tom twisted and turned, kicking out blindly, screaming in desperation. But Alex was right above him now, and kicking back. The first kick came under and into his ribs, so hard Tom was lifted off the ground, coming down hard again on the grass. He didn't get the chance to get up again. Alex was already stamping at him, then leaning in, punching at his stomach and chest, his fists heavy, the blows stunning. The wind went out of Tom and he gasped for breath, a bursting noise in his ears. Behind it, from the cars, he could hear a muffled screaming. Sara. They were doing something to her. He struggled to move out of the way, but couldn't. He felt three more kicks, heard a snapping sound in his side, then collapsed backwards and lay on the ground, the world swimming above him.

He felt Alex holding him by the T-shirt, pulling him up towards him, whispering hoarsely: '*You'll thank me for this when you think about it. I'm doing this for you. To protect you ...*' Something gave in Tom's chest and he started to cough. He took a huge breath. His vision was turning black. He rolled over and lay with his face against the dirt, dribbling into it, the breath rasping in his throat.

'*Forget you ever saw the girl,*' Alex hissed, breathing heavily, right in his face. Tom tried to shake his head. '*They've got her now. It's over. Just lie there and wait. Be calm. When we're gone you can get up and get on with your life. Forget all this. You'll hate me at first, but not when you think it through, when you see it from where I am. I'm your friend, Tom. Never forget that. It's just that I have a family too. So you do what I tell you and we'll all be OK. Got it? No telling tales afterwards. Just forget it all. You go yapping to your old Five-O mates and they'll cut her fucking throat. I'm serious. Then they'll come for you and come for Jamie. You understand? They'll break every bone in his body. They'll make him suffer. You have to believe me on this, mate. This is big, big shit. Bigger than me, bigger than you.'*

Tom sensed him move away, then there was a jarring blow to his head. He saw a bright flash of light, felt himself starting to vomit, everything spinning again. He tried to move but his limbs were like logs. He couldn't do anything. He lay panting and gasping, retching on his empty stomach, his ears filled with a frightening buzzing noise. He needed to get up, move, do something, but it was impossible. All he could do was lie in the dirt and let it wash over him.

36

He didn't hear the cars driving away. By the time the dizzying waves of blackness stopped all he could hear was a rushing noise in his ears and his own gasping breath. No voices, no car doors, no engines, no more screams from Sara. He rolled painfully on to his back and stared at the lurching night sky, trying to control the nausea. He had to lie like that for a long time before he began to feel his heart slowing and the drunken movement of the world easing. He stared at the stars, glimpsed between indistinct masses of cloud. He wished it would rain. His mouth was dry, smeared with a bitter copper taste. He could smell smoke. He turned his head very slowly and looked back through the grass towards the hedge, but it was too dark to see anything.

His legs could move now, so he forced himself to sit up. There was a sharp pain in his chest, low down, over his liver. It was possible there were broken ribs there. But it was the blows to his head that worried him most. Too many knocks in too few days. The world began to spin as he reached the sitting position. He waited for it to stop, taking deep breaths, expecting to be sick again, but managing not to be.

The only real light was from the street light past the hedge. The clouds were thick above him, obscuring the moon. He kept himself steady with one hand on the ground and dug around in his trouser pocket for the mobile. It was in pieces.

He brought them out and they fell into the trampled grass. The phone had been crushed. He spent some time finding and extracting the SIM card with trembling fingers, then had to lie back again and let his head recover.

By the time he could actually stand he calculated it might be as much as an hour since they had all driven off. Or ten minutes. He wasn't confident about his grasp of time. He walked carefully over to the hedge and stepped through, into the lay-by, feeling his way past the trees and bushes. He could still smell smoke, but there wasn't any. He could see the road well enough, though. It was empty. He leaned against a section of fencing in front of the hedge and gritted his teeth. The pains were receding, but the anger and hurt were like fire in his bloodstream. He could feel it flushing his skin, tingling in his fingertips. Only with difficulty could he resist the urge to lash out at something inanimate – one of the trees, or the fence posts. He needed to guard the rage, keep it bottled up for the right moment. Because there was nothing here to hit. What he needed to hit was Alex.

He started to walk, heading, he thought, back in the direction the car had come from. After they'd left the motorway they'd driven along deserted country roads for a while, then through a village. The name had come up on the driver's sat-nav, but he hadn't paid it any attention. He thought maybe it was a mile back to the place, maybe two. He would get there, find a phone.

As he walked the pain in his side eased. Nothing broken, he decided, though it was possible the adrenalin was drowning the pain. All he could think about was smashing his fists into Alex's face, kicking him, stamping on him. He was past being rational about it, past weighing up risks or consequences. It was a betrayal of the worst kind. He had issued threats against Jamie, threatened to cut Sara's throat. It left him speechless, so pumped full of fury that he didn't care about his head, didn't care about the other injuries.

He had trusted Alex. All his life he had trusted him. He had thought Alex was his closest friend, thought there was an unassailable bond between them. He had chucked an entire career away because of it. He was a fucking idiot. The consequences of his stupidity were overwhelming. He had to stop and crouch in the road, letting the thoughts organise themselves, lest they swamp him with fear and confusion. There were so many angles, all sickening, that it was hard to keep his mind focused. He felt dizzy again, but now it was because of what *he* had done. He had let Sara down so terribly he could barely let himself think about it. He had promised not to leave her, to protect her. And then, out of gross naivety, he had delivered her straight into Alex's hands. Alex was going to hand her over – Tom had no doubt about it – to some professional criminal group, specialists in kidnapping and extortion. *That* was how she was valuable. *That* was what Alex had meant.

He stood and looked around. The road was pitch-black, high trees meeting right overhead. Suddenly he realised just how urgent everything was. He took a breath and started to run. The jolting movement made it feel like his head would explode. But he ignored it. Ahead, through the trees, he could see faint lights. He had to get her back and there was only one way to do that. Get to Alex and threaten him so convincingly that he gave something away. Take a stick or a metal bar to him. Whatever it took. The link between them was broken.

Houses appeared. He was still running, making a lot of noise as he gasped for breath. He slowed. What time was it? Not yet three, he thought. All the houses were dark, curtains drawn. There were a few smaller ones, fronting the street, but most were set back, in gardens, big detached mansions. The street lights made him squint. He prayed there were no police patrolling here. Now that he could see himself he realised he had been bleeding from somewhere. It was all over the clothes he was in.

He got off the road and kept going, sticking to the shadows under the fences. A sign appeared, a fancy colourful thing in retro style. SHACKLEFORD, it said. 'Welcome to ...' Etc. Etc. He passed it by, searching ahead for a public phone. It wasn't guaranteed there would be one, not these days. What would he do then?

He reached a kind of village green. There was not a soul in sight. Everything was silent, bathed in yellow street light, unreal. The houses were all huge, with mock Tudor beams, or thatch, ostentatious alarm systems. He couldn't see any shops. He saw a phone box at the other side of the green, though, and picked up his pace, jumping straight over a little fence, passing the 'Keep off the Grass' signs.

It was an old red phone box, very conspicuous. Probably the only reason it still existed was that it was as retro as the rest of the place. Stockbroker-belt street furniture, to remind the wealthy what England had once been like – around the time he was ten years old – before their mobiles had completely taken over. Back then every street had a phone box stinking of piss. He pulled the door open and stepped in. He held the phone to his ear. It was a newer, modern thing. It took credit cards, notes, etc. Not coins. There was a dial tone.

He screwed his eyes shut and tried to recall the number. It was so long since he had used it. He couldn't remember. He got a fiver out of his pocket and slotted it in. The machine took it. He let his fingers press the buttons without thinking, hoping they would remember. It didn't work. He got a continuous tone. He tried again, pressing the numbers he thought might be right. He listened to it ringing. It rang about ten times then a voice answered. He sighed with relief. 'Dad,' he said.

37

Sara had fleeting flashes from a different perspective, where she could see herself in the back of the car, see what was really happening – and in those moments she felt a panic-stricken horror, because it meant that where she was, standing in the field with her mother, had to be a dream, or some kind of hideous hallucination, not real at all – and then she could feel her mother slipping away from her and had to shout out to her, holding her hands outstretched and trying to grab at her mother's clothing to stop her from vanishing, because some frightened part of her knew her mother was actually dead, not holding her hand, not smiling at her, not there at all. Instead there was this man forcing her down, whispering in her ear, doing things to her …

She was trying as hard as she could to stay with her mother, to stay where it was safe. The field was the one right outside the place near Golovchino. It was full of a blond, waist-high grass that was being blown in waves in the wind. The entire field looked like water, rippling in huge spiral waves as the wind whipped across it. Up above them there was a broken old fence between two stands of birch, and then an overgrown lawn leading to the house – a magnificent, broken, collapsing palace, with smashed windows and tarnished minarets, direct from a Russian fairy tale. Even in neglect, abandoned, it looked magical, a relic from a time that had existed many years before she was born, or even before her mother was born. But it wasn't a dream, it was a memory. Because she had been there, with her mother. She had actually stood where she was now, looking up the slope, across the huge wheat field, with her mother by her side, holding her hand, telling her that this place was where she was from, where she was *really* from, where she belonged.

Could that have happened? She could feel her mother's hand like it was real. But had it happened? Everything was confusing. The images fractured as if on a rent projector screen and she was suddenly back in the car, the man forcing her arms back. His weight was on top of her, crushing her, she had the smell of him in her nose. There was a frightening succession of blurred movements across her vision, things coming at her. Then there were more of them, more men, holding her down, pulling her T-shirt off, saying things to her, warning her to keep still. She began to gasp for air and tried to pull away, but she had no control of her limbs. She couldn't move anything properly. She felt like something had hit her head, very hard, knocking her to the ground, forcing the air from her lungs. They were pushing her arms up above her head, rolling her on to her side. She was more terrified than she had ever been in her life, yet could do nothing. They had done something to her so she couldn't move – drugged her. There was some kind of fabric over her mouth, choking her … she tried to scream, but all that came up was vomit. She was being sick and it was sticking in her throat. She would breathe it in and die.

She started coughing violently, then the images melted again and she could feel her mother's hand, hanging on to her, calming her. She took a breath. Her throat was clear now. Back in the wheat field she could breathe. She felt a sense of safety and security. It was coming from her mother, directly, going into her hand, then spreading through her body. Liz was staring down at her, her hair waving in the wind, a smile on her face, her eyes kind. *One day you will return here.* That was what she was saying. *You will bring our family home.* Pointing at the palace through the trees, moving her arm across the horizon to show what belonged to them. All of it. All the fields as far as she could see, the palace, the section of the river at the bottom of the slope where the dirt track turned into the forest.

How old was she? She was still much shorter than Liz. Maybe ten years old. Liz looked young. It had to be a memory, from a time before Liz got sick and began to obsess about dirt and disease. Sara had been twelve when her mother had bought the clinic in Paris and moved in. After that everything had changed. She had seen less and less of her, been sent off to various boarding schools. And she had hardly ever seen her father anyway. Only Felice had been there for her after that. One series of empty houses after another, full of staff and people she didn't know. If Felice had not been there she would have killed herself. She had taken an overdose when she was fifteen, but her father had just shrugged when he found out. It was de rigueur to try it, he said, when you had all that she had, when there was nothing else she could need. He'd done it himself. *So what?*

Had those really been his words, at the hospital bed, by her side, holding her hand and telling her – *so what*? She hadn't remembered that before.

Her mother had referred her to a batch of psychiatrists, but had never spoken to her about it. Or about anything. Yet up to the age of ten she had never been away from her mother. She had felt loved then. She *had* been loved. She knew that, because she had been over and over it all with the psychiatrists. But at ten years old it had all stopped. All the love, all the affection, all the contact. Suddenly her mother was gone – into her clinic – inaccessible. So this – this visit to her mother's property in Russia – if it was a memory – this must have been before the big change, before it all fell apart.

She felt a sharp pain somewhere in her body. The wheat field wavered and faded. There was urgent noise all around her. The man hissing something at her. He was speaking in Russian, so fast she could barely understand. Liz had spoken Russian to her when she was little, but no one had bothered since then, and it was maybe thirteen years since she had spoken it regularly. She still could, but not well. Was that why she was imagining this thing in Russia, because *he* was speaking Russian, because … she screamed as the pain sliced into her again. It was her arm they were cutting. Or her side. She tried to struggle, tried to speak, but there was lead in her limbs, her mouth wouldn't open. Everything was sluggish, spinning, dizzy. She was screaming in her head, but nothing was coming out of her mouth. She could feel a pulse of blood running out of her. She wanted to struggle and kick but couldn't. He was muttering to her as he did it, his voice so close it was like something *inside* her head, whispering insistently, telling her he was doing this for her, that he had to do it, that it would soon be over, that everything would soon be over …

38

When her phone began to vibrate, Arisha was in the library, sitting right opposite Freddie and the policeman at the long oak table there, listening intently, trying very hard to make it look like she was calm. She got up without saying anything and walked over to the closed, panelled door. She stepped out into the passageway, closed the door after her and moved over to the window before taking the phone from the pocket of her jeans and answering. The number had been withheld, the caller anonymous, but she knew who it would be.

'Clear,' a voice said quickly, in Russian. 'All safe.'

Max. She was sure of it. She felt a huge surge of relief, took a massive breath, let the tension begin to escape. 'And the device?' she asked, very quietly, with great self-control.

'Done,' he said. 'No worries.' Then he was gone.

She put the phone back into her pocket and leaned heavily on the windowsill. *Thank God for that*, she thought. She said a little prayer of thanks, silently, but fervently.

Outside it was the middle of the night – the early hours of the morning, in fact – but the view across the Thames was lit by the lights from Chelsea Embankment. They were in Freddie's house there, a place he hated using because it fronted the road, and despite all the soundproofing they could always hear the traffic. There wasn't much of it at this hour, comparatively, but it was still fairly constant. Streams of light flashing by. To the left, about two hundred yards away, Chelsea Bridge, lit up like a Christmas tree.

Her eyes fixed on a long, black barge sliding through the water directly in front of her. She watched the reflected yellow light rippling in its wake and felt her heart slowing for the first time since all this had started. From the end of the passageway, up in the drawing room, she could hear the lawyers talking quietly. There were two lawyers at the table up there, and three people from security. Plus the other two policemen. They were waiting for Freddie to finish with the assistant commissioner.

She got her thoughts together and turned back to the library. She had to stop herself from smiling. 'All safe' meant Max had found Sara Eaton, that he had her, that the plan was back on track. Her question about the device, and his answer, meant he had – somehow – managed to disable the tracking device that was implanted in Sara Eaton's arm. A very discreet agency – owned by a Wellbeck family company – provided this unadvertised service to a select number of clients who had well-grounded kidnap fears and enough wealth to take cutting-edge counter-measures. Arisha had never seen the device, but knew all about it. It was what Freddie Eaton was counting on. Smaller than a pacemaker, it contained a state-of-the-art GPS signalling system. She had been told that if you felt the skin beneath Sara Eaton's left armpit you could find the location of the thing quite easily, along with the small scar from when it had been fitted, three years ago. To extend battery life the device could lie in a dormant state, until remotely activated by the controlling company. Freddie had already told her to request this, of course, and up until now she had been relying on the device too, waiting for the company to call so that she could pass the coordinates to Max. But either the thing had malfunctioned or something else was interfering with it. The company hadn't been able to get a clear signal. And now Max had Sara, Arisha didn't need the thing, so it was imperative Freddie couldn't use it to trace Sara. So Max had removed it.

She sat down as Freddie started to tell the policeman what he wanted. The policeman glanced uneasily at her, again. He obviously hadn't wanted her in there with them. He'd wanted privacy. From his own men, from her. Because he was corrupt, in a straightforward way – he was Freddie's contact point, his eyes and ears on the inside of the Metropolitan Police. One of them, at any rate. The kind of influence Freddie had could get you a lot of friends in powerful places. This man was an assistant commissioner. But the commissioner himself had attended Freddie's last birthday party. His fingers could pull many strings, if he had to, even now, when he was about to lose virtually nine-tenths of his fortune. Nobody knew that, of course.

Freddie had summoned this man to explain why there was some kind of international warrant for Sara Eaton's arrest. He had found that out from friends in France and Belgium. In fact, he probably knew more about what was going on than the policeman sitting here now. They all did.

The policeman was called William Morgan. Freddie called him 'Bill'. He wasn't in uniform – everything looked pretty casual, in fact, Freddie in jeans and open-necked shirt, the policeman in smart casual gear – but he still looked uncomfortable, Freddie haranguing him gently, as if it were a fireside chat at the golf club and Freddie was his superior. 'I want it sorting, Bill. I really do,' he said now. 'It's absolutely disgraceful that this has been permitted. It's quite clear that my daughter has managed to escape a truly horrific incident on that island, only to have this happen. She is a victim, for Christ's sake. And this isn't how we should be treating the victims of crime. She told me – you should make a note of this – she told me, in effect, that they found one of our most valued former assistants dying. Alison Spencer. It was clear that there had been a burglary. A violent burglary. They found her dying. Good God! Can you imagine it? She told me ...' He paused. Bill was nodding at his words, but hadn't actually taken any notes. 'I mean it, Bill,' Freddie said, smiling. 'I think you should write this down.' He stopped.

Bill looked perplexed. 'I don't have ...' he started. His hands went through his pockets. 'I don't have ...'

'Please use this,' Arisha said, sliding a small pad of note-paper and a couple of pens across the table.

'Thank you.' He pulled the pad closer and scribbled something on it.

'Because that doesn't appear in the information the Belgians have sent to back this warrant, or whatever it is,' Freddie started again. 'I know that as a fact. They aren't even looking at the possibility that my daughter might have disturbed a violent burglary in progress ...'

'I'm not sure that's true, Freddie,' Bill said. He scratched his head. 'I think they're just covering all the bases. That's all. They have this footage of Sara and this other chap at the property and so they want to find them ...'

'Well, it's not on. "Cover all the bases"? It's simply not on. I want it stopped. I mean it. They just cannot be permitted to do that. It's a complete affront, an abuse of my daughter's liberty and rights. I won't lie down and take it. I won't have you complicit in such nonsense. Two dead people and a ransacked house. Our house, belonging to *our* family. You understand that? That property is ours. So there is absolutely no question of Sara herself somehow being classified as a trespasser. What has happened must be obvious to anyone with half a brain. My daughter and her friend arrived while the burglars were still present. They found Miss Spencer and, obviously, fled. Meanwhile the burglars – one way or another – managed to murder Miss Spencer and her friend, Mr Meyer – another trusted and highly valued family assistant, I should add. And instead of searching for the killers, the perpetrators, the Belgian police have issued a warrant to imprison my daughter. It's absolutely disgraceful. That it would happen in *that* country does not surprise me. But that you – you of all people, Bill – should be complicit – *that* I cannot tolerate.'

'I assure you, if there were anything that I could …'

'You must get the lawyers on to it at once. There will be a loophole, a procedural problem. My lawyers already advise me that it is possible to return these wretched things if there are procedural errors. Now if my people can come up with something, then surely yours can too?'

'They're looking at it. It's with the lawyers already, Freddie. I've seen to that.'

'Thank God for that.' Freddie sighed. His face was red with the effort of trying to stay calm. 'Well, there we are, then. Hopefully you will have good news for me soon.' He smiled and shuffled the little pile of loose papers beside him on the table, a signal that the meeting was finished.

But Bill was frowning. 'I have to ask you a couple of questions, Freddie,' he said, as if that were an embarrassment. 'It will speed matters up if there are things I know.'

Freddie continued organising the papers. 'Yes?'

'You've obviously had contact with Sara.'

'Yes.'

'Do you know where she is presently?'

'She wouldn't tell me. She's her father's daughter – she's careful. She wouldn't tell me over a public phone network. Not since the last time I was caught out that way.' Referring to the infamous newspaper bugging debacle. The police had

231

been implicated in that, after all. Freddie started to stand up. 'For all I know you might have been listening to our conversation. So she was right not to say. I was silly to ask.'

'How long is it since you spoke?' Morgan asked.

'A couple of hours. I told her to keep away. I told her there were security issues. I'm sorry to say that *you* ...' He pointed a finger at Bill. '... you, the police, I mean, our own British police forces, were those issues. It's dreadfully disappointing that it should come to that. But as that's how it is, I didn't want her coming anywhere near here – or our home in Surrey – until I knew I could count on you not just clapping her in irons. You understand, of course.'

'Yes. Of course.'

'And I'm so glad it's all clarified now. Now we can get on with finding out about the kidnap attempt and the atrocity on the island.'

'So you think she's in the UK? Or could be?'

'I really have no idea. She's nearly twenty-one and has considerable means. I'm not particularly worried that she's sitting in a field somewhere, shivering. She knows what she's doing. She managed to get off that island and they tell me there were ten people killed there. She should have a medal really. She'll be all right, I'm sure. But if she had come to me immediately ... well, I wasn't sure that you wouldn't have a car outside all my properties, waiting for her. I didn't know which way you would play it at all. To be brutally honest, I wasn't sure I could trust you, Bill.'

'You can trust me, Freddie. This is nothing we can't handle. The Belgians have put in a request to alert staff at entry points, in fact. So normally it wouldn't happen that we would put resources into surveillance, et cetera ...'

'You can assure me that won't happen, I trust?' Freddie stopped what he was doing and gave the man a glance.

'There is no surveillance on you. None. As far as I know your phones are clean. You have my word on that. There is presently an alert at UK entry points. That's all ...'

'And you have the lawyers working to solve that. Good. The sooner we can get this stupid thing out of the way the sooner we can start to work out who was behind this. The Belgians can be left to look at the burglary, I assume. But the people in the Seychelles will need assistance. I'm putting that in place already.' He stood and pushed his chair back. Arisha stood with him. 'Is there anything else, Bill?' he asked.

Bill stood quickly. 'The photo,' he said. 'Have you seen the photo the Belgians are using?' He started to fish inside the pocket of his sports jacket, presumably to produce a copy.

'I've seen it,' Freddie said. 'I had someone send me a copy.'

'You also have a copy?' Arisha asked the policeman. 'Let me see it, please.' She wanted to make sure it was the same one they had. Very reluctantly he took out an envelope and slid a photo from it. She came round to his side of the table and took it from him. It was the same one.

'Do you know who the man is?' the policeman asked. Arisha looked up to lie, but he wasn't asking her. He was trying to pretend she wasn't there at all. Freddie shrugged. 'No,' he said. 'A friend of Sara's, I assume. He clearly hasn't kidnapped my daughter, as the Belgian information states. Do *you* know who it is?'

'We think it's an ex-police officer, called Tom Lomax.' He looked at Freddie, waiting for a reaction, but Freddie just smiled. *She* had recognised Lomax as soon as she saw the photo, of course, but Freddie didn't have a clue who it was. She hadn't told him. He knew vaguely about the letters Liz Wellbeck had written, but didn't know that Arisha had identified the courier, bought her off, gained some idea of the content of those letters – enough to have had the name

233

Lomax ringing alarm bells in her ears, because John Lomax, she recalled all too well, was the policeman who twenty-two years ago had made the disappearance of Lauren Gower into some kind of personal crusade. She had assumed that Liz must be writing to him, with some kind of insane, death's-door confession that would sink them all. But Barsukov had made enquiries and found out it was the son Liz had named in the letter. That had puzzled everyone, so Barsukov had done some work on him and made the connections, asked to meet him, in fact, only about a week ago, though that hadn't worked out. Unfortunately. Because here he was now, Tom Lomax, a fly in the ointment, helping Sara Eaton to escape. Until a few minutes ago, at least.

'Are you looking for him also?' Arisha asked the police-man. 'For Tom Lomax?'

'The alert is for both Sara and Lomax ...'

'So that will be dealt with too,' Freddie interrupted. 'When you get the lawyers going on it. Clearly this man is a friend of my daughter's. I don't want you hassling him with some foreign crap either. We have to make a principled stand here. These European arrest warrants are a dangerous affront to British liberty ...'

'It's not an arrest warrant. Just an alert ...'

'At the moment. Can I count on you to deal with it, Bill? That's all I need to know. I want it killed dead. It's a distrac-tion. Terrible things have happened. The last thing we need right now is the fucking Belgians blundering in. Can I rely on you?' He stepped forward and took the man by the shoulders, looking into his eyes. Arisha saw the policeman lick his lips. It wasn't the size of the consultancy fee that Freddie paid him each year – though that was incentive enough, she would have thought – it was simply that it existed, that the mere fact of the payments could ruin him, if made public.

'Of course,' he said. 'I'll do what I can. You're absolutely right about it all. We should have queried the APA. No doubt about that.'

Freddie walked him out of the library, pointing him in the direction of the lawyers. One of the house assistants appeared to guide him away and Freddie stepped back inside the library. He shut the door and stared at her. 'What a fucking idiot,' he muttered. 'I can't believe we give him what we do.'

'He's worth the investment. He'll do it.' She reached forward and took hold of his hand. Inside she felt a shiver of disgust, but that was normal these days, and easily hidden. She'd had years of practice living this lie. She'd been concealing her hatred of Freddie Eaton since the moment Sasha was born. That was when it had started. It had taken her by surprise, because before then she had found him attractive enough, looked up to him, even. It had never been a question of love, of course, always something more practical. But that was still a long way from the contempt she felt now. He would be fifty-six this year, and still looked fit and comfortable with his body. He was tall, with a beautiful shock of white hair, a classic, aristocratic face. He could be charming and friendly, or manipulative and cruel. But he'd always been that way. Nothing had changed. She'd only started hating him because of Sasha, she thought, because the baby had given her a different perspective on everything. All she saw when she looked at Freddie Eaton now was some kind of moral aberration, and she didn't want that anywhere near her child. That was the heart of it. 'Don't worry,' she said, smiling reassuringly. 'We'll find her.'

'Did you check with the wretched tracker people?'

'They've got nothing. Not yet.' She squeezed his hand and saw there were tears in his eyes. He was such a pathetic emotional wreck, in private. Capable of boundless self-pity. It was truly despicable, and getting worse as he aged. 'Where's Sasha?' he asked. 'Will he sleep through all this?'

'I put him in the Star Room. He loves it.' The Star Room had a huge window set in the roof. On a clear night you could lie in bed and gaze at the heavens, light pollution permitting. 'What was the phone call?' he asked her, his eyes narrowing a little.

She frowned. 'Which?'

'You went out to answer your mobile, no?'

She thought he hadn't noticed. 'Nothing important,' she replied easily. Soon he would be getting his own call from Maxim – a little reality check. He'd had precious few of them in his life. But no need for her to warn him.

but it was useless, Tom had a pattern of his own. He wasn't a kid any longer.

but he was still John's son, no matter how old he was, still in trouble, still in pain. And if he'd done nothing else at John the same as they always had, he'd tried to trap his reactions under control. It was the first time he and son Tom in over a year.

There were complications in their relationship, a dynamic to overcome or. He couldn't just wade in and tell him what to do. "Could you please tell me something about where we're going..."

Tom sat in the front passenger seat, leaning against the window, breathing hard. John had found him where he had said he would be, on one of the exit roads from the Surrey village of Shackleford, in the shadow of a hedge. They were almost back in London now, on nearly empty night roads, and not much had been said aside from questions about the injuries. Tom had suffered John to examine him once he was in the car – and John had done his best to properly assess the mess – but there was no question of him going near a hospital or a doctor. He had other things on his mind. He was in pain, clearly, but had made it plain that didn't matter. John had seen him like this before, a couple of times, when he was a kid.

As far as John could determine he'd been kicked and punched repeatedly. It was possible he had a broken rib, maybe a broken nose. His face was a swollen mess, his clothing covered in bloodstains, but nothing was still bleeding. There were head injuries that were harder to see properly, but Tom insisted he had no double vision, no dizziness. His eyes weren't closed up and he could breathe freely enough through one nostril. He thought he might have lost consciousness momentarily, maybe not. John wondered anxiously whether he was lying to him, to minimise it all. He spent some time trying gently to persuade him that they should go to Casualty, but it was useless. Tom had a mind of his own. He wasn't a kid any longer.

But he was still John's son, no matter how old he was. Still in trouble, still in pain. And those things ate at John the same as they always had. He tried to keep his reactions under control. It was the first time he had seen Tom in over a year. There were complications in their relationship, a dynamic to watch out for. He couldn't just wade in and tell him what to do. 'Could you please tell me something about what's going on?' he asked again, quietly. It drew no response. 'I need to know, Tom. I need to know some detail.'

'I think it's better if you know as little as possible.'

'Not true. There might be stuff I *need* to know – stuff you're unaware of. Listen. Listen to what I have to say. I'll tell you what I know. Then you tell me what you think you can.' That drew a blank too, but he started talking anyway, telling him what was going through his head. 'You remember Grenser?' he said. 'It was a big case I had when you were little. Operation Grenser. It started in 1990. You were only five years old, so maybe you forgot it. It was …'

'Grenser. Your case. Obviously I remember it.' He saw Tom frown, then pull down the passenger-side sunshade and stare at his mouth in the mirror there. 'You were working it all my life, Dad. How could I forget it? The missing girl.'

'Right. Lauren Gower. Rachel is her mother. You met Rachel once, at my place …'

'Did I?' He was still frowning, fingers in his mouth now. 'Another smashed fucking tooth,' he muttered, then grimaced with pain. 'I don't recall meeting her,' he said.

'Doesn't matter. But you know what that case means to me, right?'

Tom shrugged, then folded the sunshade back up and stared out of the window.

'I spent nearly half my career trying to find out what happened that day, back in 1990,' John continued. 'Lauren Gower was kidnapped. She was thirteen months old. You probably don't recall any of the details.'

Tom sank lower in the seat. John thought he might be gritting his teeth. Was he listening? Or thinking about what he was going to do next? Thinking about getting even, somehow. He'd seen him like that before too. 'She was kidnapped from a crèche in the clinic where her mother worked,' John said. 'You remember the name of the clinic?'

Tom looked at him, eyes narrowed, as if to ask, *what the fuck has this to do with anything?*

'I imagine not,' John said, moving his eyes back to the road. They were going through the outskirts of south London now. 'But it was called the Wellbeck Clinic.' He glanced over and saw Tom still looking at him, but the expression behind the eyes was changing. The thoughts were beginning to slot into place. 'It was owned by a woman called Elizabeth Wellbeck-Eaton,' John said quietly. 'It was her clinic Lauren Gower was taken from.' He saw the penny drop, but then puzzlement replaced the anger. He kept quiet for a bit, glancing from the road to Tom and back, watching him trying to make sense of it, if there was any sense to make. Finally Tom met his eyes again. 'Go on,' he said.

'The woman you were with – just now, tonight – she was Sara Wellbeck-Eaton, right? That was her name?'

Tom nodded, then sighed. 'Yes.'

'You think it's a coincidence? My case – all the time we spent investigating the Wellbeck family and their staff – and now you're involved with them? It could be, I suppose. It doesn't have to mean anything.'

His son said nothing, and wasn't looking at him now. He was thinking, chewing his lip and running through it. John started to tell him about the enquiry. He told them Liz Wellbeck had been interviewed, told them that at the time she was staying on an island called Ile des Singes Noirs. Tom interrupted him. 'How did you know I was with Sara?'

Sara. First-name terms. John noted it, noted the body language. 'A colleague called me tonight, told me about the All Ports Alert. He gave me as much info as they had. Including facts related to Sara Eaton.' He told him then about the news item about the island, and the suspicions that Sara Eaton had been kidnapped. 'Were you there?' he asked. 'Were you on that island?'

'Yes. We were there. But she wasn't kidnapped. We got away.'

Silence. John bit his tongue. He had a file full of questions, but he said nothing. He kept his eyes on the road and they continued for minutes like that, saying nothing.

'People were killed,' Tom said eventually. 'It was bad.' He sounded dazed.

'It was a kidnap attempt?'

Tom shook his head. 'I don't know. Who knows? We just concentrated on getting away. I guess it was. They looked like Somalis, some of them. Not all of them.' Another silence, then: 'I don't want to talk about it. I just want to find her.'

'She's gone?'

'I don't want to talk about it. If you can just take me to my place. Then I'll sort it. Sorry. You were the only person I could call.'

'Your place might be risky. They might be looking for you.'

'They?'

'The police. Because of the alert. I'm not sure what the position is.'

'I'll take the risk. I have to. I need to get something, change. I'll be there a couple of minutes only. You can drop me wherever. You don't have to be involved. I don't want you to be involved. I don't want to force you into any uncomfortable decisions.'

'I know my priorities, son. I'm an ex-detective, but even when I was working I was always your father, first and foremost. You know that.'

Tom stared away again, but said nothing to that.

'What happened in Brussels?' John asked. 'Someone must have died there. That was the info.'

'They want me for that?'

'I think they're just fishing. Your mug was on a CCTV shot, with the girl. The info says you kidnapped her too.'

Tom nodded. 'Glad I didn't rely on Belgian justice, then.'

'Did someone get killed there?'

'We went to find Liz Wellbeck's PA. We found her dying, her place ransacked. Some guy appeared covered in blood, so I chased him. He fell off the roof.' He looked over at his dad and smiled crookedly, without humour. 'It's true. Sounds crap but it's true.'

John shrugged. He believed him, but he could see that Tom thought he didn't. 'Where's the girl now?'

'The girl? You mean Sara?'

'Yes.'

'She's not a girl. She's a woman.'

'OK. Where is she?'

'Alex fucking Renton said he'd help us. Instead he did this to me and then drove off with her.'

That didn't surprise him. 'Drove off? What do you mean?'

'Took her. He took her. Some fucking gangland deal.'

'Kidnapped her, you mean?'

Tom nodded. 'I tried to stop it, but couldn't. Alex knows who has her. He'll tell me who has her. I need to get to him. Quick.'

'That's not the way to handle it, son.'

'I knew I shouldn't have told you anything. You going to call it in? You'll get her killed that way.'

'He say that?'

'Kill her, hurt Jamie. That was the threat.'

'It makes no difference. Still the best thing to do would be to call it in. We should call it in quickly. How long ago …'

'They'll kill her if you do that.'

'They always say that.'

'And often they carry it out. So don't tell me what is and what isn't the case, Dad. I said I didn't want to talk to you and here we are. I knew exactly what you were going to do. I should have kept my fucking mouth shut.'

'I'm not going to do anything. Not without you saying I can.'

Tom looked sceptically at him. 'You mean that?'

'I mean it. But you need to think clearly about it. This is all crucial time lost. You know how it works as well as I do …'

'I'm not calling anything in. It would be a complete waste of time. All that would happen is I'd end up in a cell for three months, then on a boat to fucking Belgium. Then I wouldn't be able to do *anything*. I will find out where she is. I will find out who has her …'

'By going to the thug who did that to you?'

'He took me by surprise. It won't happen again. I know him well. I know how to handle him.'

'You think you do …' John shut up. Tom was no good at fighting, not aggressive. No good at standing up to bullies, or dealing with threats. He let things build up, get on top of him. But he had a threshold, and if it all got too bottled up he could blow. Then he was pretty scary. But that didn't make him any better a fighter. In the past when he'd lost it he'd usually come off worse.

'I'm not a kid any more,' Tom said. 'I can look after myself.'

John nodded. 'You could always look after yourself,' he lied.

'Let's do it like this,' Tom said. 'I'll tell you what's happened, provided you drop me near my place and give me three hours before you call it in. Three hours.'

John nodded. 'I won't call it in at all if you don't say I can.'

'You won't be able to help yourself, Dad.' Tom turned and smiled weakly at him. 'That's what you're like.'

'OK. We'll do it that way. If that's the way you want it. Three hours. Now tell me.'

Tom started to talk at once. John realised immediately that he desperately needed to tell it, because he was in some kind of shock. Until he'd told it to someone, the whole horrific tale would lack a sense of reality, and that would make him feel like he was going mad. That was how the mind handled this level of brutality. John had seen it many times in his career. The telling of the story made it real, brought it home, gave perspective. Sometimes even the criminals needed that. Very occasionally that led to a confession. Not often.

What his son was telling him had the flavour of a confession about it. Tom felt guilty about something, though from everything he was saying there was no need for that. But that was another effect of violence. John had all the technical knowledge to understand it, but that wasn't going to help much. What Tom had been through was something he had never experienced directly.

Tom recounted a terrifying kidnap attempt – if that's what it was – on the island. He described the assailants, including two white guys. He told John how Sara Eaton had shot at least two of them, killed them, then how they had fled through tropical forests and escaped in a plane. It sounded like something out of a film.

From there it moved to Brussels, and finding out that Liz Wellbeck was dead. They had gone to find a family 'PA' to get the truth about it, only to find her dying. Tom had chased someone who had fallen and died. So they'd fled from there too. It was a catalogue of disasters and fuck-ups.

They had got across the Channel on a private yacht, then been betrayed by Alex Renton. As Tom got to the last bit the shaking stopped and his voice became harder. By the time he had finished they had crossed London and were about five minutes from his home. John had asked very few questions to clarify details. There had been no need. But he knew details were missing, pieces that would make it all fit properly. Tom was keeping stuff back.

He slowed the car in Hounslow, his heart thudding with adrenalin, stunned at what he had been told. 'This is it,' he said. 'I'll stick to what we agreed, but I want you to think about what you're going to do ...' But Tom was already opening the door. John leaned over and put a hand on his arm, stopping him. He asked the single most glaring question he had. 'Why you?'

'What do you mean?'

'Why did Sara Eaton contact *you*? What did she want?'

Tom looked away quickly. 'I've no idea.' He shook his head. 'I'm sorry to have dumped all this on you.' Then he was out and walking off.

40

It was like saying a prayer before bed. Every single night since Lauren had been taken Rachel had done it. Sometimes she had been on odd shifts and slept during the day, sometimes in the early years she had fallen asleep at her desk, or on trolleys in Casualty, waiting for the pager to go off – but she had always found time for it. She had kept to it like a ritual every single night, over twenty-two years. She would lie down, close her eyes and imagine what she would do when she first saw Lauren again. Imagine it happening, coming true. Imagine Lauren standing in front of her, returned to her, safe, alive, well.

At first the images had been traumatic, reducing her to tears, but repetition had slowly turned them into something comforting, a mark of continued hope – a way, even, of keeping that spark alive. As the years had passed her mental picture of Lauren had changed effortlessly to try to match how old she would be. She had never – not even once – had a doubt about her imagined daughter, about how she would look, move or speak. At some stages disorienting, brutal thoughts had tried to get in there, to distort the image, and resisting them had become part of the nightly ritual, like shunning evil, turning her back to Satan. Because she was aware that the Lauren she dreamed up to walk and stand and smile in front of her was a happy Lauren, not a child who had lived through some twisted, perverted hell. She knew that if that had happened to her baby then she had no idea what she might look like now. But she had become practised, over the years, at keeping those thoughts at bay. They had no part in this night-time rite, which was something between only Lauren and her, something no one knew about, something intensely private.

In recent years the images had been the same ones each night, the same dream. She would be standing somewhere full of people – a place like an airport terminal or a railway station – her eyes searching the crowds of faces for the one she knew. The searching often went on for a very long time. Sometimes in the last couple of years she had even begun to panic, fearing that the face was gone, that it wouldn't ever reappear. But it always had eventually. Lauren always returned.

A tall, confident young woman with long, dark, curly hair and blue eyes. She would be twenty-three now. Her birthday was 8th March. Rachel would see her hair first, moving through the sea of people, then her face, in profile – but she would know at once that it was her and would start walking towards her. The commuters would part in front of her, getting out of her way. A mood would go through the crowd – they knew, somehow, that something momentous was about to happen – and they would gradually back off, silent, watching. Then Lauren would turn towards her and start walking in her direction. As they got closer the other faces would vanish completely, and then there would be just the two of them standing across from each other, Rachel's heart beating wildly, recognition in their eyes. Rachel would open her arms and Lauren would wrap her own around her waist. They would stand still, hugging each other, crying with relief and grief and joy. Rachel would finally feel that she had found her home again. She belonged. Because Lauren was back.

It was a myth. She knew the reality, knew that if such a

thing were to ever come about it would be very different, much more confusing, filled with an intense sadness. Because the years between would be lost to them for ever, whatever had gone on. Twenty-two years of irrevocable separation. And because they would neither of them stand a chance of recognising the other. But hope feeds on myths, and without hope she would be dead. Long ago dead, wrists slashed, unable to contemplate the horror of the truth. The myth had kept her alive.

But now it was gone. She had gone to sleep tonight, for the first time ever, without doing it, without imagining the reunion. So now, in the early hours, lying alone in John's bed while she waited for him to come back with his own child, now she felt – perhaps for the first time in her life – that she had really lost something that would never come back, something that had been taken from her so long ago – her child, her meaning, her self. The truth was only just sinking in now. Because tonight, also for the first time, she had believed that her daughter was dead. *She had thought that thought.* The invisible connection between them – the thing she had cherished like an imaginary friend down through the years, her tiny little grain of absolute madness – that link that she had been able to *actually physically sense*, as if it were a smell in her nose, or a sensation under her fingertips – that was gone. Lauren had left her.

She couldn't work out what it meant, that she had vanished. Did it mean Lauren had died, just now, this day? Or just that she was herself only now waking up to reality? She hadn't a clue. At first – when the link had first snapped – she had been with John and something else had opened up inside her, a channel to him, instead of a channel to Lauren. *When God closes one door, he opens another.* That's what the nuns had taught her at school, so long ago. But her belief in God had slipped quietly away long before Lauren had been taken, and not even all that trauma and all that need had been able to bring it back, no matter how much she had desired that.

Tonight, she had fallen asleep in John's arms and had felt only relief, an immense weight lifted from her. She had, in a way, chosen not to go there, not to think those thoughts, not to imagine her child again. She had chosen to let her go. But only because there had been no option. Because the link was already gone. She had felt that with absolute clarity. The link was gone. She had even said it to John, told him what it meant – that she no longer believed her daughter was still alive. She had somehow actually said that to another person, then gone on to do other things with him, intimate things. As if it were all finally behind her, the act no longer necessary – she had become what she had so long only pretended to be – a normal, healthy woman.

But it wasn't true. She knew now, at four in the morning, lying alone and cold, she knew now that she would never be normal, that everything was still somehow an act. What had happened between John and her had meant something profound. She had no doubt about that. It had been beautiful. Something she had never imagined would come to her again. But now it seemed only bitter, a species of disgusting animal treachery. *As if she had traded Lauren for John.* She rolled on to her side under the covers and pulled her knees up to her chest. She could feel the blackness rising up around her. She groaned and prayed that John would hurry, that he would return soon.

41

Tom leaned on the wall at the corner of the street and scrutinised the parked cars and silent spaces. The street was dead. No lights in the houses, curtains all closed. No sign of anything he should watch out for. His own car was still on his drive, where he had left it three and a half days ago. He had come full circle. As if nothing had happened.

He crossed the street and took the service alley that ran alongside number 42, then down the back of all the gardens. Some people used it for their rubbish and he heard cats, maybe even foxes, scrambling away from the wheelie bins as he made his way cautiously past the overgrown hedges and broken fence slats, watching far ahead for any sign that someone might be waiting at his house. But as he got closer he was sure he was alone. There was no one watching for him.

He walked up through his short garden until the automatic tungsten light dazzled him, then lifted the mat outside the little shed at the top of the garden, retrieved the back-door key and unlocked the door. Inside the alarm system bleeped its warning and he switched it off, then leaned on the kitchen counter for a few moments, catching his breath. His head was spinning, he felt nauseous. But it settled after a few deep breaths and he checked the house without being sick or collapsing. Everything was as it had been three days ago. No one had been in.

He pulled the soiled clothing off and went up the stairs naked. He couldn't travel around with blood all over him. That would attract unwanted attention. He needed to stay free and unimpeded. He was the only person who could get to Sara quickly enough. He was certain of that.

He turned the shower on and stood under it without waiting for it to warm up, sucking his breath in. As it warmed he washed the blood off him, stood with the water running through his hair until the dirty brown stream turned clear. Then he dried himself quickly and put fresh clothes on. He took a maximum dose of some painkillers he'd been given for a twisted ankle some years ago, something stronger than ibuprofen. He didn't actually have any pain at all right now, not even from his ribs, which had hurt with every breath all the way through the car journey with his father. The adrenalin had taken over, he thought. Or maybe this was just what happened – you got used to it. Tomorrow might be a different story. Either way, he didn't have time to think about what was hurting and what wasn't.

In the kitchen he wolfed bread, ham and cheese, without bothering to make a sandwich with it all. Then a bar of chocolate. He drank a full bottle of some sports drink, promising energy via caffeine and sugar. He was still starving. But there wasn't time to eat more. He opened the connecting door to the garage and found the baseball bat he kept there, along with other sporting kit he kept meaning to use with Jamie. From a locked cabinet he took out a spare mobile, checked it was still charged and fired it up. It had never been used, but it had a duplicate of his SIM card. It was his father who had taught him to keep spare, untraceable mobiles. He should have had one like this when he had made the call to Alex fucking Renton, three years ago.

He locked the doors and went out to his car, put the bat in

the back and started the engine. As the car slipped down his drive he checked the time on the dash. Coming up to five in the morning. He reckoned he had used up about thirty-five minutes of his three hours. It would only take another ten minutes to get to Alex's house, so if Alex was in and his dad stuck to the deal he would be OK. Plenty of time to do what he had to.

There was no question of John just driving off and waiting three hours. Did Tom really think he would do that? Maybe he hadn't even considered it. John could see that his head was filled with extreme images, all his concentration taken up with what he thought he had to do – which was rescue the girl, even if that meant confronting the thug who had just kicked seven bells out of him. There was a spark of something heroic in that, John realised, something which made him smile despite his fears. Tom had once got a judge's commendation for arresting a masked, armed robber, John remembered. The gun hadn't been loaded, but Tom hadn't known that. And there'd been some citizen's bravery thing for pulling a child out of the Thames. All this before the mistake that got him kicked out. The tosser who had just beat him was the author of that mistake. That might make for a lot of getting even in Tom's confused head. So there was no chance at all that John was just going to leave him to it.

So he had watched Tom until he had passed the end of the street, then got out of the car and followed him to the corner. He leaned on the wall Tom had only just rested against and peered down towards his house. After about five minutes lights had started to go on, downstairs, then upstairs. He had walked farther down the street, until he was in earshot. He couldn't hear blows or screams, or any other sign of immediate trouble, so he had walked quickly back to the car, started it up and moved it so that it was almost at the corner and he could see Tom's driveway without getting out. He had watched and waited.

His own head was swimming with conflicting demands. The information Tom had given him was organising itself slowly. He sifted it methodically, while he watched in silence. He put together a chronological sequence of all the events – everything his son had told him he'd been through – then a separate list of things he would follow up – if he were running an inquiry. Which he was, in a way, because Grenser had never gone away. He was still doing it, still thinking like an SIO. It was automatic.

Did all this his son was going through have something to do with Lauren Gower's kidnap twenty-two years ago? That was the huge question. His instincts told him there was no coincidence. He slotted together various key pieces of information to back that up – including his son's link to Sara Eaton. He tried to pull back from his memory everything they knew about Sara Eaton, and couldn't believe that it was hardly anything at all. She was a footnote to the inquiry, born after the event. The child of a woman who was herself a marginal witness. How old had Tom said she was? Twenty? Twenty-one on Friday. He rubbed his temples furiously. It was an easy thing to forge birth certificates. She could be twenty-three on Friday, without even knowing it.

He couldn't believe he was considering that. It made him exhale deeply. Was *that* what he was considering?

What he should have been doing was ignoring the little pact with Tom and calling it in. It was a kidnapping. The girl – whoever she was – would be in danger. This Renton had information that might be worked out of him, information that might be time-crucial. Except Tom was right on that – Renton wasn't going to give anything away without violence, and this wasn't the seventies. But to get in among the perpetrators, quickly – that might disrupt things, throw a spanner in the works. It might kill her too – his son was correct on that.

But that wasn't a concern that could stop them doing something. They had to do *something*. 'They'. Who was he kidding? He wasn't even a part of *them* any longer. And the last thing he wanted was to put Sara Eaton in danger.

The reality was that no one was going to discover anything fast. They would have to wait for the ransom demands, take it from there. But he should at least – in that case – be warning them to get in contact with her father. Right now. No delay. Delay was what turned abduction cases into murders. But this was more professional. They would be after money, not sex. They weren't going to kill her – whoever they were – unless there was a threat to them. Tom was right again.

And what if his crazy suppositions were right? *What if?* Then Freddie Eaton wasn't her father and all bets were off as to what exactly was going on here. Could he really risk contacting Freddie Eaton, given that possibility?

His thoughts were interrupted as Tom came out on to his drive, hands full. John saw a stick of some sort, a baseball bat or a metal bar, he couldn't see clearly. Tom was making no attempt to hide it. He put it in the back of his car, got in, and seconds later the car was sliding back into the road. John swallowed hard. What the fuck was Tom thinking about? He lay himself flat across the passenger seat. He wondered whether Tom knew what he drove, whether he had even noticed. He waited until he heard the car turning in front of him, then switched the engine on and sat up. He could see the tail lights ahead. He waited until they went round the bend, then pulled out after them.

42

The man was right in front of Sara, kneeling there, inches away, a plate of something held out towards her. He spoke to her quietly, said something in Russian. She didn't get it, but she recognised him. She could barely keep her eyes open, but she knew who he was, knew the scarred face, his voice. The same man who had come into the car and drugged her. The man she had shot at on the island, the man who had killed all her friends. She tried to pull away from him, to shrink back, but something was holding her in place, dragging painfully at her leg. And her head kept sinking back, her eyes rolling up. What had they given her? *'Don't drug me again,'* she pleaded, with a feeble, pathetic voice. *'No more of that ... I won't run ...'* She felt so sick. She just wanted to be able to sit up without her head spinning, open her eyes properly, wake up, work out what was happening to her. She could smell the food on the plate, but it made her stomach turn. Something was very sore at her side, or under her arm. *What had they done to her?* She could hear herself retching, but there was nothing coming up. How long was it since she had last eaten? She collapsed back into something soft and lay there panting, felt the queasy, terrifying fog creeping up again ...

*

The next thing she knew she was sitting up and drinking, her head groggy. The same man was there, holding a cup of water to her lips, speaking softly to her, again in Russian, so she still understood very little. Normally she could do it, but not now, not like this. She tried to say that – that she didn't speak Russian, only French or English. She didn't want him to know that she spoke some Russian. But then suddenly the water took effect and her head was very clear. Her eyes moved around and took in the scene – the essential elements of it. She saw the enclosed space, the mattress she was sitting on, her torn clothes, the dim light bulbs, the dirty metal walls, the thick shackle digging into her ankle and pinning her to the floor, that man's face right there beside her. She remembered at once what was happening and jolted back, away from him, so the water spilled all over. She opened her mouth to scream but he lunged towards her, knocking her backwards and pressing a rough, massive hand over her face. His body pinned her as he hissed in her ear, in English this time, telling her not to scream, to shut up. Her chest began to heave – she couldn't breathe with his hand blocking her mouth, his weight on top of her – she tried to nod to him. He took his hand away and she gasped for air. 'Don't scream – it will hurt my ears,' he said, then sighed and stood up, moving back from her. 'And it's useless,' he added. 'No one can hear you here. Besides, I'm not here to hurt you. I don't want to hurt you. You understand? You're not going to be hurt if you cooperate.'

She waited for her breathing to settle. But her head was spinning. She was too dizzy to sit up. She crawled as far back from him as she could and curled into a ball, keeping her eyes open and on him. 'What did you do to me?' she hissed. 'What have you done?' She started to retch again. The room smelled of vomit and machine oil, and something worse, lingering in the background.

'You need to drink something,' he said. 'And eat. You'll feel better then. It was a harmless sedative. An anaesthetic. You'll have a headache, feel sick – until you drink more and eat more. You need to do that to recover. There's food here …' He turned his back to her and walked over to what looked like a rusted, metal workbench with a naked light bulb dangling above it. There was a battered wooden stool placed in front of it, a small fridge to the side of it. The bench was right against the wall of the place. Her eyes took in the space beyond it. It was some kind of long, windowless room with metal walls. Six foot across, maybe thirty feet long, eight feet high. More like a corridor than a room. She couldn't work out what it was. 'What have you done to me?' She tried to shout, but the words came out feeble. 'What did you do? You fucking cunt. What have you done to me?'

He came back towards her with a plate in one hand. 'Nothing bad,' he said calmly. 'Why would I? I need you alive. So stop worrying and stop shouting. I only took this from your arm …' He held up something too small to see. 'That's all I've done. Aside from that I haven't touched you. No one has.'

She frowned, trying to see it properly. *He took it from her arm?* Her arm was throbbing, right in the armpit. She remembered the transmitter just as he spoke again.

'The transmitter,' he said. 'Believe me – the last thing you need is for your father to know where you are. So I took it out and disabled it. I was careful, the cut was clean. I used a sterilised blade. You'll be fine. Maybe some infection, but nothing your body can't handle.' He raised his arm a little higher, and she saw a tiny metal object held clumsily in his fist. Some of his fingers were crudely splinted together, pieces of wood protruding, the whole arm a mess of bloody bandages. 'I did to you a lot less than you did to me,' he said.

'I have maybe two broken fingers. Plus infection in the arm. You tried to kill me.'

She was starting to tremble violently. 'I had the crosshairs on your head for ten seconds,' she spat. 'If I'd wanted to kill you, you would be dead, believe me …' The words choked in her throat. 'I fucking spared you. I'm fucking stupid …'

She expected no reaction, but his expression changed. 'You aimed for my hand?'

'I aimed for the gun. I should have put it through your head …'

He smiled. 'You have spirit,' he said quietly. 'And ability. You hit the gun.'

'What do you want? What do you fucking want? Why am I here?'

'It won't help you to get angry and excited …'

'You want my mother to pay a ransom? Is that it? Well, she can't, because she's dead. She can't pay you anything.'

'I know Liz Wellbeck is dead. But I know your family too, know how much money there is. I knew your mother before you were even born …'

'She wasn't my mother. You're wrong. She wasn't even my mother …' She blurted it out before she could censor herself. It was the information Alison had given her – *she's not your mother …*' she had said. '*Liz Wellbeck is not your mother … that's why all this is happening …*' Her last words.

Her gift to Sara.

For a moment the information sat there in the silence between them.

'Who told you that?' he asked finally. He sounded puzzled.

'That's none of your fucking business …'

He shrugged. 'We can leave your mother out of it. Freddie Eaton is your father and he has money enough …'

'My father won't pay you anything. He has a policy. He's told me many times ...'

'He'll pay. Don't you worry about that ...'

'He won't. The money isn't even his. It was hers – Liz Wellbeck's. I *know* he won't pay anything. But *I* can pay you. Tell me how much you want. I can arrange it.'

He smiled at that, then knelt again, nearer to her. 'You should stop talking,' he said gently. She pulled away involuntarily, but the metal band wrenched at her ankle and she cried out.

'I have to keep that on you,' he said, looking at it. 'For obvious reasons. But there's no need to drag at it, no need to try to get away. I give you my word that I have no intention of harming you. This is food that you should eat ...' He held the plate towards her.

43

Tom didn't think about what he was going to have plenty of time to do once he got to Alex's place. That decision was already made. His main worry was that his dad would think better of the three-hours deal. He had told his dad the entire thing because it seemed the only way to get his cooperation. Well, not the entire thing. He'd left out crucial parts. What Alison Spencer had told Sara – that Liz Wellbeck was not her mother – for example. And that Liz Wellbeck had probably intended that he, *John* Lomax, should have ended up on the island with Sara, not his son. Why hadn't he told him that? He wasn't sure. It was like he had lied somehow – took on a job that his father was meant to have taken, assumed his identity. He'd felt ashamed about it. Knowing it would only confirm what his father already thought about him – that he was some kind of criminal. But that wasn't really a good reason not to tell him. And nor was the need to rope him in a good reason to have told him everything he had. He'd let his mouth run, of course. Because it was all sitting there in his head like a squirming monster, because he had to talk about it to someone, get it out. Because Sara was gone. Sara, the person he'd shared this whole nightmare with, the only other person in the world who could understand what he was feeling. If he hadn't spoken about it to someone his head would have exploded. How much had he given away?

he asked himself. He couldn't even recall now exactly what he'd said. Everything was confused and unreal. The passage of time, too. All he knew for certain was that he had to get to Alex and get out of him who had taken Sara.

He drove deliberately carefully, feeling the anger burn within him but not letting it interfere with his reactions. He had to look normal, drive normally, not go too fast. Not that he could see any police cars or patrolling officers. There was traffic, but not much, and nothing that he needed to be careful of.

He ran through his plan, such as it was. He needed Alex on the ground, incapacitated. That was the first step. Take him by surprise, get him down. Because Alex was bigger than him, of course, and stronger. He had a wily sort of intelligence too, but it wouldn't reach to correctly judging what Tom was now capable of. Tom would get to the house, he thought – he was almost there already – park up, ring the fucker and get him to step out. He would be waiting for him in the garden, hidden. Alex wouldn't come prepared because he would be expecting Tom, his old friend, the little wimp he had just given a good kicking. Tom knew the exact spot in the garden where he should wait. Then step out as Alex passed, swing the bat, bring him down. That was the first step.

He turned into Alex's street. A long, tree-lined avenue. Plenty of cover. He thought – *what will I do if he's not there?* He hadn't considered that. What if Alex was off with whoever had Sara? He would come back some time. Tom could wait. The rage could wait. This feeling wasn't momentary. It could last weeks, just bubbling away under the surface. He could guard it, nurture it, wait for the right time. But then it would all be too late. And anyway, his dad would have called all this in before that and then there would be other people coming for Alex. So he hoped Alex was in. He couldn't think past that right now.

Get him down – what next? Alex was a tough little fucker. Take him down with the bat, tie him with some rope. Except he hadn't brought any rope. Alex would have some, though. In his garage. But how would he get him back into the house? Drag him? He started to get confused thinking it through. He could see the trees in front of the place now. He was there. He put the thoughts to one side, but then remembered Alex's wife and kids. Garth and June. He hadn't even considered them until this moment. *What would he do about them?*

He parked the car, got the bat out and started to jog towards the gateway. He felt weird, his head pounding with real pain now, but also airy, light, as if he were floating along. He tried to ignore the confusion he felt when he thought about Alex's family seeing anything. He couldn't stop to consider all that. Not now. Sometimes you just had to act. Now he was getting his phone out to call Alex's number. Now he was going to do it.

John already knew where Alex Renton lived. He had a fat dossier of information on Alex Renton from during the disciplinary hearings against Tom. He had needed to find out what the little thug had got into since leaving school. Renton was a middle-tier lackey in some mediocre gang run by a mid-range west London mobster called Glynn Powell. Powell was into the usual mix – drugs, extortion, prostitution, fraud, trafficking of all kinds, plus attempts at laundering and legitimisation. But he wasn't up to this. He was too small to kidnap someone as big as Sara Eaton. He could command neither the loyalty nor the facilities to keep something like this under wraps once the conflicts arose – once the reward was broadcast, for example. And Powell would know that. He wouldn't even try something so risky. So if Renton organised this for Powell then Powell was doing someone else a favour, someone bigger. And that, in itself, raised interesting questions about the timings. How had this other party managed to contact Powell so quickly, for example? Was there some warning? Had someone known that Sara Eaton was going to be here?

Renton lived in a decent enough house – more decent than John would ever be able to afford – in what counted as upmarket Feltham. There were high walls, security gates, tall hedges, a long front garden, trees obscuring clear views to the building. As John turned into the long road he had to slow suddenly, because Tom had already stopped, he saw, right opposite the place, wheels on the verge. John pulled over, turning like he was going into a driveway. He went back the way he had come until a row of trees blocked his view to Tom, then got out carefully, quietly. He heard a door closing.

Tom was already jogging across the road as John came past the treeline. The road was deserted, with poor street lighting, all the houses set well back. John ducked back behind the trees, though felt there was no need. Tom wasn't looking around, wasn't being careful at all. John started to quicken his pace, going down the blind side of the line of trees. He caught intermittent glimpses of Tom walking along the front wall of the place, then a hedge got in the way. How was he going to deal with the security gates? John wondered.

As he came from behind the hedge he was only about thirty feet from Tom's car. He slowed and looked across, but couldn't see him any more. He paused, listening. He couldn't hear anything either. He stepped out and looked properly, then kept walking, quickly reaching the car. There was no sign of Tom anywhere. Had he already got over the gates somehow?

John crossed the road, noting the security camera above the gates. It was pointing down at the gates themselves. They were about ten feet high. He couldn't see how Tom would have got over them without any noise. He looked around, starting to panic. About thirty feet along he realised there was a path through trees, leading down the side between Renton's place and the gardens of the next property. He ran to it, looked down into the darkness. The route was overgrown. He began to push through. Tom must have come this way.

John was making a lot of noise as he went, so much that he couldn't hear anything ahead. To his left the wall was lower now and he kept catching glimpses of a big house, lights all off. He started to swear to himself, and right then he saw Tom. He was about forty feet ahead, past the line of the house, on a clearer area of path. He was crouched down, motionless. John stopped, holding his breath. But then immediately realised there was nothing he could do here except stop Tom – it had gone too far to do anything else – so he kept walking, gaining quickly on him.

He was almost on him before Tom looked up and saw him. He didn't register surprise. The stick was a baseball bat, John saw now, but Tom wasn't holding it – it was already discarded, lying in the foliage behind him. At the same time John realised there was another, lower gate here, a side entrance. But Tom wasn't trying to get through it. He was crouched down, head in his hands. When he raised his head the light from the moon fell across his face. It was wet. He was crying. John stopped. 'It's only me, son,' he whispered, confused. He looked across at Renton's house, but could see no signs of life.

'I can't do it,' he heard Tom mutter. 'I can't do it.'

John stepped over and crouched down beside him, put a hand on his shoulder. He felt worried about the house, about Renton hearing something, but more than that he felt a tremendous relief. He'd been foolish to worry at all, maybe.

'I would have to go in,' Tom said. 'I'd have to take him down, crush his fucking face with the bat. His kid might see, or his wife … I can't do that …'

John nodded, but said nothing.

'I can't do it,' Tom said again. 'I can only *think* about it. I can't actually *do* any of it. Not to anyone.'

John patted his shoulder, very gently. He felt like whooping with relief. 'It's good you can't,' he said. 'It means you're not like that fucker. It means you're human.'

'They'll kill her, though. I've fucked it up completely. I can't do anything.'

'That's not true. We need to talk about it. Urgently.'

44

She was starving, but she wouldn't touch the food he was offering. He kept coming back to her with the plate. She kept refusing. He was standing in front of her again now, holding it out. 'Will you eat or not?' he asked.

'Tell me how much you want,' she said to him, again. 'I can arrange it. I *will* arrange it right now. Just give me my phone. If that is what this is about … if it's only money …'

'*Only?* You have forty million sterling?'

His eyes flickered as she hesitated. He saw the truth at once. Of course, she didn't have anywhere near that. Not in liquid assets. Maybe he knew that already.

'Not yet,' she said. 'But on Friday I will have it. I'll pay you then if you let me go now. You have my word …'

He laughed now, but not unkindly. 'It's out of my hands,' he said. 'Sorry, but I can't do it. I just look after you …'

'And kill people.' She could hear herself spitting the words at him. *Shut up*, she thought, in her head. *Stop goading him.* But her mouth wouldn't obey. '*You're a fucking monster. You killed my friends …*'

'Your friends? You mean your *staff*?'

'Janine Mailot was a friend.'

He shrugged. 'I didn't do that. And I think it was you who started the shooting. No?'

'The others were already dead. She was stripped, terrified …'

'Yes. But I didn't do that. I didn't want anyone to die or be hurt. It was a mistake. All of it. I used the wrong people.' He looked at the floor, still frozen in the same position, with the plate extended towards her. Incredibly, he looked upset. She inched a fraction closer, just enough to ease the tension on her ankle, then pushed herself into a half-sitting position. If he crouched lower, she could kick him with her free leg, she thought. There was enough slack. Get him in the face, or the throat. Jean-Marc had taught her how to kick or punch people in the throat. If she was lucky she would disable him for a few minutes. But what then? She had to think about it, not just react. She had to be intelligent, use her head.

'Sometimes shit like that happens,' he said. 'I'm sorry about your friend.'

'Who are you?' she asked, her voice cracking as she fought back the tears. 'Why are you doing this?'

He looked up at her, then knelt on the floor, right in front of her, the plate still in his hand. 'Will you eat this food? Please?'

'You going to force it down me if I don't?'

'Of course not ...'

'My arm is sore. It's infected. I need antibiotics ...'

'You'll live. This should be over in a few hours, then you can use all that money you've got to get all the medicine you want ...'

How did he know about the transmitter? He knew about her family, so he was connected somehow, so she had to know him from somewhere. There had to be a link. Or was the connection to Tom Lomax? Could he have set this up? He had left her to this man, left the car and abandoned her. She forced her mind away from that. She couldn't face it. She had heard Tom shout a warning, anyway. The truth could be anything. She had no idea what was going on. She needed to know who this man was. She had thought she recognised him on the island, when he was in the sights of her gun. She should have killed him then. She was fucking stupid. He had cut out the transmitter. Her last hope, the final back-up. Now no one could find her.

She started to sob, but stopped herself at once. Appearing like a weak little girl wouldn't help. 'Who are you?' she mumbled again. 'Why are you doing this to me?'

'My name is Maxim Sidurov. Ring any bells?' He shifted position so that he was sitting on the floor where he had been kneeling. He moved the plate back on to the floor beside him.

Sidurov? Something connected to Arisha Vostrikova, she thought. Had she seen him *with* Arisha? But when? Years ago. She couldn't work out where. 'If he doesn't pay you will have to kill me,' she muttered. The words came out before she could censor them. She stifled a gasp as she thought about it, and saw him frowning at her. 'But if you wait until Friday I can pay you myself ... that's the only way we can ...'

'We've thought of it already, and that won't work. Too complicated. How would you arrange it? You would have to make a phone call, at the very least. And that's too traceable. People don't just release forty million. They would need proof of life. I would have to cut off a part of you and send it. There would need to be connections with people we don't know, negotiations. All that involves contact and traces. My DNA moving around. It would be out of our control, out of your control. Someone would inform the police, obviously. Messy, and too dangerous. The people I work for won't go for that. They've thought of it all already ...'

'Why are you telling me this?' She started to cry as she asked the question, as the implications sank in. 'Why tell me your name? Why let me see you? I know who you are now. I can identify you. That's worse than your DNA. So it must be true ... you must intend to kill me anyway ...'

'Stop crying,' he said, very gently. 'There's no need for it. Stop it. I need you to be calm and healthy. Not like this. I don't care if *you* know who I am. What can you do about that? Tell the police? But you won't do that, because there's not just me involved. There are many of us, and if you give my name away then one day one of us will come for you. Then we *will* kill you. That's a promise. You understand? Of course you do. This isn't something personal. It's just about money. You understand *that*. It's between my boss and your father. And your father has plenty of money. No one wants to hurt *you*, no one wants to kill *you*. Killing people is counterproductive. If we kill you we will be hunted until we are caught. Your family has a lot of money to throw at hunting us. But this is just like a little taxation for them. Forty million is nothing. So, you see, everything is practical, not personal. Everything is rational ... no one is going to kill you ...'

'They will already be hunting you. You killed eight people on my island. Maybe more ...'

He waved a hand in the air. 'No one is going to hunt us for that. Those people were nothing, nobody. Not like you. No one cares if a few people from an unknown tropical island are dead. That's the way of things. You know how it is. To kill *you* would be a different matter entirely. That's why we won't do it ...'

'Why are you telling me all this?'

'To calm you. To show you there's no need for you to be frightened. If you're frightened you will make my life difficult. I don't like hurting people ...' He leaned over to one side, reaching back towards the table. His hand closed around the red, insulated handles of a large crocodile clip, lying on the floor, attached to a coiled, electrical flex running out of the ceiling.

He pulled it towards her and showed her. 'This place is a container,' he said. 'A converted shipping container. But it hasn't been used recently for storage. Nothing so harmless. This was in here. I found it. It's attached to the mains.' He flicked a switch on one of the grips. 'It's live. Don't touch it.' He grinned, then flicked the switch again and placed it on the ground beside him. 'There's a dried puddle of blood behind you,' he said. 'That's what you can smell. I don't like to think what they have been doing to people here. But that's not me. I don't even want to drug you again. I don't know whether that would harm you, so I'm playing safe. And I certainly don't want to use things like that ...' His eyes flicked towards the crocodile clip. 'I want us to get on and be calm with each other. That way everything is easy. No one gets hurt. No need to use things like that.'

45

They drove back to Hammersmith in Tom's car. John left his parked in Feltham. He drove, Tom sat in the front passenger seat and tried to summon the strength to concentrate. He had assumed they would get back to the car and his father would call in the kidnapping, maybe not via 999 – better to use one of his connections, get some guarantee of a sympathetic approach, at first at least – but before he could do that Tom had quickly told him the parts he had left out. 'I think Liz Wellbeck was trying to get *you* out to the island,' he had started. 'I think it was you she wanted, not me. I think someone made a mistake with our names.' He told him then about the note, as best he could remember it, the letter from Liz to Sara. Then finally told him what Alison had told Sara – that Liz was not her mother. That changed everything. The effect was electric.

'Christ almighty! I was right! I was fucking right!' His father was shouting, instantly animated. 'Of course. Jesus. It's true. It *has* to be.' He slammed his fist against the dashboard, then immediately started to talk about his case, about Operation Grenser, some theory about it. But Tom couldn't keep up, quickly lost track. His head was pounding, he couldn't think straight. All he could see was images of Sara, in the back of some car, men around her, pinning her down.

Something shut down in his head. One minute his dad was

talking away, voice raised in excitement, the next they were outside his place in Hammersmith, the car stationary, his dad leaning over him at the open passenger door. 'Rachel is inside,' he was saying. 'She's a doctor. She'll check you out. Either that or we take you over the road to the hospital.'

Tom frowned. Had he blacked out? Slept? He asked who 'Rachel' was.

'She's Lauren Gower's mother,' his father said.

'*She's* here, at your place?'

'Yes.'

'What? You called her?'

'God, no. Don't say anything about this, son. Nothing at all. I'm probably wrong. Very wrong. We don't want to get her hopes up.'

Tom shook his head. He didn't follow. *What* was he not to mention? Had he missed something? 'Why is she here?' he asked.

Suddenly his dad looked embarrassed.

Tom sat on the balcony, looking out over the Thames with a fixed stare, while his dad disappeared somewhere – to talk to Rachel Gower. It took longer than Tom thought it would. He was having some kind of a relationship with her, Tom assumed. Maybe she even lived with him.

The sun was coming up, the noise of traffic mounting. He could see the buses going over Hammersmith Bridge. A normal day beginning, just like any other. He slept again, though only for a few minutes.

Then she was standing in front of him – Rachel Gower. Behind her, his dad was saying something, pushing something towards him. He could smell it – a mug of coffee. Rachel looked upset, he thought. Had she been crying? He'd met her before, apparently, a few times, but couldn't recall details. Had she been sleeping in his father's bed just now?

He smiled at her and sipped the coffee, burning his lip. She started speaking to him. He thought she sounded odd, like she was trembling. He realised she was asking him to explain what had happened to him. He told her the gist of it. Three blows to the head, at least, in about five days. She started to feel around in his scalp. She had very soft, careful hands. After a while it felt hypnotic, like when the nurse at school had run her hands through his hair, looking for lice. He closed his eyes and answered her questions about how much sleep he'd had, dizziness, sickness, loss of consciousness. Then she produced some instruments from somewhere and looked in his eyes and his ears and nose. She pressed the cold pad of a stethoscope against his chest and he did as she asked, taking breaths. She took his pulse, his blood pressure, his temperature. All the time his dad was watching anxiously. The end result, she decided, was that he should sleep. She didn't know for sure how concussed he was, but thought he certainly must be 'to a moderate level'. But if there was serious bleeding in his brain he would be showing more 'dysfunction'. Nevertheless, she wanted him to have X-rays, urgently. He'd lost consciousness, after all – maybe more than once. The caffeine was working already, though, or the hot liquid, or the touch of her fingers. 'There's no time for any of that just yet,' he said. He drank more of the coffee and turned to his dad. 'What are we doing?' he asked. 'What are we doing about it?'

They went up to a room his dad called his study, just Tom and his father. His father then left him there and went back downstairs to make sure Rachel was OK. Again. 'She's not so good,' he explained. 'It's complicated.' He returned looking flustered and edgy. He needed to explain what was going on to her, he said, but didn't dare.

'What *is* going on?' Tom asked. He was sitting at one side of the desk.

'Two things. Two key things. Firstly – Liz Wellbeck wanted *me*, not you ...'

'That was my guess. I might be wrong...'

'I think you're right. I have a feeling about it, about all of this.' His dad started to take folders from the bookshelves behind the desk. He placed them on the desk and opened them, one by one, looking for something. 'I think she was trying to say something before she died,' he said.

'Like what?'

'Like a confession.'

'That she kidnapped Sara when she was little?' Tom asked with obvious incredulity. Suddenly he realised where his father was headed. 'That Sara is Lauren Gower?'

His dad put a finger to his lips and looked anxiously at the closed door. 'Keep your voice down ...'

Tom spoke in a whisper: 'That's a mad idea. You're letting your imagination run away with things.'

'You reckon? Liz Wellbeck was not her mother. Was that ever mentioned to me, to my inquiry, through several years of investigations and many interviews? In 2003 we spoke to them all again. It was never mentioned. Indeed, they lied about her age.' He found some sheets of paper. 'These are copies of an interview with someone called Arisha Vostrikova, Liz Wellbeck's PA ...'

'The name rings bells. She works for Sara's father now, I think.'

'I'm not surprised. In 2003 she told us the kid – Sara Eaton – was twelve years old.'

'But that's right. She's twenty-one now. On Friday.'

'More like twenty-three, I would say. They've probably lied about her age her entire life, forged the birth documents. To put the kid out of the frame. I'd put money on it she's older. She probably doesn't even know it …'

Tom frowned. 'But you don't know that. There's nothing to prove that. Nothing at all. You're just guessing.'

'It fits. It's easily done … Plus, in the note, Liz Wellbeck wanted me to meet Sara. Why? There is no other possible reason. I have no connection to Liz Wellbeck except through this case. I'm telling you, she was trying to confess it.'

'Through Sara? It doesn't make sense. She would write to you. Why write to Sara? It's all mad, Dad. Completely fucking mad. Maybe she was trying to get something off her chest – it reads like that – maybe she wanted to confess *something*, but not *that*, not that Sara wasn't her child. It doesn't read like that at all. It's something else. And anyway, her father is still her father …'

'Is he? You said she wasn't happy about speaking to him …'

'Doesn't mean he isn't her dad.' Their eyes met, then they both looked away. 'Does any of this help with who has her?' Tom asked.

'Maybe.' He started pulling sheets of paper out of another box. Tom assumed the boxes – and there were many of them – were copies of material from Grenser. 'Maybe.' He found something, a photo. 'You told me that when you were on the island one of the two gunmen referred to the other as "Max". Right?'

'Yes.'

'That set me thinking. There was one "Max" that came up in the inquiry. Maxim, in fact, but Max could be short for Maxim. Have a look at this photo of him. Is this one of the gunmen?' His pushed across a photo, a mugshot of a young, blond-haired man. Tom looked at it, knowing it was useless.

'I've no idea,' he said. 'I didn't see them close up. I didn't see anyone close up. Except the one Sara shot, in her room. And he was black.'

'That was taken back in '90. The man is Maxim Sidurov. He was security for Freddie Eaton and Liz Wellbeck. We interviewed him. He was in the hospital on the day Lauren was taken. He's Russian. You said one of them might have been speaking Russian?'

Tom shrugged. 'Maybe. Or Polish. Or something Eastern Bloc. I don't know.'

His dad wasn't deterred – not yet. He produced another photo. 'This is Maxim Sidurov in 2003, when we reopened the inquiry. Thirteen years later. We interviewed him again. Got nothing interesting.'

Tom looked at it with a sigh. 'I told you. I didn't see anyone close enough. And besides …' He stopped. A detail in the photo caught his eye. It wasn't a mugshot photo, but a very clear image of someone slim and tall, with hard, bony features, cropped blond hair, wearing a smart suit, in a street somewhere.

'A surveillance team took that,' his dad said.

'You watched him in 2003. Why?' Tom put his finger on the feature that was bothering him. He couldn't work out what he was trying to remember. 'What's this?' he asked.

His dad came round the table and looked over his shoulder. 'A scar,' he said.

Tom felt his heart trip. He took a breath. 'A V-shaped scar,' he said, very quietly.

'Yes. It's distinctive. A war wound of some sort.' His dad looked down at him. Their eyes met. 'You've seen the scar before?' his dad asked, suddenly getting it.

'No,' Tom said. 'But Sara has. She saw it through the weapon sights. She told me. A V-shaped scar on his cheek.

Distinctive. It could be him.' But already he was thinking of all the possible coincidences that might ruin that conclusion. He was still thinking about them when his father spoke again.

'We put a team on him because in 2003 he was working security for a big-time Russian mobster called Dimitri Barsukov.'

'Barsukov?' Tom stood up quickly. 'I don't believe it. This guy works for Barsukov?'

'You know Barsukov?'

'No. But I was meant to get to know him. Less than a week ago. I'll tell you about it.'

They stood looking at each other.

'OK,' Tom said, frowning. 'That's one coincidence too many.'

His father nodded. 'You're getting the same feeling I have.'

'Not that Sara is Lauren Gower. Definitely not. There's nothing pointing to that at all.' He ran a hand through his hair. 'But maybe Barsukov has her,' he said, uncertainly. 'Maybe Barsukov is behind all of this.'

46

Her mind kept going to the crocodile clip. It was right by his leg, almost within her reach. She just had to move a little closer to him to get it. The shackle was attached to a short chain and that was bolted into the floor. There was a lock. He would have the key. She had to get him feeling safe with her, then get the clip. Attach it to him, switch it on. Electrocute the fucker.

She ate the food. She thought that might relax him a bit, make him think she trusted him, and anyway, she was starving and damaged and it would help. She needed a clear head. There was nothing to suggest he would try to poison her. He talked while she ate, sitting on the stool and rambling on in a morose, depressive voice, telling her about her family, how he had met them, where, when. He talked slowly, avoided eye contact. She stuffed a whole sandwich in and chewed without tasting, then drank about a litre of water from a bottle. She expected to be sick, but she wasn't. Instead, she very quickly started to feel better, just as he had predicted. Her head began to clear, her heart started to slow, she was able to think.

'There were rumours,' he said. 'Rumours that Liz Wellbeck couldn't have a child.' He looked directly at her. 'Maybe you heard those rumours. That she stole someone else's child?'

She frowned. She didn't know what he was talking about.

'But that was all before you were born,' he said. 'I don't

know who told you she wasn't your mother. But maybe they heard those rumours, and got it wrong.' He stood up and walked across the floor, leaned against the wall, back to her. He looked more agitated now. She had no idea why. She checked the clip again. It was in reach, she thought. But he wasn't. She shuffled forward on the mats a little, watching to see if he would notice. He didn't move from the wall.

'I was working for her when you were born,' he said, talking into the wall. 'Liz Wellbeck was your mother. There were no children stolen. Those rumours were all rubbish. You should believe me.'

She took another drink of the water, spilled some, wiped her mouth with her sleeve. 'Why do you care?' she asked him. 'She's dead. Doesn't matter if she was my mother or not – you're not going to get any money from her.'

She started to move again. If she dived, she thought she could get her hands on the clip. He turned his head slightly, looked at her, then immediately looked at the clip. Like he'd read her thoughts. She froze. He pushed himself off the wall, walked over to the clip and kicked it back, away from her. 'You're right,' he said. 'Why should I care?'

47

It was after nine by the time they could get everything ready, but still Tom hadn't been able to sleep for longer than about fifty minutes. Standing in the foyer of Barsukov's Knightsbridge address, he leaned on the counter between himself and the man he had spoken to and let his eyes close momentarily. The man was standing back from the counter, phone to his ear, speaking in hushed tones to communicate Tom's presence to Barsukov's people in the apartment far above.

Tom knew Barsukov was here, because he had called him, using an ordinary mobile number his father had provided. Barsukov hadn't answered, hadn't even spoken to him. But what Tom had said had been enough to get this meeting set up. What Tom had said was that he wanted to negotiate over Sara Eaton, that if Barsukov didn't cooperate then he would go to the police with a list of thirty-seven properties held by Barsukov. That Barsukov had bitten didn't necessarily mean he was holding Sara Eaton at one of these properties, but it *might* mean that. It might.

Tom was trying not to focus on how speculative his reasoning was. At the moment his father was going along with it all – caught up in a fever of excitement at the absurd idea that Sara might be the missing Lauren Gower. Any little glimmer of hope that might shine a chink of light on his twenty-two-year-old case had to be worth following through. He had already had meetings and phone calls with colleagues from Operation Grenser, retired and ongoing, already involved the new Grenser SIO, ostensibly on his terms. Which at the moment were that they should proceed quietly, in secret, without even telling Freddie Eaton, because this was their only chance of recovering Sara alive.

But that would have to change soon. Before long someone was going to call Freddie Eaton with a ransom demand. Eaton was highly connected. He would certainly wish to use those connections. There was a deputy assistant commissioner, or some such, who had flags against Eaton on all the systems. So he should already have been told about John Lomax's information and involvement. Maybe he had. If so, he hadn't appeared yet. But he would appear sooner or later. Then Tom's father was going to have no control over it. Tom had until then to test his hunch, to go for Barsukov.

The address was a high-profile recent development to cater for the super-rich, an address that even Tom had heard of. There had been carefully orchestrated media coverage when the place had opened, rumours that the penthouse apartments were going for over one hundred and forty million. The security was said to be provided by ex-SAS personnel, though if that was so they weren't hanging around the atrium chewing gum and looking hard. The atrium was full of activity and people, but it looked more like the foyer of an expensive hotel than a carefully guarded residential address. Everything was normal – rich-normal, at any rate. There were men standing either side of the lifts up to the apartments, true, but they didn't look like bouncers – more like off-duty waiters. Perhaps that was their skill. Tom couldn't see any indication that they might be armed, though there had been press rumours about that too. It occurred to him again that – despite everything looking relaxed and normal, despite the luxury address in the heart of London – what he was doing might still carry a risk – the man he was approaching played by different rules, as he already well understood. But the fear was just a shadow behind the urgency. This was *all* he could think of to do, so he was doing it. And he wasn't completely alone. His father was out there, on the street, in the car. And within the hour there would be proper back-up – his father was seeing to that. So there was some protection. Just not much.

The man dealing with him had been scrupulously polite, but it was obvious nevertheless that he regarded Tom with distaste, a stain on the pristine carpet, not the type they liked to let in via the main entrance. Tom was in clean clothes, but his face was a mess of cuts and bruises, one eye fat and swollen. He couldn't breathe through his nose, which was blocked with clotted blood, and his lips were swollen and wouldn't close properly, so that he had to keep wiping his sleeve across them to stop saliva dribbling all over when he spoke. He tried to keep on top of all this as discreetly as possible.

He was waiting about five minutes for the man to come back to him, and in the end it was another character who appeared at his elbow to tell him that Barsukov was ready. This one was a bit heavier, though not tall, and spoke English with an accent. He looked at Tom with hard eyes and indicated that he should follow him to a lift.

Once inside they stood side by side and took the ride to the top floor in silence. It was only when the doors opened that the fun began. There were three more waiting to greet him. Which meant drag him out and put him against the wall. It was done with enough force to make it clear that he shouldn't bother arguing. He was into it now. There would be no turning back.

Two held him, tight enough for it to hurt, two searched

him. When that was done he was propped between them and walked forcibly down a tasteful, short corridor to the door to Barsukov's apartment. This they opened by one of them standing in front of a sophisticated piece of wall-mounted kit which Tom guessed was a retina scanner. Then they were in and Tom was released into a large, very bright reception room, walls and ceiling of glass and steel. The four of them stood close to him, facing him, hands at their sides. Barsukov was already there, lounging on a long, semicircular couch done out in cream leather, a big balcony window behind him, everything chrome and glass and minimalist, spotless, reeking of luxury. Except Tom. Barsukov looked at him with a scowl, then said something in Russian. One of the four answered, then there was a further exchange and they walked off through a door to the left.

'That leaves me and you, Lomax,' Barsukov said. 'I let you up because I didn't understand the message I was given and because ...'

'We already met,' Tom said. 'You hit me about a week ago, broke a tooth ...'

'Don't interrupt me. I know who you are. What was the message – give me it again.'

Tom took a breath. 'I want to talk about Sara Eaton ...'

'I got that bit – what was the rest, the crude blackmail attempt?'

'Blackmail? Hardly. I said if you wouldn't see me then I would go to the police with a list of thirty-seven addresses owned by you ...'

'That was it. Yes.' He stood up and walked towards Tom. 'Thirty-seven addresses. That was the part I didn't understand.' He looked angry, like he was going to throw another punch.

'I'm not alone in this,' Tom said quickly. 'If I don't make a call within the next fifteen minutes then it starts. I call every ten minutes after that. Or it starts.'

'What starts?'

'The information goes to the police, along with everything we know and those addresses. The police will start an operation to search those addresses. At the very least.' He hoped.

Barsukov looked mildly surprised. He stood in front of Tom, looking up at him as if trying to read something written on his face. He was wearing a suit, no tie. After a little he sighed and nodded. 'I don't understand anything you've said,' he said, quite loudly. He looked at the floor. 'There is some error, surely. You've come to the wrong place, the wrong person. I've never heard of this Sara Eaton person ...'

'I meant it. We will go straight to the police ...'

Barsukov looked sharply at him, then put a finger to his lips. Tom shut his mouth. 'You do what you have to Mr Lomax,' he said. 'As I said, I have no idea what you're talking about.' He smiled, then pointed off to a door – adjacent to the one the security had gone through. Tom frowned. What was he saying? That the place wasn't secure, that there might be surveillance devices? Tom shrugged. That didn't bother him. But then Barsukov suddenly leaned closer to him and whispered, so low Tom had to lean forward to hear – '*We talk through there, or not at all. Your choice.*'

'OK,' Tom said. 'But remember ...' He took his phone out and looked at the time on it. 'Nine minutes now. I call in nine minutes or it's out of my hands.'

'Yes. Yes. Of course.' Barsukov replied, smiling again, as if there might be cameras on him too. 'You do whatever you have to. But I think we're finished here now.' He walked over to the door, a big glass thing, inviting Tom to follow. Tom paused, unsure how to assess the risk. Barsukov opened it and

Tom saw beyond an empty room, a toilet, or bathroom, it seemed, though big enough to be his living room.

He sighed then followed Barsukov through, the phone still in his hand. Once inside he saw that they were in a beautifully tiled bathroom/toilet – the guest toilet, presumably – with neat towels and soaps, like something in a hotel, fine art on the walls, separate shower, big circular bathtub and jacuzzi, two toilets, two bidets, flatscreen to watch while you did your business, a shelf full of medicines, or toiletries, even a little bar with drinks. There was nothing to suggest why this room would be any more secure than the last – from a surveillance point of view. But as Barsukov closed the door on the reception room he started to talk at once. 'Just a precaution,' he said. 'This room is perfectly secure. No one can hear us here. No one at all.' He wasn't smiling any more. Almost as soon as he shut it the door opened again and the four heavies came in. Then there were five of them standing in front of Tom and he was feeling distinctly afraid. He was in the middle of the room, back to the toilets. There were no windows. The door closed again with a smooth click. One of the men turned and pressed a button on the wall, to lock it.

'What's the matter?' Barsukov asked. 'You look nervous.'

Tom held his phone up. 'I meant what I said about the call.' He wiped his sleeve across his lips. His heart was beating very fast now.

'Take the phone off him,' Barsukov said calmly. 'Strip him and put him in the bathtub.'

'Wait!' Tom shouted. 'Wait!' But they weren't waiting for anything. In a second they had tripped and pushed him, were pinning him to the floor and the phone was out of his hands. He started to struggle, kick out and shout, writhing around while they strained to get their hands on to his arms and legs, to hold him still, muttering instructions to each other in Russian. One of them caught hold of his head and told him to calm down, over and over again, but Tom was frantic now, his heart going crazy. He succeeded in getting a hand free and lashed out wildly. The one holding his head pushed harder, grinding his face into the tiled floor. He started to yell with pain and panic, still thrashing the arm around, blindly trying to hit or grab anything he could feel. He thought he could hear them laughing at him, like it was all some kind of schoolboy bullying prank.

It went on like that for a few seconds more before someone finally hit or kicked him in the upper belly so hard the blow left him prone. After that all he could do was curl into a ball and gasp. He could hear Barsukov talking, then feel them pulling his clothes off. As he got his breath back they picked him up and actually threw him across the room. They gave a shout as they did it. He caught the side of the big bathtub with a hard blow to his hip, then slid over and into it. Immediately he staggered to his feet and tried to get out. But they were right in front of him, blocking him in. As he stepped forward one jabbed into his face. The punch looked almost casual, but Tom's vision went black, and when it came back he found he was sitting in the tub in a half-collapsed position, sucking in air, a terrible pain radiating out from his left cheekbone. He brought his hand up to his face and held it there, groaning.

One of them pressed buttons on a control panel and water started to gush from two taps. Tom looked down at himself. He was in his underwear with the water swirling around him. Above him Barsukov pushed between the men and sneered. 'You stupid little man,' he said. 'We can drown you in this. Did you think of that? They will just hold you under until you drown.' He was holding Tom's jacket in his hands, going through the pockets as he spoke. He found and pulled out the folded paperwork Tom had brought with him, the proof that they really did have the details of thirty-seven addresses belonging to Barsukov. His father had taken it from copied material he had at home, information put together from the 2003 inquiry which had involved surveillance on Maxim Sidurov and Barsukov himself. Other teams had already been working Barsukov, of course, had already compiled masses of material preparatory to getting financial orders against him. Nothing had come of that, but Grenser had taken copies of substantial parts of it.

Tom saw Barsukov looking at some of the paperwork now. He said a silent, useless prayer. It was all old material. How much of it would still be current? His safety in coming here rested on the risk that one of those addresses or details might mean something. If Barsukov had Sara, then, even though she might not be being held at one of those places, she might have been through one, leaving enough traces – in DNA and prints and suchlike – to make it too risky for Barsukov to ignore the threat of the police showing up there looking for her. Or maybe if there was just enough material there to convince him that Tom really wasn't alone, that there were police resources behind him – maybe that would be enough to make him cautious. Any police inquiry at all would be damaging for him. Even if he had nothing to do with kidnapping Sara, then that prospect might still make him think twice about doing anything further to Tom. That was the idea, anyway. Back at Tom's father's place it had seemed like a good idea.

And anyway, in a few minutes his father was going to make the call. He was outside, in the car, waiting. He would make the call. But how long would it then take for help to get up here? Ten minutes, fifteen? He had to stop them for that long. If they tried to kill or seriously injure him that was how long he had to fight for. In a kind of stunned daze, he watched Barsukov frown as he read through the paperwork, then push past the heavies and walk away, back to the door. He heard the door close behind him as he left, without saying anything, without giving any instructions.

Tom looked at the heavies and didn't know what to do, what to say. They were staring at him, not doing anything. The water crept up around his boxer shorts. It was freezing. He started to shiver. He sat like that for four minutes, panting, his head and heart pounding. He counted the minutes in his head. He calculated that if he didn't call within the next two minutes then the game was over, the gamble played out. His father would call his friends, the connections would be made. It would start. He tried not to think about what that might mean for Sara.

He didn't hear the door open again, but suddenly Barsukov was back, saying things in Russian. The water was switched off, towels were held out to him, two of the heavies left. Everyone seemed to relax a little. Barsukov stood in front of him, holding his phone out, still looking very angry. 'Not so stupid after all,' he said. 'You had better make your little call. Then we'll talk.'

48

When the call came in, Arisha was sitting in the top study with Freddie, watching it happen, watching her plan unfolding perfectly in front of her, feeling like she might pass out with relief. It had been two hours since Freddie had taken the call from Max and he had been frantic the entire time since then. He was sitting on the phone now, delivering instructions to a broker in Monaco in a desperate, cracking voice.

He hadn't been off the phone since Max had called. She had thought there would be some hesitation, that she might have to put some effort into persuading him, but he had swallowed it at once, not even querying the amount. Forty million sterling. It was – as she understood it – just about all he would be able to put together in the time frame available. It would clean him out. He wouldn't look cleaned out, of course. Not yet. He would still live in big houses, still have yachts in harbours all over the world, still enjoy all the trappings of this absurd life, with no concern whatsoever for the price of things. But only for a little while. Because all that was an illusion. None of it belonged to him. Aside from roughly forty million sterling – an amount barely enough to maintain the annual expenditure for even one of his London homes – the reality was everything in his life had belonged to Liz Wellbeck and was destined elsewhere.

And Freddie knew that. Because what had started all this

was that he had managed to get his hands on her will. He'd suspected for years that Liz had made some kind of provision for Sara. He assumed that the provision would be held in trust until Sara reached a certain age – probably twenty-one, which was now only two days away. But he had imagined, of course, that the sum would be negligible, that the rest of the staggering Wellbeck fortune would all come to him in due course. Then his contacts had got hold of the will and the mountain of other secret arrangements Liz had put in place to cut him off. He'd discovered that if Liz had her way, he wasn't going to get a penny. What he had owned when he married her – or what was left of it – was what he would get when she died.

Emergency meetings had followed. Lawyers were found who would examine the stolen documents. But all they told him was that Liz had done nothing more than what he had agreed to before their wedding in New York in 1985. He had signed the paperwork, he had taken advice. He had walked into it with his eyes open. There were no bankable loopholes. Liz had been scrupulous, as ever. She had paid a small fortune to top lawyers to make sure she kept control of her family assets, that *she* decided who it would all go to.

And what she had decided was that every cent of it would go to Sara, on her twenty-first birthday. That was assuming the cancer killed Liz before then. Which it had. Sort of. But even if that hadn't happened there would have been separate, secret trust provisions to ensure the same result. In that case, she would have retained enough to fund her palliative care in her own private clinic, but the rest would still have gone to Sara. All of it. On Friday this week.

So the money Freddie was desperately trying to transfer now was all he had, all that was actually his to dispose of. And twenty-five million of it was owed to Barsukov, according to Barsukov. That was why Dima was in on this, why his authority and resources were backing the entire enterprise. Freddie had always denied the debt to Dima, always laughed at the idea. There had been an arms deal somewhere in the past, something massive that had gone wrong owing to political issues in the corrupt African states they had been trying to sell to, back in the days before Arisha had sight of Freddie's accounts. Freddie's version was that he hadn't seen a penny of Dima's millions, he'd been a broker for Dima, nothing more. If it had all worked he would have taken a percentage. He spoke of it like it was a little game he'd played, and lost. Like a night at the casino. But Dima was exceptionally bitter about it, felt betrayed and tricked. The money Freddie had used as some kind of obscene bribery fund had been his. How Dima had got his hands on it wouldn't bear close scrutiny, she imagined, but Dima had nursed his resentment very carefully, because that was what he was like – he never forgot.

So Dima would take his cut of the forty million, plus the pleasure of cleaning Freddie out. But the rest was for Arisha and Max. Max thought he was getting Arisha as well, she realised – that was really why *he* was so committed – Arisha and a straight half of fifteen million. In fact, she planned to take ten of that. For her and Sasha alone. She wanted them all out of her life, Max and Freddie. She wanted rid of them. Max would have to live with five million as consolation. She would take her fifteen and make do. She would go back to Russia with Dima's protection. She would take her child and start over. Fifteen million was chicken feed compared to the sums she'd been handling for the Eatons, compared to what it cost to fund the life she'd been leading with Freddie, but there was a lot you could do with fifteen million in modern Russia. Russia wasn't what it had been when she'd left. She would thrive. She would be free of them all and thrive. Just herself and Sasha.

That was the plan.

And it was working. Max had called him, so Freddie now understood what was happening – Max held Sara. Freddie was doing exactly what was demanded, arranging the transfer of forty million sterling. She was sitting in the room with him watching every move, listening to every word, willing it on. The money was going to come to her, she was going to escape.

And then her mobile was buzzing, Dima's number on the screen. She stepped out to speak to him and listened in stunned silence to what he told her. He spoke in very rapid Russian: 'It's off. I'm cancelling. Can you hear me? Do you get that? It's all off.'

She managed to grunt something. She could feel her throat closing up on her.

'We'll release her,' he said. 'I'm on my way there now to do it. No option. I want you to call Max at once, give him the instruction. You understand?'

She couldn't reply.

'Do you understand, Arisha?'

'I … I don't … what …'

'No discussion. Call him and warn him. Then I want you there, in case he takes it badly. He will listen to you. I want you there urgently. You understand?'

'Yes. But …'

'After all, it was your idea. I always knew it wouldn't work.'

Then he was gone. She leaned against the wall and felt like she would collapse. Behind her she could hear Freddie shouting at someone, still trying to rake together the needed amount. She gasped and clutched at her throat. What had happened? What had gone wrong?

She thought she would suffocate. The implications came at her all at once, an avalanche of consequences. She would have to remain with this disgusting man, watch his perverse ideas about childhood and humanity corrupt her son. She would have to pretend, lie, act her way through this sickening charade for the rest of her life. She would go insane.

He must have heard her, because the next thing he was at the door, staring down at her. She had sunk to the floor by now and was sitting in a little heap.

'That won't fucking help,' he said harshly. 'We can't give in to this. Stand up, for Christ's sake. I need your assistance in here.' He didn't even help her up. Gone was the weepy dependency. There was money involved now, and everything came down to that, in the end. Everything he was. Take away the wealth and he was an utter failure. He was the most despicable man she had ever met. The father of her son. How could it be? How could Sasha be so perfect and still have this man's miserable genetic material inside him?

She pushed herself up the wall. 'I had a phone call,' she muttered, trying desperately to think what she should say. But then it just came out: 'I know where she is. I know where he's holding her.'

'What?' He took a sudden step backwards, like she'd hit him. 'You know? How do you know? Are you serious?'

She nodded. 'I made calls. I told you.' She had lied to him that she was trying to do just that – to find out where Max was. 'Now I know.'

For a moment they were staring at each other. She could see him working through it, his brain racing. He started to turn crimson. She thought he might have a heart attack, or explode with anger. His fists clenched and unclenched. He had to lean against the door frame. But her mind was blank. What was she doing? *She was crossing Dima.* For the first time ever, she was going against him, disobeying his instructions.

Because Dima was offering her nothing. But this way she was still in with a chance. Or because she hadn't even thought it through, more likely. Because she couldn't. Because the alternative was so desperate. So the words had just come out. And there was no getting them back in now. She had said it, told him, started it. Now she would have to follow through.

She slotted the responses into her brain, adjusted her breathing, let the role slip over her. She could tell as many lies as were necessary, she could look Freddie in the eye and tell the lies and know, for certain, that he would never guess. Because he was stupid. She would take this chance on him. Try it. Find another way to get what she needed from him. There would be a way. As long as there was money, there would be a way. There was nothing else she could do.

'Tell me where,' he hissed. 'Tell me where that fucking bastard Sidurov has her.'

'It's a storage facility. Out past Barking, on the Thames. I'll drive you. We can go now.'

'You're fucking damn right we can.' He stepped out of the room. His face was quivering. He was trying to keep it under control, trying not to let it out. She had never seen him so enraged. 'I'll see you down in the garage,' he said. 'Tell no one.'

'Where are you going?'

'To get my shotgun. I'll fucking kill him.'

49

Tom sat rigidly in the front seat of the Volvo, his eyes on the packed London streets crawling past through the tinted glass, but registering only basic details. The city, the glass and steel and concrete, the hordes of commuters flowing out of the tube stations, lost in their ordinary, normal lives, the clear blue sky, the roads gridlocked with traffic, the dirty short-cut streets east of Docklands before they were on the road out to Barking and Essex, following the line of the river, travelling east. His brain was racing, thoughts and fears flashing across it as in some broken cinema reel, everything confused and disorganised.

Barsukov was driving. No staff for this job, no involvement of anyone who might pose a risk later. That was how he had explained it. He had insisted Tom ride with him, or no deal. He had already had ample opportunity to kill Tom, of course, and hadn't done it. Nevertheless, Tom didn't like the arrangement – but since refusing would mean the end of the entire gamble, that was that. There were no witnesses, no weak links. Just Tom and Barsukov. And Tom's father, close behind. But Barsukov didn't know that. Barsukov thought he had cleared the boards, got himself and Tom into an armour-plated car and was now taking him to some unknown destination across the other side of London. What they had agreed would happen once they got there was that Barsukov would release Sara to Tom, then they would simply go their separate ways. That was the agreement.

'You have to understand the position I'm in,' Barsukov was saying. 'It's crucial that you understand it, understand who I am. This is a practical arrangement we have come to. The least said about it the better. You played your cards and you played them well. Maybe you were a bit lucky – who knows? It doesn't matter. The point is you outflanked me ...' He turned to Tom and gave him a nasty smile. 'Not many people manage that. But you did it. I congratulate you on that. What I was trying to do here was set something straight. You don't know the players involved, you don't know how filthy they are, how completely without honour. Maybe you're different. I know about you, about you and your father and family. I made it my business to know. You had a little trouble in the police, you had to leave that route. But that was down to the actions of people who had no honour. You probably understand that now. We Russians are not like that. We believe in honour. We believe when you give your word then that is something final and binding. You understand? And you gave me your word, you recall that?'

'Of course.'

'And I gave you mine. But I have to know that you understand the same thing by that. So I'll tell you how it works in Russia. I'll give you an example, in fact. Once I had the misfortune to have a business deal with a man who was in a very prominent position in the old Russia. This was back in the bad old days. You are too young to remember, no doubt, but in the early nineties, when it all started to fall apart, there was *only* honour. You had to do business on that basis because the law didn't exist. The law wasn't an option. No law, no police to enforce things. Just honour. Anyway, this man, because he was at the heart of power, he had lost his sense of honour and personal dignity and he decided to cross me. He thought he was safe. In fact, I shall tell you, his actual job was that he was a police investigator. He was entrusted with a position investigating crimes, very close to the chief prosecutor's office. A powerful man, in other words. He imagined he was untouchable, because all power corrupts. We know that. We see it every day, in every country. So he crossed me and I lost the equivalent of several million euros. Not a large sum, but that's not the point. It was an issue of principle. Now, I am – I assure you – as respectful and wary of authority as the next person. I know what these people can do to you. They have the power to fuck up lives, destroy businesses. It's still the same in Russia. That hasn't changed. But how are we to react in the face of this kind of abuse of power? What are we to do? My approach has always been to stick to principles. So I took this man. I took him myself, in a car, just like this, like I am doing with you now. With no witnesses, no one who might later turn on me. I took him and I myself saw to it that he was made an example of. I did this because I believe that honour is paramount. Without it nothing can function properly. The deal I had with this man was for the sale of several million fridges – crappy communist bloc junk, but there existed an opportunity, so I took it. To make sure that the connection was made I arranged that this man was put inside one of these fridges, with the door secured. Then they left him there. It was cold, and there was no air supply. They told me it took fifteen hours before he was dead. I wasn't there for that, obviously. I don't mind confessing that. I am not good at that sort of thing. I feel sick when I see death, when I watch it, but if it has to be done, it has to be done. You understand?'

'Perfectly. You have my word, believe me.' His eyes went to the wing mirror, but his father wasn't stupid. Tom couldn't see him there, tagging along behind, obvious. But Barsukov had taken no evasives, hadn't done anything sneaky, so surely he was there, somewhere.

'Good,' Barsukov said, giving that smile again. 'Because I know about your boy, your little kid. I've seen him, in fact. He looked like a good kid. A little weak, perhaps ...'

'I told you, you have my word.'

'Good. I'm glad about that. But I should add just one more thing – I have witnesses, as many witnesses as I could need. They will say, to the police, to a court, to whoever it is necessary to say it to, they will say exactly the same thing as me about what happened here: you came to me saying you were police and I believed you. I didn't have a clue you were ex-police, that you were corrupt, kicked out of the police for corruption, a man with no credibility at all as a witness. You told me you had reason to believe a woman was being held on premises owned by one of my interests. You asked for my help to go there and gain entry and check. I gave that help as a matter of urgency, because I'm a good citizen, with a spotless record, because I love this country and its police. Indeed, I have many, many friends in the police and the judicial system, friends higher and more powerful than you could imagine. Even the man who is there, with her, will say that I was completely ignorant of his reckless actions. I know this for certain ...'

'I get the picture ...'

'I'm glad. I'm glad we understand each other. This business was a mistake. We can rectify it, turn our backs on it and walk away. That's what we'll do.'

'That's what I want to do. That's all I want to do. All I want is Sara Eaton. The rest doesn't interest me. I have no friends at all in high places.'

'You have your father, though. I know about him. I know who he is. You keep looking in the mirror. You are worried about us being followed, perhaps? Don't be. I've taken pre-cautions.'

Tom stared at him. The nasty smile slipped on to Barsukov's face. 'Just in case,' he added. 'It's what I always do. So don't worry. We will be perfectly alone. Your life is in my hands. But ...' He paused while he manouevred round a parked truck. Tom squirmed in his seat, took a deeper lungful of air. 'But you have my word,' Barsukov continued. 'So please don't worry. Now – isn't it time for you to make your call?'

John felt relatively relaxed, he thought, considering all that was going on. He wasn't relaxed, of course – far from it – he was existing on a kind of adrenalin overdose, all his senses tuned up, all his muscles tight and ready. Maybe relaxed was the wrong term, then. He was in control. Or felt relatively in control. He was eight cars behind his son and Barsukov, confident enough to let them get well ahead every now and then, and then still be sure of catching up. Barsukov had made some quick turns, taken some odd routes, but only to avoid traffic, John thought. He had satnav, presumably, and was doing what it told him to do. John had easily been able to keep up. And he knew the final destination. At least, Tom had told him what Barsukov had told him was the final destination. Not a precise address, but a business description, and the area. *A container storage facility near Creekmouth* was what he had said. John wasn't relying on that. That could be a trick. But they were headed in that direction, towards an industrial area he vaguely knew, just south of Barking. So there was no need to panic. He kept telling himself that.

Barsukov had basically followed the A13 out of the city, a living history tour of modern destruction and development. John could remember clearly back to the early eighties when the entire East End had been a dirty slum with nasty immigration issues. He wasn't sure he hadn't preferred it then. It had been run-down, crime-ridden, shabby England in all its cheap brown colours, with its drab shops and tatty products – but there had been the last remains within that, in the communities that hung on there, of something older, some surer, pre-war identity that was now utterly vanished. New Docklands looked like a science-fiction fortress slung together overnight from glass and steel cladding. From a distance, it was shiny and impressive, but up close there was something alien about it, like it had skipped history, just suddenly appeared there overnight. If it was a monument to something then it wasn't to renewal, he thought. More like the power of raw cash – new cash. Which was always coming and going these days. These days nothing was certain. In thirty, fifty years those offices could easily be empty, unneeded, the cash gone elsewhere – then they would pull it all down again.

They had passed the turn for the Olympic Park – the roof of the new stadium clearly visible off to the right, construction still feverish with only a couple of months to go – then London City airport, over the North Circular and down towards Creekmouth and areas east of the city where the job was only half done – the old slums were nearly all levelled, but so far only replaced by temporary structures. Here they were caught between the old London and the new; progress hadn't quite arrived, but the past was already flattened.

The route was exactly the one John thought they would take. The muddy little river – the Roding – that came around Barking was off to the right somewhere. John caught glimpses of the tall Roding flood defence gates, then a sewage works in among the mess of scrappy light-industrial developments, the prefabs and sheds and warehouse blocks, the auto parts businesses and VW and Volvo dealerships. It was the usual sprawl of ugly functional land, the same now all the way up to Dagenham and Tilbury, all along the borders of the river, where only a century ago the sky would have bristled with the masts of shipping. There was not a single building that might claim to be beautiful. Everything looked thrown up and neglected, temporary. There were half-finished building sites all over, functional mesh fences ringing low-rise industrial blocks slung together from corrugated iron, guard dog signs – the whole area looked like a wasteland, though hardly a foot of space was in fact wasted. Even the river itself, when he caught a glimpse of it, looked forgotten and forlorn – a big, black, polluted mudflat. He could smell the low-tide stench.

Ahead of him he saw Barsukov slow to manoeuvre past a truck, then he had to slow himself to answer his mobile. It was Tom, sticking to their plan. John spoke quietly to him, tried to sound reassuring. 'I have you in sight,' he said. 'No problems.'

'No problems here,' Tom said. He sounded worried, though. 'Next call in twenty-five minutes. We're almost there.'

Then he was gone. John placed the phone on the passenger seat and eased round the truck. It was almost blocking the narrow road, so he had to mount the kerb. As he came off he no longer had Barsukov's car in sight, but that didn't worry him too much. He could see there was a choice of two turn-offs within range. They must be very close to the destination now. He drove slowly past the first turn-off, peering past a flat-roofed Indian restaurant that must have been a choice location for a relaxing meal, then turned back to the road ahead just as a big dark blue Mercedes came steaming past him. It slowed as if turning off, into the yard of a building supplies firm, and John felt his heart skip a beat.

It had only half-turned across the road, so his way was blocked. He hit the horn, but that produced no response.

Why had it stopped? There was no obvious obstruction in front of it. He horned it again, trying to peer round it. Then the passenger door opened and a big guy in a smart suit got out. He walked casually over. John wound his window down. The man was speaking to him, holding his hands up as if to advise John to be calm. John shouted at him, telling him to fucking move. He couldn't understand a word the man was saying. But still the Merc wasn't budging. Was it Russian the guy was speaking?

He wound the window up and put the car into reverse. But already there was someone behind him. He almost backed into them – a truck. He was horning the guy as well. John banged his fists off the steering wheel. The man from the car was right by his passenger door now. At the instant John thought to lock it, right when his finger was on the button, the man opened the door, picked his mobile off the seat and leaned his head in. 'Take it easy, mate,' he said, in a very thick accent. 'Take it easy. OK?'

'Put my fucking phone down,' John yelled. 'What the fuck do you think you're doing?'

The man stepped back, looking at the phone. He was trying to get the back off it, John thought.

Suddenly he realised what was happening. He got out at once and ran round the car. The man saw him and started backing off, hands in the air. The driver of the truck behind was still leaning on the horn, the Mercedes was still stuck across the road. John started yelling at the man, demanding his phone. It registered how big the guy was just as he got up to him. By then he was already pulling his arm back to thump him. He didn't get that far. The man dropped the phone to the ground, breaking it into pieces, then held both hands up in a submissive gesture. 'Sorry. Sorry,' he was saying. 'Just a little misunderstanding. Sorry.' John picked up the phone pieces, fuming. He knew exactly what had happened. He looked over the top of the Merc and felt his heart go into overdrive. There was definitely no sign of Barsukov now.

50

The place Barsukov turned into must have been right on the river, Tom calculated. As they drove past the outlet for Barking Creek, he kept catching glimpses of grey water and the mudflats on the far bank. There was a nine-foot security fence at the front, electrified along the top, according to warning signs, twisted through with razor wire, with CCTV cameras prominently displayed. Beyond it there were low brick buildings and, over the top of them, Tom could see rows and rows of rusting, used shipping containers, stacked on top of each other, as in a dockyard, sometimes into structures five or six high, the names of shipping lines and export companies still partially visible in big letters on their sides. They were painted a variety of dull colours – off-white, yellow, black, blue – making a chequerboard of random patterns where there were groups stacked closely together. The predominant impression, though, was of a chaotic dump of rust-red, forty-foot-long metal containers piled into an area about the size of two football fields, stacked tightly on top of each other, or side by side in rows and blocks, so high that the whole thing was like a massive, irregular fortress. There were a couple of cranes standing over the biggest stacks, and high floodlight pylons. A sign at the entrance said the place housed EXPRO CONTAINER STORAGE – one of the addresses on the list Barsukov had taken from him. There didn't seem to be any sign of life within the compound – no movement, no people.

Barsukov had some kind of remote to open the gates. As they slid back and the Volvo pulled alongside a security cabin, a private security guard in a creased brown uniform appeared from somewhere. Tom kept his eyes moving, trying to take in as much as he could. The guard came to the driver's-side window. Barsukov and he had a short exchange in Russian, then Barsukov drove past the admin buildings and into a wide concrete yard, overgrown with weeds. The rows of containers started at the edges of the yard, towering corridors of metal with giant forklifts and mobile cranes parked haphazardly at intervals. Tom counted twenty-five rows of containers stretching off towards the river. 'I told them to take a break,' Barsukov said as he cut the engine. 'We don't want any witnesses. They're used to that. But they'll be back. We have about half an hour.'

Tom nodded nervously and glanced back to the gates. He would have preferred them to have stayed, maybe. Barsukov seemed to have left the gates open, though. 'This is all storage?' Tom asked, clearing his voice. 'That's what this place is?'

'The Olympics have generated a lot of storage opportunities. We have nearly five hundred containers here. It's a little sideline. I would get rid of it, but the privacy is useful. You could keep anyone in here, lost in there ...' He pointed to the maze of stacked containers. 'No one can see or hear. Sometimes that is useful. You understand?'

Tom looked away. 'She's here?' he asked. 'Sara is here?'

Barsukov smiled. 'Tell me, Lomax, how did you know to come to me? Not a lucky guess, I assume?'

Tom swallowed. He'd thought already of a response to that, though. 'Alex Renton told me.'

Barsukov frowned.

'He works for Glynn Powell.'

'Ah. Of course. Small-time people. Little people. No standards. I have very few dealings with this man Powell.' He paused. 'But you don't expect me to believe that Renton just gave you my name?'

'He had to be persuaded,' Tom said, without looking at him.

Barsukov laughed, then exited the car. Tom got out on his side and stood there, scanning the place, watching out for anyone who might appear from between the rows of containers. Behind them he saw two men walk out of the gates. The security guards. But still the gates were left open. Barsukov had turned the car in the yard so that it was pointing back at the gates. He was leaving the gates open so he could get out fast, Tom thought.

Barsukov walked round to him. 'You are a poor liar,' he said, standing right in front of him, too close. 'I very much doubt *persuading* is one of your strengths. But you have done well in this. You persuaded *me*. When all this is over you should come back to me. I could use your abilities.' Another one of those nasty little smiles. 'I mean that. That is an offer you should not refuse.'

Tom took a step back. 'When all this over?' he said. 'Let's keep our focus on that right now. What happens now? Is the idea that we just find Sara and I walk off with her?'

'You don't trust me?' Barsukov pointed back to the gates. 'You can leave. The gates are open.' He looked around, squinting into the sunlight, then shaded his eyes and stared at the rows of containers. 'Otherwise you can follow,' he said. He started to walk. 'Let's get it over with.' Tom went after him. He could feel the skin prickling at the back of his neck. 'Like I said, I know about you,' Barsukov called over his shoulder. 'I had some research carried out, on both you and your father. That was why I wanted to meet you, a week ago.'

'Why?'

'Elizabeth Wellbeck was trying to make contact with your father. That concerned me, because it touched on another matter. But you don't need to know about that. Not now. Because of that, however, I wouldn't have needed your paperwork to be convinced that this should be stopped. I just needed to know your father was with you. That's what I checked this morning. He was in a car outside my apartment. Easy to spot.'

Tom tried to work out what that might mean for the back-up plan, but Barsukov wasn't giving him time to think. 'I calculated that his connections might still be effective enough to make the increased risk not worth my while,' he said. 'So it was a simple choice for me. The money involved is negligible. My interest was always in revenge, not the money.'

'Revenge? On Sara?' Barsukov had entered one of the long canyons of stacked containers now. They were in shadow, the sun cut from view. Barsukov was walking quickly, Tom still a few paces behind him. The corridor was wide, big enough to turn a forklift in, but the space still felt claustrophobic, the huge metal structures leaning in on them. Their footsteps and voices were dampened. Tom saw things scurrying away in the spaces between the stacks.

'Rats,' Barsukov said. 'The place is infested.' He stopped, looking around as if he were lost.

'Revenge on who?' Tom asked again. 'What has Sara done to you?'

'I couldn't care less about Sara Eaton,' Barsukov said. He started walking again. 'It's her father I despise. This would have ruined him, financially. That would be nice, but not nice enough, not once you changed the equation. So I can wait. I'm very patient, where revenge is concerned. I never forget.'

They passed a big forklift and kept going. At the end of

the row, about four hundred yards away, Tom could see the river glinting in the sunlight. But on the broken concrete surface between the walls of containers it was cold. He was still shivering. It hadn't completely stopped since he had got out of Barsukov's bathtub. 'Where are we going?' he asked. He sounded frightened, tried to change his tone. 'Where is she? Are you sure she's here?'

Barsukov made an impatient noise. 'You think I brought you here to kill you? I gave you my word – remember? Of course she's here.'

He turned suddenly into a much narrower corridor between two very tall stacks of containers. Tom glanced up – they were five or six high, reaching at least fifty feet into the air.

'Come on,' Barsukov shouted to him. 'Be quick.' He was in front of a container, holding a metal ladder that was leaning against it.

'We go up there?' Tom asked.

But Barsukov was already climbing.

Tom went to the bottom of the ladder and looked up. Barsukov was going quickly, the ladder bouncing and shaking with his weight. It was an ordinary two-stage aluminium ladder and it went straight up the side of two containers. When Barsukov got to the top he leaned over and shouted for Tom to follow. Tom hesitated, then started up. There wasn't much choice. At the top he crawled on to the roof of the container and stood up. There was no rail, no protection from the drop. Barsukov was already walking away.

They had come out on to a platform created by the roofs of multiple rows of containers, all placed together and surrounded by higher stacks. Barsukov was headed for another ladder, lying on the roof of the farthest part of the platform. As he crossed the containers his footsteps made a booming sound in the cavities below. 'A good warning system,' he said. 'They will be able to hear us coming.' There were narrow gaps between the containers – two feet at most – which he simply jumped across. He picked the ladder up and placed it against the side of another container, then started to climb. He knew where he was going. Tom followed more quickly this time. Once on the roof of the next level they walked to the far end of that container and then down another ladder, taking them back to the first level, but now they were completely surrounded by containers, completely cut off from the access route they had used to get here, with only a square of sky visible above. It reminded him of when he had been little and he and his brother had played in a giant haystack on a cousin's farm. They had moved rectangular bales into walls and towers to make a secluded fortress in the middle. Just like this. But this was a more sinister attempt at secrecy.

Barsukov was already at the other side, positioning another ladder. This led up to a gap between the walls of higher stacks of containers, ending in another enclosed platform, one level higher. There were containers stacked very high around this – two further levels on each side, but on the farthest side there was a wide gap between the platform and the wall of containers opposite– at least two yards wide. To get across to the farther containers you would need some kind of bridge or gangplank. These containers were facing the platform end-on, their doors all bolted. Barsukov stood right on the edge of the drop, facing them. Tom followed him more cautiously and peered over. There was a drop down to an area of ground, the height of three containers, about thirty-five feet. Enough to break your neck if you were unlucky, and he knew how that could happen. He could see rats crawling around down there. Maybe they'd fallen and got stuck. 'So where is she?' he demanded, out of breath. He was very tense now.

Barsukov pointed up, to a container across the other side of the gap, a level higher than them. 'She's up there,' he said.

In a fucking shipping container, Tom thought. His heart was very loud now. She would be terrified. 'You'd better not have hurt her,' he said.

Barsukov ignored him, started to shout up. Tom caught a man's name – 'Max' – but the rest was in Russian again.

'You didn't call him first?' Tom asked. 'He doesn't know you're doing this?'

'Obviously I do not have direct contact. There are no direct links between myself and this man. But someone else has called. He knows I'm coming.'

Tom heard bolts sliding, then the door of the container cracked open. There was a moment's pause before it swung back on its hinges, banging off the front of the container adjacent. A man stepped into view, his legs at a level twelve feet above Tom's head, so Tom could see nothing inside the container itself but a section of roof. The man may have been the man he had seen on the island, or may not have. He was certainly the man from his father's photo. The scar was obvious. So was the gun, a short machine pistol with a magazine jutting from it. He looked at Tom and Barsukov, the gun pointed down at them. He looked puzzled, wary, angry. He started to speak back to Barsukov, who was already talking to him very fast, all in Russian. Tom couldn't understand a word of it, but it didn't look like the two were in agreement. It didn't look like things were going to be as easy as Barsukov had thought.

51

All the way across town Arisha was having doubts. She could remember holding Sara Eaton when she was too small to even talk, could remember her in her arms, remember the smell of her baby hair and skin. In a way she had loved her then. There had been hardly any contact since – at least, not contact like that – but she knew the person Sara had grown up to be. There was nothing wrong with her, nothing spiteful, evil or malicious. She had managed to turn out completely different to Liz Wellbeck and Freddie Eaton. She didn't resemble them at all. Whenever Arisha came across her, she was always polite, friendly, generous, and all that despite the rumours about Arisha and Freddie, which she must know of, since everyone else did.

Sara didn't know about Sasha, of course – they had been extremely careful to keep Sasha a secret while Liz was still alive. That was one of the reasons she suspected Freddie had killed Liz, or set it up. She wasn't sure – and she had played no part in that – but she had seen paperwork which made her suspicious. Freddie wanted Sasha out in the open, wanted everyone to know about him, wanted him 'legitimised'. And Liz wasn't dying to schedule, wasn't rotting away as quickly as her doctors had predicted. It was possible that Freddie would do that – pay the doctors to overdose her. He was capable of it. And the PA too – Liz's ex-assistant? Had Freddie had something to do with that? Everything had happened so quickly over the last few days she had lost control of it. Now she didn't know what was going on.

But even if Sara knew about Sasha, Arisha had no reason to think she would behave any differently. Her character was due to the nanny, maybe – Felice Cotte. She had been a good mother, the real mother to Sara when she was a child. That was the way it always was in rich families – it couldn't be avoided – there was always paid help to bring up the children, to replace the missing maternal love. It was happening now with Sasha. At this moment he was with a young American woman they had employed to care for him. She had two others who helped her, who she used on the basis of a rota they drew up. Arisha had very little to do with it. How often did she actually spend time with Sasha, each week, or each day? It wasn't more than two hours a day, normally, a little longer at weekends. It wasn't enough, she knew that. She had always known that, always felt it in her heart. She was doing no better for him than her mother had done for her, that odious woman. And that was because of the money, because Freddie needed her the whole time to manage his affairs. The money was the root of all this evil, that was for sure.

Could she do without it? Could she change her mind, turn her back on it? Why shouldn't she? This hadn't been her plan. *Her* idea – kicking off from Freddie's twisted plans – had been to spoil his intentions, to turn them against him. She had gone to Dima with information about Freddie's monstrous plot and with a really simple quick-hit idea – take Sara, hold her harmlessly on a boat off the island for a few hours, get Freddie to pay for her. Then release her. Dima had gone along with that because he was owed, because he hated Freddie. There had never been an intention to hurt Sara.

What had happened on that island? Stupid fucking Max, with his guns. He couldn't be trusted. The war had savaged him, done something to his brain as well as his balls. He had screwed it up. She still didn't know how or why. She should have stopped it then. Dima had wanted to, when she visited him. But what would have happened to Sara if she had stopped it then? In a way everything she had done was to protect Sara. Sara had no idea who her worst enemy was. It was the same now. What was going to happen when Freddie went in with his shotgun? Would he kill Dima? Where would that leave her?

She was driving as she fretted about it all, the sweat pouring out of her, soaking her back and under her arms. Just her and Freddie in the car. He was ranting the whole way, but she couldn't hear it. Her thoughts were too fearful, she had no space for him. And they were here now. Here already. The time for choosing was past. She could see the sign – EXPRO CONTAINER STORAGE – hear Freddie demanding if this was the place. The gates were open, no one in sight. Dima would already be here. He had left the gates open for her. She slowed down in front of them and looked in, saw his car parked farther into the yard there, facing her. But no Dima. No sign of him.

'This is it,' she said. 'This is the place.'

'You wait here,' he said, through gritted teeth. 'Wait here until I come back.'

She nodded frantically. Should she wish him luck or something? Should that be part of the act? It didn't matter, because he was already getting out, already popping the boot, taking out the gun. It wasn't even in a bag. He was a complete idiot. Crossing the road in full view with a gun.

An idiot, but not incapable of harm. He had been a soldier

at some point, a paratrooper, he'd even been given a medal for doing something brutal, somewhere – possibly in the Falklands. He wouldn't speak about it. But he knew how to shoot. He might kill Dima. Dima would be unarmed. Freddie was an idiot, but he was cunning. The way he had handled the police, to get them off Sara – that had been very assured. As if he had been concerned only for Sara's safety. She couldn't assume Dima and Max could handle him. It might be Freddie who walked out alive.

She watched him run into the yard. Wait for him? She should just drive off, leave them all to it. But she couldn't. Freddie she could ignore, and Max. But Sara? Could she do this to Sara? She didn't want to. *She didn't want to.* She was realising that only now. It wasn't the plan. And Dima – she would never get away from him. To cross him was insane. She took her phone out, her hands trembling. She could see Freddie trying to open the doors to Dima's car. She assumed it was Dima's car. She got his number up. She would have to warn him. She couldn't let it happen like this. Warn him, then drive off. Get Sasha, get to the airport. Get away while it happened. Back to Russia without any of their money. She had some savings, her own money. That would have to do. She had to protect Sasha, get away from all this, start again. She didn't want these people coming between them.

She started the engine. Freddie was running into the place now, disappearing into the rows of containers. It would take him a while. The place was massive. Maybe he would never find them. But she couldn't take the chance. Dima would find her, wherever she was in the world, eventually he would find her. If she crossed him and he lived, he would get her. Get her, get Sasha. So she had to call him, warn him now. Tell him – lie to him – that Freddie knew her role, that he had monitored her phones, that he knew everything, that she had fled in fear of him, that he was coming here to kill right now. Warn him and then get out.

52

When the banging started Sara was concentrating on how she could get the shackle off her ankle. The crocodile clip was still lying there, just past the metal bench, where he'd kicked it. She couldn't reach it now, so she had to get the shackle off instead. She had begged through tears to use a toilet, to see if that would do it. But that only led to him giving her a bucket and some paper, and turning his back. 'I do the same,' he said. 'Now's not the time for delicacy.'

Her tears bothered him, though, made him say reassuring things, make promises, give her more food, or water. She had some leverage because he didn't want noise, she thought. Maybe no one could hear from outside, as he claimed – though she had noticed that the entire floor of the container was covered with thick rubberised matting, presumably to muffle any sound – but the noise still disturbed him. When he couldn't stop her he didn't start screaming at her or lashing out, he just sat at the bench with his head in his hands.

Unfortunately, he hadn't used his mobile yet. She assumed he would have to, at some point, that he would speak in Russian and she would understand. Unless he went outside to speak. He hadn't been out at all yet. If he went out it wouldn't help her much – the shackle chain was so short she couldn't even reach as far as the container walls – but she still hoped he would go, leave her alone for a moment to think clearly.

He was on his feet as soon as the banging started. She didn't know what it was, but he obviously did. He produced a gun from behind the bench and pulled the slide back, cocking it. It looked like the same sort of thing he had been holding back on the island when she had shot his hand. He was using the other hand now. He didn't point it at her. Instead, he padded to the far end of the container and started sliding the bolts across the door. Now she could hear someone shouting something outside. The door swung open and light flooded in. She had to squint. She heard him talking, then saw him moving forward, into the door frame. Her eyes started to adjust, but all she could see outside was the sides of more shipping containers, like the one she was in. She kept perfectly still, listening hard.

Someone was saying things to him in Russian, talking very loudly. Her head was clearer now and she got some of it – something about problems and a change of plan. When he replied she realised he was looking down, speaking to someone below him. Their container must be on top of something, raised off the ground. She wondered how he had got her up here. He would have needed help, she thought. She had been out cold, could recall nothing of the journey.

She understood all of his reply, perfectly. 'Arisha has to call,' he said. 'We stay here until she calls.'

Vostrikova, he meant. What did she have to do with him? But that was right, she thought – she had seen him with her at some point.

'Arisha told me she would call you,' the other voice said, still in Russian. 'She should already have called…'

'She hasn't called. I've heard nothing…'

'You take your instructions from me, not her…'

'Everything I've done on this I've had the instructions

from her. You know that. I need to know what she thinks. This isn't right ...'

'It's a waste of time, Max. Do as I say. It's no longer worth the risk ...'

'Why? Because of *him*?'

'Not just him. You don't know the detail. It's not worth the risk to my interests. It's too risky now. That's my decision, my judgement ...'

'So you've done some deal with him. I understand that. But where does that leave me? I need to know the details. Where does it leave Arisha? Does she know anything about this?'

'She knows everything. I told you – she will be here soon. But I told her to call you also. Was your phone off? Maybe the reception in there is bad. Check. See if she has called you ...'

'No one has called. And I don't like it. What does your deal say about Arisha and me?'

'Nothing. There's no need. The deal is simple. We just call it off and we all walk away ...'

'Just like that? But she has seen me. She can identify me. And now *he* has seen me too. You should not have brought him here.'

Who were they referring to? she wondered.

'He has seen me as well,' the other said. 'It doesn't matter. He knows the situation. He knows what will happen. He can be trusted ...'

'But you made no deal with *her*. Can *she* be trusted? I don't think so. This is sloppy, Dimitri Alexandrovich, sloppy and unusual. It's not how I would handle it ...'

'It doesn't matter how you would handle it. You are being impertinent ...'

'I'm sorry. But I can't do it. I need to hear from Arisha. Ring her. Tell her that ...'

'You ring her.'

'I have my hands full …'

Suddenly the argument was interrupted by another voice, shouting in English. 'Is Sara in there? I want to see her. This goes no farther unless I see her. Right now.' Tom. It was Tom. She felt her heart jump with sudden hope, some of the argument between the other two now making sense. Now she knew who they had been talking about. She was on the point of shouting to him, but just caught herself. The man – Max – was looking back at her.

'I want to see her,' Tom shouted again. 'If you've hurt her in any way this is all off …'

'You see,' Max said in Russian. 'You think you can trust him? He will see her and go crazy …'

'She is not hurt, though,' the other man said – the one Max had called Dimitri Alexandrovich.

'She is cut,' Max replied calmly. 'Where I took out the transmitter … there is blood on her …'

'It's nothing. Let him come up and see her …'

'No one comes up here until I've heard from Arisha …'

'Why? Don't be an idiot, Max. What are you going to do if you think I'm wrong? Shoot everyone? Don't be fucking mad …'

'No one comes up here. Contact Arisha. If I hear it from her – that we are safe, both of us – then I will do what you want. I'm sorry, Dimitri Alexandrovich. I have been with you many years, but this is different. I am exposed here …'

'You have my word …'

'And I know your word is good. But I can't abandon Arisha. Call her …'

'I'm walking,' Tom shouted. 'I'm going back. It's off. I don't like it …'

'No, wait!' It was the one called Dimitri, that she couldn't see, who replied. 'Wait a moment. Everything will be cool.

Wait! Maxim Fedorovich, get her to shout or something. Get her to shout to him that she is OK ...'

Max turned back to her and spoke in English; 'Shout that you are OK. Now.'

She shrunk back and curled into a ball. It was a gamble. But it worked – he didn't ask again.

'Or bring her forward so he can see her,' Dimitri yelled. 'Do that, then I'll call Arisha. She should be here soon anyway. Bring her forward so he waits until she gets here. Please.'

'I can stop him leaving. I can make sure he waits.'

'Not without shooting him, or coming down, so don't be stupid. Just show him the fucking girl, then we'll get Arisha here.'

Max turned back suddenly, away from the door, and strode over to her, one hand digging in his pocket. He looked very nervous now. He got a key out and his hand was shaking badly. 'Any fucking around and I will kill you,' he whispered. 'You understand?'

She nodded her head frantically, like a terrified little useless girl, but her heart was racing, her mind supercharged with adrenalin. Now she would be able to act. The shackle was coming off. She watched him unlock it with difficulty, then her foot was out. There was a moment when she thought she might kick him right then, take her chances, but the gun was in her belly immediately and he was dragging her roughly to her feet. He marched her very quickly to the front – before she could even think about it – and then held her a little back from the entrance. She heard someone gasp outside, looked down, saw two men there, about ten to fifteen feet away, below her – Tom and someone she didn't know. Tom was speaking to her, his face etched with distress as he looked at her. Then he was screaming at the other man, the one beside him.

'She is completely unhurt,' Max shouted down, in English.

'She is alive and well ...' She realised from his stance and his grip on her that he was going to march her back, straight away, shackle her again. She couldn't let that happen. But right at that moment the one called Dimitri – a short, squat, older man – pulled a mobile from a pocket and held it up. 'It's Arisha, Max,' he shouted with obvious relief. 'She's calling now. Wait!'

He put the phone to his ear and started to speak to her in Russian, then shut up suddenly. At exactly the same time Sara heard the banging again, the same banging they had heard from inside. She knew now it must be the noise made by someone walking across the tops of the hollow containers. It meant someone was coming, someone else.

'Who is coming?' Max shouted. She could feel his body tightening with fear. 'Who is it? Is that Arisha? Who is it?'

But Dimitri had closed the phone, his face suddenly pale. He started to walk quickly back to the edge of the area he was standing on. Tom was shouting some questions now, and Max had tightened his grip on Sara's shoulder so that his splinted fingers were digging into her, hurting. Tom was asking her if she was OK, Dimitri was shouting something she couldn't catch, in Russian. They were about ten feet below her and on the other side of a six-foot gap between stacked shipping containers. But the containers they were standing on, close against each other to make a kind of platform, were themselves piled on others and surrounded by even higher piles of the rusting metal boxes. Dimitri ran to the farthest edge of the platform, where there was a space at their level and the top of a ladder showing, but even as he got there a figure appeared to the side of them all, surprising everybody. He hadn't come from the ladder Dimitri was heading for – he was on the roof of one of the higher containers. She looked up in shock.

It was her father, with a gun. He shouted down at them all and pointed the gun at the one called Dimitri. She thought he was going to just shoot him. There was a split second of stillness, everyone waiting for the shot, then Max spun round to bring his gun up. Dimitri shouted a warning. Tom started screaming something, his hands in the air. Max shifted his grip and pulled her brutally in front of him, holding the gun to her head. His damaged arm was round her neck now.

53

The gun was a shotgun, pointed at Barsukov. But Barsukov didn't look frightened. Tom was right behind him. Tom *was* frightened. He stepped sideways, quickly, out of the line of fire.

'Who is that?' the man shouted. 'Is that Lomax, the idiot who was with her?'

'He's police, Freddie,' Barsukov said quickly, calmly.

To the side of Tom he heard Sara yelling, speaking for the first time since the man had dragged her forward. 'Don't kill anyone, Daddy. They're going to free me. Don't shoot.'

Barsukov started to laugh. Tom edged farther away from him. The man was Freddie Eaton, he realised.

'You fucking double-crossing fuckers!' Eaton shouted in crisp Etonian. 'Trying to rip me off! Fucking Russian scum!' He looked like he was drunk, but the gun was real, and was held perfectly steady. Two barrels, one on top of the other. Barsukov held his hands up, still laughing. Sara shouted something else, something about it all being under control.

'I'm not police,' Tom shouted up to him. 'I came here to free your daughter ...'

Barsukov laughed again. 'He doesn't want her free,' he said, loud enough for Sara to hear. 'He paid us to kill her. That's how all this started – he paid Maxim to kill his daughter. Arranged it through Arisha.'

There was a terrible silence. Eaton had his eyes on Barsukov, the gun held steady. 'Shut the fuck up,' he said.

'He has a son,' Barsukov said. 'He has a son with Arisha. So you're in the way, Sara Eaton. On Friday every penny of your mother's fortune goes to you – didn't you know that? Freddie would have nothing left, so he paid Max to kill you. If you're dead it all comes to him.'

Tom looked up at the open container. Sara was still standing in front of Sidurov, held there with a gun against her head. Her face was working, the muscles moving fast, clamping her jaw. She looked stunned. She'd heard it all.

'We thought we would just take a little cash off him instead,' Barsukov said, speaking to Sara, but looking up at Eaton. 'That was Arisha's idea.'

That seemed to have an impact. Eaton started to turn crimson.

'You didn't know that, Freddie?' Barsukov went on. 'Arisha came to me with your twisted idea – to kidnap and kill your own daughter. She suggested we twist it a little ourselves. Kidnap her, tell you we had her but wouldn't kill her unless you paid us a little sweetener ...'

'You fucking Russian bastard,' Eaton interrupted. 'I told you I would pay you your stupid money. I told you I would pay you ...'

'But that's not what I wanted. I wanted to rectify an injustice. We thought we would have you pay what was yours, *everything* that was yours, then simply release Miss Eaton. She would inherit and you would be fucked. That was what I wanted, Freddie. Nice scheme, eh? You have to admit it's nice.' He looked over at Sara. 'We didn't want to hurt you,' he said. 'In fact, if it hadn't been for our little kidnap he'd have killed you already ...'

'Shut up, Barsukov!' Eaton shouted. 'Shut up!'

'Don't be stupid, Eaton. Put the gun down. We've all had our fun, but it's over now. This story between us will have to continue elsewhere. You're not going to start killing everybody here. That's not you. Besides, you only have two shots.'

'Two is enough. One for you …'

'And one for her?' Barsukov interjected, then laughed again.

Sidurov shouted something in Russian, but Barsukov didn't reply.

'*You* do what we agreed you would do,' Eaton yelled at Sidurov, glancing in his direction. 'You carry it out as we agreed and we will all walk away.'

'But what about him?' Barsukov asked, pointing at Tom. 'You'd have to kill him as well now.'

'Daddy?' Sara said, her voice tiny. 'Daddy. What is going on? What are you telling him to do?'

'Shut up, Sara,' Eaton said, not even glancing at her.

'He wants you dead,' Barsukov said. 'He's telling Max to kill you, to do what he's already paid him to do. Don't you understand that? Aren't you listening? That's what this is all about. He paid us to kill you.'

'Daddy? Tell me it's not true …'

'I'm not your father,' Eaton snapped at her, brutally. But his eyes and the gun never left Barsukov. 'Shut her up, Sidurov,' he yelled. 'Do what you were paid to do!'

Tom looked up at Sara. She was starting to cry. He himself felt nothing but confusion and fear. It looked like Sidurov was experiencing the same. He had a gun to Sara's head, but it was dropping now. He was unsure where he stood. What was the point of holding her hostage when Eaton wanted him to shoot her anyway?

'You're not my blood,' Eaton grunted, his mouth twisting. 'You're nothing to fucking do with me. I have a son to think of, a real son. He needs to live, he needs what is rightfully his. It's not me you should be blaming. That mad bitch who was my wife has done all this. She left us nothing. While you're alive we get nothing. She wanted it all to go to you. All she could see was you. It's the most monstrous, unnatural spite I've ever come across. It's insane. Because nothing belongs to you. Nothing. There's not a drop of my blood in you. I swear that I shall die before you inherit a penny. I can't allow it. I have my son to provide for. No father would allow it.' He moved the gun suddenly away from Barsukov, turning it towards Sara. Tom saw her flinch, saw the surprise in Sidurov's eyes. He was right behind her. If Eaton fired now it would kill them both. Sidurov shouted again in Russian, maybe asking Barsukov what to do. He sounded desperate.

'Pull that ladder up and put it here, Barsukov,' Eaton said. 'Or I'll let them both have a barrel now.'

Barsukov sighed. Tom couldn't believe how calm he was. His own heart was beating so heavily he could barely hear anything else. Barsukov walked to the ladder and pulled it up, then rested it against the container near Eaton's feet. 'Yes. Come down here, Freddie,' he said, tiredly. 'Let's talk about debts, shall we? Debts and betrayals.'

Tom was frozen to the spot, didn't have a clue what to do or say. Eaton held the gun in one hand and started to come down the ladder, his body twisted so that he could still shoot. He barked instructions to Barsukov, telling him to move farther off. He was almost at the bottom of the ladder when there was movement off to the right, where Sara was. She must have hit Sidurov, because when Tom looked he was doubled up, still clutching at her, still holding on. Tom started to step towards her, horrified, saw her wrenching an arm from Sidurov's grasp then stepping in front of him to the edge of the container. He realised suddenly what was going to happen. *She was going to jump*. He turned his head and saw Eaton shouting, bringing the gun up with one hand. Sara went into a crouch.

She leapt a split second before he fired. Tom was ducking, his hands in the air over his head, his eyes on her. He could see her pushing off, straightening, reaching out ahead of her to grab the ledge if she fell short. The blast was deafening. He thought it would blow her head off. But she was already past it. Instead Sidurov took the shot full on, reeling backwards into the side of the container. As Sara landed Sidurov dropped his weapon and keeled over, clutching at his head. A moment later he was toppling into the gap.

She was quickly on her feet, rushing away from them all, across the platform towards where the ladder had been. Eaton was spinning where he stood at the base of the ladder, tracking her, trying to get a clear second shot. Barsukov ducked and dived flat out, under the line of the gun. The distance between Tom and Eaton was only a few feet. He saw Eaton raising the gun to aim better, both hands on it now. Tom hurled himself forward – two, three steps – barging into Eaton with all the force he could gather, knocking him against the side of the container. The gun went off again, firing high and wide. Out of the corner of his eye Tom saw Sara leap straight off the edge of the container, down on to the one below. He struggled to get a hand up to Eaton's face, across his mouth, forcing his head back, his other hand going for the gun. Eaton was shouting and grunting, opening his mouth to bite Tom's hand. He looked old, but he was stronger than Tom had guessed, and fighting with a desperate energy. He twisted free, easily, then swung the gun round, stock first, smacking the thing into the side of Tom's head.

Tom felt his legs crumple. He fell against the container and slipped slowly to the ground, his coordination gone, the world spinning all over again. He had a premonition of Eaton stepping back, reloading, shooting him where he lay, but Eaton didn't even look at him. The gun dropped with a clatter and he was running after Sara. Tom rolled over and started to retch. He needed to get up, chase after them, but it was too much. He managed to stand with his arms against the side of the container, his legs quivering. He couldn't see where Eaton had gone. He sank to his knees and sucked at the air. He had to get up. But his vision went and he couldn't see a thing. He thought he was spinning through the air, thought he too might have fallen into the gap with Sidurov.

But when it stopped he was still on the metal surface where Eaton had hit him, flat out. He couldn't see anyone now. Above him, the container door where Sidurov had stood was swinging on its hinges, the metal beside it splattered with blood. There was no other noise, just the squeaking of the door's hinges. No sign of Sidurov, Barsukov or Freddie Eaton. He waited a moment, until he could breathe better, then forced himself to his feet.

He had to pull the ladder over to the edge. He was halfway down it when his balance gave out and he slipped off. He fell painfully, twisting his right knee. But he managed to stand, and started to limp back in the direction he had come, going as fast as he could, his feet resounding off the container roofs. All the time he was listening, trying to hear anything that might give him a clue which direction they had gone.

He got off the long ladder and back into the main corridor at ground level – the one with the forklift – just in time to see Barsukov getting into his car in the distance. He didn't wait for it to move. They couldn't have gone that way. He started to run in the other direction, a lopsided movement that wasn't very fast. Before he got to the end of the row he had tripped twice and landed flat on his face.

Clear of the last container he ran into a high mesh fence. Beyond it he could see a low wall, then the Thames. The tide was out, the river itself only visible at the edge of a long, sloping mudflat. But they couldn't have got over the fence. It was too high. He stuck his hands through the mesh and hung on it, catching his breath, trying to get his head to clear.

There was a sharp noise from off to the right. He looked over. There were a few makeshift buildings there, breeze-block walls, plank roofs. One of them stuck out towards the river on a concrete pier of some sort. He started to shuffle towards it, then heard a scream. He began to run, gasping and panting, his heart jerking inside his chest. He shouted Sara's name at the top of his voice. He thought he would keel over and pass out at any moment, but instead he kept going, started to get faster as he got used to the pain in his knee, the way his head was trying to trick his balance. He still collided with the side of the building, though, misjudging the distance. He flopped on to the ground again, terribly dizzy and out of breath.

There was a wooden door, swinging on its hinges with a broken lock. He could see it from where he was lying. He heard her scream again, heard her shouting something. It all sounded muffled, far away. He thought she must be inside the building and started to crawl towards the door. After a few seconds he could get to his knees again, then stand by leaning against the wall. He stumbled through the door and almost fell straight over an edge.

It was some kind of deserted, dilapidated dock. The high roof was falling in, planks hanging precariously, shafts of light slanting into the cold gloom. He picked out two dank concrete walls going straight down into the low-tide mud, about twelve feet below, with ladders leading down. He could see where the mud stretched towards the front of the place and joined the riverbank. There was a tall iron fence across the entrance, strung with flotsam left there by the high tide, plastic bags, bits of planking, a broken bicycle, all caught up in the mesh and just hanging there. The fence would block access to the river, but still let the water in at high tide. At high tide the whole area between the two walls would be under water. In the past, they had moored boats here, unloaded them. There was a jagged hole in the fence blocking the river end. As long as the tide was out someone could get through it, squeeze through, get on to the riverbank, escape. Was that what Sara had done?

He was starting to move towards the end of the dock to check when he heard her right below him. Maybe she had been trying to get out to the river, but she hadn't made it. He had to step forward and look over the edge to see her. They were in the mud, both of them, right below him, Sara and her father, struggling wildly with each other. It was like something happening in slow motion, with muted sound – a slow, desperate floundering in the stinking, sucking mud. Sara was up to her waist, her face covered in it, gasping for air. Eaton was right beside her, striking at her, hissing through his teeth. It took Tom a moment to interpret it correctly. Eaton was trying to push her under, trying to drown her in the stuff.

They were both sinking, slowly. Even as he watched, Sara twisted backwards and sank a little deeper. She was flailing around urgently, begging with Eaton, crying, pleading, still calling him 'Daddy'. The mud was up to her waist. Eaton wasn't saying anything. He was up to his knees in it, right in front of her, his back to Tom, his head about five feet lower than Tom's feet. He was catching her arms, hitting her, pushing her back. He managed to get his hands over her face and she fell sideways with a dull slapping noise. Tom could hear Eaton panting with the effort.

There was a half-brick on the edge, just in front of Tom.

He picked it up and stepped unsteadily towards the edge. He could throw it from there, but didn't trust his aim. He staggered sideways and found the ladder down, then swung himself round and over, holding on with one hand, taking the rungs too quickly, expecting to fall. Sara started to scream at the top of her voice. He looked over, heart in his mouth. She was flat on her back now, lying in the mud. It was already closing over her. There were fallen planks on the surface, but too far for her to reach. He had to get them to her.

He stepped off the ladder and felt his feet go under. He started to drag himself towards the planks, wrenching his feet out of the mire. By the time he was behind them he was in it up to his knees, but could still get his legs clear. He was only a couple of feet away from them when he yelled at the top of his voice. Eaton turned, his mud-streaked face wide with surprise. Tom's arm was pulled back, ready to throw the half-brick. In a split second he took in the miserable, sad brutality of it all. A woman fighting for her life in stagnant mud, someone stronger trying to hold her under, trying to kill her. He let his arm snap forwards. It happened very quickly – the stone curling through the air, Eaton ducking and turning, but not fast enough. The brick hit the side of his head with a soft crack. He fell immediately.

Tom waited momentarily, to see if he would get up, try again. But the man was flat out, his face in the mud, motionless. Tom lurched towards the planking. Sara was thrashing around on the surface, completely trapped. 'I'm coming,' he gasped, breathless. 'I'm coming.' He got to the planks, grabbed one, stepped back to her, but suddenly sank lower, up to his waist, in one gulping movement. The stuff was pressing around him, freezing cold. How deep was it? He couldn't feel the bottom. Sara had her arms out of it now, her head clear. She saw him as if for the first time and started begging him to help.

But he couldn't get any closer. He was stuck. He pushed the plank over to her, squeezing it under her arm, then reached back for another one. It was farther away. He had to lean out across the mud to get it, and felt himself sinking deeper. He twisted on the mud and threw it towards her. It actually hit her shoulder. 'Put it under your arm,' he shouted. It was absurd. Already he could hardly move. What was he going to do now?

She got it under her other arm. That would hold her, but for how long? Her eyes looked wild, insane. She was coughing and spluttering.

He only remembered Eaton as he turned back to get another plank. The man was still face down in the mud, arms splayed, sinking very slowly. For the first time it occurred to Tom what that meant. But he couldn't do anything about it. He was out of energy, out of range. He couldn't even do anything for himself. His eyes kept rolling up, his vision clouding. Sara started to shout something at him. He collapsed backwards into the mud, sitting in it, his legs already underneath. He didn't think he could do anything else. It was over. Whatever happened, it was over.

54

He had a hard head, one of the doctors said. It was a joke, maybe – maybe not. He could remember the doctor leaning over him and saying that, after another round of CAT scans and X-rays. He could remember the doctor's face, how cheerful she had looked, how young. At the time he had been crushed beneath the worst headache he had ever experienced, flat out on a hospital trolley, moaning to himself, suffering extreme nausea – but he could recall her talking very calmly to him, as if everything were normal.

Other details were vague. When he had first come round, still in the mud, with his father tugging at him, he had been completely bewildered, with no recollection at all of where he was or how he had got there. Other men were pulling Sara out – and he saw her, and remembered who she was – but he had no idea how they had ended up drowning in mud.

Over the last week most of it had come back in fits and starts, but there were still gaps. He could remember standing on top of the containers, for instance, but not how he got down from there, or what had happened in between. A different doctor had assured him it was all 'routine', that he shouldn't fret about it – he might never remember some things. But that didn't mean he wasn't lucky.

They said he had suffered multiple impact lesions, but nothing they would classify as worse than concussion. No skull fractures. No subdural haematoma extensive enough to require immediate surgical intervention – observation had been necessary, though, and repeat scans, hence the long stay. So maybe that did mean he had a hard head.

Now, seven days after the events, the headaches had finally eased and he could see properly. But it had taken a whole week to get there. For the first few days he really had been sick – unable to eat without throwing up, unable to stand straight. A nurse had taken him on toilet trips. It was Saturday before all that had stopped. He had to count the days off on his fingers to be sure. There was a lingering confusion about time. Now, finally – Wednesday, was it? – he was sitting on the edge of the bed, fully clothed, waiting for his father to sort out the admin, then take him home.

Jamie was sitting next to him. He had come with his grandfather, though on Sunday it had been Tom's mother who had brought him. She had travelled up from Devon and stayed two days, during which period there had been a couple of awkward visits with both his dad and mother present at the same time. It was the third time he had seen Jamie since coming here. 'Here', he had learned, was Guy's – he had been admitted here via its A&E department, brought there by ambulance. He couldn't recall any of that. Even Jamie's first visit was unclear. When had it been? Maybe Friday, when he was still quite confused. Sally had been with them, sitting at the edge of the bed with a permanent scowl on her face, tutting her disapproval between sarcastic comments. No love lost there, then.

There had been unpleasant visits from police officers too. One snide DI had sat at his bedside and spoken for what seemed like hours about how dangerous he was. There was a massive international murder inquiry under way and his position in it was far from determined. He had killed Frederick Eaton, maybe other people. That's what they said. Eaton had been dead before his face hit the mud, according to the autopsy. There was none of it in his lungs or throat. So Tom had killed him, with a simple brick to the head. He had taken multiple blows to his own head, and survived practically unscathed. But one lucky shot with a half-brick had switched Eaton off, just like that. Tom felt peculiarly untouched by that fact – at the moment.

Maxim Sidurov was dead too. It had taken him longer to die, from blood loss and shock, down in the rathole, half his face taken off by Eaton's first shot. Except there had been a suggestion that Tom might have fired that shot. A female DS said they would have charged him already, if it hadn't been for pressure from his father. Tom couldn't believe that was true. In his experience, nothing stopped the cogs of a homicide inquiry. But it had been on Thursday they had said all these things, when nothing had been clear, his brain scrambled. They'd tried to get what they could out of him before the doctors kicked them out. Fair enough. Since then, he knew, they had taken long statements from Sara and his father, and no one had returned to accuse him.

Now, Wednesday morning, he had spent the last half-hour talking to Jamie, hearing an account of his holiday in Ibiza, or wherever it had been. There were a lot of snorkelling stories, not many references to Sally. Jamie knew the diplomacy already. If she had been with another guy Jamie didn't mention him, and Tom didn't ask. He sat with his arm round his son and listened in a kind of dopey, dreamy state. He wasn't taking anything but painkillers now, but he still tired quickly if he had to concentrate. It was a huge relief to see Jamie again, to hear his voice, to mark the irritating turns of phrase picked up from American movies and computer games. Normal life. Someone he loved, who loved him.

His phone buzzed and he looked at the number. Sara. She had called him at least twice a day for the last four days. He hadn't really been up to speaking to her at first, so had just listened for as long as he could, the phone pressed to his ear. But the conversations were lengthening now he was getting back to normal. Last night they had spoken for three hours.

It wasn't what Tom had expected. When her number had first come up while he was lying here alone, head pounding, the first night in this place, his heart had skipped like he was a teenager all over again.

55

She spoke to him for a few seconds only, from where she was sitting, halfway across London, in a waiting room in New Charing Cross Hospital, in Hammersmith. She told him where she was, what she was doing, then listened to his response. Calling him was like holding his hand. It calmed her. And she needed calming. She ended the call, took a breath.

She was in a part of the paediatric department, her eyes on the corridor full of little doors that led to consulting rooms. The room was full, full of parents with worried faces, kids who were sick of waiting. There was a little play area off to one side, with three or four kids making quite a bit of noise there. So far, no one had said anything to her – such as 'Why are you here? Where's your child?' Nor had anyone asked who the guy at the door was – tall, smart, discreet, with an earpiece; one of a retinue of security personnel and assistants that she was becoming increasingly irritated with.

They were all over her now, all the people her mother – Liz Wellbeck (she could not stop thinking of her as her mother) – had also loathed. The PAs and advisers and security managers. Necessary, she knew that. She was more like a business now, a living, walking conglomerate of global assets, at the peak of an entity that kept over a hundred thousand people in direct employment. She didn't want anything to do with it. She still had to think it all through, work out if she had any options.

Her birthday had brought it all to her, all Liz's property, more than she had even guessed existed. Liz Wellbeck – a woman who had wanted *her*, and not Freddie Eaton, to control it all – a woman who had tricked her into thinking she was her mother. But that had been nothing compared to her father. Except he wasn't her father. *Freddie Eaton*. She had to start thinking of him like that, as something detached from her. A name. Not her father at all. *Freddie Eaton* had tried to kill her, to drown her in mud. For money. She closed her eyes and had an image of Tom, diving into him as he tried to shoot at her, then later throwing the brick that had stopped it all. He had saved her life.

She took a breath, tried to get her head clear of it all, to focus on the reason she was here instead. Part of why she felt so desperate at the moment, so completely unable to hold it together, was because there was just too much to deal with, to try to assimilate.

She shouldn't have come here at all, of course. Would this do any good? The assistants had told her that this was where the woman worked. That was why she was here. One of them had come in here earlier and had somehow or other found out that she was here right now, in Cubicle 3, working. So far she hadn't emerged to call out the name of the next patient. But she was going to, any minute now.

She bent forward and tried not to cry again. Every time she thought about what had happened she wanted to cry. She felt stupid, dirty, violated. She wasn't even the age she had always thought she was. She was two years older. Where had those two years gone? Lost somewhere in her blurred childhood, on the Ile des Singes Noirs. She had passed her first years there as a kind of infant recluse, isolated from the world. Just her and her mother. Now she knew why. Her entire life had been a disgusting deception. And two of the monsters behind it all had been her parents. *Elizabeth Wellbeck. Freddie Eaton.*

They were not her real parents. That was why she was here. She dug her hand in the pocket of the long cashmere cardigan she was wearing and unfolded the sheets of paper she had there. John Lomax – Tom's father – had spent a long time talking to her about a case, a child who had vanished in 1990. That had been on Saturday. She had agreed to a doctor from his inquiry taking a blood sample from her, for the purpose of running DNA tests. They had promised to expedite the results. They were comparing her DNA to Freddie Eaton's, and to the DNA held from John Lomax's old inquiry, the DNA of the missing girl's mother. She was still waiting for the results of that, but didn't really need to. Not now. Because on Sunday this letter had arrived.

A letter from Liz, another of her near-illegible missives, this time from the grave. It had been in a safety deposit box in Switzerland for over ten years. It was different to anything else Liz had written in that it had been composed over ten years ago, when she had first been diagnosed with her cancer, before she had changed. Only Felice Cotte, Sara's old nanny, had known about this letter. But she knew nothing of the contents, and had promised absolute secrecy as to the letter's existence, and kept that promise. Her responsibility had been to deliver it when Liz was dead. And she had done that. On Sunday. At least arranged it, in accordance with Liz's wishes of ten years previously, her fingers and commands reaching out even from her grave.

Except she wasn't in her grave any longer. Her body had been exhumed. It was in some police morgue somewhere in Paris. They needed to do an autopsy, to find out if she had been poisoned. That was what Sara's new principal PA was calling 'the Belgian inquiry'. It was hard to keep track of how many inquiries there were. A document had been found on the body of the man Tom and she had surprised at Alison Spencer's place, the man who had run and fallen off the roof, Stefan Meyer. A communication from Liz to Alison. Sara didn't know the contents – no one had told her – but they had led to Hulpe – her cancer consultant – being arrested in Brussels, and Liz's corpse being unceremoniously dug up. The suspicion was that Freddie Eaton and Hulpe had killed her off. Because Freddie knew what Sara had never known. He knew that on her birthday everything was coming to her – a woman who wasn't even his daughter – and he was getting nothing.

'Madeleine?'

Sara looked up. The door was open and the doctor had come out, standing there in a white coat and flat shoes, a clipboard in hand, a stethoscope hung around her neck. 'Madeleine?' she asked again. Nearer to her a mother turned and started to get up, holding the hand of a little girl sitting beside her. Sara watched with her heart in her throat, her breathing stopped, as the doctor stepped forward, smiling, and greeted the little girl.

She was about twelve feet away from her. Sara could see her clearly. She was tall, with white hair, completely white, and a thin, drawn face. It didn't look like there was an ounce of fat on her. She looked as though she might be in her fifties, though Sara knew she had to be younger than that. The first impression was of someone severe, but then she stooped to the little girl and said something to her, smiling. The smile transformed her, a glint of something warmer inside. The little girl seemed to take to her at once. They walked back to the cubicle hand in hand, the mother following. The doctor hadn't looked at Sara at all.

The door closed and Sara let herself breathe. It was as though she were suspended in time. She wasn't feeling anything. Her heart was banging against her chest, her face flushed and burning, her scalp prickling. But she wasn't feeling anything. Or rather it was like there was a massive hole in the centre of her chest. She stood up and walked to the door of the cubicle. She read the name on the plate there, to be sure – Dr Rachel Gower. That was her. Her child had been called Lauren Gower. Sara turned away and walked out.

She went to the main hospital lobby, ignoring Danny, the second bodyguard, who had been out in the corridor, walking past Katarina, the new PA, who was waiting down there for her. She sat in a seat there and took the letter out again. She read it.

56

My love, my sweetest little love. My Sara. You are going to hate
me when you read this, you are going to think that I must have
hated you, but you must never believe that. I have loved you, as
my own, with all my heart, from the first moment you came into
my care. I have loved you completely, as a mother should, as only
a mother can. I truly believe that.

You cast everything that existed in my life before you into
shadow, lit my life with your beauty and joy. I cannot stress to
you enough that this is true, that all this is true. You are the
most beautiful thing that ever happened to me, maybe the only
truly pure thing that has ever entered my miserable life.

Because it has been miserable. All the Wellbecks are miser-
able people. That you are not like that, not like me, that you
have, already, such a generous heart, cannot have had much to
do with me. But I have at least tried not to crush your spirit, to
let it grow, and breathe. If everything had worked out you might
have proved the salvation of my entire family. No one would
know the secret. Maybe it can still be like that, but now – if you
are reading this – that will be up to you. It will be your choice.
That is the only thing I can do for you now.

Because if you are reading this then I am dead. Last month
they diagnosed a form of cancer that they have warned me will
be passed on to you. They say you will die of it too, because you
are my daughter, my flesh and blood. So I write you this letter

now so that you will not have that shadow hanging over you, and the only way to do that is to tell you the whole truth. I should tell you it now, while I am alive, face to face. I know. But I am too much of a coward for that. I cannot. I could not bear to see your face sour and your gaze turn to hatred. So here is this letter, instead. Sorry.

I could not have babies. Not because of this latest illness, but because of some other genetic malformation seeded into the Wellbeck line. Nothing good ever came from my family. You should know that. I hardly knew my parents. Your 'grandparents'. You never knew them at all. You missed nothing. What they gave me was faulty genes. And money. Maybe nature is trying to kill us off, in her own way. She will succeed, because they tell me I will die of this cancer, sooner or later, and already I cannot have children of my own. Frederick – a man I married when he still had some spirit – knows this. It would make him leave me, sue for divorce, if he had any honesty. But he only ever wanted the money from me, I think. I can hardly bear to look at him now. He has his purposes, but you must be a little wary of him. He will resent you. And he is not your father. Remember that. He has had little concern for you because he cannot step beyond himself sufficiently to know how beautiful you are. It does not matter whose blood you have. It does not matter.

He is not your father and I am not your natural mother, though I have tried my best to fill that role as the only thing worthy of my life. I hope I have made you feel loved and wanted. There has been a lie involved, yes, but it was all for a purpose. It makes me bitter to think of it, bitter to the point of tears. I wish it could have been otherwise, but you could never have come from me, and that's that. It was something money could not buy.

Anybody could know that you were not mine simply by looking at you, by watching you. That nobody has commented says something brutal about all of them. Trust yourself, Sara.

Trust your own heart. Don't listen to any of the people who are there because of the money. Which is nearly everyone you know. The money alone will never bring you anything but misery and loneliness.

I would be ashamed of what I have done, if it were possible to feel shame about anything that touches on you. But it's not. I can't regret what I did. I'm sorry. I can only feel grateful that I have had ten years with you. Maybe there will be more. Everything is so very uncertain right now. So I write this letter and entrust its transmission to Felice. What else can I do? I'm not expressing myself very clearly, I know. But it will have to do.

First, they brought me a little girl I had never seen before. From Russia. She was an orphan, they said – they didn't even know who her parents were. So they said. I called her Elizabeth, after me, because we didn't know her real name. I had asked Arisha to find me someone who would need me, and she did. I don't know now whether she told me the truth, though. She went to Russia to do it with Maxim Sidurov, a cruel man, who could easily steal a child and feel nothing. Maybe that was what they did. Maybe there is a mother somewhere in Russia who mourns that baby.

I shouldn't have called her after me. That was bad luck. The poor baby died of a flu, an ordinary flu. She was in my arms less than three weeks. She had black curls and blue eyes. I asked them to find a dark-haired girl with blue eyes – to be as much like me as possible – and they did. But she was torn from me. There was nothing I could do. This was on Ile des Singes Noirs, the island you already love so much, though I can, as you know, no longer stand to be there. The baby is buried there, under the steps up to the house. That is something I wish I could fix, and now leave to you. I'm sorry. She should have a marked grave at least, my little Elizabeth. This will all sound brutal and in-human to you. I realise that.

When she died I thought I would never be able to look at another child again. I was devastated. But only four days later I met you. You were in a crèche in my London clinic. Your mother, your real mother, was a doctor there. Her name is Rachel Gower. Your father was a doctor also – Roger Gower – though I have never met him. I did meet your mother. I felt only an intense jealousy. She had you. I didn't. I had just lost my little baby. I was under a black cloud, grieving. I didn't want to go anywhere near children. But the visit had been organised many months previously. So I tried to muddle my way through it. I looked at all the children and all I wanted to do was cry. And in the midst of all that, there you were, reaching out to me. I knew that you should be mine from the first moment I held you, which was there, in that crèche. I looked at you and the blackness started to lift away from me. It will all sound monstrous to you. But I cannot hide it, the truth is what it is. I don't make any excuses for my nature or circumstances. I found you, or you found me – shouting out to me with your little blue eyes – they were blue then – in a room full of children. You couldn't speak much, but you were so beautiful, already so perfect. I felt resentment then, towards Rachel Gower, but now I see that she has made you what you are. Of the good things that shine out of you I had no part. You are all hers. I wish there was some way I could help her now. I don't regret taking you, but I wish there was some way I could help her. She was very young then. I thought she would get over you. An absurd, selfish thought. I thought she would simply have another 'you'. Because that's what normal women can do. But I know she hasn't done that. I know her life has been blighted by what I did, while my life has been charged with an impossible happiness.

But there's not much of it left now. So perhaps that's some kind of justice. You are free to do what you wish, of course. You can meet her. I don't know whether you will want that. But whatever you want, you at least know that all the curses that have lived in my blood do not live in yours. You can live your life without all that hanging over you. That's all I seek to achieve with this letter. The love I have for you is like something that could burst my heart. Today I sat with you in the reading room and I felt truly content. We were there for three hours, reading Jane Eyre, *just you and I. Perhaps you remember the moment? Perhaps not. I needed nothing else. It's enough to have had that time with you. So don't feel sorry for me.*

Try to forget me, perhaps.

A last kiss from me. A last apology. Then this is done.

Liz

57

Thursday, 26 April 2012

John stood at the kitchen table in Rachel's house and tried to keep still. He was so exhausted he could hardly see straight. He needed to sit down, rest, relax, give his heart an adrenalin break. More than anything, he needed to sleep. But he was charged with nervous, excited energy. If he closed his eyes he could see lights jumping behind his eyelids. He felt stretched like a wire, ready to snap. When he spoke everything came out in a rush. Sleep had been impossible for several nights. So much happening. He had hardly seen Rachel. But now it was here. It was here. It was happening.

He took a huge breath. His heart was like a massive drum, thumping in his ears. He wanted to burst out laughing, giggle, jump around her kitchen. But at the same time he didn't want to. Because he was frightened. Frightened of all sorts of things. So he was just standing there, sweating, trying to control the strangest fear he had ever experienced. Rachel knew something was up, of course. She knew he had come here to say something big. She could see what he was like just looking at him. And he had come with Ian Bilsborough, after all, the current SIO for Grenser. Ian had actually come to him with this job, only forty minutes ago, asked him to do it. Ian had looked frightened too. He was waiting out in the hallway. John had told him about what Rachel had said, only last week, about her knowing that Lauren was dead.

The kitchen had a counter cutting across it, and an adjoining space with a big table in it. A breakfast table, perhaps, since she had another room which she called the dining room. He'd never eaten in there with her. Always when he came over they ate here. He wondered what happened in the dining room. Everything was always very neat in there. There was a dresser, he knew, with fancy plates and stuff, and also a photo of Lauren, when she was first born. It was the only photo of Lauren he had ever seen in the house. He put his fist into his mouth and bit down on it.

Rachel was fussing around in the kitchen part, making coffee. She was getting very nervous. He could see the warning signs. He resisted the urge to yell at her.

'It doesn't matter, Rachel,' he said, speaking as carefully as he could. 'I don't need coffee. Please. Just come and sit down. Please.'

She kept going, though, washing the coffee pot, head down, caught in a little loop of panic. 'Who is that man out there?' she asked, her voice trembling.

'It's Ian. I told you. Ian Bilsborough. He's the SIO now.'

'The SIO? For Grenser?'

'Yes.'

'Why is he waiting out there? I feel like he's come to arrest me or something.'

'It's so we can talk better. Please. Leave that. Sit down.' He had to have her sitting, in case she passed out.

She dropped the coffee jug, with a bang, into the sink. 'It's cracked,' she said. 'It's broken now. See what I've done ...'

'Doesn't matter.'

'What's that in your hand?' she demanded. 'You keep fiddling with it.'

347

She came from behind the counter and walked over to the table. She was breathing unevenly. He felt very worried. He looked down at the sheaf of papers he was holding, among them the DNA results. 'It's these I want to talk to you about,' he said, holding them up.

She sat down, finally. He sat right next to her and leaned on the table. He took another exaggerated breath, but still when he started to talk his voice was all over the place. 'The thing with Tom,' he said. 'What's been happening. That's why I haven't been able to see you. You don't know the details, but I'll tell you. This is the very, very short version.' She put her elbows on the table too. Her arms were shaking. There was a little twitch at the corner of her mouth.

'This isn't going to be bad, Rachel,' he said, very quietly. 'Believe me.'

She shook her head, like she didn't understand that. 'Tell me. Say what you came to say.'

'Tom got a message from a woman called Sara Eaton ...'

'You told me. Her mother was Elizabeth Wellbeck. I know that.'

'I told you that. Yes. But Tom went to her and there was a lot of shit happening. A lot of shit. Freddie Eaton tried to kill her. Tom rescued her, in fact. If it hadn't been for Tom she would be dead, but she's not dead. She's alive. She's a beautiful, living, twenty-three-year-old woman ...'

'Her father tried to kill her? Is that what you said just now? Her own father? Didn't you tell me Freddie Eaton was her father?'

'Yes. That's what I said. But he's not her father. And Elizabeth Wellbeck was not her mother.' He pushed the DNA results over to her. She didn't look at them. She was turning bright red. 'What is that?' she asked, rigidly. 'What is it?'

'It's DNA results. They show Freddie Eaton was not her father...'

'The DNA results for this girl you're talking about? For Sara Eaton?'

'Yes.'

'You compared her DNA and Freddie Eaton's? That's the man who was married to Elizabeth Wellbeck?'

'Yes. And he's not Sara Eaton's father. But we didn't just run that comparison...' He took a gulp and clutched the side of the table. 'We ran yours too. Your DNA, from the inquiry. We ran a comparison...'

She started to cry immediately. She saw it coming.

'It's *her*, Rachel,' he said. 'Sara Eaton is Lauren. It's *her*.' His voice was like a strangled gasp. He realised suddenly he was going to start crying as well.

'I can't believe it...' she stuttered. 'I thought it was going to be a body... the remains...'

'No. No body. She's alive and well. She's beautiful. She even looks like you. In her eyes. I can see you in her eyes. There's no doubt. No doubt at all. The DNA is certain. We found her, Rachel. We found her ...' He couldn't keep still any longer. He thought he was going to explode, burst out of the top of his head. He jumped up from the table, pulled her to him and held her face between his hands. 'It's Lauren,' he said, laughing. 'It's Lauren. She's alive. She's alive, Rachel. It really is her.'

She closed her eyes, the tears really pouring now. She started to giggle through them. He pulled her to him and let it start to come, let twenty years of it rise to the surface. They were laughing and crying, holding each other so tightly that it was painful.

58

When she had thought about it, imagined it – this moment – Rachel had forgotten about Roger. Lauren's father. John had reminded her yesterday that he would have to be present too when she met Sara, unless they could both agree something different. There was no need for that – he should be there, of course – but she just hadn't imagined him there.

She'd forgotten the press problems too. There had been a lot of that twenty-two years ago, and again in 2003, when John had reviewed the case. She had been used to it all then, learned how to deal with it as a necessity, because publicity was something that could help find Lauren. But now it bewildered her. She had got up this morning and there they were, hanging around outside her house, more and more of them. Cameras flashing as she pulled the curtains. John had been annoyed, though not surprised. Someone at the police had leaked it, he said. It was all good publicity for the police, though they'd in fact had little to do with it.

By midday it was a scrum and the local police were putting up barriers. John assured her they would leave her after the meeting. They changed the location of the meeting, though. Sara Eaton had said she would meet them anywhere, apparently. Rachel hadn't known what to do about that. When she had imagined it they were always in a crowded public space. But that was just her silly dreams. In the end she'd asked if Sara could just come here, to Fulham, to her home. Now they had changed it at the last minute to John's place on the river in Hammersmith. She had managed to get out of her house the back way, with police assistance, and, as far as she knew, no one had followed them. They were in John's main room now, Roger and her, sitting at John's table, waiting. John was down in the hallway, keeping a discreet distance, talking to the people who were there from Grenser. It was all very odd, very uncomfortable. She wished Roger were not here at all. She wished it were John sitting beside her. She wanted him to hold her hand. Roger had given up on Lauren long ago. John hadn't.

Roger was talking a lot. She just wanted to sit in silence. She felt very calm, much calmer than she imagined she would be. There was a powerful sensation of unreality, but she had anticipated that – like she was floating through a story someone else had written, someone else's story, or like she wasn't really there, couldn't really hear or see properly, though she could, of course. She could see and hear everything with great clarity, every tiny detail. She had thought about all the possible issues and problems that might arise – over the years she had thought about them all, over and over again, imagining every possibility. She had expected, waking up this morning, to feel grim. That was how she had imagined it. Because the reality of what had happened was grim. She was waiting now to meet a daughter she really could no longer do anything for, that she had no relationship with. Because someone had taken away all the years when she was meant to have been there for Sara, or Lauren, all the years she was meant to give her love and be her mother. They had been stolen, with the child. And there was no going back on any of that, no recovery of what was gone. It was gone for ever. The woman who would arrive was an adult. She didn't need a mother any more. What *did* she need? Maybe just to fill in some gaps in her history, to satisfy a curiosity. Maybe she wouldn't want anything to do with Rachel at all. John had told her all about Sara's wealth. She lived in a different world to the sad, deformed thing that Rachel had been moving around in for the past twenty-two years. She hadn't been stricken with loss. Until a few days ago she hadn't even known that Rachel was her real mother.

In fact, she'd had – until recently – a different mother. Liz Wellbeck. A woman Rachel had met many times. She had even met her – years ago now – during the period when Liz Wellbeck must already have had Sara, stashed away somewhere secret, her child. Liz had stood in her clinic and spoken to her and sympathised with Rachel, and all the time she had known that back at her home, somewhere, Rachel's child was there, alive and well. It brought a terrible lump to Rachel's throat when she considered this – that Liz Wellbeck, a woman who had enough money to buy almost anything you could name, her ex-employer, someone she had always respected for her charity work – this woman had wreaked this misery on her, knowingly. It brought a lump to her throat because it shattered at a stroke illusions that might still have remained hers, a source of some kind of optimism about humanity. It said something about evil, about its existence. It wasn't just the taking of her child, more the keeping her in the dark about Lauren, deliberately refusing her any succour, so that Rachel hadn't ever known whether her baby was dead, alive, or in the hands of some child abuser. Liz Wellbeck had looked her in the eyes, with all that going on, knowing that was what Rachel was suffering, and said absolutely nothing. The woman was monstrous, an embodiment of a kind of evil that Rachel hadn't thought real. Or had only imagined. And that idea was very hard to reconcile with the fact that Liz Wellbeck – however evil she seemed to Rachel – had brought up her child, had probably loved her (how could you not love her – and why steal her if you didn't?), had been Lauren's actual mother. How was she meant to skate around that subject with Sara Eaton?

Roger didn't seem to have these worries. He was excited like a little kid, talking away about it. There didn't seem to be any resentment of John. But why should there be? Roger had left her. He had a new wife now, two kids of his own. He had a successful career. He had decided long ago that Lauren was dead and he had dealt with that. This now was like some fantastic surprise, a gift he had never expected. She resisted the urge to turn to him and say, *But what about our lives, Roger, our ruined lives?*

If she could have exerted more control over this whole process she would have taken things much more slowly. This meeting – this thing that was about to happen to them – wasn't really a meeting for her, or for Roger or Sara. It was like a wedding, she thought. Some kind of public ritual. It was what happened when they found someone who had been lost, it was what had to happen – there had to be a publicised first meeting, *the reunion*. It existed because there was a social expectation about it, a social rule. Just like the wedding cere-mony. That wasn't for the two people getting married – it was for everyone else. What she was about to go through would be private, of course, but the fact that it was happening was very public. There would even be press statements later, she assumed. The detectives from the inquiry would need to say something to the world. And the world was right to want to know. There was nothing prurient about it. What had hap-pened was massive. She understood it all. But if she could have kicked against it what she would have preferred was to have seen pictures of Sara first, so as to know what to expect. John had said he would arrange that, but in the end it had all just steamed ahead and rolled right over him too, so she now had no idea what Sara Eaton looked like. She would have preferred to have emailed her maybe. Email was such an easy way to communicate, at a distance. Or speak to her by phone. Why did intermediaries have to organise this meeting for her? There was no need for that. She should have just been able to speak to her daughter, find out what she thought about it all. They could have arranged something for a couple of weeks' time. That would have given them both time to get used to it all, to assimilate the shock. But instead, here they all were, a day after the DNA tests were confirmed.

And yet, despite all that, she didn't feel grim, or depressed. The overwhelming expectation she was experiencing wasn't quite joyful – there was too much uncertainty around it for it to get anywhere near that – but it felt like it could be something new, not something old, the start of something, not the end. And that was a positive feeling, one she hadn't expected at all.

There were noises from the stairs now, people coming up. The time was coming. She stood up. Roger stood too, suddenly silent. The door opened and John walked in, smiling. Behind him was a tall, young woman with a very pale face and short, blonde hair – it was dyed, someone had told her, and naturally dark. She was wearing a pair of black jeans, a green sweater with a polo neck, flat black shoes. She was looking at her, staring straight at Rachel as she walked across the room.

Rachel collapsed back into her chair. She saw it at once, in the eyes, in the face. She saw herself. She realised with a jolting shock that until right now, this very moment, a part of her hadn't believed it. There was the science, the DNA, everything they were telling her. But she hadn't believed it.

Now she could see it. It was Lauren, it was her daughter.

She started to cry stupidly, still looking at the woman. Roger was going forward to her, his hand held out to shake her hand like she were a friend, introducing himself, stammering nervously. The woman looked away from her, tears in her eyes now, but a smile on her face. She shook Roger's hand and held it, spoke to him, then embraced him and put her head against his shoulder. Rachel couldn't hear what she was saying to him. She could only hear the blood rushing through her ears. Sara came past Roger and sat down next to her. But Rachel couldn't look at her. All she could see was the day she had vanished. The daffodil she had picked for her, Lauren's little legs kicking in delight as she had held it. It was the same baby sitting next to her now, grown up into something incredible. She was beautiful, so beautiful and self-assured that Rachel thought her face might burn if she looked directly at her. As if she were an angel. She hung her head instead and wept while Sara just sat beside her, a hand on her arm, waiting.

Enid Blyton ®

Malory Towers

Winter Term

Written by Pamela Cox

Hodder
Children's
Books

Contents

On the train

'Mother, there's Susan!' cried Felicity Rivers, as she and her mother made their way along the station platform. 'Susan! Hi, Susan!'

'Felicity, don't run!' called Mrs Rivers. 'It's far too crowded and you will bump into someone!'

But it was too late. Felicity was determined to reach her friend Susan and she ran along the platform, dodging the groups of people that stood here and there. Many of them were girls in the Malory Towers uniform, waiting for the train that would take them back to school for the winter term.

But Mrs Rivers was right, and it wasn't long before Felicity *did* bump into someone – a tall, red-haired girl with a serious expression and grey eyes.

'Felicity Rivers!' said the girl, looking rather cross. 'Do watch where you are going! And what do you mean by running around like a mad thing?'

'Sorry, Fenella,' said Felicity meekly, turning red. Of all the people she could have bumped into, why did she have to pick Fenella Thornton, the new Head Girl?

Fenella glared at her for a moment. Then, suddenly, her face broke into a wide smile, making her look quite different.

'Go on, push off!' she said with a chuckle. 'And this time, walk! Remember, you're a fourth former now, Felicity, not a silly little third former any more.'

Golly, so I am! thought Felicity, walking over to join Susan and her mother. Fancy *me* being a fourth former!

She and Susan greeted one another noisily, for they had to tell one another *everything* that had happened in the holidays. Then Mrs Rivers came up and chatted to Susan's mother, and at last it was time for the two girls to board the train.

Each of them hugged her mother, and Mrs Rivers said, 'Do write, won't you, darling? And I know that Darrell would love to hear from you, too.'

'I'll see you at half-term, dear,' said Susan's mother. 'Have a marvellous time!'

Felicity and Susan waved their mothers off, then grinned at one another as they walked down the train to find their carriage.

'The beginning of a new term,' said Susan. 'And now we are fourth formers!'

'Yes, we are, so why are you going towards the third-form carriage?' laughed Felicity, pulling her friend back. 'We don't want to sit with *those* babies!'

'Of course not,' said Susan loftily. 'Babies!'

Just then, the guard outside blew his whistle and, with a lurch, the train began to move forward slowly – on its way to Malory Towers!

'I say, isn't it exciting to be getting the train all on our own?' said Felicity.

'Much better than being in a stuffy old car,' agreed Susan.

The girls usually came to school by car, but Felicity's father had needed to drive to an urgent appointment, so she was getting the train for the first time. And, as she and Susan were quite inseparable, Susan's parents had agreed that she could catch the train with Felicity, too.

A sudden shout of laughter came from one of the carriages further along the train, and Felicity said, 'I'd know that laugh anywhere!'

'So would I,' grinned Susan. 'It's June!'

Quickly, Felicity and Susan made their way to the carriage that the laughter had come from, and slid open the door. And there, all chuckling their heads off, sat three of their fellow fourth formers – June, Freddie and Nora. There was another girl sitting in the corner of the carriage too, one that the girls hadn't seen before, but she wasn't laughing. In fact, her expression was very sullen indeed.

Heavens, she doesn't look very friendly, thought Felicity. I do hope that she isn't in North Tower with us.

The new girl, who was rather plain, with straight, mousey-brown hair, which fell to her shoulders, looked up as Felicity and Susan took their seats. Then she looked away again almost immediately, without so much as smiling at the newcomers. The two girls looked at one another and grimaced, but there was no time to worry about the new girl now, for their friends were welcoming them noisily.

'Hallo there, you two! Had good hols?'

3

'Isn't it grand to be going back to good old Malory Towers?'

'And this time we shall be in the fourth form! My goodness, we *are* going up in the world!'

'I don't know that I want to be a fourth former,' said Nora, frowning a little. 'We shall have to settle down a little and be more responsible now that we are in the upper school. It won't be nearly as much fun!'

The sullen-looking girl, who had been huddled miserably in the corner, looking out of the window, turned her head again at this, and threw Nora a scornful look. Fortunately, Nora didn't see it, but Felicity did, and felt quite shocked. Whatever had Nora done to deserve *that*?

'I have no intention at all of settling down,' said June. 'I don't see why we can't have a little fun, just because we are fourth formers.'

'Quite right!' said her friend, Freddie. 'We can still play the odd trick . . .'

'And have the occasional joke,' put in June.

'And, perhaps, we might even arrange a midnight feast!' said Freddie, her blue eyes lighting up.

The eyes of Felicity, Susan and Nora lit up too. A midnight feast would be simply too marvellous for words! They hadn't had one for absolutely ages. On the other hand, though, what Nora had said was quite true. The girls *were* expected to settle down a little once they were in the fourth form. But then Felicity remembered that when her sister Darrell had been in the upper fourth, they had held a feast. And if it was good enough for Darrell, it was good enough for Felicity!

'Perhaps we *could* have a feast,' she said, grinning. 'It's not as if we would be doing any harm. And as long as we keep it to ourselves, we can't be accused of setting a bad example to the lower forms.'

'My sentiments exactly!' cried June, clapping her on the back. 'My word, we're in for some fun this term.'

June's wicked, dark eyes were shining. She and Freddie were the jokers of the form, and fun was never far away when they were around!

'There's a very mischievous look about you this term, June,' said Susan, watching the girl.

'June *always* looks mischievous,' laughed Nora.

'Yes, but she looks even more mischievous than usual,' said Susan. 'And so do you, Freddie! Secretly planning lots of tricks, I expect!'

'Us?' said June, making her eyes very wide and innocent. 'Of course not!'

'As if we would!' said Freddie, also looking very innocent.

But the others knew that Freddie had spent the last few days of the holidays at June's. And June's brothers, who were also great jokers, had been there too. No doubt the two girls had come back with all kinds of jokes and tricks up their sleeves!

The new girl, who had sat in silence while the chatter went on around her, gave a sniff, and Felicity and Susan looked at the others enquiringly.

'Oh yes,' said June, as though she had only just

remembered that the girl was there. 'I haven't introduced you to our new member of the form, have I? This is Olive Witherspoon.'

Felicity and Susan said hallo, and the girl returned their greeting unsmilingly, in a tight little voice.

'Have you been to boarding school before, Olive?' asked Felicity, pleasantly.

'Yes,' said Olive shortly.

'Well, that's good,' said Susan, brightly. 'As you're used to it, I don't suppose you will feel too homesick, will you?'

'No,' came Olive's curt reply, and June muttered under her breath, 'Don't waste your time. She won't volunteer any information, and all you will get out of her are one-word answers. I gave up after about five minutes.'

'Yes, cheerful little soul, isn't she?' murmured Freddie.

Nora pulled a face and said in a low voice, 'Never mind about her! We've tried to be friendly, but she obviously doesn't want our company. Let's talk about something else instead. I say, did you know that Fenella Thornton has been made Head Girl, now that Kay Foster has left?'

'Yes, and old Amanda's gone, too,' said June. 'Ruth Grainger is taking her place as games captain.'

'I like Ruth,' said Freddie. 'And Fenella's not a bad sort, although she has a bit of a temper.'

'Yes, Fenella can be hot-tempered at times,' laughed Felicity. 'I bumped into her on the platform, quite literally! She was cross with me at first, but she soon got over it.'

'I wonder who will be head of the form?' said Susan.

'Well, it won't be me,' said Felicity. 'I had my turn in

the third form. I must say, I'm quite looking forward to taking a back seat this year.'

'And it certainly won't be me,' said June comfortably. 'I'm far too irresponsible.'

'And it won't be me, either,' laughed Freddie. 'For the same reason.'

'I'm much too scatterbrained,' said Nora. 'Potty and Miss Williams would never choose me.'

'Perhaps it will be Pam,' suggested Susan. 'She's so steady and good-tempered. And she was head girl when we were in the second form.'

'Pam was a super head-girl,' said Felicity. 'But I think that Miss Williams should give someone else a chance this term. It might be you, Susan!'

'No!' said June at once, with a horrified expression. 'Why, Susan would be no good at all as head-girl.'

'She would be marvellous!' retorted the normally even-tempered Felicity, firing up in defence of her friend. She had turned rather red, and June gave her a push, saying, 'Ass! I was only joking. Of course I know that Susan would be a splendid head-girl. I say, just imagine if Miss Williams made Bonnie head of the form? Or Amy?'

'I don't know which of them would be worse,' said Susan, with a shudder. 'It would certainly be an entertaining term if one of those two were chosen, but somehow I can't quite picture it happening!'

The chatter continued as the train went on its way, but still Olive took no part. Felicity, who thought that perhaps the girl was just very shy, felt a little sorry for her. Every now and then she tried to draw Olive into conversation, but, as before, the girl responded with terse answers, and asked no questions of her own.

She really was rather odd, decided Felicity, giving up. She remembered how excited she had felt about starting at Malory Towers, and how she had bombarded her older sister, Darrell, with questions. Yet Olive wasn't at all excited, and she didn't seem remotely curious about her new school either. It was very strange!

At last the train drew up at the little station near Malory Towers and, dragging their trunks and carrying their night cases, the girls alighted. Several big coaches were waiting to take the girls to the school, and Felicity and her friends boarded the first one, Olive following. Felicity and Susan sat together, of course, and so did June and Freddie. Which left Nora to sit next to the new girl, something which neither of them looked very pleased about.

Felicity and Susan felt sorry for Nora, for they would not have liked to sit next to the surly Olive either. They sat behind the two girls, and did their best to include Nora in their conversation, for which she was very grateful.

The coach journey was only a short one, and the girls grew very excited as the coach rounded a bend in the road, and their beloved Malory Towers came into view.

Felicity always loved this first glimpse of her school, thinking how magnificent it looked – almost like a castle, with its four towers, one at each corner.

In excitement, she cried out, 'Olive, look! There is Malory Towers, up on the cliff. Isn't it just the most beautiful building you have ever seen?'

Olive looked, but she made no comment. And Nora, stealing a sideways glance at the new girl, thought that her frown seemed to deepen.

There was great excitement as the coaches pulled up in the driveway, those girls who had arrived earlier by car gathering round to greet their friends.

'Felicity! I wondered where you were!'

'And there's Susan! Had good hols, Susan?'

'Hallo, June! And Freddie! My, isn't it good to be back?'

'Nora, old girl! Hurry up, and let's take our night cases to Matron.'

This was Nora's friend, the placid, even-tempered Pam. She looked with interest at Olive, who was coming down the steps behind Nora, and said in her friendly way, 'Hallo there! Welcome to Malory Towers. Are you going to be in the fourth form with us?'

'Yes,' answered Olive, in her funny, stiff little voice.

'Got your night case? Good, you can come along to Matron with the rest of us. I say, where did Felicity and Susan get to?'

Felicity and Susan had been swallowed up by a group of fourth formers. There was pretty little Bonnie, the haughty Amy, and freckle-faced Julie, with her friend, Lucy.

Julie and Lucy had brought their horses to school with them, and all of the girls were eager to go down to the stables and greet them.

'Thank goodness that there was room in the stables this term for Jack and Sandy,' said Felicity.

'Yes, it's wonderful to have him with me again,' said Julie. 'I don't blame Bill and Clarissa one little bit for what happened last term, of course, and I know that it won't happen again. But I just feel happier knowing that Jack is here, at Malory Towers.'

Last term there had been no room in the school stables for Jack and Sandy, so Julie and Lucy had stabled their horses at Five Oaks, a nearby riding school, which was run by two old girls. But there had been great consternation when Jack had gone missing. Fortunately, he had been found, and the culprit arrested, so everything had ended happily.

Now, though, Julie was even more reluctant to let Jack out of her sight than usual.

'Come along, everyone!' came Pam's voice from behind the little group. 'Let's take our health certificates to Matron and unpack our things. I'm simply dying to see our new dormitory and common-room.'

So the girls picked up their night cases and trooped inside North Tower to the big hall. A small group of first formers stood there, all of them looking nervous and a little lost.

'Poor little dears,' said Susan to Felicity. 'Shall we offer to take them upstairs to Matron?'

Felicity nodded, but before they had time to approach the first formers, a large, fair girl with a round face and very rosy cheeks strode up to them.

'Come on, kids!' she commanded, in a loud, very hearty voice. 'Follow me, and I'll take you to Matron's room. No lagging behind now!'

'Heavens, who's that?' asked Susan.

'Must be a new girl,' said June. 'Probably a fifth or sixth former by the look of her. I say, she looks like a mother duck, with all her little ducklings following behind her, doesn't she?'

The fourth formers burst out laughing, for that was exactly what the big girl did look like! Susan, however, was a little put out. It simply wasn't done for a new girl to be so bossy, and take charge of the young ones like that – even if she was a top former!

Just then, someone called out, 'Hallo, you kids! No loitering in the hall now, or I shall dish out a punishment.'

The girls turned to see a tall, graceful girl standing there, a wide smile on her face.

'Esme!' they cried. 'How marvellous to see you!'

Lucy, who was Esme's cousin, punched the girl gently on the shoulder, and said, 'I'm surprised that you even bother with us small fry now that you're a fifth former.'

'It's only because there's no one else around,' said Esme with a perfectly straight face. 'Of course, if I should happen to pass you when I'm with any of my form I shall simply walk past with my nose in the air.'

Then she laughed, and the others laughed with her, for they knew that Esme – who had been in their form last term – would never go all high-and-mighty on them, no matter what.

When the girls arrived at Matron's room, the big, fair-haired girl was there, still fussing over the first formers. Matron herself was looking rather irritated, but her stern face relaxed into a smile when she saw the fourth formers. 'All got your health certificates?' she said, in her brisk tone. 'Good. Now, I want no illnesses, and no broken bones this term. Is that clear?'

'Yes, Matron,' chorused the girls, all except Olive, who hung back and looked at Matron suspiciously. The others knew that Matron was only joking, and there was no one they would rather have look after them if they fell ill. But, to Olive, she seemed a most unsympathetic person. Matron noticed the girl watching her, and, looking at the list in her hand, said with a smile, 'You must be Olive Witherspoon. And I have another new girl here for the fourth form, too. Sylvia, come and meet the rest of your form.'

The girls followed Matron's gaze and realised, with surprise, that she was talking to the rather bossy girl who had borne the first formers off. Heavens, was she going to be in the fourth form too?

The first evening

The girl turned at once, and strode across to the others, a broad smile on her round face. 'How lovely to meet you all!' she boomed, in her hearty voice. 'I'm Sylvia Chalmers, and I'm so happy to be at Malory Towers. I was at St Hilda's until the end of last term, you know, but our Head was taken ill and it had to be closed down. So sad! It was a simply super school, but I'm sure that Malory Towers will be every bit as nice.'

Sylvia paused to take a breath, and Matron seized the chance to say, 'Well, Sylvia, the girls will show you and Olive to your dormitory, then you can all unpack.'

'Oh, I know where the dormitory is, Matron,' said Sylvia. 'I arrived early this morning, you know. And my things are already unpacked. I was just going to show the youngsters to their dormitory, because I always like to help out if I can.' She beamed round at the others, who were all staring at her open-mouthed. Heavens, what a chatterbox!

Bonnie put a hand to her forehead, and murmured to Amy, 'I'm beginning to get a headache.'

'Oh, poor you!' said Sylvia, whose sharp ears had caught this. 'My mother suffers dreadfully from headaches, so I know just what you should do! You need to take –'

But Bonnie never found out what she needed to take, for Matron, quite affronted, cut in, to say crisply, 'Thank you, Sylvia, but *I* am Matron of North Tower, and if Bonnie has a headache she can come to me for a remedy.'

Then she reached up and took a large bottle of green medicine down from one of her shelves, shaking it in Bonnie's direction. 'A dose of this will cure your headache, Bonnie,' she said.

But, miraculously, Bonnie found that her headache had suddenly disappeared!

'I thought it might,' said Matron drily, putting the bottle back on her shelf. 'Now, off you go, all of you, for the first day of term is a very busy one for me, and you are all in my way.'

The fourth formers went out, but Sylvia lingered, saying, 'Matron, I was hoping that I might show the first formers where their dormitory is, and help them to settle in.'

Matron, who was growing a little tired of Sylvia and her pushy manner, said firmly, 'The first formers can learn to find their own way around, Sylvia. They certainly don't need you chivvying them round. Now do, please, go and join the others.'

'Well, what a know-it-all!' said Nora, as the rest of the fourth form made their way along the corridor.

'Isn't she just?' said Susan. 'And she acts as if she has been at Malory Towers for years, not just a few hours.'

'I can see that she's going to be jolly trying,' said Felicity. 'I wonder how she knows her way around so well?'

'You can ask her,' said June. 'Here she comes!'

And, when Sylvia caught up with them, Felicity *did* ask her.

'Oh, whenever I go anywhere new, I always make a point of exploring, so that I can find my way around,' explained Sylvia in her loud voice. 'I do so hate having to ask where I'm supposed to be going all the time, don't you?'

Felicity opened her mouth to answer, but Sylvia swept on, 'It can be quite uncomfortable being the new girl, among so many others who have been here for a long time, especially when you have been used to being *somebody* at your old school.'

'*Somebody?*' repeated Julie, with rather a dazed expression.

'Oh yes, I was head-girl in several forms at my old school,' said Sylvia airily. 'I'm afraid I do have rather a tendency to rule the roost.'

'Really?' said June in a smooth little voice. 'I would never have guessed.'

The others giggled, and before Sylvia could hold forth again, Susan said, 'Well, let's get along to our dormitory, or we shan't have time to see anything before tea.' Then, in a lower tone, she murmured to Felicity, 'My word, if Sylvia tries to rule the roost in the fourth form she'll be in for a shock!'

Indeed she would, thought Felicity, smiling to herself. There were several very strong characters in the fourth, and they would have no hesitation in putting Sylvia in her place if she became too bossy!

The fourth-form dormitory was a very pleasant room, large and airy, with cream-painted walls. Each bed had a brightly coloured bedspread on it, and a locker beside it, so that the girls had somewhere to keep their personal belongings.

Sylvia, of course, had already unpacked and arranged several things on top of her locker, and she hovered round the others now, saying brightly, 'If anyone wants a hand with their unpacking, they only have to say the word.'

'If they can get one in edgeways,' muttered June darkly, making the others laugh.

Olive, in complete contrast to Sylvia, had remained very much in the background and, as the fourth formers entered their dormitory, Felicity turned to the girl.

'Settling in all right?' she asked, with a smile.

Olive merely nodded, and Felicity, determined to draw her out, tried again, asking, 'Which school did you go to before you came here?'

'Chartley Manor,' answered Olive.

'What made you leave and come to Malory Towers?' asked Susan, coming over to help Felicity in her efforts.

And, quite suddenly, Olive's face lost its sullen, uninterested expression, becoming angry and red, as she hissed at Susan, 'Mind your own business!'

Then she turned away, flung her night case on to the nearest bed and began furiously pulling things out.

'Well!' said Susan, annoyed and rather shaken. 'What on earth brought that outburst on? Of all the nerve! Olive can remain in her shell now, for all I care! I certainly won't bother trying to make conversation with her again.'

Felicity, angry on her friend's behalf, glared at Olive. But the girl kept her head down as she concentrated on her unpacking, and didn't even notice.

'I've a jolly good mind to go and tell her what I think of her!' said Felicity, her cheeks glowing red.

But Susan said, 'Don't let's bother about her, Felicity. I'm certainly not going to let her spoil our first day back at school. Besides, at least I managed to get *four* words out of her, instead of just one!'

Felicity laughed at this, but she still felt sore with the new girl, sitting as far away from her as possible at the tea table later.

The girls rubbed their hands together happily as they went into the dining-room, Nora sniffing the air appreciatively. 'Sausages and mash, with gravy, unless I'm much mistaken,' she said. 'And treacle sponge for pudding. Yummy!'

Mam'zelle Dupont, the plump little French mistress, was already at the head of the fourth-form table when the girls seated themselves, and she smiled round, delighted to see everyone again, crying, *'Bonjour, mes enfants!'*

The fourth formers were very fond of Mam'zelle, and smiled back. But they didn't have a chance to return her greeting, for, once again, Sylvia pushed herself forward, saying brightly, *'Bonjour,* Mam'zelle! I'm Sylvia Chalmers, and we met earlier.'

'Ah yes,' began Mam'zelle. 'I remember. Miss Potts –'

'Miss Potts introduced us,' interrupted Sylvia. 'And you

and I had a lovely, long chat about France, for I spent my summer holiday there, and I was telling you all about it.'

Mam'zelle's smile began to slide a little, and she murmured, '*Oui* – it was a very, *very* long chat indeed.'

'I simply must show you the photographs I took, Mam'zelle,' Sylvia chattered on. Then she looked round the table, and said, 'I'm sure that you would all find them most interesting, girls. You see, we stayed in the most beautiful chateau, and . . .'

Then, to Sylvia's astonishment, the fourth formers all began to talk to one another, very loudly and very pointedly. Even Mam'zelle turned away and began to talk rapidly to Nora, taking care not to meet Sylvia's eye again.

As for Sylvia herself, she began to eat her sausages and mashed potato, feeling puzzled and a little hurt. She wanted *so* badly to fit in here, and really had gone out of her way to be friendly. Poor Sylvia! She simply couldn't see that she was trying just a little *too* hard.

It was a strange meal, thought Felicity. Normally the fourth formers would have pointed out all the mistresses to the new girls, telling them which ones to beware of, and which ones were easy to get round, or good to play tricks on. But Olive didn't seem in the slightest bit interested, while Sylvia seemed to know all there was to know already!

Just then, June glanced towards the first-form table, and noticed that there was a new mistress sitting there, beside Miss Potts, the head of North Tower.

'I wonder who that is, with Miss Potts?' she said, and

the others turned to look. The mistress looked very young, and had tightly curled blonde hair, which looked very striking with her dark brows and brown eyes.

'Do you know who she is, Sylvia?' asked June.

'Of course not,' said Sylvia, rather defensively. 'Why should I?'

'Well, you seem to know everything else,' said June.

'She looks awfully young,' said Nora. 'I wonder what she is going to teach?'

'Ah, I know who this new mistress must be!' cried Mam'zelle, who had been listening, and surveying the new teacher with great interest. 'Perhaps you do not know, *mes filles*, but our good Miss Hibbert was taken ill during the holidays, and has been ordered to stay at home and rest.'

The fourth formers were sorry to hear this, for Miss Hibbert, who taught English and Drama, was an excellent teacher, with a knack of making her lessons very interesting indeed.

'That's bad news!' said Felicity, looking very grave. 'I do hope that there is nothing seriously wrong with Miss Hibbert, Mam'zelle?'

'*Non*, but she must not return to Malory Towers until she has fully recovered,' said the French mistress. 'That is why Miss Grayling has engaged someone else to take her place this term. Her name, I think, is Miss Tallant.'

'She's very pretty,' said Bonnie, surveying the mistress critically.

'In a rather common sort of way,' said Amy with a sniff. 'I bet her hair is dyed.'

'She looks as if she might be good fun,' said Lucy. 'The younger mistresses often are.'

'I think she looks rather hard,' said June to Freddie, in a low voice that could not be overheard by Mam'zelle. 'Mark my words, our Miss Tallant is going to be trouble, and not fun at all!'

Olive, meanwhile, sat silently and ate very little, merely pushing the food around her plate. She wasn't interested in the new mistress. She didn't like Malory Towers. And she didn't like the girls! Not that nosy Susan, nor snobbish Amy, and certainly not the bossy Sylvia. As for Nora and Bonnie, they were both the kind of girls that Olive disliked most, with their big eyes, pretty faces and sweet, innocent expressions. Olive knew all about girls like them. She knew how they used their sweetness and prettiness to get their own way, and to make themselves the centre of attention. While plainer girls, like Olive herself, had to find other ways to make themselves noticed, or be ignored altogether.

Certainly the new girl had not made any impression on Mam'zelle, who had barely noticed that she was there. Felicity suddenly realised, with a pang of guilt, that no one had bothered to introduce Olive to the French mistress. Really, she thought, it was quite Olive's own fault if she was left out of things, for she had made no effort at all to respond to the others' attempts at making friends. All the same, someone ought to make the introduction, and as Felicity had been head of the form last year, she decided that it was up to her.

'Mam'zelle,' she said. 'I don't think that you've met our other new girl, Olive Witherspoon.'

'Ah, you are so quiet, *ma petite*, that I did not notice you!' said Mam'zelle, smiling at the girl. 'Well, these fourth formers will make you welcome, for they are good girls, and soon you will be just like them.'

Just then, Bonnie let out a squeal that made everyone jump, and leapt up from her chair, wailing, 'Oh no, I've spilled my tea all over my skirt!'

'You are scalded, *ma chère*!' cried Mam'zelle dramatically, getting to her feet. 'I shall take you to Matron at once!'

'I'm not scalded, Mam'zelle, for the tea was almost cold,' said Bonnie, dabbing rather ineffectually at the damp patch on her skirt with a handkerchief. 'It was just such a shock, that's all. Thank heavens I have another skirt in my trunk. Amy, be a dear and pour me another cup of tea, would you?'

How typical, thought Olive, watching the little by-play with a sour expression. Bonnie was quite obviously one of Mam'zelle's favourites, and the girl simply couldn't bear to see the French mistress paying attention to someone else. So she had purposely spilled her tea in her lap and then made a big – and quite unnecessary – fuss about it. Olive's lip curled scornfully and, seeing this, Felicity nudged Susan, murmuring, 'Just look at Olive's face! It's enough to turn the milk sour!'

In fact, Olive was being extremely unjust, for Bonnie had been deep in conversation with Amy, and hadn't even realised that Mam'zelle was speaking to Olive. Nor had she spilled the tea on purpose, for it really *had* been an accident.

But the new girl had taken a completely irrational dislike to both Bonnie and Nora, and it came to the fore again when the girls were relaxing in the common-room that evening.

'I must say, this is a jolly nice common-room,' said Sylvia, whose hurt silence at the tea-table had lasted all of five minutes. She liked the sound of her own voice far too much to be quiet for any longer! 'Very cosy! I'm sure we shall have some wonderful times in here, all chattering away together!'

'What Sylvia means is that *she* will chatter, while *we* are forced to listen to her,' muttered Amy under her breath, scowling at the new girl. 'I think it's dreadfully vulgar, the way that she pushes herself to the fore all the time!'

'Of course, when I was head of the form at St Hilda's, we used to have all kinds of fun and games in the common-room,' the new girl went on. 'I organised most of them myself, for if there is one thing I pride myself on it's being a good organiser. And, if I do say so myself, I'm jolly good at thinking up games to play. I could show you some of them, if you like, and . . .'

'Thanks. If we ever feel that we need someone to organise us, or tell us what to do in our free time, we'll let you know,' said June, with heavy sarcasm.

But Sylvia was too thick-skinned to recognise sarcasm, and she continued to talk and talk and talk! At last it became too much for Nora, who jumped up and put a gramophone record on.

'Good show, Nora!' called out Freddie.

Then, to the amusement of the fourth formers, Nora began to do a little tap dance in the middle of the floor.

'You're full of beans tonight!' said Pam, in surprise. 'Usually it's all you can do to keep your eyes open after the journey back to Malory Towers.'

'Ah yes, but I have been staying at my aunt's, and she doesn't live many miles from here, so it was only a short drive back,' explained Nora, stopping in mid-dance. 'So I feel quite wide awake, for once!'

'You're not a bad dancer, Nora,' said Sylvia – rather patronisingly, the others thought. In fact, Nora, who was naturally graceful, was a very good dancer and had been taking lessons in the holidays. She opened her mouth to tell the others this, but Sylvia got in first, saying, 'I simply love dancing, and, if I do say so myself, I have quite a talent for it.'

'My gosh, can you imagine it?' muttered Lucy, under her breath. 'It would be like watching a baby elephant!'

This was a little unkind, but Julie couldn't help laughing, and Sylvia, quite oblivious, went on, 'I coached some of the youngsters in dancing, for their part in the school concert last year, and it all went swimmingly. The parents thought that it was marvellous, and I do think that I have a knack for teaching people things, even if –'

'Even if you do say so yourself,' interrupted June smoothly, as muffled laughter ran round the room.

Sylvia looked a little puzzled at this, and while she was temporarily lost for words, Nora cried, 'Let me show you all a dance I learned in the holidays. Turn the music up, Felicity.'

Felicity obeyed, and the others moved back to make room for Nora. Then they watched, entranced, as she danced for them, her movements very graceful and balletic. Nora was a complete scatterbrain, and a bit of a duffer at most of her lessons, so it was very nice to see her excel at something, thought Felicity.

As Nora curtseyed daintily, the fourth formers clapped and cheered. All except Olive, who sat with her arms folded, her mouth set in a thin line and an expression of scorn on her face.

Susan, who still felt angry with the girl because of her earlier outburst, nudged Olive rather sharply and said, 'What's the matter with you? You could at least join us in clapping Nora.'

'Why should I?' said Olive sullenly. 'Nora is a show-off, and I don't like show-offs!'

The others gasped and muttered angrily, Pam saying hotly, 'How dare you, Olive! You take that back at once!'

'I shan't,' said Olive obstinately. 'She *is* a show-off, and so is Bonnie! Both of them have to be the centre of attention, all the time.'

Poor little Bonnie looked quite stunned, for she couldn't think what she had done to make the new girl dislike her so. Why, she had barely exchanged more than a few words with her.

'I see what it is!' said Amy, suddenly. 'You're jealous. Bonnie and Nora are both pretty, and dainty, while as for you . . .' The girl paused as she looked Olive up and down, rather scornfully. 'Well, no one could call *you* pretty!'

Olive turned pale, and shrank back as though Amy had struck her. Everyone else was quiet, for – although Nora and Bonnie felt grateful to Amy for sticking up for them – most of the girls felt that she had gone a little too far. Olive *was* very plain, but it had been rather cruel to point it out in front of everyone like that.

'That's enough!' said Felicity sharply. 'There are only five minutes until bedtime, so let's not waste them in arguing.'

'Well done,' said Susan, grinning at Felicity, as everyone dispersed. 'Once a head-girl, always a head-girl!'

Felicity laughed and said, 'Well, *someone* had to take charge, before things got out of hand. I must say, though, that I think we've been rather unlucky in our new girls this term.'

'Haven't we just!' agreed Susan. 'Olive is a real misery, and I'm afraid it looks as if she's going to be rather spiteful, too. And Sylvia is simply too pushy for words! She'll try and take over everything if we aren't careful.'

Felicity nodded, and said, 'I've a feeling that this is going to be quite a difficult term!'

Exciting news

After breakfast the following day, all of the new girls had to go and see Miss Grayling, the Head mistress. Fenella Thornton, the Head Girl, rounded them all up from the four towers and took them along to the Head's study.

There were six girls altogether, from various forms, most of them looking a little nervous as Fenella lead them to Miss Grayling's room. Olive, wearing her habitual sulky expression, walked a little way behind the rest, dragging her feet. She hadn't wanted to come to this stupid school in the first place, and she couldn't think that anything the Head mistress had to say would be of the slightest interest to her. Sylvia, on the other hand, was very eager to meet Miss Grayling, and felt quite certain that she would make a good impression on her.

She strode along confidently beside Fenella, and said brightly, 'I've heard that Miss Grayling is a wonderful person.'

'She is,' said Fenella. 'There is no one I would rather go to if I was in any kind of trouble, and –'

'Our headmistress at St Hilda's was just the same,' cut in Sylvia. 'So wise and kind.' Fenella, who was not accustomed to being interrupted when she spoke to a lower-form girl, looked rather taken aback. A sharp retort sprang to her lips, then she reminded herself that Sylvia was new and rather over-enthusiastic, so she held her tongue.

But even Sylvia was silent in the presence of Miss Grayling. The Head was a calm, dignified woman, with a rather serious face, which could, at times, break into the most beautiful smile. She could also be very stern indeed, when the need arose, and although Miss Grayling looked perfectly serene now, each of the new girls hoped fervently that they would never be called before her for misbehaviour!

Fenella left the room, and the Head spoke to each girl individually, asking her name and form. Even Olive found that she did not dare address Miss Grayling in her usual, surly manner, and answered politely. But she still looked rather miserable, and the Head stared at her hard. She knew far more about Olive Witherspoon than that young lady realised! Sylvia, for once, was quite subdued, and confined herself to answering the questions that Miss Grayling asked her, rather than chattering endlessly about herself.

Then the Head addressed the group as a whole, saying gravely, 'One day you will leave school, and go out into the world as young women. You should take with you a good understanding of many things, along with a willingness to accept responsibility and help others. I do not count as our successes those who have won scholarships and passed exams, though these are worthy achievements. I count as our successes those who learn to be good-hearted and kind, sensible and trustworthy – good, sound women the world can lean on.'

The six girls before Miss Grayling listened intently, her words making a great impression on them. Sylvia felt quite determined to become one of Malory Towers' successes.

Olive was quite certain that *she* would not be one. But Miss Grayling's words were so inspiring that, just for a moment, she wished that she could be.

By the time that the new girls joined the others, in the fourth-form class-room, all of the seats had been taken, apart from three, side-by-side, in the front row. Another new girl called Sarah, who was in East Tower, quickly slipped into the one nearest the window, leaving the two North Tower girls to take the others.

'I think that Sylvia and Olive are going to be thrown together quite a lot,' said Susan to Felicity, as the new girls slipped into the empty seats. 'They are the only two who don't have a special friend to pair up with.'

'Well, perhaps they will be good for one another,' said Felicity. 'In spite of her faults, Sylvia seems jolly and good-hearted, so perhaps some of that will rub off on to Olive.'

'Let's hope so,' said Susan. 'And, with a bit of luck, Olive might quieten Sylvia down a little.'

'Shh!' hissed Freddie, who was standing by the door. 'Miss Williams is coming!'

At once everyone stopped talking and stood up very

straight, while Freddie politely held the door open for the fourth-form mistress.

Miss Williams thanked her, and walked to the big desk at the front of the class. She was a scholarly woman, with a rather prim appearance and a gentle manner. But she also had a quiet air of authority, and certainly knew how to keep her class in order.

'Good morning, girls,' she said, smiling round.

'Good morning, Miss Williams,' chorused the girls.

'Please sit down. Now, before we get on with the business of making out timetables and handing out books, there are one or two things that I have to say to you.'

'I bet that she's going to announce who will be head of the form!' whispered Nora to Pam.

'Quiet please, Nora,' said Miss Williams, without raising her voice.

Heavens, thought Felicity, she must have awfully sharp ears, for Nora sat near the back of the class.

'First of all,' began the mistress, 'I am sure that you are all eager to know who is to be head-girl of the fourth form.'

Everyone sat up straight in their seats, and Miss Williams went on, 'I consulted Miss Potts and Miss Peters before making a decision, and, in the end, we all agreed that we would like to try Susan Blake.'

A cheer went up, and those nearest to Susan patted her on the back, while Felicity cried, 'Well done, old girl! You'll be first-rate, I just know it.'

Susan, who had turned quite pink with pleasure, could

hardly speak for a moment, then, at last, she said, 'Thank you, Miss Williams. You won't regret your decision, I promise you. I shall do my very best.'

'I am quite sure that you will,' said the mistress, smiling at the girl. 'And now, I have something else to tell you all. At the end of the term, the three top forms will be putting on a Christmas concert, which the parents will be coming to watch. The concert will last for approximately an hour and a half, so each form will have to fill half an hour. It is entirely up to you what you choose to do – sing carols, recite, or perform a short play. But I want every member of the form involved in some way, either as a performer, or behind the scenes.'

The fourth formers looked at one another, absolutely thrilled, as an excited murmur ran round the class. My word, what fun this was going to be! Each of the girls was absolutely determined that their contribution to the concert, whatever it was, would far outshine the fifth and sixth formers.

Miss Williams smiled at the girls' enthusiasm and went on, 'Susan, as head-girl, you will be in charge of the whole project, of course. And I am quite sure that you will have no shortage of willing helpers.'

There was no doubt about that! Half a dozen voices cried, 'We'll help you all right, Susan!'

Sylvia was just as excited and interested as the others. Why, at her old school she had produced a play and it had been a roaring success. If only Susan would hand over the reins and let her, Sylvia, produce the fourth's contribution to the Christmas concert, she would really be able to show the others what she could do!

Miss Williams rapped on the desk with a ruler and said, 'Well, I'm very pleased that you are all so eager. But we really must settle down and get on with more mundane matters. However, before we do so, I should just mention that we have a new English and Drama teacher this term. Her name is Miss Tallant, and she will be replacing Miss Hibbert for a little while. Miss Tallant will, of course, be happy to give you – and the other forms – any help that you require with your contribution to the concert.'

'Thank you, Miss Williams,' said Susan, whose head was in a perfect whirl. 'It's nice to know that there is someone we can call on if we need advice.'

The fourth formers crowded round Susan at break-time.

'I say, what a marvellous term this is going to be!'

'I simply can't wait to get started on our piece for the concert.'

'Yes, we'll show the fifth and sixth formers how it should be done, all right!'

'Well, we'd better have a meeting in the common-room, after prep this evening,' said Susan. 'Bring plenty of ideas with you, everyone, for we shall need them.'

'We'd better find out what the fifth and sixth formers intend to do as well,' said Felicity. 'I mean to say, it will be no use if all three forms decide to sing carols, or something. That will be terribly boring for the audience.'

'Yes, you're right,' said Susan. 'Well, I'll have to have a word with Fenella, and Katie Ellis, who is head of the fifth, then we can all make sure that we are doing different things.'

So, when the fourth formers gathered for their meeting that evening, Susan was armed with the necessary information.

The girls sat on the chairs and sofas, while Susan perched on the edge of a table, a notebook and pen in her hand. There was a good deal of excited chatter going on, and Susan clapped her hands together for silence.

'Well,' she began. 'I've found out that the fifth form are going to sing carols, and the sixth are planning to do a selection of Christmas readings.'

'Sounds a bit dry,' said Freddie, pulling a face.

'That's exactly what I thought,' said Susan, with a grin. 'Though, of course, I didn't say that to Katie and Fenella!'

'So, it looks as if it's up to us fourth formers to add a little fun to the proceedings,' said June, looking thoughtful.

'I say!' said Julie. 'Remember that splendid pantomime that Darrell, Alicia and the others put on when they were in the fifth? Wouldn't it be marvellous if we could do something like that?'

'We could never squeeze a whole pantomime into half an hour,' said Felicity.

'No, it would be impossible,' said Pam. 'Besides, super though their pantomime was, I don't think that any of us really want to copy Darrell and the others. It would be much better if we came up with a completely original idea.'

There were murmurs of agreement, and Nora piped up,

'How about a display of dancing? We could all dress up as fairies, and angels, and what-not, and . . .'

'And you could take centre-stage,' said Olive, with a sneer.

Nora turned bright red, stung by the injustice of this. She had made the suggestion because of her love of dancing, but she certainly wasn't the kind of person who wanted to steal the limelight all the time! Fortunately, the others knew her well enough to realise this, and Susan said coolly, 'Do you have any ideas about what we could do as our contribution to the concert, Olive?'

'No,' muttered Olive, sulkily.

'I thought as much. Well, if you don't have anything useful to say, kindly keep quiet.'

Then Susan turned to Nora and said, 'Thanks for the suggestion, but most of us can't dance as well as you can, so I really don't think it would work. We need something that we can all be involved in.'

'What about putting on a short play?' said Felicity. 'There are lots of scripts for plays in the library, so we could try and find one with a Christmassy theme.'

This sounded more like it, and the girls looked at one another excitedly.

'Marvellous idea!' cried June. 'And if we can find something that has a bit of humour in it, so much the better.'

Sylvia, who had been unusually silent, perked up at this and said, 'That sounds super! We put a play on at St Hilda's once, and it brought the house down. Of course, I produced it, and –'

'And I expect you wrote it yourself, too, didn't you?' said Freddie.

'Oh no, though I did add a few lines of my own,' said Sylvia, looking pleased at Freddie's apparent interest. 'You see –'

'I bet you designed all the costumes,' put in Bonnie.

'And painted the scenery yourself,' said Lucy.

'And probably took the leading role, too,' said Nora.

'Oh no, that would have been far too much work for just one person!' said the thick-skinned Sylvia, still completely unaware that the others were making fun of her. 'Naturally I supervised everything, for I think it's so important to have someone in charge who can organise things, and see that they go smoothly. And everything really did go like clockwork, if I do say so myself.'

'If she says that once more, I shall go mad,' muttered Amy savagely, while Susan went on smoothly, 'I do so agree with you, Sylvia. It's *very* important to have someone who can organise things at the helm. And, as Miss Williams has put me in charge, *I* am that someone. But that doesn't mean to say that I intend to go all bossy on you, and take over everything. This is going to be *our* play, and I will welcome any sensible suggestions, and listen to them.'

That was the right way to run things, thought Felicity. Susan was firm, yet not the slightest bit domineering, and she was determined that this was going to be a form effort.

'We really need to decide on a play as quickly as possible,' said Pam. 'We can't start casting parts, or deciding who is going to do what, until that has been sorted out.'

'Right,' said Susan. 'So, what I suggest is that as many of us as possible go along to the library over the next few days, and read through some of the scripts that are stored there. If anyone finds anything that they think might be suitable, please bring it to me. Then we'll hold another meeting in here on Saturday, and make a decision.'

'Good show!' someone called out, and Susan grinned.

'That's just what I hope it will be,' she said. 'A good show. The best show that Malory Towers has ever seen!'

The new mistress

Soon the old girls felt as if they had been back at school for weeks, not just days. Sylvia, too, settled down in her own way, though she often irritated the others with her never-ending chatter, and the way she always tried to take the lead.

This was particularly galling to Felicity, Susan and June, who had always been the leaders of their form, and the three of them often found it necessary to put Sylvia in her place.

'I thought that June was going to explode yesterday, when Sylvia took it upon herself to show her the best way to hold her lacrosse stick,' said Felicity, smiling, as she remembered.

Susan grinned too, and said, 'She *will* explode, one day, if Sylvia keeps it up. And I can't honestly say that I blame her! Sylvia is such an expert on everything – even things she's not very good at, like lacrosse.'

'It's difficult to dislike her wholeheartedly, though,' said Felicity, looking thoughtful. 'She's annoying, but she doesn't have any mean, petty faults.'

'Unlike dear Olive,' said Susan, with a sigh. 'Who has so many mean, petty faults that it is quite impossible to like her!'

'I really don't think I've ever met anyone so unfriendly in my life,' Felicity said. 'I tried to start a friendly conversation with her in the dorm yesterday morning, just to see if I could get through to her, and almost got my head bitten off!'

Felicity had seen the girl putting a photograph on her bedside cabinet, and went over to take a look. It was a picture of Olive, with a man and woman, whom Felicity took to be her parents. Her mother and father were smiling happily, but Olive's mouth was set in its usual, sullen droop.

'Are these your parents?' asked Felicity, pleasantly.

'That's my father,' Olive answered flatly. 'And my stepmother.'

As Felicity leaned forward to take a closer look, she noticed something odd about the photograph. Mr Witherspoon had his right arm out at an odd angle, as if he had it around someone's shoulders. But there was no one on his right side at all. In fact, the edge of the photograph was jagged, as if a piece had been torn off.

'There's someone missing,' said Felicity, mildly curious. And Olive's temper had flared up at once.

'No, there isn't!' she had cried. 'I tore part of the photograph off so that I could fit it into the frame, that's all. Not that it has anything to do with you – interfering little busybody!' With that, Olive had snatched up the photograph and flung it into her bedside cabinet, slamming the door shut.

'I wish I had never been sent to this beastly school!' she

raged, angry tears starting to her eyes. 'I knew exactly how it would be, with everyone poking their noses into my private business!'

Felicity was quite flabbergasted, of course. She hadn't meant to pry at all, and had only been making polite conversation. Just as she was on the verge of giving the new girl a thorough dressing-down for her rudeness, Felicity received some unexpected support.

'Pooh!' said a small, lisping voice. 'Who on earth is interested in *your* business, Olive?'

It was Bonnie, of course, her little nose wrinkled in disdain, as she went on, 'I think that you are quite the rudest girl I have ever met.'

Olive had turned on Bonnie, saying scornfully, 'Do you think I care what people like *you* think of me? Why, you're nothing but a silly, babyish little doll!'

'*Doll?*' Bonnie had squeaked. '*Doll?* How dare you! Do you know, Olive, I'm beginning to think that Amy was right, and you are jealous! I can't think of any other reason why you dislike me so much.'

And Bonnie had flounced off, while Felicity said to Olive, 'I'd be careful, if I were you. Bonnie is nowhere near as silly as you seem to imagine, and she can be a dangerous enemy. Watch out, Olive!'

But Olive had merely shrugged, so Felicity had left her to it, thinking that it was just impossible to help some people.

'Yes, she's a strange one, all right,' said Susan now. 'And I, for one, am quite tired of her and her unpleasant ways.'

'Let's not waste any more time talking about her, then,' said Felicity, slipping her arm through Susan's. 'We have our first Drama lesson with the new mistress shortly. That should be interesting.'

As it turned out, it was a *very* interesting lesson indeed!

Bonnie held the door open for Miss Tallant, as she entered the class-room, and gave the mistress one of her sweet smiles. Miss Tallant smiled back, and went to the front of the class, her dark, dramatic eyes sweeping round.

The girls eyed her just as keenly, for they had never seen a teacher quite like Miss Tallant before. Most of the mistresses at Malory Towers dressed neatly and sensibly, in quite plain clothes. The new mistress, though, was wearing a flowing, brightly patterned skirt and a very fussy blouse, with lots of frills. She also wore big, dangling earrings, which swung to and fro every time she moved her head, and Pam murmured to Nora, 'Heavens! She looks as if she has a couple of dinner gongs hanging from her ears!'

Nora gave one of her explosive snorts of laughter, and Miss Tallant turned her head.

'Do you find something amusing?' she asked softly, a smile on her face.

'N-no, Miss Tallant,' stammered Nora, looking rather apprehensive now. 'I'm sorry, I didn't mean –'

'Stand up when you address me,' said the mistress, still in the same calm voice, and still smiling.

Very red now, Nora got to her feet, and Miss Tallant asked, 'What is your name?'

'Nora Woods, Miss Tallant,' answered poor Nora.

The mistress's smile grew wider, and she said, 'Well, Nora Woods, it might interest you to know that I don't stand for any nonsense in my classes. Come and see me after the lesson, and I will think of a suitable punishment for you. Sit down.'

A gasp ran round the class as Miss Tallant turned to face the blackboard, and a great many sympathetic glances were sent in Nora's direction. But nobody dared to speak to the girl, for fear that they would be punished too.

The mistress turned to Bonnie, her ridiculously large earrings swinging, and she asked, 'What is your name, my dear?'

'Bonnie Meadows, Miss Tallant,' lisped Bonnie, her wide gaze fixed admiringly on the mistress.

'Bonnie, please hand these round to everyone,' said Miss Tallant, indicating a pile of books on her desk. 'As quickly as you can, there's a good girl.'

Nimbly, Bonnie skipped round the room, handing a book to each girl, before returning to her seat.

'Thank you,' said Miss Tallant, smiling at her with approval. 'Now, girls, we are going to begin reading a play. You will all take it in turns to read, until I tell you to stop. I really want to see you get into character as you read each part, so that I know what you can do. Bonnie, dear, you go first.'

The play was an extremely dramatic historical one, and normally the fourth formers would have enjoyed reading it enormously. But they could not forgive the new mistress for her harsh treatment of Nora, who was an extremely popular member of the form, and – with the exception of Bonnie, who seemed determined to impress Miss Tallant – they read their parts as sullenly as they dared. After a particularly poor show from Pam, who had read her part in an expressionless monotone, Miss Tallant shook her head, and sighed. 'Dear me! Bonnie seems to be the only member of the form with any dramatic flair at all. It is your turn next.' The mistress pointed at June. 'And for goodness' sake, do try and put a little *expression* into it.'

The corners of June's mouth twitched humorously. So, Miss Tallant wanted her to be expressive, did she? Well, she would give the drama teacher just what she had asked for.

'Do you mind if I stand up, Miss Tallant?' the girl asked politely. 'I feel that I will be able to throw myself into the part more.'

'Very well,' said the mistress. 'But do hurry up, for there are only ten minutes of the lesson left.'

Winking at Freddie, June got to her feet – then what a surprise the class, and Miss Tallant, had. For June really *did* throw herself into the part of the dashing young hero! Putting on a deep, booming voice, she read the lines loudly – so loudly that Mam'zelle Rougier, who was taking a class in the room next door, wondered who on earth could be speaking. The only male teacher in the school was Mr Young, the music master, and that, most certainly, wasn't his voice!

Enjoying herself hugely, June began to add some actions to her performance – clutching at her brow, throwing her arms out, and even, during one particularly moving moment in her speech, falling to her knees.

Miss Tallant stared at her in astonishment, wondering if the girl really meant to be taken seriously, or if she was playing the fool. The fourth formers, of course, were in no doubt at all, feeling laughter bubble up inside them, though they did their best to hide it. It was fortunate for Nora that June's voice completely drowned out her sudden snort of laughter, or she would probably have been given a second punishment!

'June . . .' began Miss Tallant, in her low, calm voice. But it was no use, for June pretended not to hear, and simply carried on with her impassioned speech.

'June!' said the mistress, speaking a little more loudly. 'I really think . . .'

But, to the amusement of the others, the girl ignored Miss Tallant, almost smacking poor Freddie in the face as she flung her arm back, in a dramatic gesture.

'Here, watch out, June!' cried a startled Freddie, moving her chair back a little, while the others were now quite unable to control their mirth.

Felicity and Susan were holding their sides, while tears slid down Pam's cheeks. Nora had stuffed a hanky into her mouth to stifle her giggles, and even the miserable Olive had a smile on her face. Only Sylvia, who did not have much of a sense of humour, did not seem to understand that June was fooling, and looked puzzled rather than amused.

Miss Tallant, however, noticed none of this, for her attention was all on June. Really, the girl was quite dreadful! And it seemed as if she would go on and on, right through the morning break and into the next lesson! Miss Tallant pursed her lips. She hated to raise her voice, or appear that she was losing control in front of her class, but it seemed as if she would have to!

'JUNE!' shouted the mistress and, at last, June stopped, looking round the class as if she had just woken from a dream.

'So sorry, Miss Tallant,' she said. 'I tend to get rather carried away when I'm acting a part. Perhaps next time I can show you how I would tackle a humorous role.'

'Thank you, June,' said the mistress rather frostily. 'I think that you have now given us a quite adequate display of your – er – talents.'

Just then the bell sounded to signal the end of the lesson, and the girls waited expectantly for Miss Tallant to tell them that they could leave. The mistress looked round the class, her eyes going from one girl to another. At last, she said, 'Well, if this form is an example of the standard at Malory Towers, I can see that I am going to have my work cut out. What Miss Hibbert taught you, I simply don't know.'

Of course, this little speech did nothing at all to endear the new teacher to the girls. Not only had she insulted their beloved Malory Towers, but she had found fault with Miss Hibbert. The fourth formers felt what little respect they had for Miss Tallant waning, for they knew that there was a strict rule among the staff that they did not speak against one another in front of the girls.

'Dreadful woman,' said Pam, as the fourth form went

to the cloakroom to fetch their coats. 'I wonder what she has in store for poor old Nora?'

Nora was not with the others, for, of course, she had had to stay behind to learn what her punishment would be. Sylvia was not there either, for she had gone to speak to Matron about something.

'Well, perhaps it will be a lesson to Nora,' said Olive, rather smugly. 'It will do her good to learn that there is one of the mistresses who won't let her get away with anything!'

'Don't tell me that you're a fan of our spiteful Miss Tallant, Olive?' said Susan, looking at the girl rather hard.

'Of course not,' said Olive hastily, turning a little red. 'I'm just pleased that she can see through Nora, that's all.'

'You keep that nasty tongue of yours still,' said Pam, angrily, giving the girl a little push. It was most unusual for the placid, good-natured Pam to lose her temper, but Nora was her best friend and the girl already felt annoyed with Miss Tallant for picking on her, without this spiteful new girl saying beastly things about her as well.

Seeing that Pam was really upset, Felicity gave her arm a squeeze, saying, 'We'll all back Nora up against Miss Tallant, Pam, you know that. And against anyone else who is mean to her as well.'

This last remark was obviously meant for Olive, who scowled at Felicity, before putting on her coat and going outside.

'Mean beast!' said Bonnie, pulling a face, as the door shut behind the new girl. 'What a lot of spite we are going to have to deal with this term, what with Olive *and* that horrid Miss Tallant.'

'Well, you're a fine one to talk!' said June, quite astonished. 'You were sucking up to Miss Tallant no end.'

'Of course I was,' replied Bonnie, calmly. 'Someone has to.'

'Whatever do you mean, Bonnie?' asked Susan.

'People like Miss Tallant always have to have a favourite,' explained Bonnie. And everyone listened intently. Bonnie might be silly in some ways, but she was surprisingly shrewd, and very good at sizing people up.

'She is the kind of person who needs to have someone who thinks that she is wonderful, and will stick up for her. So, I thought that it might as well be me. It might be useful to us, if she thinks that she has someone on her side.'

'Sort of like a spy in the enemy camp, you mean?' said Felicity.

'Exactly!' said Bonnie.

'I think that's a very good idea,' said Freddie, who had been listening thoughtfully. 'I really do. And Bonnie is certainly the right person to carry it off.'

The others murmured their agreement. With her charming manner, innocent air and sweet smile, Bonnie found it quite easy to get people to confide in her. Often far more than they intended to!

'We had better keep this a secret from Olive,' said Felicity. 'I don't trust her, and she might go running to Miss Tallant and tell her the plan, just to stir up trouble for Bonnie.'

'Perhaps we had better not let Sylvia in on it either,' Julie said. 'She *seems* decent enough, but we don't really know her very well.'

'We know that she can't keep her mouth shut!' said Amy, with a haughty toss of her head. 'I don't know which of the two new girls I dislike more – Olive, or that awful Sylvia.'

'Oh, come off your high horse, Amy,' said Lucy. 'Sylvia might be annoying in a lot of ways, but I don't think she's a bad sort.'

'Neither do I, but perhaps we had better not tell her any secrets just yet, just to be on the safe side,' said Susan. 'She's such a chatterbox that she might let something slip out without meaning to.'

The others agreed, and just then the door opened. Nora came into the cloakroom, a very woebegone expression on her face.

'Fifty lines!' she groaned, sinking down on to one of the wooden benches. 'Just for laughing! Honestly, girls, I'm beginning to think that I'm jinxed this term! First Olive takes a dislike to me, and now Miss Tallant. Am I really so horrible?'

The fourth formers crowded round Nora at once, anxious to reassure her.

'It certainly isn't you who is at fault!' cried Julie. 'Miss Tallant is quite the most unpleasant grown-up that I have ever met, while Olive seems to dislike *everyone*! Though, I must say, you and Bonnie do seem to get under her skin more than the rest of us. I can't think why!'

'I told you – it's because she's jealous,' put in Amy. 'She's so unattractive herself that anyone who is pretty simply makes her *green* with envy.'

June gave a crow of laughter. 'Olive-green!' she cried. 'That's a jolly good nickname for her. Next time she makes one of her spiteful remarks about Nora, or Bonnie, or anyone else for that matter, that's what we'll call her!'

The others approved wholeheartedly of this, and even Nora managed a smile. She cheered up even more when the girls told her about Bonnie's plan to suck up to the new mistress.

'I just hope that it pays off,' she said.

'Well, one thing I am absolutely determined about is that we shan't be asking Miss Tallant to help us with our play, or give us any advice at all,' said Susan firmly. 'I don't want her taking any of the credit for our hard work – we shall do it all by ourselves, and we shan't tell her anything about it at all!'

'Hear, hear!' cried the others, and Lucy asked, 'When are we going to have our next meeting, Susan? We're all simply dying to get started.'

'Well, I've looked at a few scripts, and there is one in particular that I think might be just right for us,' said Susan. 'Let's meet in the common-room on Saturday afternoon, and we can make a decision.'

'Good idea,' said Felicity. 'Now, come along, everyone, let's go out and get some fresh air, or our break will be over.'

'I'm looking forward to starting rehearsals for our play,

aren't you?' said June to Freddie, as the two of them followed the others outside.

'Yes, and that's not all I'm looking forward to,' said June, a wicked expression on her face.

Freddie knew that expression well, and, with a grin, she asked, 'What mischief are you plotting now?'

'Well, Freddie, I was just thinking that this is the last term where we will really be able to let ourselves go and have fun at Malory Towers,' answered June. 'Next term we will all have to knuckle down and study for School Cert. And, once we go up into the fifth form, things like tricks and midnight feasts will be out of the question. We shall have to go all serious and dignified, and set a good example to the lower forms.'

'Golly, so we shall!' said Freddie, much struck.

'And that is why I intend to have as much fun as possible *this* term,' said June. 'Are you with me, Freddie?'

'I should say!' said Freddie, her eyes alight with laughter. 'June, it's your birthday in November, isn't it? Wouldn't it be marvellous to celebrate it with a midnight feast?' Then she frowned. 'As long as Susan agrees to it, of course.'

'She will,' said June, confidently. 'Susan might be a bit goody-goody at times, but she's a sport.'

'And just think of the tricks that we can play on Mam'zelle Dupont!' breathed Freddie, looking quite ecstatic.

June laughed, and said, 'Oh, I have quite a few tricks up my sleeve. And Mam'zelle isn't the only one who is going to be on the receiving end! I think that both of our new girls need taking down a peg or two. And as for that beastly Miss Tallant – well, she had better be jolly careful. We're going to have to think up something very special for her.'

'We will,' vowed Freddie. 'She's going to be really sorry that she was so mean to Nora. The Malory Towers mischief makers are out for revenge!'

Olive is annoying

Of course, it wasn't long before Miss Tallant discovered that June's dramatic performance in her class had been a joke – and she felt extremely angry about it. It was Miss Potts, the stern head of North Tower, who set the new mistress straight. The two were in the mistresses' common-room together when Mam'zelle Rougier walked in and cried, 'Miss Tallant! Was there a man in your class this morning?'

'A man?' repeated Miss Tallant, puzzled. 'Of course not, Mam'zelle Rougier. I was taking the fourth form for drama this morning, and there was certainly no man present.'

'But yes, I heard him,' said Mam'zelle Rougier. 'His voice, it was deep and booming, and he talked, and talked, and . . .'

'Ah, that was June,' said Miss Tallant, her brow clearing. 'She was reading the part of the hero, in the play that we are learning. She gave a most extraordinary performance, flinging herself around all over the place and over-acting like nobody's business! It's quite obvious that she considers herself a very talented actress, but I am afraid that she is nothing of the kind! Why, even her friends were laughing at her! June didn't seem to notice, though, and just kept on going. She didn't strike me as terribly bright, I must say!'

Miss Potts looked up sharply from the work she was marking, and said drily, 'I am afraid that you have been taken in. June is very bright indeed, but unfortunately she chooses to use her good brains to amuse the others, rather than on her work. Watch out for her, Miss Tallant, for now that June has succeeded in duping you once, she will certainly try to do so again.'

'Ah yes, she is a bad girl, that June,' said Mam'zelle Rougier, shaking her head. 'A *very* bad girl. When I think of the tricks that she has played on poor, foolish Mam'zelle Dupont! Of course, *I* am not so easy to fool, and June knows that she would be punished most harshly if she tried any of her tricks on me! But you, Miss Tallant, you are young, and not so experienced in the ways of girls as Miss Potts and myself. Be on your guard, for if June thinks that you are weak, she will certainly take advantage of you, and try to make you look stupid – just as she does with Mam'zelle Dupont!'

The new mistress turned scarlet with humiliation. So, that wretched June had duped her! Well, she would very soon come to regret it! As for Mam'zelle Rougier – how dare she couple her, Miss Tallant, with the weak and silly Mam'zelle Dupont?

'I can assure you that June won't find it so easy to take me in again,' said the mistress rather stiffly. 'Nor will any of the others. I fully intend to nip such silliness in the bud.'

Fortunately, the fourth formers were quite unaware of

Miss Tallant's plans as they gathered in the common-room on Saturday to discuss their contribution to the Christmas concert. Once again, Susan was in charge of the meeting, and she sat at the table in the common-room, with a small pile of scripts in front of her.

The fourth formers from the other towers were there too, as it was to be a joint effort, and the common-room seemed very crowded indeed, with girls perched on top of cabinets and on the arms of chairs. Susan began, 'There are several good plays here, but this is the one that I think would be the best, for it is very short and gives us plenty of scope to add a few touches of our own. Felicity has read it as well, and she agrees with me. The play is called *The Christmas Tree Fairy*, and I'd like to read it out to you all now, and see what you think.'

And, in her low, clear voice, Susan began to read the play. The story was quite a simple one, about a fairy doll who has been abandoned in a dusty attic, along with lots of other old toys, and is rescued by a lonely little girl.

'I like it,' said Pam decidedly, as Susan finished her reading. 'It really captures the spirit of Christmas somehow.'

'And I love it when the toys come to life, when there's no one around!' squeaked Bonnie excitedly.

'We won't have to worry about shifting scenery either,' said Felicity. 'For the whole thing takes place in the attic.'

'Yes, but it's far too short,' complained Mary from South Tower. 'It certainly won't fill half an hour.'

'It will by the time we've finished with it,' said Susan.

'We can add a few jokes, and perhaps a song and dance routine. I think it'll be super.'

'Good idea,' said Mary. 'But who is going to write the song?'

'How about you, Mary?' suggested Felicity. 'You're excellent at music.'

'Good idea!' said Susan. 'That's settled, Mary. You are our official songwriter.'

'Oh, my word!' cried Mary, a comical expression of dismay on her face. 'What *have* I let myself in for?'

The others laughed, and Mary's friend Doreen clapped her on the shoulder, crying, 'Don't make a song and dance about it, old girl! I'll help you out.'

'June and Freddie, I have a job for you two as well,' said Susan.

'Us?' chorused the two girls, looking very surprised. 'What do you want us to do, Susan?'

'I want you to take the script away and add a few jokes here and there,' said Susan. 'It's quite a sentimental play, and I think it needs a touch of humour. And who better than the two form jokers to add one!'

Everyone cheered at this, and June and Freddie grinned, both of them absolutely delighted with the task they had been given.

'I'm going to produce the play, with Felicity as my assistant,' said Susan. 'And, of course we will –'

But Susan got no further, for Sylvia called out, 'Susan! If you need anyone else to help produce the play, I am only too keen to help. As you know, I've done this kind of thing before, and you know what they say about many hands making light work.'

'Yes, and I know what they say about too many cooks spoiling the broth,' muttered Susan under her breath to Felicity.

But Felicity was rather touched by the earnest, eager-to-please expression on Sylvia's round, rosy face and she said in a low voice, 'It seems a shame to discourage her when she's so willing. And, who knows, she might prove very useful indeed. Perhaps we should give Sylvia a chance to show what she can do.'

Susan didn't look entirely convinced, but she said, 'Perhaps you're right. But if she becomes too bossy I simply won't stand for it!' Then she raised her voice and said, 'Thank you, Sylvia. A third producer might come in very handy. Now, everyone, I'm going to ask if we can use the big hall for our next meeting, for it really is dreadfully cramped in here. Then we will cast the parts, and decide who is going to help backstage and so on. Any questions?'

There were no questions, but, after the girls from the other three towers had left, there was a good deal of excited chatter. Nora was hoping that she would be considered for the role of the fairy, and said to Pam, 'I do hope that Susan will let me try out for it.'

'Of course she will,' said the loyal Pam, at once. 'You're a marvellous actress, and you can dance beautifully. In fact, I can't think of anyone who could play the fairy as well as you could.'

But someone else was quite certain that *she* was destined to play the role of the fairy – and that someone was Bonnie. 'I have a fairy costume at home that I wore to a fancy-dress party once,' she told Amy, breathlessly. 'I must ask Mother to send it to me.'

'You would certainly make a lovely fairy,' said Amy, looking the pretty, dainty girl over with approval. 'I don't think any other girl in the form would fit the role as perfectly as you.'

Bonnie beamed with pleasure and said, 'Will you be trying out for any of the parts, Amy?'

'No, I don't want to push myself forward,' answered Amy rather piously. 'Let the others have a chance.'

The truth was that Amy wasn't particularly good at drama, dancing or singing, and she was well aware that she didn't stand a chance of getting one of the lead parts. And as she wasn't going to be centre stage, the girl would have preferred not to be involved in the project at all. But this was a vain hope, for Susan wanted everyone to play a part in the success of the form's play, however small.

'Though I can't imagine what we are going to find for Olive to do,' she said to Felicity, as the fourth formers got ready for bed that evening. 'The only talent she seems to have is for rubbing people up the wrong way!'

Felicity laughed and said, 'Well, if all she's going to do is stir things up and cause ill feeling, perhaps it would be best just to leave her out altogether.'

But Susan wouldn't hear of this, and she said stubbornly, 'No, Olive is a member of our form, whether she likes it or not. And she is jolly well going to take part in our play!'

'I wonder why she is so bad-tempered and angry all the time?' said Felicity, with a frown. 'I do hope that she settles down and cheers up a bit, for the sight of her miserable, scowling face puts a damper on everything!'

But, as Pam remarked a few days later, Olive only seemed happy if someone else was getting into trouble.

'She's so spiteful and mean-spirited,' said Pam, with distaste, as the fourth formers got changed after lacrosse practice. 'Did you see the smirk on her face when Miss Maxwell ticked Amy off for not trying hard enough?'

'And she nearly laughed herself sick when June got Mam'zelle Dupont to use that trick pencil in French this morning,' said Nora.

'Well, we *all* laughed at that,' pointed out Julie. 'That was the whole idea, after all!'

'Yes, but Olive wasn't laughing at the joke,' said Nora. 'She was gloating over the tremendous scolding that June got from Mam'zelle afterwards.'

'Good!' said Bonnie, with satisfaction. Then, as the others turned to look at her in surprise, she went on, 'Because June will have it in for Olive, and will get her own back on her. And I, for one, am looking forward to it!'

As Bonnie flounced off with Amy, Susan gave a sigh and said, 'I do so hate all this spite and bad feeling that seems to be brewing.'

'Horrible, isn't it?' agreed Felicity. 'Though I must say, Olive has rather brought it on herself. Petty spite is one of the hardest faults to forgive, and it always stirs up more spite in return.'

'Yes, you're quite right,' said Susan. 'And I think that Bonnie was right, too, when she said that June will try to get her own back on Olive. I say, where *is* June?'

'She and Freddie got changed in a trice, and dashed off somewhere,' said Lucy. 'I wouldn't be a bit surprised if they're plotting revenge on Olive this very minute.'

'You know, Susan, as head of the form, I really think that it's your duty to speak to Olive about her behaviour,' said Sylvia, an earnest expression on her face.

Susan was rather taken aback, and not at all pleased at this unwanted piece of advice from the new girl. Felicity, too, felt annoyed, and she said, 'Really, Sylvia, I don't think that it's your place –'

But Sylvia didn't even realise that Felicity was speaking, and went on, in her rather loud voice, 'We had a girl just like Olive at my old school. Of course, as head-girl, I had to reprimand her pretty severely. It did the trick, though, if I do say so myself.' She smiled at Susan and said sympathetically, 'There is such a lot to learn when one first becomes head-girl, isn't there? Especially if one has never held a position of responsibility before. But I am always on hand to give help and advice, Susan.'

And, leaving the fourth formers staring after her, open-mouthed, Sylvia put on her coat and went out of the changing room.

Felicity made an explosive little sound of irritation as the door closed behind the new girl, while Susan scoffed,

'As if I would ask Sylvia for advice about anything! If I needed anyone to help me, I would ask you, Felicity, or Pam. You have both had a turn as head-girl, and I'll bet you both made a better job of it than Say-So Sylvia!'

A shout of laughter went up at this, and Nora cried, 'What a marvellous nickname – Say-So Sylvia!'

'I suppose it *is* rather a good nickname,' said Susan, with a pleased grin, and the others chorused, 'IF YOU DO SAY SO YOURSELF!'

June and Freddie, meanwhile, were indeed plotting revenge on Olive. They were up in the dormitory, looking through June's box of tricks, the pair of them chuckling as they recalled jokes that they had played in the past.

'Do you remember the time that Mam'zelle used that soap, which made her face look as if it was streaked with dirt?' laughed Freddie. 'I say! I don't suppose you have any more of it, do you June? That would be a super trick to play on Olive.'

'No, I lent it to my brother, Peter, in the holidays,' answered June, before lapsing into a thoughtful silence. Olive's unpleasant habit of gloating over those who got into trouble rankled with her. Perhaps the girl would think twice about doing it again if *she* was on the receiving end of a scold from one of the mistresses!

June said as much to Freddie, who agreed heartily. 'It would certainly serve her right,' she said. 'I say, can't we think of something to do in Miss Tallant's class tomorrow?

There must be a way that we can get her to lose her temper with Olive.'

June clicked her fingers suddenly. 'I think that there is,' she said, grinning. 'Have you noticed how frightened Olive is of the mice in the biology room?'

'I know that she always sits as far away from their cage as possible,' said Freddie. 'And she jumps every time one of them moves. What have you got in mind, June?'

'Well,' said June, her eyes glinting wickedly. 'Just suppose that one of those mice found its way into Olive's desk. My word, wouldn't she squeal!'

'June!' gasped Freddie. 'It would be a marvellous trick to play, but dare we?'

June, who was bold enough for anything, said at once, 'Of course we dare. Miss Tallant's lesson is right after break, so we can slip along to the biology room at break-time, get one of the mice out and put it into Olive's desk.'

'Poor little mouse,' giggled Freddie. 'Fancy having to face the wrath of Olive! I say, June, he will be able to breathe inside the desk, won't he?'

'Of course,' answered June. 'He won't be in there for long, and I shall return him to his cage as soon as I can.'

'Shall we tell the others?' asked Freddie.

'Yes, let's,' said June. 'But we had better do it when Sylvia is not about. I don't think that they went in much for jokes and tricks at her old school, for, in spite of her jolly, hearty attitude, she doesn't have much of a sense of humour. And we certainly don't want her warning Olive of what's in store for her!'

Freddie nodded and said, 'You're absolutely right about Sylvia. I told her one of my best jokes the other day, and when I had finished she simply looked puzzled. It was quite obvious that she didn't understand it at all. A waste of a perfectly good joke, I thought!'

'Well, when Sylvia has been in the fourth form for a while, perhaps her sense of humour will come to the fore,' said June.

'I don't see how it can fail to,' said Freddie. 'Not once Sylvia realises what fun it is to play tricks and share jokes. That's one of the good things about laughter – it's infectious!'

'Well, one person certainly won't be laughing tomorrow,' said June, with a touch of malice. 'And that will be dear Olive!'

A very successful trick

The fourth formers were in a great state of excitement as they went into Miss Tallant's class the next morning. Everyone but Sylvia – and Olive herself, of course – knew about the trick, and Olive looked puzzled as a few sly glances came her way.

All the mice in the biology room were quite tame, and the one that June had picked up didn't seem to mind being handled at all. He liked it in Olive's desk as well, for there was plenty of room to run around, and lots of interesting things for him to sniff at. 'Quiet, everyone!' hissed Felicity, who was standing by the door. 'Miss Tallant is coming.'

The girls stood up politely as the mistress swept into the room. As usual, she was wearing one of the fussy, frilly blouses that she was so fond of, and a pair of earrings with enormous pink stones in them hung from her ears.

Bonnie, playing up to Miss Tallant for all she was worth, said admiringly, 'Oh, what a lovely blouse, Miss Tallant! You do look so pretty.'

'Why, thank you, Bonnie,' said the mistress, preening a little, while the fourth formers grinned at one another. 'Good morning, girls. Sit down, and we will continue with the play that we began reading the other day. Get your books out, please.'

The fourth formers watched with bated breath as Olive lifted the lid of her desk. But the little white mouse was hiding behind her pencil case, and the girl closed the lid again, without even realising that he was there.

'Never mind,' whispered June to Freddie, Felicity and Susan. 'Olive will have to open her desk again later to put the book away. She's certain to spot the mouse then.'

But the mouse had ideas of his own, and had no intention of waiting until the end of the lesson to make his appearance!

After about ten minutes, he grew rather bored with his new surroundings, and, feeling lonely, decided that he would like to go back to his friends. But how was he to get out? The mouse scuttled into a corner, the sound he made startling Olive very much indeed. What on earth could it be, she wondered? It seemed to be coming from underneath her ink-well. Cautiously, Olive removed the ink-well from its hole in the lid of the desk and the mouse, seeing daylight, stuck his head up through the hole.

Olive's expression of terror was quite comical. For a second she could only sit there, frozen in horror, then she let out a blood-curdling scream, jumping up so hastily that she knocked her chair over.

Miss Tallant, who had been listening intently as Lucy read out part of the play, jumped violently and cried, 'Olive! How dare you disturb the class in this way? Whatever is the matter with you?'

Her eyes wide with horror and her hand trembling, Olive pointed at her desk and stammered, 'A m-mouse! In my d-desk!'

The little mouse had been quite as frightened of Olive as she had been of him, particularly when she screamed so loudly, and he had swiftly retreated back through the hole, into the safety of the desk. He moved so quickly that even Sylvia, who sat next to Olive and turned her head sharply as the girl screamed, hadn't spotted him.

As for Miss Tallant, she didn't quite know what to think. On the one hand, she sincerely hoped that there wasn't a mouse in the desk, for she didn't like them any better than Olive did. But if, on the other hand, there was no mouse, that would mean that Olive was playing a trick, for no other purpose than to disrupt the class.

June, seeing the uncertainty on the mistress's face, was quick to take advantage of it.

'I'll take a look, if you like, Miss Tallant,' she offered, standing up. 'I'm not afraid of mice, and if there is one in Olive's desk I shall be able to remove it.'

The mistress had made up her mind that she didn't like June at all, after learning that her peculiar performance in class the other day had been a joke, but she felt extremely grateful to her now, and said in a relieved tone, 'Thank you, June. Please do so at once.'

June strode up to Olive's desk, saying, 'Better stand aside, Olive, just in case he makes a dash for it. You don't want him running up your leg.'

Olive certainly didn't want that, and she hastily stepped

into the aisle, moving towards the back of the room. June opened the desk, and immediately spotted the poor little mouse, cowering in a corner. Standing with her back to Olive, so that the girl couldn't see what she was doing, she swiftly picked up the tiny creature, slipping it into the deep pocket of her skirt. If only he didn't poke his head out and give the game away! But the mouse, quite worn out by his adventure, rather liked the warmth and softness of June's pocket and decided to settle down there for a nap!

Some of the others had seen what June had done, though, and were now struggling to contain their laughter! This became extremely difficult for them when the wicked June began rummaging violently in Olive's desk for the mouse, scattering books, pencils and all kinds of belongings over the floor. At last she straightened up and, facing Miss Tallant, said solemnly, 'There is most definitely no mouse in Olive's desk.'

'There is!' cried Olive. 'I saw it, I tell you.'

Miss Tallant, feeling bolder now that June had assured her there was no mouse, moved towards Olive's desk and peered in. Of course, there was nothing to be seen, and Miss Tallant pursed her lips, turning to Olive.

'Pick up your belongings from the floor at once,' she said coldly. 'And put them back in your desk.'

The mistress looked and sounded so angry that Olive didn't dare to argue. But as the girl turned away, her eye caught June's and she saw the glint of malice there. Suddenly she realised the truth. June was responsible for the mouse being in her desk. And June must have removed it. But where was the creature now? Olive's eyes fell on the suspicious-looking bulge in June's pocket, and she thought that she saw a slight movement. So that was it, she thought, her eyes narrowing. June had somehow managed to slip the mouse into her pocket. Olive opened her mouth to tell Miss Tallant what had happened, but June hissed, under her breath, 'If you sneak it will be the worse for you.'

She sounded so menacing that Olive felt quite alarmed. Sneaks were not looked upon favourably at any school, she knew that. And there was no point in making her life at Malory Towers any more difficult than it already was. So Olive shut her mouth, said nothing and turned to the task of putting her things back in her desk.

June, meanwhile, went back to her place, winking at the others, who grinned back at her. 'Olive!' snapped Miss Tallant. 'Come and see me when you have finished your lunch.'

'Yes, Miss Tallant,' said Olive bleakly. What a beastly school this was!

'That was simply marvellous, June,' laughed Felicity, as the fourth formers made their way down the corridor after the lesson.

'Yes, and now I had better get this little fellow back to his home,' said June, taking the mouse from her pocket and stroking him with one finger. 'Unless, of course, you want to do it, Olive?'

Olive scowled, then, as June held the mouse out towards her, gave a squeal and ran off down the corridor, the laughter of the fourth formers following her.

'Serves her jolly well right!' said Nora. 'Let's hope that she will think twice before laughing when one of us gets scolded now!'

Sylvia, who had watched in amazement as June produced the mouse from her pocket, said now, 'So there was a mouse, after all! But why did June pretend that she couldn't find it? I don't understand.'

'It was a trick, Sylvia,' explained Pam patiently. 'To pay Olive back for all the times she has crowed over other people when they have got into trouble.'

'Oh,' said Sylvia rather blankly. 'I do hope that June is going to own up to Miss Tallant.'

'Of course she's not, idiot,' said Freddie scornfully. 'The whole idea was to teach Olive a lesson. And that is exactly what we have done!'

'It seems rather mean to me,' said Sylvia, with a frown. 'I really think . . .'

'Sylvia, if you're thinking of sneaking to Miss Tallant, don't!' Susan warned her. 'Because we don't take kindly to sneaks at Malory Towers, and if you aren't careful you might find that *you* become just as unpopular as Olive!'

'I wouldn't dream of sneaking,' said Sylvia stiffly, her rosy complexion turning even redder. 'I just think that June ought to be persuaded to own up. If I were head-girl –'

'Well, you're not,' Felicity interrupted rudely. 'Susan is, and she agrees that Olive needed to be taught a lesson.'

'We *all* agreed,' said Susan, glaring at Sylvia. 'Of course, if you want to go against the whole form, that is quite up to you, Sylvia.'

But Sylvia didn't want to do anything of the sort. She so badly wanted to fit in at Malory Towers and make friends. At once she said, 'Naturally, I shall go along with what the rest of the form decides. I don't like Olive any more than you do, you know, but I think that I would have chosen a different way of dealing with her. I'm not awfully fond of jokes and tricks, you see.'

'How odd!' exclaimed Bonnie. 'That's rather a shame, because we play quite a lot of them in our form. Well, June and Freddie do. Really super ones, too!'

Unsurprisingly, Sylvia didn't look terribly thrilled by this, but as the fourth formers had reached the dining-room by this time, she said no more.

The girl was unusually silent during the meal, lost in her own thoughts. Olive, too, was quiet and sullen, but then she usually was, so the others didn't take much notice of this. As soon as she had finished her meal, Olive left the table and went to find Miss Tallant, to discover what her punishment would be.

'Well, if Miss Tallant gave me fifty lines just for laughing, she's certain to come down much harder on Olive,' said Nora, quite unable to keep the note of glee from her voice.

'After all, she did disrupt the whole class.'

'I think that what Olive did is worth two hundred lines at least,' said Bonnie, happily.

'That ought to keep her busy while we are in the

common-room this evening, so she won't have time to make any of her spiteful remarks!'

But when the fourth formers gathered in the common-room that evening, it seemed that Miss Tallant had not punished Olive at all, for the girl sat down in an armchair and began reading a book.

Felicity nudged Susan and whispered, 'I say, look at Olive. You don't think that she's going to be so silly as to ignore Miss Tallant's punishment, do you?'

Susan frowned at this and, raising her voice, called out, 'Olive! Why aren't you doing the lines that Miss Tallant gave you as a punishment?'

'She didn't give me any lines,' said the girl, sullenly.

'Don't tell me that she let you off scot-free!' exclaimed Pam.

'Olive, you had better not have sneaked on me,' said June sternly. 'I warned you what would happen if you did.'

'I haven't sneaked on you,' retorted Olive, glaring at June. 'But Miss Tallant has given me another punishment, instead of lines.'

'What is it?' asked Felicity. 'Are you to go to bed early?'

'No, I'm to do extra prep with Miss Tallant on Saturday morning,' said Olive gloomily. 'Not that it's any of your business!'

This really was a horrid punishment, for the girls enjoyed having their weekends all to themselves. They were happy, jolly times where everyone could do as they pleased, whether they chose to play games, go horse-riding or simply sit around laughing and joking in the common-room. And next Saturday would be even more fun than usual, for the casting of the Christmas play was to take place that afternoon. But nobody felt in the slightest bit sorry for Olive, for all of the fourth formers thought that she had well and truly earned her punishment.

The girl ignored the grins of the fourth formers and went back to her book, though Felicity, who stole several glances at her, noticed that she didn't turn the pages at all. She's only pretending to be engrossed in her book, thought Felicity. I wonder what is going on in Olive's head? What a odd girl she is!

Most of the fourth formers were looking forward to the meeting on Saturday afternoon, and the rest of the week seemed to pass by very slowly indeed!

But, at last, it was Saturday, and June, looking out of the common-room window after breakfast, said, 'It looks quite sunny for the time of year. Freddie, shall we take a walk along the cliffs in a little while?'

'That would be super,' answered Freddie. 'Would anyone else like to come?'

Amy and Bonnie, neither of whom cared for exercise and fresh air, both shook their heads, but several of the others agreed eagerly to the suggestion.

'Lucy and I will join you,' said Julie. 'But, of course, we will be on horseback.'

'What about you, Olive?' asked June, in a deceptively sweet tone. 'Would you like to come with us? Oh no, half a minute! I completely forgot – you have to do extra prep for Miss Tallant, don't you?'

Everyone laughed, and Olive scowled, before stalking angrily to the door and flouncing out. As the door slammed behind her, Felicity said, 'Miss Tallant will keep her nose to the grindstone, all right, while we are all out enjoying the fresh air.'

'It seems a jolly odd punishment to me, though,' said Bonnie, who had been looking thoughtful. 'I know that Miss Tallant is not on duty this weekend, for she told me so herself. Yet she has chosen to give up part of her Saturday too, so that she can sit in the classroom with Olive.'

This seemed very strange indeed, for the girls knew how hard the mistresses worked, and how they treasured their free time.

'I never thought of that!' exclaimed Lucy. 'Fancy wanting to give up part of a weekend off to spend time with a sourpuss like Olive.'

'Perhaps Miss Tallant has nothing better to do,' said June. 'The mistresses sometimes go home to visit their family or friends when they have a weekend off. Miss Tallant might not have a family. And I'm quite sure that she can't have any friends. I don't think she's awfully popular with the mistresses here either.'

'She's not,' piped up Bonnie. 'I stayed behind to help her tidy the classroom the other day, and she told me that Mam'zelle Dupont dislikes her. So does Miss Potts.'

'She really shouldn't say such things to you, Bonnie,' said Susan disapprovingly. 'I'm quite sure that none of the other mistresses would!'

'I think it's a jolly good thing that she did,' said June

warmly. 'After all, the whole point of Bonnie sucking up to Miss Tallant was so that she could get to know things about her. Well done, Bonnie!'

Of course, this was the first that Sylvia had heard about Bonnie's plan to become Miss Tallant's favourite, and she looked extremely startled.

Seeing her expression, Freddie said, 'I suppose you don't approve, Sylvia?'

'You're wrong,' said Sylvia, to everyone's surprise. 'I don't like Miss Tallant. She's sly, and if Bonnie can find out what she's up to that will be a very good thing.'

Bonnie smiled, and said, 'Actually, it's rather lucky for us that she doesn't seem to have any friends, for that means that I am the only person she has to talk to.'

'I don't think it's lucky at all,' said Nora, dismayed. 'If Miss Tallant is going to start dishing out Saturday morning preps as punishment simply because she has nothing better to occupy her time, we shall all have to watch our step!'

'Golly, yes,' said Julie, horrified. 'I always spend Saturdays with Jack, and Lucy with Sandy. And I'm not very good at English or Drama, so I'm certain to get a row from Miss Tallant sooner or later.'

'Well, perhaps we had better give our dear Miss Tallant something to do,' said June thoughtfully.

'Do you have anything in mind?' asked Felicity.

'Not yet,' said June. 'But I'll think of something, you may be sure. Now, let's go and get our hats and coats on and enjoy the sunshine.'

Miss Tallant interferes

The fourth formers enjoyed their lunch, for their walk in the fresh air had made them very hungry indeed. Only Olive seemed to have no appetite, pushing the food around her plate with a fork, but eating very little. She looked even more miserable than usual, thought Felicity. Miss Tallant had probably given her a really bad time. Despite her dislike of Olive, Felicity couldn't help feeling a little sorry for her, and said kindly, 'You must feel glad that your punishment is over, Olive. Did Miss Tallant give you a lot of extra work to do?'

'Quite a lot,' answered Olive, who was surprised to discover that she felt a little cheered by Felicity's interest. Then Bonnie, who was sitting nearby, said, 'Well, I walked by the classroom earlier, and you certainly didn't seem to be working very hard then. You were standing by Miss Tallant's desk, and the two of you were talking about something.'

'She was explaining the work to me,' snapped Olive, giving Bonnie a look of dislike. 'And how dare you spy on me?'

'I wasn't spying,' said Bonnie, with a disdainful little laugh. 'I just happened to be passing. As if I would want to spy on *you*.'

Olive flushed angrily, and lapsed into her usual morose silence. When the meal was over and the girls left the dining-room, Olive turned to go towards the common-room. Susan called her name, and said, 'Where do you think you're going? Have you forgotten that we are holding auditions for our play in the hall?'

Olive hadn't forgotten, for the girls had talked of little else for days. But she had been hoping to slip away unnoticed, and avoid having anything to do with the stupid play.

'Do I have to come?' she asked Susan now, her mouth set in a discontented droop.

'Yes, you jolly well do,' answered Susan sternly. 'Just for once, Olive, show a bit of team spirit, and do something to help the form.'

So, reluctantly, Olive followed the others over to the big hall. There was a stage at one end of the room, with several rows of chairs set out in front of it. Felicity, Susan and Sylvia, as producers, took three chairs in the front row, while the rest of the fourth form filed into the seats behind. There was a great deal of scraping of chairs and shuffling of feet, but once the noise died down, Susan stood up and addressed everyone. 'Well, girls, you all know why we are here,' she said in her clear voice. 'So let's begin casting the parts, and not waste any time. Of course, the two most important roles in the play are those of the fairy doll, and Amelia, the little girl who finds her. Now, who is interested in auditioning for the part of the fairy?'

Three girls put their hands up at once. One was Jenny,

a tall, dark, West Tower girl, who had a beautiful singing voice. The second was Nora. And the third, of course, was Bonnie.

'Very well, we shall try all three of you out in the part,' said Susan. 'As you know, whoever plays the fairy has to sing and dance, as well as act, so we really need someone who is a good all-rounder. Jenny, if you would like to take the stage first, please, we can –'

Just then the big door at the back of the hall opened, and Susan stared in surprise as Miss Tallant entered. The rest of the girls turned to see who had come in, getting politely to their feet when they realised that it was one of the mistresses. But whatever was she doing here?

They soon found out! Miss Tallant strode briskly to the front of the hall and said, 'Sit down, please, Susan.'

Astonished, and none too pleased, Susan did as she was told, and Miss Tallant faced the fourth formers.

'I understand that you have decided to perform a play called *The Christmas Tree Fairy*,' she said. 'Quite a good little play, though rather short.'

The fourth formers looked at one another in consternation. This was *their* play. What business of Miss Tallant's was it? Susan spoke up. 'We are going to make it longer by adding a few touches of our own, Miss Tallant.'

'I see,' said the mistress. 'What do you have in mind?'

'Well, we are going to add a song and dance, and June and Freddie are going to write a few jokes,' explained Susan.

Miss Tallant gave a cold little smile and said, 'Indeed?

Well, I shall have to approve them first. Now, I suggest that we begin casting the parts.'

The girls began to mutter among themselves, quite horrified now. Miss Tallant was trying to take over their play!

Susan, however, had other ideas. As head of the form, it was up to her to take the lead and she stood up and faced the mistress. This was really very brave of Susan, for she knew that Miss Tallant could be spiteful and vindictive, and her knees shook a little. But her voice was steady as she said firmly, 'Excuse me, Miss Tallant. I don't mean to be rude, but Felicity, Sylvia and I are going to produce the play, and the three of us would like to decide who to cast in the different parts.'

Miss Tallant stared at Susan as if she was something extremely nasty, and said coldly, 'And just what do you girls know about producing a play?'

June, whose temper had been rising as she listened to the mistress, got to her feet and said, 'Nothing at all, Miss Tallant. And we won't have the chance to learn anything if we aren't left alone to make our own mistakes.'

Miss Tallant turned quite white with anger and hissed, 'How dare you cheek me like that, June? I should watch your step, if I were you, or I might feel compelled to enquire a little more closely into that affair of the mouse in Olive's desk.'

June blinked, quite lost for words, for once. How on earth had Miss Tallant come to suspect that she, June, was behind that? Suddenly, yet another interruption occurred.

Miss Williams, the fourth-form mistress, had seen Miss

Tallant go into the hall, and had frowned to herself. She knew very well that her form was holding a meeting about the play, and wondered what Miss Tallant was doing there. Only that morning, Miss Williams had spoken to Susan about the play, and the girl had said politely, but very decidedly, that the fourth formers wanted to do everything themselves, without asking for any assistance from Miss Tallant. Miss Williams had been pleased to hear this, for it would be a very good thing for the girls to take responsibility for their play, and learn how to organise themselves. Moreover, the fourth-form mistress did not like Miss Tallant, and she felt that the new mistress might well be more of a hindrance than a help to the girls. Miss Williams went across to the door of the big hall and pushed it open a crack, so she heard what Miss Tallant said to Susan. She had been about to intervene herself when she heard the way that Susan coolly stood up to the mistress, and she smiled to herself. Then June spoke, and Miss Williams, opening the door a little wider, saw the angry, spiteful look on Miss Tallant's face. The trouble with June was that she was likely to get carried away, and perhaps go too far in her rebellion against Miss Tallant. And then the girl would only end up getting herself into trouble.

So Miss Williams strode briskly into the room and said, 'I am sorry to interrupt your meeting, but . . . Why, Miss Tallant, what are you doing here? Susan, I distinctly remember you telling me that you intended to produce the play yourself, with assistance from Felicity and Sylvia.

And I must say that I was very pleased to hear it. Don't tell me that you have changed your minds?'

'No, Miss Williams,' said Susan, noticing a glint in Miss Williams's eye and realising that the mistress was well aware of what had been happening. 'Miss Tallant very kindly offered her services, but I was just telling her that there was no need for her to trouble herself over us.'

'Most commendable!' said Miss Williams warmly. 'It's always nice to see you girls using your initiative and doing things for yourselves. Miss Tallant and I shan't hold you up any longer.' Then she turned to the other mistress, and said brightly, 'Come along, Miss Tallant. The girls are very busy, so let's leave them to it.'

Miss Tallant had no choice but to follow Miss Williams from the hall. And once the door had closed behind the two mistresses, a perfect hubbub broke out.

'Of all the nerve!'

'Who does Miss Tallant think she is? How dare she try to order us about like that?'

'Thank heavens that Miss Williams turned up when she did.'

'Yes, she has sized Miss Tallant up, all right,' said Susan. 'And now that they have both gone, let's get down to business!'

So, one by one, Jennifer, Bonnie and Nora took to the stage, as the rest of the fourth form watched with interest.

Jennifer's singing was so lovely that the fourth formers cheered when she came to the end of her song. She read a few lines from the play, too, and Felicity murmured to

Susan and Sylvia, 'She's not a bad actress. A little stiff, perhaps, but I daresay that's because she feels nervous.'

Then Mary sat down at the piano and played a lively tune, while Jennifer danced. Alas, her dancing was nowhere near as good as her singing or her acting, and Sylvia said, 'Well, I suppose it would be too much to expect her to be good at everything.'

'That's just it, though,' said Susan. 'The girl who takes this part *has* to be good at everything.' Then she raised her voice and said, 'Thank you, Jennifer, you may sit down now. Bonnie! Your turn next.'

There was no doubt that little Bonnie certainly looked the part of the fairy to perfection. She seemed even smaller and daintier than usual as she stood alone on the big stage. She danced gracefully and, when it came to reading the lines, the girl really threw herself into the part. Alas, Bonnie floundered when it came to the song, for not only was she out of tune, her voice was so high pitched that some of the listening girls covered their ears. Grimacing, Susan said, 'Simply awful! A pity, because she acts and dances well.'

Then it was Nora's turn. Nora's singing voice was not as pure as Jennifer's, but it was very pleasant, and the fourth formers clapped eagerly when she finished her song. And she was by far the best dancer of the three girls. Nora proved, too, that she was a fine little actress, and Felicity said, 'Nora is very humorous, too, and I feel quite sure that she will be excellent at doing the jokes and the funny lines that June and Freddie are going to write.'

Susan and Sylvia agreed with this at once, and Susan said happily, 'Well, it looks as if we have found our fairy! I shan't tell Nora yet, though. We shall audition for the other parts first, and let everyone know what we have decided at the end.'

'Bonnie isn't going to be too pleased,' said Felicity. 'I just hope that she doesn't throw a tantrum. You know how difficult she can be if things don't go her way.'

'Don't you worry about Bonnie, Felicity,' said Susan firmly. 'I shall deal with her when the time comes.'

Felicity felt a little apprehensive. Susan had a blunt way of speaking at times, and didn't always see that it was sometimes necessary to handle things with a little tact.

The auditions went very smoothly indeed, and both Felicity and Susan found themselves warming to Sylvia. The girl hadn't tried to push herself forward at all, and had worked amicably alongside Felicity and Susan. Soon all of the parts had been cast, and it was time to let the fourth formers in on the decisions that had been reached.

Susan stood up to face the girls, and said, 'Thank you to all of you who auditioned. Everyone did very well indeed. And now it's time to tell you who is going to play each part.'

The listening girls sat in expectant silence, those who had auditioned feeling both nervous and excited. At last Susan said, 'We have decided that the lead role of the fairy doll will be given to . . . Nora!'

A great cheer went up at this, while Nora looked as if she simply couldn't believe her ears. Those closest to the girl clapped her on the back, and Pam cried, 'Splendid choice! You'll be marvellous, Nora, old girl.'

Jennifer managed to hide her disappointment, and congratulated Nora, but Bonnie was quite unable to hide hers. Her bottom lip jutted out, and she scowled fiercely at Susan.

'Horrid beast!' she lisped to Amy. 'Susan has never liked me, because I used to be friends with Felicity, and this is her way of getting back at me. I don't like Miss Tallant, but perhaps it would have been a good thing if she had stayed after all, for I'm sure that *she* would have chosen me for the part.'

Once the noise and excitement had died down, Susan announced, 'Amelia, the little girl, is to be played by Molly.'

Molly, a very small girl from East Tower, with rather a serious expression, suddenly found herself beaming from ear to ear, as a rousing 'hurrah!' went up from the East Tower girls.

Quickly Susan gave out the other parts. Pam was to play Amelia's aunt, Julie was going to be a toy soldier, and Lucy laughed out loud when she learned that she was to dress up in a big, furry costume and play a teddy bear!

'There will be something for everyone to do,' said Susan. 'Mary is writing a song for us, of course, while June and Freddie are adding some humorous touches to the script. And we're going to need plenty of people to help paint scenery and do hair and make-up, and so on.'

'I've a good mind not to do anything at all to help,' muttered a disgruntled Bonnie to Amy.

But Susan hadn't finished. 'There is one more thing,' she said. 'There is one person I haven't mentioned, who is going to be very important to our little play. In fact, I would go so far as to say that she is vital.'

The fourth formers looked at one another in surprise. Who on earth could Susan be talking about?

'That person is our wardrobe mistress,' said Susan, looking very serious indeed.

'Because there are so many costumes, we really need someone who is an expert at needlework. Someone who has flair and taste, and a good eye for detail. Someone who, once she sets her mind to a task, works tirelessly to complete it. There is only one person in the form – in the whole *school*, in fact – who fits that description. And that person is Bonnie Meadows.'

Bonnie gave a gasp, her big brown eyes growing even bigger. Instantly, her disappointment at not being cast as the fairy was forgotten. And Susan was no longer a mean beast. On the contrary, she was very shrewd and perceptive indeed. Bonnie couldn't imagine how she had ever thought that she didn't like her!

Felicity grinned to herself. Good old Susan! She was learning that, with some people, a little tact worked wonders. Now she had turned Bonnie's sulks to smiles, and made sure that the fourth formers had an excellent wardrobe mistress, in the neatest possible way! Most of the others guessed what Susan was up to as well, and played along by cheering Bonnie, and praising her extravagantly.

'Simply marvellous! I can't think of anyone who would do a better job!'

'Yes, we can be sure of having just the right costumes now, with old Bonnie in charge.'

'I should say! Good for you, Bonnie!'

Bonnie beamed round and thanked everyone prettily. 'I shan't let you down,' she said. 'And I shall be glad of some help from anyone who is good with a needle, for there will be a lot of work to do.'

Several girls from other towers immediately volunteered their services, and Bonnie said, 'Perhaps tomorrow afternoon we can all go and look in that little room behind the stage, where all the old costumes from past Malory Towers plays are stored. We are sure to find some things that will be useful to us in there.'

'My word, you're eager, Bonnie,' called out Julie.

'If a job's worth doing, it's worth doing well,' said Bonnie, briskly. 'I intend to take my responsibility as wardrobe mistress very seriously indeed. Now, if you'll excuse me, the library has a fine book on play costumes, so I think I shall pop along there and borrow it.' Then she called out to the girls who had offered to help her, 'Two o'clock sharp, tomorrow afternoon, you girls.'

And with that, she walked purposefully from the room, as Felicity chuckled, 'Bonnie really *does* go all out when she takes on a task. I feel quite sorry for the girls who have offered to help her, for I think that she may turn out to be quite a slave-driver!'

Susan laughed at that, and said, 'Well, I call that a

highly successful meeting – in spite of Miss Tallant's attempts to sabotage it! Mary told me that she has almost finished writing the song, and June and Freddie have already written a few jokes into the script – and very funny they are, too. At this rate, it won't be long before we are able to hold our first rehearsal. Shall we go back to the common-room before tea?'

Felicity agreed to this at once, and as the two girls were walking along the corridor, June and Freddie caught them up. June's expression was unusually serious, and Felicity asked, 'Anything up, old girl?'

'Yes, there is, actually,' said June. 'It has just occurred to me that Miss Tallant knew the name of the play we are doing. But how *could* she know, for we haven't told anyone outside the form. And we agreed that we weren't going to tell Miss Tallant anything.'

'Perhaps someone let something slip out by accident,' suggested Susan.

'Who would do *that*?' asked Freddie rather scornfully. 'It's not as if any of us are in the habit of having cosy chats with Miss Tallant, for none of us can bear her.'

June's brow cleared suddenly, and she snapped her fingers. 'Bonnie!' she cried. 'She's always hanging round Miss Tallant, offering to help tidy the classroom and what-not.'

'Yes, but only as part of her plan to suck up to her,' Felicity reminded June. 'She certainly doesn't do it because she has any real liking for Miss Tallant.'

'I know that,' said June. 'But she could easily have

given something away by accident. And there's something else, too. Miss Tallant mentioned that business with the mouse, and it was pretty clear that she suspected I was involved. I don't see how she can have reached that conclusion unless someone told her.'

'Yes, we all heard her say that,' said Susan, looking grave. 'I didn't think anything of it at the time, but you're quite right, of course. We certainly don't want our dear Miss Tallant poking her nose into fourth-form business.'

The others were in wholehearted agreement with this, and June said, 'Bonnie said that she was going to the library, didn't she? Well, let's find her and tackle her about it. She has to learn that it simply isn't on to give away fourth-form secrets!'

Bonnie in trouble

June stormed off down the corridor, the other three in hot pursuit. Susan caught up with her as they reached the library, and grabbed her arm.

'Now look here, June,' she began. 'Don't go rushing in and accusing Bonnie of things, when, for all we know, she may be quite innocent.'

'Susan is quite right,' said Felicity. 'I know that Bonnie can be devious in some ways, but I really don't think . . .'

Her voice tailed off suddenly, for through the glass pane in the library door, Felicity had spotted Bonnie sitting at a table with a book. And bending over to speak to her, her blonde head very close to Bonnie's darker one, was Miss Tallant. Both of them were smiling, and Miss Tallant patted Bonnie's shoulder, before reaching into her bag and pulling out a bar of chocolate. She handed this to Bonnie, then walked towards the door. Swiftly, the four girls outside retreated along the corridor before they were spotted, and went into one of the empty music-rooms.

'Well!' said Freddie, looking astonished. 'Did you see that?'

The other three nodded, and June said grimly, 'Well, that seems to point to Bonnie being the culprit. And from the look of things, the information she passed to Miss Tallant certainly didn't slip out by accident.'

June felt just as shocked and dismayed as the others, for although she had suspected Bonnie, she had never, for one second, imagined that the girl's actions had been deliberate.

'It certainly looks that way,' said Susan, frowning deeply. 'Why would Miss Tallant have given Bonnie chocolate, unless it was in return for a favour?'

No one could imagine, and Felicity said thoughtfully, 'This puts a different complexion on things. If Bonnie *is* sneaking fourth-form secrets to Miss Tallant, it might be best not to tackle her just yet, for it will put her on her guard.'

'Quite right,' said June. 'Until we can think of a way of catching Bonnie out, we must carry on as usual, and all behave in a perfectly normal way towards her.'

'What do you think, Susan?' asked Freddie. 'You are head of the form, after all.'

'Yes, I agree with Felicity and June,' said Susan, who was looking very upset indeed. 'I must say that I am terribly disappointed in Bonnie. I know that she and I have had our differences, but I really didn't think that she would stoop this low.'

'Shall we tell the others?' asked Felicity.

Susan thought for a moment, then said, 'No. Obviously we can't say anything in front of Amy, for she is Bonnie's friend. We can't rely on Sylvia to keep her mouth shut either, and as for Olive – well, I certainly don't trust *her*!'

All the same, the four girls found it very difficult to stick to their word and behave normally with Bonnie. They had very strict ideas of honour, and anyone who sneaked, or gave away secrets, was beneath contempt, as far as they were concerned. It was June who came up with an idea to trap Bonnie, a few days later. She and Freddie got into a huddle with Felicity and Susan in the courtyard one break-time.

'We will pretend that we are planning to play a trick on Miss Tallant, and make sure that Bonnie overhears us,' explained June. 'Then Bonnie will run off and tell her tales, and Miss Tallant will try to foil our trick.'

'And that will prove that Bonnie is working against the fourth form,' said Felicity with a sigh. 'What do you have in mind, June?'

'Well, I thought we could pretend that we are going to do something similar to the mouse trick that we played on Olive,' answered June. 'We could say that we are going to put a big spider in the drawer of Miss Tallant's desk, perhaps.'

'Good idea,' said Freddie. 'Miss Tallant is very like Mam'zelle Dupont in that she doesn't care for spiders, or mice or anything like that.'

'Exactly!' said June. 'We will make sure that Bonnie is nearby when we are plotting, and we shall be able to judge from Miss Tallant's reaction when she goes to her desk whether Bonnie has sneaked.'

'Very well,' said Susan. 'The sooner we get definite proof that Bonnie is the one giving things away to Miss Tallant, the better, I suppose.'

So when the four girls went into the common-room that evening, they made a point of sitting close to Bonnie. The girl had her head bent over her needlework, as usual, and was chattering away to Amy as she sewed. Pam, Sylvia and Olive were there as well, while the others had gone off to see a slide show in the big hall.

'I simply can't wait to see Miss Tallant's face when she opens her drawer tomorrow and that spider runs towards her,' said June, in rather a loud voice.

Freddie giggled. 'We're going to find a spider in the gardener's shed,' she said. 'A big, fat one, with thick, hairy legs.'

'Ugh!' said Susan, giving a shudder. 'I can't say that I'm awfully keen on spiders myself. It will be funny to see how Miss Tallant reacts, though. And it will jolly well serve her right for trying to spoil our meeting the other day.'

'When are you going to play the trick?' asked Felicity. 'Monday morning? Jolly good.'

The four moved away then, to join Pam, who raised her eyebrows and said, 'What's this? Hatching a plot?'

The four girls looked at one another, and Susan said, 'Shall we tell Pam our secret? Let's, for we know we can trust her.'

Quickly, June explained that they suspected Bonnie of telling tales to Miss Tallant, and of their plan to catch her out.

Pam listened intently, her expression very serious. At last, she said, 'I simply can't believe that Bonnie is on Miss Tallant's side.'

'None of us wants to believe it, Pam,' said Felicity, earnestly. 'I know that Bonnie has some funny ways, but I honestly believed that she was completely straight. But if you had seen her in the library with Miss Tallant, you would agree that her behaviour was most suspicious.'

'Hush!' hissed Freddie. 'She's coming over.'

Bonnie joined them, saying excitedly, 'Susan, I have some super ideas for costumes. I've made some sketches and must show them to you.'

'I'm looking forward to seeing them,' said Susan, forcing herself to smile at the girl. 'Bring them to me tomorrow, if you like.'

'I will,' said Bonnie. 'I say, did I hear you talking about playing a trick on that horrid Miss Tallant.'

'Yes,' said June, winking slyly at the others. 'We are going to put a huge spider in her desk on Monday, but you must promise to keep it to yourself.'

'Of course,' said Bonnie, clapping her hands together in excitement. 'I shan't say a word. Oh, how I shall enjoy hearing her squeal!'

With that Bonnie went back to join Amy, and Freddie said, 'See! Even more proof, if we needed it. What a nerve, coming over like that to try and get more information out of us.'

Pam looked thoughtful, and said, 'I must say, she's a jolly convincing actress.'

'Well, we'll see how convincing she is when she's been well and truly caught out,' said June, in a hard voice. 'And then we will decide how to punish her.'

All of those who were in on the secret were looking forward to Miss Tallant's Drama class on Monday. As usual, Bonnie held the door open for the mistress, receiving a warm smile and a word of praise. June, who was watching Miss Tallant closely, thought that there was a triumphant glint in the mistress's eye as she walked towards her desk. She didn't go right up to it, though, noticed June, but stopped a few feet away from it – almost as if she was afraid that there was something unpleasant in there.

'Sit down girls,' she said. The girls did as they were told and, for a moment, the mistress stood watching them, her eyes hard and cold. They seemed to linger on June, and, at last, she said, 'June, please come out to the front of the class.'

June stood up, her head bowed so that the mistress would not see the little smile on her lips, and walked to the front of the room. Miss Tallant looked her up and down coldly, then said, 'Please open the drawer of my desk.'

June put on a puzzled look, and said, 'Open your drawer, Miss Tallant? But why?'

'Don't ask questions, June,' said the mistress. 'Just do as you are told.'

So June pulled open the drawer, noticing as she did so that Miss Tallant shrank back a little. Then the mistress peered over June's shoulder and said, 'Now kindly remove the spider that is lurking in there.'

'Spider? What spider?' said June, looking so puzzled, and so innocent, that Felicity had to clamp her lips tightly together to stop her laughter escaping.

'The spider that I know very well you have hidden

there,' said Miss Tallant, a triumphant note in her voice.

'Miss Tallant, I would never do such a thing!' said June, sounding so outraged that Freddie grinned. 'Why, the very thought of playing a trick on a mistress is –'

'June, your reputation for playing tricks and jokes on mistresses is well known to me,' interrupted Miss Tallant. 'So please don't waste your breath. I know that you have put a spider in that drawer, and I insist that you remove it immediately. After you have done so, I shall inform you what your punishment is to be.'

'But Miss Tallant, there is no spider there,' said June, looking down into the drawer. 'See for yourself.'

Rather gingerly, Miss Tallant looked. 'It must be hiding in one of the corners. Remove everything from the drawer, June, and put it on top of the desk.'

Obediently, June did so, then at last she stood back and said, 'There is no spider there, Miss Tallant.'

Miss Tallant was reluctantly forced to agree that there wasn't, and she said crossly, 'I believe that you have hidden it, just as you did the mouse. Turn out your pockets, at once.'

June turned out her pockets but, of course, there was no spider, and she said cheekily, 'You're quite welcome to feel in them yourself, Miss Tallant, if you think that I am hiding anything else.'

But Miss Tallant had no intention at all of doing this. If she did find a spider in June's pocket, she would simply die! Yet she couldn't let this wretched girl get the better of her.

Miss Tallant had been reliably informed that June intended to put a spider in her drawer today, and she was going to punish her for it.

'June, you will go to bed one hour early tonight,' said the mistress spitefully, and the fourth formers gasped in outrage.

'You can't punish June without any evidence!' cried Susan, stung by the injustice of this, and Miss Tallant glared at her.

'I can do anything I please,' she said in an icy tone, before turning back to June. 'Put your belongings back in your pocket,' she said. 'Then go back to your seat and we will get on with the lesson.'

Susan opened her mouth to protest again, but Felicity whispered, 'Don't, Susan. You will only earn a punishment for yourself. We are going to have to think of some other way to defeat Miss Tallant.'

So, reluctantly, Susan remained silent.

June, meanwhile, stole a glance at Bonnie's face as she made her way back to her seat. The girl really *was* a good actress, for she looked just as shocked as everyone else. June made up her mind that she was going to tackle her later over her deceit – and, my goodness, wouldn't she give her something to look shocked about! The girl wasn't terribly upset about her punishment, though having to go to bed early was a frightful bore. But she *was* upset by the fact that the punishment was an unjust one. She intended to use her hour of peace and quiet to good purpose, however – in thinking up a way to get back at Miss Tallant!

'Phew!' said Pam, when the girls emerged from the classroom. 'What a lesson! How I dislike that woman.'

'It's so terribly unfair!' cried Susan. 'June is being punished for something that she hasn't even done.'

'Don't worry about me, Susan,' said June. 'The main thing is that it proved our suspicions are correct, and that Bonnie is giving our secrets away to Miss Tallant. Where *is* Bonnie, anyway?'

'Oh, she stayed behind to help Miss Tallant tidy up the classroom,' said Nora. 'But what's all this about Bonnie telling her our secrets?'

'Of course, you don't know, do you?' said Felicity. And she and Susan told Nora, Julie and Lucy what had been happening.

They were very shocked, of course, and Lucy said gravely, 'What are we going to do about it?'

'Speak to her about it, of course,' said June. 'And I vote we punish the little beast by sending her to Coventry.'

'That will be a very hard punishment for her to bear, because Bonnie loves to chatter,' said Julie.

'I wonder if Amy will stand out against the punishment?' said Nora. 'After all, Bonnie is her friend.'

'Well, if she does, then I'm afraid we shall have to send Amy to Coventry, too,' said Susan, her expression grim. 'We'll tackle her in the common-room after tea tonight.'

So, after tea that night, the girls gathered in the common-room.

Susan was sitting with Felicity, Pam and a few others, and she said, 'Well, I vote that we get this whole beastly business over with as quickly as possible.'

The others agreed, and Susan called out, 'Bonnie, can you come over here a minute, please? There is something we need to talk to you about.'

Surprised, Bonnie went over to Susan, who decided that it was no use beating about the bush, and said, 'Bonnie, I need to ask you something. Have you been letting Miss Tallant in on some of our form's secrets?'

Bonnie gave a gasp, and said at once, 'Of course not! What makes you ask such a thing, Susan?'

'She's fibbing!' said June. 'There's no one who can play innocent as well as Bonnie can. And we all know how good she is at acting.'

'That's enough, June,' said Susan sharply. 'The thing is, Bonnie, someone told Miss Tallant the name of the play that we are doing.'

'And they sneaked to her about the mouse that I put in Olive's desk,' said June, who was far too angry to stay silent. 'And we saw her with you in the library on the day of our meeting. She gave you a bar of chocolate.'

'Yes, because she had asked me to do something for her, and said that she would give me a bar of chocolate if I did,' said Bonnie, who had turned pale. 'It was all part of my plan to suck up to her.'

Freddie gave a harsh laugh. 'Yes, but you went a little too far in your plan, didn't you? You decided that you had more to gain from being on Miss Tallant's side than ours.'

'That's a horrid lie!' cried Bonnie, tears starting to her big, brown eyes.

'Of course it is,' said Amy, entering the battle. 'How dare you accuse Bonnie of such a thing?'

'I realise that you want to stick up for your friend, Amy,' said Felicity. 'But we know that Bonnie is the culprit. You see, we let her overhear us talking about June's plan to put a spider in Miss Tallant's desk. And, sure enough, word reached Miss Tallant's ears.'

'But it wasn't me!' protested Bonnie, tears beginning to trickle down her cheeks now. 'I wasn't the only one who overheard you. Sylvia was there that night, and so was Olive. And Pam! It could just as easily have been one of them.'

Of course, the others knew that it wasn't Pam, for she had come up through the school with them and would never dream of such a thing. Felicity couldn't help glancing at Sylvia and Olive, though. Sylvia was looking extremely startled, while Olive wore her usual miserable expression. *Could* it have been one of them? She said to Bonnie, 'All right then, you tell us what this mysterious job was that Miss Tallant asked you to do. Then, perhaps, we will believe you.'

But Bonnie had a stubborn streak, and she pursed her lips, saying through her tears, 'I shan't tell you, for if you were true friends you would believe me, and wouldn't expect me to explain myself to you like this.'

'So you are refusing to tell us?' said Susan, looking grave.

Bonnie's soft, brown curls shook as she nodded her head.

'Don't be an ass, Bonnie!' begged Felicity. 'Just tell us what Miss Tallant wanted you to do, and that will be an end to all of this.'

This time Bonnie shook her head, a stubborn set to her firm little chin.

'Then I am afraid, Bonnie, that we will have to assume that you are the sneak,' said Susan heavily. 'And your punishment is that you will be sent to Coventry. Not one girl in the form is to talk to you, or have anything to do with you, for a whole week.'

Then Amy surprised everyone by putting her arm around Bonnie's heaving shoulders, and saying loyally, 'Well, I am not joining in your silly punishment, and I don't care if you send me to Coventry as well! Come along, Bonnie, let's go somewhere where we can be alone.'

With that, she led the weeping girl from the room and, as the door closed behind them, Susan grimaced and said, 'Well, that was simply beastly, but it had to be done.'

Most of the others agreed at once, but Felicity remained silent. She remembered how Bonnie had played a big part in reuniting Julie with her missing horse, Jack, last term. The girl had certainly proved her loyalty to the form then. And there were several other past incidents when Bonnie had shown that, although she could be rather unscrupulous when it came to getting what she wanted, she was absolutely straight and honest – in her own, rather strange way!

Oh dear, thought Felicity, I do hope that we haven't made a dreadful mistake!

A shock for the fourth form

Several days later Felicity and Susan learned some startling news. It was a pleasant, if cold, afternoon, and the two of them were wrapped up in coats, hats and scarves as they walked through the grounds.

'I shall be glad when Bonnie's period of Coventry is over,' said Susan with a sigh. 'It really is horrible. And it is making things awfully difficult as far as the play is concerned, for I can't discuss the costumes with her until I can speak to her again.'

'Yes, but even when we are allowed to speak to Bonnie again, things will never be the same,' said Felicity thoughtfully. 'For this incident will always be at the back of our minds. It's a shame, because although I didn't like Bonnie much when she first came to Malory Towers, I've grown quite fond of her now.'

'Yes, she has many good qualities, although she has a funny way of going about things sometimes,' said Susan. 'Still, I suppose that no one is completely good, or completely bad. And once Bonnie's punishment is over, we shall all have to do our best to try to forget what she has done, and help her try to make amends.'

Just then, the two girls saw a figure coming towards

them, and both groaned inwardly. For it was none other than Miss Tallant!

'Susan!' said the mistress sharply, as she drew level with the two girls. 'I understand that you took a book about play production from my desk yesterday, without permission. Not a very good example for a head-girl to set her form.'

Susan flushed bright red. She had sneaked the book from Miss Tallant's desk, for she knew very well that the mistress did not like her, and would certainly have refused to lend it to her if she had asked.

She had flicked through it in the common-room yesterday evening, and had meant to put it back on Miss Tallant's desk this morning, before the mistress even realised it had gone. But, alas for Susan, she had completely forgotten about it, and now she could have kicked herself!

'Kindly ask permission before borrowing anything again, Susan,' said Miss Tallant coldly. 'And please bring the book to me in the mistresses' common-room before prep this evening.'

'When I will no doubt be given lines, or some other beastly punishment!' muttered Susan as the mistress walked briskly away. 'Blow! Why didn't I remember to put it back this morning?'

'Susan,' said Felicity, with a frown. 'How did Miss Tallant know that you had taken her book?'

'Well, she noticed it wasn't there, I suppose,' said Susan, shrugging.

'Yes, I know *that*,' said Felicity, a little impatiently. 'But how did she know that *you* took it, when it could have been any one of us fourth formers?'

'Golly, I didn't think of that!' exclaimed Susan. 'Well, there is only one explanation. Bonnie must have been tittle-tattling again. Which means that, even after being sent to Coventry, she *still* hasn't learned her lesson! Honestly, that girl is a glutton for punishment!'

'Half a minute, though!' said Felicity. 'Bonnie couldn't have known that it was you who took the book, for she wasn't there when you took it. I was, and so were Pam and Nora – but not Bonnie.'

Susan thought this over for a moment, then said, 'But she *was* in the common-room last night, while I was sitting there reading it. I noticed that she kept glaring across at me, and thought it was because she was still sore at being ignored by everyone. But, of course, she must have been planning to tell on me to Miss Tallant all along.'

Felicity brooded on this as the two girls walked on. They had almost walked as far as the stables, and could see a slim, red-haired girl patting the nose of one of the horses, who had stuck his head over the stable door.

'I say, there's old Clarissa!' cried Susan. 'Hi, Clarissa!'

The girl turned her head, smiling when she saw Felicity and Susan coming towards her. 'Hallo, you two!' she said brightly. 'You only just caught me. I've just been to see Miss Peters, and was about to go back to Five Oaks.'

'How are things at Five Oaks?' asked Susan. 'Bill all right?'

The three chatted together for a while, then Clarissa

said, 'I met that new teacher of yours in town, the other day – Miss Tallant. We had quite a chat.'

'Really?' said Felicity. 'How did you come to meet her, Clarissa?'

'Well, I was in the little tea-shop, waiting for Bill, and Miss Tallant sat down at the table next to mine. I didn't realise who she was at first, of course, but then we fell into conversation. Very pleasant woman!'

Felicity and Susan exchanged startled glances and, noticing this, Clarissa laughed. 'Do I detect that Miss Tallant is not very popular?'

'She's extremely *un*popular!' said Susan, pulling a face.

She and Felicity went on to tell Clarissa about some of the things Miss Tallant had done, and Clarissa exclaimed in surprise. 'Well, I never! She seemed awfully nice when she was talking to me. And, having a niece of her own here, you would think that she would know the best way to handle young girls.'

'A *niece*!' exclaimed the two girls in unison, completely taken aback.

'Well, that's the first we've heard of it!' said Felicity. 'Who is this niece, Clarissa? Which form is she in?'

'Why, the fourth form,' answered Clarissa. 'Apparently she has just started this term.' Clarissa soon went on her way, leaving Felicity and Susan to stare at one another in horror.

'You know what this means, don't you, Felicity?' said Susan in a very serious tone.

'Yes,' said Felicity, also sounding very grave. 'Either

Sylvia or Olive is Miss Tallant's niece. And whichever one of them it is must also be the person who has been sneaking to her.'

'Which means that we accused poor little Bonnie unjustly,' said Susan, with a groan. 'I feel simply dreadful! Felicity, we must round up the others at once, and call a form meeting.'

'Of course,' said Felicity. 'Wait a minute, though! There are two of the others that we don't want at our meeting – Sylvia and Olive themselves. Whichever one of them is the mysterious niece, she obviously doesn't want anyone to know about the connection. And if we ask straight out she is likely to deny it.'

'Yes,' said Susan, looking thoughtful. 'We need to set a trap for her, just as we did for Bonnie. And this time we need to make sure that nothing goes wrong.'

Susan called a meeting of the North Tower fourth formers in one of the music-rooms that evening. Sylvia and Olive, alone in the common-room, wondered where everyone had disappeared to.

'Perhaps there's a debate in the hall, or a slide show, or something,' said Sylvia, sounding puzzled. 'Though I'm quite sure I would have remembered. Do you know where they can all be, Olive?'

Olive shook her head and hoped that Sylvia wasn't going to chatter all evening. She wanted to be alone with her thoughts.

'They can't be holding a rehearsal for the play,' Sylvia went on. 'Or we would have been invited too. Perhaps they're planning some sort of trick, and don't want to let us in on it.'

Olive's ears pricked up at this. 'Perhaps they are,' she said, sounding more friendly. 'Jolly mean of them to leave us out.'

'Well, they know that I'm not awfully fond of jokes and tricks,' said Sylvia. 'I wish that I was, but I never seem to see the funny side of things.'

'I say! Perhaps they are planning to play a trick on us,' said Olive. 'That would explain why they don't want us involved.'

Sylvia looked extremely dismayed at this, and said, 'Surely they wouldn't be so mean?'

'They probably just see it as a bit of fun, and don't think that it's mean at all,' said Olive. 'All the same, after that business with the mouse, I don't really want to be the victim of another of June's pranks. I vote that we go and look for them, Sylvia, and see if we can overhear what they are up to.'

'That seems rather sneaky, don't you think?' said Sylvia, looking rather uncomfortable.

'Nonsense! They are the ones who are being sneaky, plotting things behind our backs,' said Olive. 'Come on, Sylvia! Imagine how uncomfortable you are going to feel tomorrow, knowing that something may be going to happen to you, but not knowing where or when. Why, you'll be on tenterhooks.'

This was quite true. Sylvia really did find the thought of a trick being played on her quite horrid. So, reluctantly, she stood up and said, 'Very well. Let's see if we can track them down.'

But the fourth formers had hidden themselves well. Susan had chosen a music-room right at the top of North Tower, which hardly anybody used. There was no glass in the door, and once all the girls had filed in, she locked the door behind them.

Bonnie had been most surprised to be invited to this meeting, and had said to Susan, 'I thought you weren't supposed to speak to me.'

'Yes, well, I'm afraid there's been a bit of a mis-understanding, Bonnie,' Susan had said, turning red. 'Amy is invited too, of course. I'll explain it all to you both later, at the meeting.'

Bonnie had shrugged, and said, 'You may not get the chance. I don't know if I shall bother turning up.'

And with that, she had walked off, her little nose in the air.

But curiosity had got the better of Bonnie, and now she was in the little music-room with all the others, waiting to hear what Susan had to say.

'It's awfully cramped in here,' complained Amy. 'And it smells dreadfully musty.'

'Well, I shall be as quick as possible,' said Susan. 'Then we can all go back to the comfort of the common-room.'

'I say, Susan, Sylvia and Olive aren't here,' said Julie.

'They weren't invited,' said Felicity. 'And you will understand why, in a moment.'

Swiftly, Susan told the fourth formers what she and

Felicity had learned from Clarissa, and, of course, there was a perfect outcry.

'I wish I knew which one of them it was!'

'Yes, wouldn't I like to tell her what I think of her.'

'To think that she let us blame poor Bonnie,' said June, who was feeling rather ashamed of herself, for she had been the first to accuse Bonnie. She went up to the girl now and held out her hand, saying forthrightly, 'I'm most terribly sorry, Bonnie. I should have known that you wouldn't betray the form like that. I just hope that you will accept my apology.'

Bonnie stared solemnly at June and, for a moment, the others thought that she was going to reject the girl's frank apology. But then she smiled and took June's hand, and a sigh of relief went round the room.

'We are all very sorry, Bonnie,' said Susan. 'We misjudged you badly, and we will all do what we can to make it up to you. Amy, too, for we sent her to Coventry as well. She was the only one who had the good sense to realise that you couldn't possibly have been the sneak, and she was courageous and loyal in sticking by you.'

Amy, unaccustomed to being praised for these good qualities, found herself turning quite pink with pleasure, and graciously inclined her head.

'Well, thank goodness that is sorted out, at least,' said Felicity, thankfully. 'Jolly decent of you to forgive us, Bonnie.'

Bonnie smiled and said, 'I shall expect you all to make it up to me, though, just as Susan said. You are all to be especially nice to me this term.'

'We shall be,' said Pam, giving the girl a pat.

'Bonnie,' said Freddie. 'What *was* the job that you were doing for Miss Tallant? The one that she gave you the chocolate for?'

'It was nothing, really,' said Bonnie. 'She had torn her skirt, and I mended it for her, because she doesn't like sewing. That's all.'

'But why on earth didn't you tell us this in the first place?' said Julie, astonished. 'It would have saved so much unpleasantness.'

Bonnie's little rosebud mouth set in a stubborn line, and she lifted her chin.

'I was cross,' she said. 'Because you thought I was a sneak. And when I get cross I can be awfully stubborn. I thought that you should have believed me, without me having to prove myself.'

'Well, you were quite right,' said Nora. 'But now, the question is, what are we going to do about finding out which of the new girls is Miss Tallant's niece?'

'We shall all have to put our thinking caps on,' said Lucy. 'June, you are usually good at coming up with ideas.'

June, who had been looking rather thoughtful, said, 'I'm afraid someone else will have to think of something, for I have another thing on my mind.'

'What?' asked the others, curiously.

'I'm going to get my own back on Miss Tallant,' said June. 'I don't know how yet, but I'm going to play the biggest, best trick that I have ever played – on her. If only

I knew what her weaknesses are.'

'Well, we know that she doesn't care for mice and spiders, and things like that,' said Felicity.

'Yes, but we have already used those this term,' said June. 'And I do like to be original.'

'There is something that she is even more afraid of,' piped up Bonnie. 'She was talking to me one day when I helped her to tidy the classroom, and I happen to know that Miss Tallant is simply terrified of ghosts.'

'Really?' said June, her quick brain turning over all sorts of ideas instantly. 'How very interesting!'

'How silly of her,' said Susan, rather scornfully. 'There are no such things as ghosts.'

'Well,' said Bonnie. 'Miss Tallant says that she once saw one. It nearly frightened the life out of her.'

'I believe in ghosts,' said Nora, her eyes big and scared-looking. 'I remember once, when I was little –'

'Tell us another time, Nora,' said Susan, who didn't particularly want to spend the rest of the evening in this cramped, musty little room, listening to ghost stories. 'We really should get back to the common-room now, for it won't be long until bedtime.'

She unlocked the door, and the girls filed out. When they reached the bottom of the stairs, Felicity said, 'Now, we must all behave perfectly normally towards Sylvia and Olive for the time being. We don't know which of them is guilty, and it would be terrible if we accused someone wrongly a second time.'

June appeared to have drifted off into a kind of dream,

and Susan said sharply, 'June! Are you listening? We don't want any accusations flying around until we are absolutely certain which of the new girls is the sneak.'

'Of course,' said June. 'Don't worry, Susan, I've learned my lesson. In fact, I wasn't even thinking about the sneak.'

'What *were* you thinking about, June?' asked Freddie, noticing the mischievous glint in her friend's eye.

June grinned, and said, 'I was thinking about the ghost of Malory Towers.'

Miss Tallant strikes again

Sylvia and Olive had returned to the common-room, having failed in their search for the fourth formers. Olive, in particular, felt very disgruntled. She looked across at Sylvia, and thought what a dreadful chatterbox the girl was. Sylvia had kept up a constant stream of talk throughout the search, endlessly speculating on where the girls could be, what they could be doing, and what form any trick they were planning might take. Olive had soon grown heartily tired of her, and thought what bad luck it was that they were thrown together so much.

Just then the door opened, and the rest of the fourth form poured noisily in.

Sylvia and Olive eyed them suspiciously, but Susan grinned warmly and said, 'Did you think that we had got lost?'

'Well, Olive and I did wonder where you had got to,' said Sylvia. 'It's been awfully quiet in here.'

The girls had already decided what story they were going to tell, and Julie said, 'We all popped down to the stables. You see, Lucy has taught her horse Sandy the most marvellous trick. He can count up to five by pawing the ground with his hoof.'

'Yes, I taught him how to do it in the holidays,' said Lucy. 'And, of course, the others were simply dying to see it.'

'I should have liked to see it too,' said Sylvia, looking a little put out. 'I'm very fond of horses, you know.'

'I didn't realise,' said Lucy. 'If I had known I should have asked you to come along too, Sylvia. Never mind, perhaps I can take you to see Sandy tomorrow.'

That cheered Sylvia up, and she was able to dismiss her worries about the girls playing a trick on her. Julie sat down beside her and asked, 'Do you have a horse at home, Sylvia?'

'No, for we don't have any stables,' Sylvia answered. 'My young brother and sister and I go to a local riding school in the holidays, though.'

'How old are your brother and sister?' asked Julie with interest.

Of course, Sylvia needed very little encouragement to talk about herself, and was soon telling Julie all about her home and family.

Felicity, nearby, turned to Susan and said, 'Clever Julie! She is getting Sylvia to talk about her family in the hope that she might let something slip.'

'Good idea!' said Susan. 'If only we could do the same with Olive, but she will just clam up, as she always does.'

'Perhaps the reason she never talks about her family much is because she has something to hide,' suggested Felicity. 'Like an aunt, who also happens to be the most unpopular mistress at Malory Towers.'

'I wouldn't be at all surprised,' said Susan. 'I must

admit, I feel far more inclined to suspect Olive than Sylvia. Sylvia is so open, and will chatter away about herself to anyone who will listen. Hardly the behaviour of someone who is hiding a dark secret!'

'Miss Tallant never seems to take much notice of Sylvia,' observed Felicity thoughtfully. 'Yet she came down hard on Olive over the mouse trick.'

'Did she, though?' said Susan, frowning. 'She may have just pretended to give her a punishment to throw us off the scent. Bonnie said that when she passed the classroom that morning, Olive and Miss Tallant were just talking. Do you remember?'

'Yes,' said Felicity slowly. 'And I've just remembered something else! That photo that Olive put on her locker. I asked her about it, and she bit my head off. She threw it in her locker, in a fit of temper, and I haven't seen it since.'

'What are you getting at, Felicity?' asked Susan, puzzled.

'Well, it looked as if someone was missing from the photograph,' Felicity said. 'Olive's father had his arm outstretched, as though it were around someone's shoulders, but there was no one there. It was as if someone had been cut off. What if that's it, Susan? What if the person missing from the photograph is Miss Tallant?'

Susan gave a gasp, and said, 'I wonder if you could be right, Felicity.'

'Hallo, you two look very serious!' said Pam, coming over with Nora. 'What's up?'

Felicity told the two girls, and Nora said, 'So, it's

looking more and more likely that Olive is the culprit. I must say, I don't altogether blame her for not wanting to own up to having Miss Tallant as an aunt. I certainly wouldn't, if she was mine.'

'Well, we still can't be absolutely certain that it is Olive who is Miss Tallant's niece,' Susan said. 'And until we *are* certain it might be wise to keep our suspicions to ourselves.'

'Yes, I suppose it would,' agreed Pam. 'Actually, Susan, Nora and I came over to ask when we are going to have our first rehearsal. I know it's only short play, and no one has many lines to learn, but we all want it to be perfect.'

'I was thinking about that myself, actually,' said Susan. 'Mary has finished her song, and very good it is too. So now we are just waiting for June and Freddie to add their jokes.' She raised her voice, and called out, 'Hi, June! Freddie!'

The two girls, who were sitting side by side on a sofa, their heads close together as they talked, looked up, and Susan said, 'How are the jokes coming along for our play?'

'Almost finished,' said June, who had thoroughly enjoyed the task that Susan had given her. Ably assisted by Freddie, she had come up with several very funny lines and jokes to add to the script. Now she said, 'Another day or two, and we should be finished.'

'Excellent!' said Susan, happily. 'In that case, we could hold our first rehearsal on Saturday, if the hall is free.'

There were 'oohs' and 'aahs' at this, and Nora clapped her hands together, crying, 'Marvellous! I simply can't wait to begin. Bonnie, how are the costumes coming along?'

'I have made a start on yours, Nora,' answered Bonnie. 'I found the most beautiful dress in the store-room – all white and sparkly. With a little alteration, it will be perfect.'

'I say, I wonder if that was the dress Mary-Lou wore, when she played Cinderella in the pantomime that Darrell wrote,' said Felicity, her eyes shining.

'I'll bet it was,' said Pam. 'My word, that was a jolly good pantomime. I hope our little play will be as big a success.'

'I'm quite determined that it shall be,' said Susan, and everyone agreed.

'We shall spend every spare moment tomorrow finishing our work on the script,' said June to Freddie. 'For once that is done, there is something else I need to concentrate on.'

'How to get back at Miss Tallant?' said Freddie.

'Yes,' said June, her wicked dark eyes glittering. 'My goodness, I'm going to make her wish that she had never crossed me!'

Freddie grinned, and said, 'So, when is the ghost of Malory Towers going to make an appearance?'

'Not until he – or she – is ready,' said June, grinning back at her friend. 'This trick is going to be more carefully planned than any trick I have ever played. I really do intend to give that horrid woman the shock of her life!'

'Well, your brother is coming to see you at half-term, isn't he?' said Freddie. 'He's always full of good ideas, so perhaps the two of you should put your heads together.'

'The *three* of us,' said June. 'Don't forget that you are coming with us at half-term, because your people will be on holiday. And I may need your help, Freddie.'

'You know that you can rely on me,' said Freddie loyally. 'I would like to see Miss Tallant brought down a peg or two as well.'

And Miss Tallant struck again, the day before the first rehearsal was due to take place. The mistress caught Julie whispering to Lucy, and promptly dished out a hundred lines. 'I have to hand them in tomorrow morning!' groaned Lucy. 'And I was hoping to learn my lines for the play tonight.'

'Look here,' said Julie. 'Why don't I do half of them for you, Lucy? My writing is a bit like yours and I bet Miss Tallant will never notice the difference.'

'Oh, would you, Julie?' said Lucy happily. 'You are a sport! If we do them as quickly as we can, we shall both have time to go through our lines.'

The plan was duly carried out, and once the lines were finished, the two girls sat down together in the common-room and read through their parts in the play.

But they were in for a shock the following morning, when Lucy handed two sheets of paper to Miss Tallant, both covered in large, rather sprawling handwriting. The mistress did not even glance at them, but smiled at Lucy, saying, 'I hope that you did not have to waste too much of your evening on these lines, Lucy.'

'No, Miss Tallant,' said Lucy a little nervously.

'Of course you didn't,' said Miss Tallant, her smile

growing broader. 'Because Julie did half of them for you, didn't she?'

Lucy gasped. How on earth could Miss Tallant possibly know *that*? The girls' writing was almost identical, and even if there *was* the very slightest difference, the mistress couldn't have noticed it, for she hadn't so much as glanced at the pages. There was only one way Miss Tallant could know, Lucy realised suddenly, her lips tightening grimly. The sneak had struck again!

Just then, a small second former walked past the classroom, and Miss Tallant called out, 'Elizabeth! Please go and find Julie of the fourth form, and tell her to come to me at once.'

The nervous second former sped off at once, and then Lucy endured a very uncomfortable five minutes indeed! Miss Tallant sat down at her desk and picked up a book, neither looking at Lucy, nor speaking to her. So the girl had to stand in silence, until a puzzled and rather worried-looking Julie arrived. Miss Tallant laid her book aside and got to her feet, and one look at the mistress's face was enough to tell Julie that she was in serious trouble.

'Well, Julie!' said Miss Tallant, looking sternly at the girl. 'I understand that you were foolish enough to help Lucy with her punishment yesterday evening.'

Startled, Julie looked at Lucy. Surely her friend couldn't have been so foolish as to tell Miss Tallant the truth? But Lucy, guessing what Julie was thinking, gave the tiniest shake of her head.

Miss Tallant spoke again, a smile of satisfaction on her face, as she said smoothly, 'Of course, you must both be punished for such deceit. And your punishment will be that you are both forbidden to take part in the rehearsal this afternoon. Instead you will sit here, under my eye, and write an essay on the importance of obeying one's elders and betters.' The girls stared at Miss Tallant in dismay. Julie actually groaned out loud, and opened her mouth to say something, but Lucy gave her a nudge. There was no point in antagonising the mistress, for they would only end up with an even worse punishment. If there *was* anything worse than missing their first rehearsal! They had been looking forward to it so much, and now they were going to miss it. Not only that, but they had let the rest of their form down too, and all through their own deceit.

'I know that what we did was wrong,' said Julie angrily, as the two girls escaped from Miss Tallant's presence, her instructions to come back to the classroom at two o'clock sharp ringing in their ears. 'But we did it for the good of the play, so that you could learn your lines. The mean beast who split on us to Miss Tallant had no good intentions at all!'

'No,' said Lucy miserably. 'She just intended to cause trouble for us with Miss Tallant – *and* to spoil our rehearsal.'

'Well, she has succeeded,' said Julie, who felt very angry and upset.

Felicity and Susan were angry, too, when the two girls

told them that they had been forbidden to attend the rehearsal.

'What rotten luck!' cried Felicity. 'We can't possibly rehearse properly without the whole cast there.'

'Oh, Julie!' wailed Susan. 'I know that you were trying to help, and did it for the good of the play, but I do wish that you hadn't offered to do half of Lucy's lines for her. There are so few characters in the play, that I really don't know if it is worth carrying on with the rehearsal now.'

Julie hung her head and said, 'I'm sorry, Susan. I wish that I hadn't done it now.'

'It's not all our fault, Susan,' said Lucy. 'The person who sneaked on us is to blame, too.'

'I realise that,' said Susan, looking angry. 'But as we don't know who is to blame, we can't deal with them as they deserve.'

'Were both Sylvia and Olive in the common-room last night?' said Felicity, thinking hard.

'Yes, they were,' said Lucy. 'I remember seeing them.'

'Lucy and I were sitting at the table doing our lines,' said Julie. 'I suppose it would have been easy enough for one of them to peep over my shoulder and see that I was helping Lucy. Bother, why couldn't I have been more careful? Susan, you aren't really going to cancel the rehearsal, are you? Do say that you aren't, or I shall feel even more dreadful than I do already.'

'Well, I suppose we shall have to go ahead with it, as all the others are looking forward to it,' said Susan, still sounding rather disgruntled. 'We shall just have to get someone to stand in for you two, though they won't know the lines, of course. For heaven's sake, do take care not to get on the wrong side of Miss Tallant again, for I shouldn't be at all surprised if she is deliberately setting out to spoil our play, simply because we wouldn't let her be involved.'

Fortunately the rehearsal went smoothly, though Olive was not at all happy when Felicity told her that she was going to stand in for Julie, and take the part of the toy soldier.

'Can't you get someone else to do it?' said Olive, sullenly.

'Everyone else is busy with their own parts, or with jobs behind the scenes, so I'm afraid you really have no choice, Olive,' said Felicity firmly. 'And it doesn't matter if you can't act well, because you're only standing in for Julie. All you have to do is read the lines.'

And with that, Felicity pushed a script into Olive's hands and walked away to check that all was well behind the scenes.

A girl called April, from South Tower, was taking Lucy's part – much more graciously than Olive was taking Julie's – and once the two girls joined the rest of the cast on stage, the rehearsal began.

The three producers sat at the front of the hall, and all of them were very pleased with the way things turned out.

There were a few mistakes, of course. Several of the girls fluffed their lines, and Olive somehow managed to trip Nora up during her dance. She hotly denied doing it on purpose, when Nora accused her of this, but most of the girls were quite certain that it had been deliberate.

117

Susan gave the girl a scold, and Sylvia intervened, saying in a low voice, 'Susan, there's no point in losing your temper. We can't prove that Olive tripped Nora on purpose, and all we're doing is wasting valuable time.' Then she clapped her hands together briskly, and said in her loud voice, 'Come along, girls, back to your places, please, and let's start the dance again. Olive, you stand further back, then if Nora *should* happen to trip again, you can't be held responsible.'

Both Susan and Felicity looked rather taken aback, and none too pleased at this, but as one of the producers, Sylvia was quite within her rights. And both girls had to admit that what she said was very wise and sensible.

The rest of the rehearsal went without mishap, and at the end of it Susan said, 'Well, that wasn't bad at all!'

'I thought that it went very well indeed,' said Sylvia. 'Of course, the girls aren't word perfect yet, but that is only to be expected.'

Felicity, who felt cheered by how well the rehearsal had gone, said, 'You were very good, too, Sylvia. You handled the incident with Nora and Olive perfectly.'

Sylvia shrugged, and said, 'Well, of course, I'm quite an old hand at all of this, you know. Being a former head-girl, and having produced a play myself, I'm used to being a bit of a bossy-boots!'

But both girls noticed that Sylvia had turned pink with pleasure at Felicity's remark and, as she walked away, Susan said, 'Actually, although she can be dreadfully pushy and bossy at times, I think Sylvia is rather nice.'

'So do I,' agreed Felicity. 'And I know it's a horrid thing to say, but I actually *want* Olive to be Miss Tallant's niece, for that would be so much easier to bear than finding out that it is Sylvia.'

'Yes, I feel the same,' said Susan with a sigh. 'What a beastly business it is!'

'Cheer up!' said Felicity, slipping her arm through her friend's. 'There is still an awful lot to look forward to this term, you know. As well as our play, it will be half-term very shortly.'

'So it will!' said Susan, brightening. 'I had almost forgotten about that.'

She chuckled suddenly, and went on, 'And I must say, I'm rather looking forward to finding out how June intends to pay Miss Tallant back. Whatever she has in mind, I'll bet it's something quite ingenious. And I, for one, can't wait to see Miss Tallant get her comeuppance!'

An interesting half-term

The fourth formers took great care not to give Miss Tallant any cause to punish them over the next couple of weeks. They didn't want anyone else missing rehearsals, so they were polite, well-behaved and worked hard in her classes. But, as Pam remarked in the common-room on the evening before half-term, 'She doesn't seem terribly pleased! Any other mistress in the school would be delighted to teach such model schoolgirls.'

'Of course she's not pleased!' said June. 'She *likes* punishing us, and she's disappointed that we haven't given her any opportunity to vent her spite.'

'Well, Miss Tallant might not be pleased, but I certainly am,' said Susan, beaming round. 'Our play is really taking shape, and the last two rehearsals have gone swimmingly.'

'Shh!' hissed Freddie suddenly. 'Sylvia is coming this way, so don't mention Miss Tallant. Change the subject, quickly!'

At once the girls began to talk about the forthcoming half-term, and Sylvia joined in, saying in her hearty way, 'I simply can't tell you how much I am looking forward to my first half-term at Malory Towers, and to showing my people round properly.'

'It's going to be super,' said Julie happily. 'Lucy's parents aren't able to come, so she is coming on a picnic with my people.'

'And I bet Jack and Sandy will be going along too,' laughed Felicity, knowing that the two girls never went anywhere without their beloved horses unless they absolutely had to. Susan glanced round at that moment, and caught sight of Olive, sitting alone, as usual, a sour expression on her plain face.

'Are your people coming tomorrow, Olive?' Susan asked.

'Yes,' answered Olive, in her curiously flat voice. But she volunteered no more information, and discouraged the others from asking any more questions by immediately burying her head in a book. And she didn't look as if she was terribly excited about seeing her family again, thought Susan. She turned to Felicity, and murmured in a low voice, 'I'm jolly well going to keep an eye on Olive and her people tomorrow. If she *is* Miss Tallant's niece, then one of them may give something away.'

'Good idea,' said Felicity. 'And I suppose we had better watch Sylvia's parents too, for we can't rule her out yet.'

But as it turned out, there was no need to watch Sylvia's parents.

The girls leaped out of bed eagerly on the morning of half-term, even lazy Nora, who hated leaving her warm bed on cold mornings.

'Thank heavens it isn't raining,' said June, pulling the curtains open. 'Otherwise the upper-school lacrosse match would have to be cancelled.'

Ruth Grainger, the games captain, had chosen two teams from the upper school to play an exhibition match for the parents, and June had the honour of being the only fourth former to be chosen.

'Just make sure you play up, June!' called out Felicity.

'Yes, we'll all give you three cheers if you shoot a goal,' said Pam.

'I shall do my best,' said June, in her usual off-hand manner. But the others knew that June was as pleased as punch to have been chosen, and felt very proud indeed, though she would never admit it.

After breakfast, Sylvia was called to Miss Grayling's study, and when she returned to the common-room afterwards, she looked so woebegone that the others felt quite alarmed.

'What's up, Sylvia, old girl?' asked Felicity kindly.

'My parents aren't able to come today, after all,' said Sylvia miserably. 'My grandmother has been taken ill, so they have had to go and look after her.'

The others were terribly sorry to hear this, for they knew how disappointed Sylvia must feel.

'I say, what rotten luck!'

'Awfully sorry to hear that, Sylvia.'

'I do hope that your grandmother isn't seriously ill?'

'No, I think it's just a bad dose of flu, but she's too ill to do anything for herself,' answered Sylvia with a sigh. 'Of course, I quite see that Mother and Father have to go to her, but I can't help feeling upset that they won't be here.'

The kindly Pam gave Sylvia a pat on the shoulder, and

said, 'Cheer up, Sylvia! I know it's awful to have news like this at the last minute, but why don't you come out with me and my people instead?'

Sylvia's face lit up and she said, 'Thank you, Pam. That's jolly decent of you, if you're sure your parents won't mind.'

Since Pam's parents were as good-natured and easygoing as their daughter, Pam was able to reassure Sylvia on this point, and the girl cheered up considerably.

'There are some cars coming up the drive!' cried an excited Bonnie, who was peering out of the window. 'Amy, your parents are here! And June, yours are right behind.'

With an excited whoop, June ran from the room, Freddie – who was spending the day with June's people – right behind her. Amy followed at a more dignified pace, while Felicity and Susan went to join Bonnie at the window.

'I do hope my mother and father aren't going to be late,' said Bonnie fretfully. 'They promised to be here early.'

Felicity laughed, and ruffled Bonnie's curly hair. 'Don't worry, Bonnie,' she said. 'Your parents always keep their promises, for you know how to wrap them round your little finger.'

Olive, nearby, muttered under her breath, 'Spoilt brat!' Fortunately for her, no one overheard, for at that moment Bonnie's father's car drew up beneath the window, and the girl squealed loudly in excitement, before darting from the room.

'Someone else's people are here too,' said Susan, leaning out of the window. 'I don't think they belong to anyone here, though, for I don't recognise them.'

Felicity followed Susan's gaze, to where a man and woman were getting out of a car.

With them was a very pretty, dainty girl of about thirteen, with curly golden hair and big eyes.

'The two grown-ups look vaguely familiar to me,' said Felicity. 'Though I don't recognise the girl with them. Oh, I know who they are! Olive, it's your father and step-mother. I remember them from your photograph. Is the girl with them your sister? How pretty she is!'

'She's not my sister!' snapped Olive, her pale skin turning a dull red. 'She's not related to me at all!'

'Well!' exclaimed Nora, as the girl stomped out of the room. 'How odd!'

'Olive *is* odd,' said Susan in disgust. 'Her behaviour gets more peculiar by the day.'

'I wonder who that girl is,' said Felicity. 'Why on earth would Olive's father and step-mother bring someone who isn't related to Olive to visit her at half-term? It doesn't make sense.'

'Oh, who wants to worry about silly old Olive on a day like this?' said Nora. 'If she wants to act all odd and bad-tempered, let her! But I intend to enjoy half-term.'

The others felt exactly the same, and, as more and more parents arrived, went off to greet them excitedly.

Felicity, of course, was delighted to see her own pretty, sensible mother and her tall, distinguished-looking father, and flew into their arms as soon as they got out of the car.

'Mother! Daddy! How super to see you both again!' she

cried. 'Do come and say hallo to Susan and her people.'

Felicity's parents and Susan's parents knew and liked one another, and the two girls were thrilled when both families agreed to join up and go for lunch together at a restaurant.

But before that, there was plenty to see and do.

Parents had to be shown around the dormitory, common-room and classroom, then there were displays of art and needlework to admire, and mistresses to talk to.

Felicity spotted Olive and her family talking to Miss Tallant, and noticed that the mistress was laughing and joking.

'Hmm, that looks very suspicious,' said a low voice behind Felicity. She turned to see that June had come up behind her, and was also watching the little group.

'Miss Tallant spoke to *my* parents a little while ago, and she wasn't nearly as friendly, I can tell you,' June went on. 'Just look how relaxed and jolly she is with Olive's people, though. But then, I suppose she would be if she is related to them!'

'It does look suspicious,' said Felicity. 'Look, she is even talking to the girl that Olive's parents brought with them, as if she is very familiar with her.'

'Well, it looks as if we have discovered who Miss Tallant's niece is,' said June in a hard little voice. 'All we have to do now is catch her out.'

There was no time to say any more just then, for Freddie came over with June's parents, and the four of them went off together.

So Felicity went to join her own parents, who were chatting with Mam'zelle Dupont, feeling rather troubled.

But it was half-term, and Felicity found it impossible to stay troubled for long. Especially when her mother gave her a hug, and said, 'You're doing marvellously, dear. I have had glowing reports of you from every mistress I have spoken to.'

'Yes, Miss Potts said that she is delighted to have you in North Tower,' added Mr Rivers. 'She told me that it is girls like you who makes Malory Towers what it is, for you bring a wonderful spirit to the school. And I must say, darling, I agree with her.'

Felicity felt as if she would burst with pride! Fancy Miss Potts, the strict head of North Tower, saying that about her. She simply couldn't wait to tell Susan.

The two families went off to a restaurant for lunch together, and had an absolutely marvellous time.

'I don't want half-term to end,' said Felicity to Susan, as the two girls tucked into ice-creams. 'What a super day it's been!'

'Well, it's not over yet,' said Susan. 'We still have the lacrosse match this afternoon, then a scrumptious tea to look forward to, and all of tomorrow as well. Marvellous!'

Bonnie was also enjoying herself, for her parents spoiled her dreadfully, hanging on her every word as she chattered away to them. She was taken to a restaurant for lunch too, and was surprised – and none too pleased – to find that Olive and her family had chosen the same one.

'Is anything wrong, darling?' asked Mrs Meadows, noticing Bonnie's frown.

'Oh, it's just that I've seen someone I don't like very much, Mummy,' said Bonnie. 'That girl at the table in the corner. She's in my form and she's simply horrid. No one can bear her.'

'Well, we shall sit as far away from her as possible,' said Mrs Meadows, patting Bonnie's arm. 'What a plain girl she is. Her sister is very pretty, though. Actually, she reminds me a little of you, Bonnie.'

Bonnie hadn't noticed the other girl with Olive, and she looked across at her table again now, spotting the golden-haired girl. Heavens, could that really be Olive's sister? There was absolutely no resemblance between them at all.

'I shouldn't be at all surprised if she was jealous of her sister,' Mrs Meadows was saying now. 'Perhaps that is why she is so horrid to everyone, poor girl.'

'Yes,' said Bonnie, looking thoughtful. 'I think that you may be right, Mummy.' Bonnie watched Olive's family from the corner of her eye as she ate her lunch. Olive remained largely silent throughout, though Bonnie noticed that her father and step-mother addressed a great many remarks to her. But they were treated to the same one-word answers that the Malory Towers girls always got from Olive. The younger girl, however, kept up a stream of bright chatter, much to Olive's evident displeasure, for she scowled constantly.

Bonnie was in a pensive mood on the way back to Malory Towers, and her father glanced at her in the driving mirror, asking, 'Is everything all right, my dear? You're awfully quiet.'

'I'm all right, Daddy,' said Bonnie, smiling angelically at Mr Meadows. 'I was just thinking about something, that's all.'

Bonnie had been thinking about what her mother had said. Mrs Meadows was rather a silly woman at times, but she had a streak of shrewdness in her nature. And Bonnie felt that her mother might have hit the nail on the head with Olive. The girl made up her mind that she was going to try to talk to Olive's sister – if the golden-haired girl *was* her sister – before half-term was over.

And her chance came later that very afternoon. The two girls found themselves side by side while they were watching the lacrosse match. Bonnie disliked all games, and had only brought her parents to watch so that she could support June.

For most of the watching girls, however, it was a thrilling game, and very close. And June proved that she was worthy of being selected for the team by scoring the winning goal in the last minute. While the rest of the fourth formers yelled themselves hoarse, Bonnie clapped politely and heaved a sigh of relief that it was over. And she wasn't the only one, for the golden-haired girl looked relieved too, and the two girls exchanged sympathetic smiles.

As everyone began to move away, Bonnie fell into step beside the girl and said softly, 'I do so hate lacrosse, don't you?'

The girl nodded in agreement, and said in a soft, childish voice, 'I don't like *any* games. Nor does Olive, really. I think she only brought us to watch to spite me, for she knew that I would be simply bored to tears.'

There was a petulant note in the girl's voice, and Bonnie asked, 'Is Olive your sister? You don't look very much alike.'

'Oh no, she's my step-sister,' explained the girl. 'My mother married her father. He's an absolute dear, but Olive simply detests me.'

'Really?' said Bonnie, opening her eyes wide. 'I can't think why.'

'She's horribly jealous of me,' confided the girl, lowering her voice a little. 'You see, she and her father were all-in-all to one another, until Mummy and I came along. Olive simply can't bear it when he pays me any attention.'

She gave a high little giggle, and went on, 'I must admit I do play up to him at times, just to annoy Olive, for I dislike her every bit as much as she dislikes me.'

'She's not an easy person to like,' said Bonnie, wrinkling her nose.

'No, but it is *very* easy to make her lose her temper,' said the girl, pleased that Bonnie seemed to dislike Olive too, and deciding that she was a safe person to confide in. 'And such fun. I like to get her into trouble, too.'

'What kind of things do you do?' asked Bonnie, thinking that this was a very interesting conversation.

'Well,' said the girl. 'Olive deliberately smashed my

favourite doll once, because we had had a row. Of course, I was dreadfully upset, and told Mummy, who insisted that Daddy punish her. He was absolutely furious with her for being so spiteful, and she was sent to bed without any supper that night. Once she had shown that she had a bad temper and a spiteful nature, it was easy. Sometimes things get broken, or go missing, and somehow poor Olive always gets the blame. No one ever suspects that it is me.'

'I see,' said Bonnie. She would have liked to continue talking to the girl, but at that moment her mother called out, 'Annabel! Do hurry up, dear, or we shall be late for tea.' And, with a wave of her dainty little hand, Annabel darted off to catch up with her mother, and Bonnie's own parents appeared, her father saying, 'There you are, Bonnie! You must have fallen behind. Mummy and I thought that we had lost you.'

Bonnie smiled her sweet smile and tucked her hand into the crook of her father's arm, but her thoughts were racing. No wonder poor Olive was so ill-tempered! What a mean-spirited girl Annabel was. And it was quite clear now why Olive despised Bonnie herself, and Nora. The two of them were very like Annabel in looks, though not – Bonnie hoped – in character.

Well, thought Bonnie, quite astonished. Perhaps Olive wasn't as bad as she was painted after all!

Exciting plans

It was a very busy time for the fourth formers once half-term was over. There were rehearsals for the play, of course, with those girls who weren't taking part working hard behind the scenes. Bonnie and her assistants worked like beavers to produce the costumes, those who were good at art helped paint the scenery, and others searched the school from top to bottom for props that could be used.

Then there were school lacrosse matches coming up, and many of the girls were practising hard in the hope that they would be chosen to play.

June and Freddie were full of exciting plans too. They had come back from half-term their eyes alight with mischief, and when Pam had said, 'Oho! What are you two up to?' the two had shaken their heads and replied aggravatingly, 'Wouldn't you like to know!' But they did share one of their plans with the others, in the common-room one evening. Sylvia, who had a sore throat and had gone off to see Matron, was not there. Neither was Olive, who had been called away by Miss Williams over the matter of some poorly written work.

'Gather round, everyone!' cried June. 'With Sylvia and Olive out of the way, it seems as good a time as any to tell you that I intend to hold a midnight feast on my birthday next week, and you are all invited.'

There were 'oohs' and 'aahs' as the fourth formers exchanged excited glances.

'A feast, how thrilling!'

'Yes, we haven't had one in simply ages!'

'We will all bring something, of course, June.'

'Thanks,' said June, beaming round at her friends. 'Mother and Father have given me some money to get what I like, but it won't be enough to feed everyone, so if all you others can bring something, that will be a big help.'

'Jolly decent of you to invite us all, June,' called out Nora.

'Well, that's the thing,' said June. 'I'm *not* inviting all of you. Sylvia and Olive must be kept in the dark for now, for I don't want either of them running off to tell tales to Miss Tallant.'

Then she grinned, and added, 'Actually, that's not quite true. I *do* want the sneak to go to Miss Tallant. But I want to make sure that she tells the *right* tale.'

'What are you planning, June?' asked Felicity.

'I can't say just yet,' said June. 'For Freddie and I haven't quite thought it all out yet. But as soon as we have come up with a way to trick Miss Tallant and her beastly niece, I shall let you know. Personally, I am almost certain that Olive is the culprit.'

Several of the girls murmured in agreement, and everyone looked most surprised when Bonnie piped up, 'I feel rather sorry for Olive.'

'Bonnie, dear, are you feeling quite well?' asked Amy, looking at her little friend in surprise.

'Yes, perhaps you ought to pop along and see Matron, too,' said Nora. 'You're delirious.'

'Nothing of the sort!' said Bonnie. 'It's just that I happened to speak to Olive's step-sister, Annabel, at half-term. And what she told me put quite a different complexion on things.'

'Do tell us,' said June.

So Bonnie told the fourth formers what she had learned from Annabel, and very shocked they looked when she had finished.

'What a mean little beast Annabel sounds!' said Susan, in disgust.

'Poor Olive!' said Pam, her ready sympathy stirred. 'It must be quite dreadful to take the blame for everything that goes wrong, and to know that you are innocent.'

'I daresay it must have seemed to Olive that there was no point in being good and well-behaved,' said Susan, shrewdly. 'So she decided that if she was going to be treated as a bad girl, then she might as well become one.'

Suddenly Felicity snapped her fingers, and cried, 'Of course! The person who is missing from Olive's family photograph isn't Miss Tallant at all! It's Annabel!'

'Yes, that makes sense,' said Susan. 'And to be quite honest, I can't say that I blame Olive for wanting to cut her out.'

'You may be right,' said June. 'But all the evidence still points to Olive being Miss Tallant's niece. And, whatever problems she may have at home with her horrid little step-sister, it doesn't excuse her behaviour towards us.'

'I agree with June,' said Nora. 'I do understand Olive's behaviour a little better now, and I know why she has such a down on Bonnie and me. But, even though I feel sorry for her, the fact remains that we can't trust her.'

Felicity, who had been looking thoughtful, said, 'The best possible outcome of all of this would be for Olive herself to own up that she is Miss Tallant's niece. It would make us all think better of her if she told the truth, and then we could let her know that we felt proud of her for doing the right thing.'

'Marvellous idea!' cried Julie. 'And once we had praised her up a bit, Olive would surely start to feel more confident, and she might find the courage to tell her father about the mean tricks Annabel has been playing.'

Most of the fourth formers thought that this was a very good idea indeed, only June looking rather doubtful.

'If you are all agreed, I will go along with it, of course,' said June. 'But *not* until after the feast, for I'm sure that we are all looking forward to that and we can't risk having it spoiled.'

'That *would* be a terrible shame,' said Lucy. 'I really think that we will have to leave Olive out of it, you know, girls.'

'Yes, I suppose that we better had,' said Susan. 'June, you said that you were working on an idea to trick Olive and Miss Tallant, didn't you?'

'Yes,' answered June. 'If it works, it will keep Miss Tallant nicely out of the way while we enjoy our feast, *and* it will teach Olive that sneaking can sometimes backfire on the sneak, so we shall kill two birds with one stone.'

'That sounds super,' said Susan. 'And once the feast is over, we can all set to work to make Olive own up, and try to set her on the right track.'

Just then the common-room door opened, and in walked Olive, wearing her customary sullen expression.

At once all the girls began to chatter about something else, while Olive sat down in a chair, looking miserably at the returned work that Miss Williams had given her.

Kindly Pam went across to her and said, 'Bad luck, Olive. Those sums that Miss Williams gave us this morning were awfully difficult. I found them quite hard, and I'm not too bad at maths. I say, perhaps I could help you with them?'

For a second it seemed as though Olive was going to bite Pam's head off, but, looking into the girl's friendly, open face, she saw real kindness there and it warmed her. So Olive swallowed her pride, and said, 'Thanks, that's awfully kind of you.'

'Good old Pam,' said Felicity, as she saw the girl sit down next to Olive and begin to patiently explain how best to do the rather complicated sums that Miss Williams had set. 'She really is a decent sort.'

'Yes,' said June. 'Just so long as her decency doesn't carry her away. We don't want Olive turning over a new leaf until *after* the feast!'

Naturally, the feast became the main topic of conversation for the fourth formers. There was a big cupboard just outside the dormitory, which the girls used as a hiding place for all their food. It had a key, which June kept in her pocket at all times so that no one could pry and find the hidden goodies.

The girls were allowed to go into town in their free time, as long as they went in pairs, and June was forever going to the cupboard to hide packets of biscuits, tins of sardines, and bottles of lemonade that one girl or another had brought back with her.

Amy, who had a great deal of pocket money, bought a simply enormous box of chocolates as her contribution to the feast, and she handed them to June when she and Bonnie returned from town.

'Gosh, thanks, Amy!' said June. 'These look simply gorgeous! I'll run up and pop them in the cupboard now, before tea.'

June did so, then she locked the cupboard carefully and slipped the key back into her pocket, before turning to go back downstairs. Then what a shock she had! For Sylvia was standing behind her, and it was quite clear that she must have seen the contents of the cupboard.

June could feel herself turning red, but said breezily, 'Hallo there, Sylvia.'

'Hallo, June,' said Sylvia, her eyes alight with curiosity. 'I say, what on earth is going on? Are you using that cupboard to store food?'

June thought quickly and said, 'Yes, but please don't say anything to anyone, Sylvia. The South Tower girls are planning a feast next week, and they wanted somewhere to store the goodies where their matron wouldn't find them. She's a real nosey-parker, you know, always snooping round, and she's far stricter than our Matron.'

Fortunately, Sylvia, who had never met the placid, good-humoured matron of South Tower, accepted this readily, and said, 'Oh, of course. I shan't say a word.'

June breathed a sigh of relief and went off to tea, catching up with Freddie just as she was entering the dining-room.

'I say!' she whispered. 'I've just had a jolly close shave with Sylvia.'

And, quickly, she told Freddie what had happened.

'That was quick thinking, June,' said Freddie admiringly.

'Wasn't it just?' agreed June, with a cheeky grin. 'And it's given me an idea. How would you like a walk around the grounds before tea, Freddie, old girl?'

Freddie, seeing the gleam of mischief in June's eyes, said at once, 'If I agree, will you tell me what you're up to?'

June nodded, and said, 'Quiet now! Here come the others, and I don't want to let them in on what I'm going to do until I have it all worked out properly.'

It was a chilly evening, and, after tea, the two girls put on their hats and coats, June fetched a torch, and off they went, out into the garden.

'Where are we going?' asked Freddie, curiously.

June glanced over her shoulder, to make sure that no one was around, and said, 'We're going right over in the corner, by South Tower. There is a small gap in the wall there, just big enough for someone to slip through, which leads down to the beach.'

'Is there?' said Freddie, surprised. 'I didn't know that!'

'Hardly anyone does,' said June. 'It's almost completely overgrown by the ivy that hangs down the wall, so it's invisible.'

'Go on,' said Freddie, now very curious indeed.

But June said, 'No, I'll wait until we get there before I tell you what I mean to do. It will be easier to explain if you can see exactly what I mean. Thank heavens that it's a cold evening, and nearly everyone is indoors. No one will be able to see what we are up to.'

But someone *was* about! As the two girls approached the wall, they spotted plump little Mam'zelle Dupont a few yards in front of it.

'Blow!' said Freddie. 'Whatever is Mam'zelle doing here? She likes to be all nice and cosy indoors in the cold weather. It's not like her to take an evening stroll.'

Mam'zelle was well wrapped up in a thick, heavy overcoat, a long woollen scarf around her neck and a fur hat pushed firmly over her neat roll of hair. She was looking a little perplexed, but her face cleared when she saw the two girls, and she cried out, 'Ah, *mes filles*! How happy I am to see you both. You may help me in my search.'

'What are you searching for, Mam'zelle?' asked June.

'My brooch,' answered the French mistress, looking rather unhappy. 'I lost it this afternoon, and now I come to look for it.'

'How can you be sure that you lost it *here*, precisely?' asked Freddie.

'I came this way earlier with Mam'zelle Rougier,' explained Mam'zelle Dupont. 'And I distinctly remember her remarking on how unusual my brooch was shortly before we reached this very spot. Then, when we entered the school, she cried, "Why, Mam'zelle Dupont, your brooch – it is gone!" And so it was – quite vanished. I retraced my steps, but there was no sign of it, so I must have dropped it in the undergrowth here.'

'But, Mam'zelle, why didn't you search for it then, when it was still light?' asked June. 'You don't have a hope of finding it in the dark, especially as you don't even have a torch with you.'

'There was no time then, for I had to teach the third formers,' said Mam'zelle, looking agitated. 'And I see that you have a torch, *ma chère* June. You will switch it on and help me find my brooch, yes?'

Well, this wasn't what the two girls had planned at all, but they couldn't very well say no to the French mistress, so June switched on her torch and played the beam over the bushes that grew next to the wall. Suddenly, her sharp eyes spotted the gap in the wall that she had spoken to Freddie about, and a wicked idea came into her head.

'Here, Freddie,' she said. 'You hold the torch for a bit, and I'll hunt around in the bushes and see if I can spot Mam'zelle's brooch.'

Then, unseen by the French mistress, she winked at Freddie, who wondered what on earth she was up to.

Keeping one eye on Freddie and Mam'zelle, June picked up a stick and poked around in the bushes, then cried, 'I think I see something sparkling – over there!'

Freddie and Mam'zelle both peered in the direction that June had indicated and, quick as a flash, June darted through the little gap in the wall, disappearing from their view.

'I see nothing!' complained Mam'zelle. 'Do you, Freddie?'

'No, not a thing, Mam'zelle,' answered Freddie. 'June, where exactly did you say it was?'

Both she and Mam'zelle Dupont looked towards the spot where June had been standing – but she had gone!

'*Tiens!*' cried Mam'zelle, giving a little start. 'What has happened to June?'

Quick-witted Freddie realised at once what had happened, and distracted Mam'zelle by saying, 'I think I see your brooch down there, Mam'zelle.'

And once again, poor, unsuspecting Mam'zelle, who never seemed to realise when she was having her leg pulled, obligingly turned her head, allowing June to emerge from her hiding place.

'Haven't you found your brooch yet, Mam'zelle?' she asked, and the French mistress spun round sharply, crying, 'There you are, June. Where have you been?'

'Why, nowhere, Mam'zelle,' answered the girl, her lips twitching humorously. 'I've been here all the time. Isn't that so, Freddie?'

Freddie nodded, and Mam'zelle fixed June with a stern

stare, before shaking her head and crying, *'Non! Méchante fille!* You are trying to trick your poor Mam'zelle, once again! I saw you, over there by the wall. I looked away for a split second, and you disappeared – poof!'

'Mam'zelle, I really think that the poor light is making your eyes play tricks on you,' said Freddie, so gravely that June wanted to burst out laughing. 'June most certainly did not disappear.'

'Of course I didn't,' said June. 'You know, Mam'zelle, tricks take quite a lot of planning, and I didn't even know that I was going to bump into you, so I couldn't possibly have prepared anything.'

This gave Mam'zelle pause for thought. She knew how carefully June worked out her tricks, and the girls had come upon her quite by chance. So, she was forced to agree that, in the gathering gloom, her eyes had indeed deceived her.

'And still I have not found my brooch,' she said, rather forlornly. 'It is a very special one, for my nephew gave me it for my birthday.'

Freddie, who, like most of the other girls, was very fond of Mam'zelle Dupont, felt sorry for her, and said kindly, 'Look here, Mam'zelle, why don't you go indoors and get warm? June and I will carry on looking for your brooch, and we will come and tell you if we find it.'

'Ah, you are indeed good, kind girls!' cried Mam'zelle, quite forgetting that, a few moments ago, she had accused June of tricking her. The thought of going indoors and sitting before a roaring fire, with a mug of hot cocoa, was so pleasant that she could almost have hugged the two girls.

June was less pleased, though, and said rather crossly to Freddie, 'Why on earth did you volunteer us to find Mam'zelle's brooch? It's getting jolly cold now, and I was looking forward to sitting in the common-room for a bit, now that we've done what we came for.'

'I know, but poor old Mam'zelle looked so miserable,' said Freddie, who was much more soft-hearted than her friend. 'The brooch must be around here somewhere, so if we hurry up and find it we'll still have time for a sit down before prep. Besides, after the trick you played on Mam'zelle, I think that the least we can do is help her.'

June grinned at this, and said, 'Yes, I suppose you're right. Did it really look as if I had vanished into thin air, Freddie?'

Freddie nodded and gave a shiver, 'It was quite creepy, actually, the way you suddenly disappeared and then reappeared again.'

'Good,' said June. 'I was hoping you would say that, for I intend to give Miss Tallant the fright of her life! Let me tell you what I am going to do.'

As the two girls talked, they began to hunt for the missing brooch. In a very short time their efforts were rewarded. Freddie gave a cry and yelled, 'I've found it! My word, won't Mam'zelle be pleased?'

Mam'zelle was highly delighted when June and Freddie took the brooch to her, patting the girls on their shoulders.

'Ah, you may be bad sometimes, but you are good girls

at heart!' she cried, beaming at the two girls. 'I only wish that there was some little reward I could give you.'

'There is, Mam'zelle,' said June promptly. 'You can let the two of us off French prep for a week.'

But even big-hearted Mam'zelle was not that generous, and she wagged her finger at June, saying, 'Now you try to take advantage of me! One minute you are good, June, and the next you are bad again! I do not know whether I am on my heels or my head with you! But I shall not forget the favour that you and the dear Freddie have done me, and you may be sure that I shall think of something I can do to repay you.'

A trap is set

And Mam'zelle was as good as her word, for a few days later, when the girls were at tea, the French mistress produced the most enormous chocolate cake, which she placed in the centre of the fourth form's table.

'Heavens, Mam'zelle, that looks simply delicious!' said Nora. 'What have we done to deserve this?'

'You have June and Freddie to thank,' said Mam'zelle, cutting the cake into big slices. 'They found my brooch the other day, and I promised them a reward.'

'Jolly decent of you, Mam'zelle,' said Freddie.

'Yes, thanks, Mam'zelle,' said June. 'Though I don't see why the others should share it, for they did nothing. Really, Freddie and I should have half each.'

Of course, June was joking, and the others laughed as Mam'zelle handed round slices of cake, Lucy saying, 'Good show, June and Freddie! Mam'zelle, you should lose your jewellery more often, if this is what happens.'

'I say, June!' said Sylvia, who was sitting beside the girl. 'Speaking of cake, that was a fine, big fruit cake that I saw you put in the cupboard this morning. My word, the South Tower girls must have enough food to feed an army.'

'Sh! Keep your voice down, Sylvia!' hissed June. 'Do you want Mam'zelle to overhear, and spoil the feast for the South Tower girls?'

'Sorry, June,' said Sylvia, lowering her voice and looking rather sheepish.

But Felicity and Susan, on the opposite side of the table, had heard Sylvia's remark and were puzzled by it. What on earth did Sylvia mean about the cake that the two of them had bought being meant for the South Tower girls' feast?

They caught up with June after tea and asked her about it.

'Sylvia caught me stowing some food in the cupboard,' explained June. 'I told her that the South Tower girls were having a feast to throw her off the scent. And I'm going to make sure that Olive thinks the same. Then whichever of the two girls is our sneak is sure to tell Miss Tallant.'

'So she will be thrown off the scent, too,' said Susan. 'And we can have our feast in peace, because Miss Tallant will be over at South Tower on a wild goose chase!'

'June, what a super idea!' laughed Felicity. 'I would love to see Miss Tallant burst into South Tower to spoil the feast, only to find the girls tucked up in bed. How foolish she is going to look!'

'That is going to be the least of Miss Tallant's problems,' said June, with a wicked grin. 'Just wait and see what I have in store for her!'

'June, do tell!' begged Felicity and Susan.

'I shall tell you, but not now,' promised June. 'I have

something else to do at the moment. Has anyone seen Bonnie?'

June eventually found Bonnie in the dormitory, where she was brushing out her curly hair in front of a mirror.

'Bonnie,' said June. 'Thank goodness I've found you.'

Bonnie looked round at the girl in surprise, and said in her lisping voice, 'Is something the matter, June?'

'Not exactly,' answered June, sitting on the edge of one of the beds. 'But I need you to do something for me. I want you to help me set up this trick that I'm going to play on Miss Tallant.'

Bonnie clapped her hands together in glee, and said, 'Goody! Just tell me what you want me to do, June.'

'Well, Bonnie,' began June. 'I know that you talk to Miss Tallant a lot, and I want you to tell her a little story – all about the ghost of Malory Towers.'

'Ooh!' said Bonnie, thrilled, her big eyes growing wide. '*Is* there a ghost at Malory Towers, June?'

'Not as far as I know,' said June, grinning at Bonnie. 'But we are going to make Miss Tallant *think* that there is! Next time you have a chance to speak to her in private, Bonnie, I want you to tell her that you woke up in the middle of the night and went to look out of the window. And you saw a pale, ghostly figure over by South Tower.'

Bonnie was so excited that she couldn't speak, but she nodded vigorously, and June went on, 'Tell Miss Tallant that it looked up at you watching from the window, then disappeared into thin air.'

'Yes, I can do that, all right, June,' said Bonnie, eagerly. 'Anything else?'

'Yes,' said June. 'I think it would be a good idea if we were to make up a tragic story about a young girl who died at Malory Towers many, many years ago, and whose spirit is said to haunt the school.'

'We could say that she died by falling off the cliff!' cried Bonnie, struck by sudden inspiration.

'Brilliant!' said June. 'Yes, I see it all. She quarrelled bitterly with her sister, and was so upset that, one dark, stormy night, she ran away. But the wind was so fierce that it blew out the lantern she carried with her and, in the pitch darkness, she stumbled off the cliff.'

'Oh, the poor, poor girl!' cried Bonnie, looking as if she was about to burst into tears.

'Ass!' said June, giving her a shove. 'It's only a story, remember!'

'Yes, but you told it so convincingly, June, that I felt quite moved,' sighed Bonnie. 'And I think I know what comes next. The girl's tormented, restless spirit haunts the school, seeking out her sister so that they can make up their quarrel.'

'Actually I hadn't thought of that, but it's very good,' said June approvingly.

'I shall tell Miss Tallant tomorrow that I saw the ghost,' said Bonnie. 'Just to unsettle her a little. Then, the next day, I shall tell her the story of the dead girl. I really think that she will be frightened, June, because of the ghost that she saw when she was younger.'

June, who was far too down-to-earth to believe in ghosts, gave a snort, and said, 'I daresay it was a shadow, or a trick of the light. But it's a jolly good thing that it happened, for it has given us a way to punish Miss Tallant for being so mean to the fourth form.'

Bonnie carried out her part of the plan faithfully, and had the satisfaction of seeing Miss Tallant's face turn white as she told her tale.

'She looked like a ghost herself,' laughed Bonnie, as she related what had happened to June and Freddie.

'Well done, Bonnie,' said June, pleased with the girl. 'And now, Freddie, we must make preparations to carry out *our* part of the plan.'

There was a rehearsal for the play that afternoon, and Bonnie, in her role of wardrobe mistress, was most surprised when June and Freddie came backstage and began showing a great interest in the costumes, wigs and greasepaint that were there.

'I say, June!' called out Freddie. 'This would be simply perfect.'

Freddie was holding up an old-fashioned, white nightdress, and Bonnie gave a squeal.

'Freddie Holmes, if you get dirty finger-marks on that, I shall never forgive you!' she said. 'That's Molly's costume and I have just had it washed.'

'Bonnie, dear,' said June, putting an arm round the girl's shoulders. 'May I borrow it, please?'

'Whatever for?' asked Bonnie, puzzled. 'You have perfectly good pyjamas of your own.'

'I don't want to wear it to bed,' chuckled June. 'You see, Bonnie, I am going to dress up as a ghost, and scare the living daylights out of Miss Tallant!'

'When?' asked Bonnie.

'On the night of our feast,' said June. 'You see, she is going to be under the impression that the South Tower fourth formers are holding a feast, and she will rush over there at midnight to stop it. But Freddie and I are going to prepare a little surprise for her.'

Bonnie was torn. On the one hand, she felt quite thrilled at the thought of the unpleasant Miss Tallant being punished for her nasty ways. On the other, the thought of the exquisite nightdress that she had painstakingly altered to fit Molly becoming damaged or dirty quite filled her with horror.

As though sensing what she was thinking, June said, 'I promise that I shall take great care of it, Bonnie, and if it should become dirty I will wash it myself.'

'Very well,' said Bonnie, at last, handing the nightdress over. 'And just see that you *do* take care of it, June.'

'We could borrow some of this greasepaint, too,' said Freddie. 'The white one would give you a ghostly pallor, June, and we could use this purple one to make dark hollows under your eyes.'

'Good idea!' said June.

'And you could really do with a wig,' said Bonnie. 'For you don't want to run the risk of Miss Tallant recognising you. Try this.'

And Bonnie picked up a long, dark wig, which she put on June's head.

'Marvellous!' said Freddie, happily. 'With the wig and some greasepaint, I really don't think that your own mother would know you, June.'

When the rehearsal was over, June and Freddie ran up to the dormitory with the things that they had found for June's disguise, and hid everything away carefully.

As they walked out on to the landing, June spotted Olive coming up the stairs, and, putting a finger to her lips, quickly pulled Freddie into an alcove. Then she waited until Olive had gone into the dormitory, leaving the door open behind her. Beckoning to Freddie to follow, June went over to the cupboard where the food for the feast was being stored.

Unlocking the door, and opening it with a lot of quite unnecessary noise, June said loudly, 'My word, what a lot of food! Those South Tower girls are going to have a marvellous feast.'

Following June's lead, Freddie said, 'What a pity that we can't join them, for it all looks super. Thank goodness we were able to help them out by storing their food for them. When did you say that they are holding the feast, June?'

'On Friday night, at midnight exactly,' said June, in her clear voice, as she locked the door again.

The two girls walked away, and as they reached the bottom of the stairs, June said, 'Well, Miss Tallant is bound to get the false information now, either from Olive or Sylvia. Everything is working out perfectly!'

Friday was June's birthday, and most of the girls had bought her a little gift of some sort.

Felicity gave her a bottle of bath salts, and Susan gave her an enormous bar of chocolate.

Freddie, who had noticed that June's old purse was looking very shabby indeed, had bought her a new one, while Bonnie presented her with a set of handkerchiefs that she had embroidered herself. The only person who didn't give June a present was Olive, but as June said, 'I didn't really expect anything from her. And, to be honest, I'm quite glad that she didn't give me anything, for I shouldn't have liked to have accepted a gift from someone I don't like, and who I believe to be a sneak.'

'Well, you've had some jolly nice presents, anyway,' said Nora, looking rather enviously at the things June had received.

'Yes, thanks awfully everyone,' said June, smiling round at her friends. 'You've all been very generous.'

'And the best part of your birthday is still to come,' said Freddie, in a low voice. 'The feast tonight.'

'Yes,' said June, looking round to make sure that Sylvia and Olive could not overhear. 'I don't know which I'm looking forward to most – that, or the trick that we are going to play on Miss Tallant.'

Felicity and Susan, standing nearby, *did* overhear, though, and Felicity said at once, 'Is the ghost of Malory Towers going to make an appearance tonight, then?'

'She certainly is,' said June, her eyes sparkling with mischief. 'She's going to appear in the grounds, while Miss Tallant is making her way to South Tower. And then she is going to vanish again.'

'But June, you'll miss your own birthday feast if you are out in the grounds playing a trick on Miss Tallant,' said Felicity, with a frown.

'No, I shan't,' said June. 'Freddie and I are going to wake up before you others, so that I can get dressed up in my ghost costume. And the actual trick itself will only take a few moments, so we shall be back in the common-room with the rest of you in a trice.'

'What a pity that we shan't all be there to see the trick,' said Susan with a sigh. 'I should love to see Miss Tallant's face when she sees the ghost!'

'Well, Freddie and I will tell you all about it,' promised June.

'What about Sylvia and Olive?' said Felicity, looking worried. 'One of them is Miss Tallant's niece, and the sneak, and if she wakes up and finds us out of our beds she is bound to cause trouble for us.'

'Oh, I've thought about that,' said June coolly. 'Just make sure that whoever is last out of the dormitory locks the door behind them.'

Susan gave a gasp, and said, 'June, we can't do that!'

'We must,' said June firmly. 'Probably neither of them *will* wake up and everything will be all right, but I don't want to take any chances. Of course, if they should happen to wake, tomorrow the sneak will probably tell Miss Tallant about the feast, but by then it will be too late. It will simply be our word against her niece's. And Miss Tallant's niece is not going to be in her good books, for having sent her over to South Tower for nothing.'

'That's true,' said Felicity. 'I must say, I'm still not entirely happy about locking the two of them in the dorm, but it would be too bad if the feast was spoiled.'

As things turned out, there was no question of locking Sylvia in the dormitory, for later that day she was sent to Matron by Miss Williams.

'Sylvia will be spending a couple of days in the San,' Miss Williams informed her class that afternoon. 'The poor girl has had a dreadful sore throat for several days now, and she has quite a temperature.'

'Poor old Sylvia!' said Pam. 'I thought that she didn't look very well earlier on.'

Everyone was sorry to hear that Sylvia was ill, but as Lucy said to Julie, 'At least it means that she is safely out of the way now, and won't have to be locked in the dormitory with Olive.'

Most of the fourth formers now knew of the plan to lock Olive in the dormitory while the feast took place, and they also knew that June meant to give Miss Tallant a scare.

Everyone was very excited, and found it hard to keep their mind on lessons that day.

'Nora!' said Miss Williams sharply, in the maths lesson. 'Is your knowledge of the maths that we are doing so great that you can afford to waste time by whispering to Pam?'

'No, Miss Williams,' said Nora meekly.

'Then kindly pay attention to what I am saying,' said the mistress. 'Unless you want to come to me for extra coaching after tea?'

Nora didn't want that at all, so she bent her head over her book and did her best to concentrate for the rest of the lesson.

Bonnie also found her mind wandering in French, but as she was one of Mam'zelle Dupont's favourites, she found it quite easy to talk her way out of trouble.

'*Ma chère* Bonnie, you are restless!' complained Mam'zelle. 'You do not concentrate. What is the matter with you?'

Bonnie turned her large, brown eyes on the French mistress, and said in a sad tone, 'I'm sorry, Mam'zelle. You know how much I love your French lessons, but I am just so worried about poor Sylvia. I expect you have heard that she has been taken ill.'

Of course, Bonnie had not been thinking about Sylvia at all. She had been thinking about the midnight feast, and the trick that June was going to play on Miss Tallant. But Mam'zelle, as usual, was quite taken in, and cried, 'Ah, it is kind of you to be concerned for *la pauvre* Sylvia. But you must not worry your head, Bonnie, for Matron will take the greatest care of her.'

Olive, hearing this, threw an angry glance in the girl's direction. If it wasn't just like Bonnie to worm her way out of trouble! She was just like her beastly step-sister, Annabel, and how Olive detested them both.

Surprisingly, though, no one was scolded in Miss Tallant's class. Julie and Lucy whispered together, and June flipped a paper dart at Olive, but Miss Tallant, for once, didn't even notice, seeming quite preoccupied.

'She was thinking of tonight, I expect,' said June scornfully, once the lesson was over.

'And of how she is going to ruin things for the South Tower girls.'

'What a shock she is going to get!' laughed Nora. 'My word, I simply can't wait for tonight to come!'

The ghost of Malory Towers

Some of the girls found it very hard to get to sleep that night, for they were all thoroughly overexcited. At last, one by one, they dropped off. Susan, who was to be responsible for waking the girls in time for the feast, had set her alarm clock for ten minutes to midnight. She had placed it under her pillow, so that the sound did not disturb Olive. June also had an alarm clock under her pillow, but hers was set for half past eleven. When it went off, she awoke at once, and nudged Freddie, in the next bed. The two girls got out of bed, then put bolsters down the middle of their beds, just in case Matron or one of the mistresses should peep in.

The things that they needed for June's disguise were in a box under her bed, and she picked it up. Then the two girls tiptoed silently from the room, and went into a little bathroom at the end of the corridor.

There, they worked swiftly. Freddie rubbed the white greasepaint all over June's face, then carefully smudged some of the purple around her eyes.

'Golly!' said Freddie, standing back to admire her handiwork. 'You look simply ghastly!'

'Thank you,' said June with a grin.

Then June changed into the long, white nightdress, pulling it very carefully over her head, so as not to get greasepaint on it.

'Bonnie will be simply wild with me if I get it dirty,' she said.

Finally, she placed the wig on her head, smoothing the hair into place, and Freddie said, 'Thank goodness it's not windy tonight. It really would give the game away if your wig blew off!'

But it was a perfectly calm, still night as the two girls crept out of a side door and, under cover of the trees, made their way to South Tower.

There, they crouched behind a hedge, and Freddie whispered, 'It's five minutes to midnight. Do you suppose that Miss Tallant is already in South Tower?'

'No,' whispered June. 'She thinks that the feast is starting at midnight, and she will want to catch the girls in the act. I think that she will appear shortly after midnight. Freddie, I'm going to take my place now. You know what you need to do.'

'You can count on me, June,' said Freddie solemnly. 'Now, off you go.'

June darted over to the wall, slipping swiftly through the hidden gap there and disappearing from view. Freddie, still in her hiding-place, gave a shiver. June really did look like a very realistic ghost, and watching her vanish like that was very creepy indeed! The night was cold, and Freddie hoped that they would not have to wait too long for Miss Tallant to arrive.

But, as June had predicted, the mistress came into view shortly after midnight, looking over her shoulder with many nervous glances as she approached South Tower. Freddie grinned to herself in the darkness. Miss Tallant was no doubt thinking of Bonnie's ghost story, for she was evidently very uneasy indeed.

Freddie crouched down lower, to make sure that the mistress couldn't possibly spot her, then she let out a high-pitched wail. This was both to scare Miss Tallant, and to warn June that their victim had arrived. And the unearthly wail certainly succeeded in its first objective, for the mistress jumped violently, and put a hand to her heart.

'Who is there?' she demanded, her voice quavering.

But no answer came and, with one last, scared look round, Miss Tallant put her head down and strode briskly into South Tower.

With the mistress safely out of earshot, Freddie gave a low whistle, which told June that Miss Tallant had gone inside. Now, all they had to do was wait.

Five minutes later, a red-faced Miss Tallant emerged, escorted to the door by Miss Markham, the stern head of South Tower.

Miss Markham looked even sterner than usual, and her voice carried on the still night air to the listening Freddie.

'I find your behaviour quite extraordinary, Miss Tallant,' the mistress said coldly. 'If you had reason to suspect that my girls were holding a midnight feast, you should have come to me, instead of bursting into their dormitory like that and waking them all up. I don't feel that Miss Grayling will be impressed by your conduct.'

Miss Tallant mumbled something which might have been an apology, then Miss Markham bade her a frosty goodnight, before going back inside and closing the door.

Freddie put a hand over her mouth to stifle her laughter at the mistress's disgruntled expression. The person who had wrongly informed Miss Tallant that there was to be a feast in South Tower was certainly going to get it tomorrow!

As Miss Tallant moved forward, Freddie let out another wail, which stopped the mistress in her tracks. And this was the signal for June to come out. She slid silently through the gap in the wall, standing several yards from Miss Tallant.

And Miss Tallant, rooted to the spot in terror, was too frightened even to scream as she stared at the apparition before her, with its deathly pallor and big, hollow eyes.

June took a small step in the direction of Miss Tallant, who let out a sound between a moan and a whimper, then she turned away and vanished through the gap again.

Miss Tallant remained frozen in horror for a moment, then she let out a piercing shriek, so loud that both June and Freddie had to clap their hands over their ears.

Miss Markham, who had just reached her bedroom, gave a start and quickly made her way downstairs and outside again, where she found a pale, trembling Miss Tallant.

'Good heavens!' cried Miss Markham. 'What on earth has happened, Miss Tallant?'

'A g-ghost!' stammered Miss Tallant. 'I – I saw a ghost!'

Miss Markham, who had long ago sized Miss Tallant up as a rather silly, spiteful woman, pursed her lips. She knew that there were no such things as ghosts, and would very much have liked to give the mistress a piece of her mind. But there was no doubt that the woman had suffered a great shock, for she was as white as a sheet, and was shaking from head to foot. Miss Markham said crisply, 'I daresay that your imagination was playing tricks on you, Miss Tallant. Still, it is quite clear that you cannot return to North Tower in this state. Come up to my room, and I shall make you some hot cocoa, and then I will walk back to North Tower with you.'

Miss Tallant was only too happy to let Miss Markham lead her inside, and as soon as the two mistresses had disappeared, Freddie crept out from behind the hedge, and went across to the wall.

'June come out!' she hissed. 'Let's get back to North Tower quickly, while Miss Tallant and Miss Markham are both inside.'

The ghostly June emerged, her enormous grin making her look even more frightening than she had before, as she said, 'That went well. Did you see her face, Freddie?'

'Yes, but do hurry, June,' begged Freddie, taking her friend's arm and beginning to run. 'The feast will have started by now, and I don't want to miss another minute of it. I don't know why, but this midnight haunting has made me awfully hungry!'

The feast had indeed started, and the fourth formers were enjoying themselves enormously.

Susan had gone round quickly and quietly, waking everyone up and taking great care not to disturb the sleeping Olive. June had given Susan the key to the store cupboard, and she, Felicity, Pam and Nora had got all the food out, while the rest of the girls put on dressing-gowns and slippers and padded down to the common-room.

Then Susan had taken a last look into the dormitory to make sure that Olive was still asleep, before locking the door behind her and following the others downstairs.

Someone had lit candles and closed the heavy curtains, so that nothing could be seen from outside. Bonnie, who was a great favourite with the kitchen staff, had coaxed the cook into lending her some plates and cups, and the girls set everything out on them.

Then Felicity said, 'It doesn't seem right starting until June gets here. It is her birthday feast, after all.'

'Yes, but she did tell us not to wait,' said Susan, eyeing the plates of food longingly.

How delicious everything looked! There was an enormous pork pie, biscuits, tins of sardines and pineapple, cake, chocolate and all kinds of goodies!

'She won't be very long,' said Julie. 'And we shall make sure that there is plenty left for her, and for Freddie.'

So the girls munched away happily, all the time wondering what was happening to June and Freddie.

'I do hope that the trick went well,' said Lucy. 'My

161

goodness, wouldn't it be dreadful if they got caught!'

'June won't get caught,' said Bonnie confidently. 'She always plans everything so carefully.'

And it was soon seen that Bonnie was quite right, for June and Freddie joined them, and the girls gasped to see June dressed up as a ghost.

Bonnie and Amy shrieked so loudly that Susan had to tick them off.

'Idiots!' she hissed. 'Do you want to wake up the whole of North Tower?'

'Sorry, Susan,' said Bonnie. 'But really, June looks so frightening that I simply couldn't help myself.'

June grinned and said, 'Miss Tallant screamed too – much more loudly than you, Bonnie.'

She and Freddie sat down and began to eat, while the fourth formers clamoured to know what had happened.

Assisted by Freddie, June told them, and the listening girls gasped as June told the tale.

'Well!' said Pam. 'All the years I've been at Malory Towers, and I didn't know that there was a gap in the wall by South Tower.'

'Well, we fourth formers will keep it to ourselves,' said Susan. 'Who knows when we may need to use it again.'

'I expect Miss Markham will be bringing Miss Tallant back to North Tower soon,' said Freddie, tucking into a slice of pork pie. 'But we have nothing to fear, because her room is at the other side of the building, and she will come in at the door over there.'

'Perhaps I should go and wait for her,' said June, with

a smile. 'Just to see her jump out of her skin.'

The others laughed at this, but Susan said, 'I don't think we had better risk any more wandering around. It's jolly lucky that you two didn't get caught outside, June and Freddie, for you know that there is a strict rule forbidding any girl to leave her tower at night.'

'I wonder if dear Olive is still sleeping peacefully?' said Amy.

'She must be,' said Nora. 'Or we should have heard her banging at the dormitory door by now.'

'Gosh, I never thought of that,' said Felicity, looking alarmed. 'What are we to do if she starts banging at the door?'

'I suppose I shall have to go up and unlock the door,' said Susan with a grimace. 'And then I will have to tell Olive why she wasn't invited to our feast, and warn her what will happen if she splits on us.'

But there was not a sound to be heard from upstairs, and the girls finished their feast in peace, until there was hardly anything left. Then they sat around eating the chocolates, finishing the lemonade and chatting idly.

At last, Susan said, 'I suppose we had better clear up now.'

Nora gave a groan and said, 'This is the part of midnight feasts that I always hate.'

'Come on, lazybones,' said Pam, giving her a nudge. 'If we all pitch in, it shouldn't take long.'

So the fourth formers got to work, sweeping up the crumbs, piling up the plates and collecting up the empty lemonade bottles. Lucy put them into a cupboard, saying, 'I'll get rid of these tomorrow.'

'And I will take the plates and cups back to Cook in the morning,' said Bonnie. 'My goodness, my first midnight feast! What fun it's been!'

Everyone agreed to that, as, tired and happy, they tiptoed upstairs. Susan unlocked the door very quietly, feeling relieved when she saw that Olive was still fast asleep and didn't appear to have stirred. Tomorrow, she thought, getting into bed, she would have to try and think of a way of getting either Olive or Sylvia to own up to being Miss Tallant's niece. But, at the moment, she was just too tired to think, falling asleep almost as soon as her head touched the pillow. So did the others, for it had been a very tiring evening and they were quite worn out.

And all of them had great difficulty in getting up the following morning! Olive, who was awake bright and early, simply couldn't understand why the others were so sluggish.

Even Julie and Lucy, who liked to race down to the stables before breakfast to see their horses, couldn't get out of bed. At last, Susan sat up and said, 'Come on, girls, we must get a move on or we shall be late for breakfast.'

There were moans and groans at this, but most of the girls got out of bed and began to get ready. Only Amy and Nora stayed put, but they always hated getting up anyway.

'I don't want any breakfast,' muttered Amy, turning over and closing her eyes. 'I would much rather have an extra hour in bed.'

'Amy, it doesn't matter whether you actually *want* breakfast or not, you must put in an appearance, or Miss Williams will come looking for you,' said Felicity. 'And if she finds you in bed, it will mean an order mark against the whole form.'

'The same goes for you, Nora,' said Pam to her friend. 'Do get up.'

'I can't!' wailed Nora. 'I feel sick.'

'Well, it jolly well serves you right for eating six chocolate biscuits,' said Pam, bending her head close to Nora's, so that Olive could not overhear. 'Do come along now!'

At last everyone was ready, and the girls trooped down to breakfast. They cast several interested glances Miss Tallant's way, for all of them were curious to know how she was feeling after her ordeal last night.

She looked very pale indeed, and there were dark circles under her eyes, as though she had not slept well.

June noticed too, with satisfaction, that her hand shook slightly as she picked up her cup of tea. She pointed this out to Freddie, who said, 'Serves her right. At least she won't be snooping around at night in future. I shouldn't be at all surprised if she is afraid to leave her bedroom now!'

None of the girls ate very much breakfast, for they all felt full from the feast the night before, and one or two of them really did feel sick. Mam'zelle Dupont, at the head of the table, looked quite concerned when Nora refused to eat her toast, saying, 'Ah, *la pauvre*! You are sick. You shall go to Matron immediately.'

But Nora had no intention of doing this, for Matron had a knack of knowing when a midnight feast had been held, and kept a bottle of especially nasty-tasting medicine for anyone who complained of feeling ill afterwards. So, to put Mam'zelle's mind at rest, the girl nibbled at a corner of her toast and sipped a cup of tea.

It was as the girls were leaving the dining-room that Miss Tallant approached them and snapped, 'Olive! I want a word with you.'

The listening fourth formers noticed how the girl turned pale, and stammered, 'But Miss Tallant, I have to take some work to Miss Williams.'

'Come and see me immediately afterwards,' said the mistress, a cold, angry look on her face. 'And please don't keep me waiting!'

Olive went off to find the work that she had to give to Miss Williams, looking very unhappy, and the others exchanged glances.

'Well!' said June, raising her dark eyebrows. 'I'll bet you anything you like that Miss Tallant is going to give Olive a scold for sending her on a wild goose chase last night.'

'Yes, I think you're right,' said Felicity. 'It looks as if Olive is her niece all right. And I wouldn't like to be in her shoes when she faces her aunt!'

'I've been trying to think of a way to get her to own up,' said Susan. 'But I really can't.'

'Well, let's have a try in the common-room later,' said Pam. 'And if she won't admit to being Miss Tallant's niece and sneaking on us, then we will just have to tackle her about it, I'm afraid.'

As it was Saturday, there were no lessons, but a rehearsal for the play was scheduled for the afternoon. And several of the girls thought that it would be a nice idea to go and see Sylvia.

'Let's pop across to the San now,' said Felicity to Susan. 'I think that there is a bar of chocolate in the common-room, left over from the feast. Perhaps if we take it to her it might cheer her up a bit.'

'Good idea,' said Susan. 'I feel a lot happier about visiting her now that we know for certain that she isn't the sneak.'

So the two girls went into the common-room to fetch the chocolate, then went along to the San. But they were in for a shock!

Miss Tallant's niece

'Hallo, girls,' said Matron to Felicity and Susan, as they entered the San. 'Come to see Sylvia? Well, she is feeling a little better today, and I daresay a visit will cheer her up.' They found the invalid sitting up in bed reading a book, and looking rather down in the dumps. But she brightened when she saw her visitors and put the book aside, saying in a rather croaky voice, 'Do come and sit down! You can't imagine how marvellous it is to see you. Matron is a dear, but –'

'But she can be awfully bossy at times,' Felicity finished for her, and Sylvia smiled.

Susan handed her the chocolate, for which Sylvia was extremely grateful, then the three girls chatted. For once, Sylvia was quiet, letting the other two do most of the talking, as she had been ordered by Matron not to strain her throat.

Susan began to tell the girl about a trick that June was planning to play on Mam'zelle Dupont the following week, but she realised that Sylvia's polite smile was becoming rather strained, and said, 'Of course, I forgot! You don't like jokes and tricks, do you, Sylvia?'

'I know it makes me seem frightfully dull and

boring, but no, I don't,' Sylvia admitted.

'It seems very odd to me,' said Felicity. 'I don't think I've ever met anyone who doesn't like jokes and tricks before.'

'Well, it's because of something that happened when I was younger,' said Sylvia.

'Did someone play a trick on you that went wrong, or hurt you?' asked Susan curiously.

'No, it was *I* who played a trick on someone else,' was Sylvia's surprising answer. 'And it went terribly wrong.'

'What happened?' asked Felicity.

'Well, I played a trick on my aunt,' said Sylvia. 'My father's younger sister. You see, we live in a big, old house, and my aunt always used to complain that it gave her the creeps. Though it never stopped her coming to stay with us! I love the house, and I became fed up of hearing her criticise it, so one night I decided that I would *really* give Aunt Aggie the creeps!'

'Whatever did you do?' asked Susan, quite unable to imagine Sylvia playing a trick.

'I dressed up as a ghost one night, and ran around in the garden under her window,' said Sylvia, looking rather ashamed now.

Felicity and Susan, with June's trick on Miss Tallant in mind, laughed, and Felicity said, 'Well, that doesn't seem so very bad.'

'Oh, but it was,' said Sylvia gravely. 'You see, Aunt Aggie was so terrified that she fainted, and banged her head as she fell. She was quite ill for a while, and had to stay with us for simply ages!'

'Heavens!' cried Felicity. 'What bad luck. But it wasn't your fault, Sylvia. I mean to say, you didn't harm your aunt on purpose.'

'No, but it quite put me off playing any tricks,' said the girl miserably.

'Yes, I can see that it would,' said Susan. 'Did you own up?'

Sylvia shook her head unhappily. 'I was too afraid,' she said guiltily. 'My aunt has quite a temper, you know, and would have been terribly angry with me. Awfully cowardly of me, I know.'

'Well, you were younger then,' said Susan, attempting to give the girl's thoughts a happier direction. 'And I'm sure that we have all done foolish things that we are not proud of at some time or other.'

Sylvia cheered up at this, and the rest of the visit passed pleasantly, until Matron came in to throw them out.

'Sylvia must rest for a little now,' she said. 'But she may have more visitors later, if some of the others would like to come.'

It was as the two girls were making their way to the common-room that Felicity suddenly stopped dead in her tracks.

'Oh, my gosh!' she cried.

'What's up?' asked Susan, looking at her in surprise.

'I've just remembered something,' said Felicity. 'Bonnie told us that Miss Tallant is afraid of ghosts because she saw one when she was younger.'

'Yes?' said Susan, a puzzled look on her face.

'And Sylvia dressed up as a ghost to frighten her aunt!' exclaimed Felicity. 'Her *aunt*, Susan! Don't you see?'

Light dawned on Susan, and she gasped. 'Olive is innocent, after all. *Sylvia* is Miss Tallant's niece.'

'Which means that Sylvia is also the sneak,' said Felicity grimly. 'Susan, we must tell the others at once.'

But while Felicity and Susan had been visiting Sylvia, a quite dreadful row had broken out in the common room.

It started over a very little thing indeed, as big rows often do. Nora, not realising that Olive was standing behind her, had stepped back and accidentally stood on the girl's toe.

'Gosh, I'm awfully sorry, Olive!' Nora had said at once. 'I do hope that I didn't hurt you.'

'Well, you did,' snapped Olive, who seemed to be in a blacker mood than usual since she had been to see Miss Tallant. 'Why on earth can't you look where you are going?'

Nora tried to apologise again, but Olive cut her short, an unpleasant sneer on her face, as she said spitefully, 'For someone who thinks that she is *so* graceful, and *such* a marvellous dancer, you're terribly clumsy, Nora. I don't know what Susan and the others were thinking of, to let you play the fairy, for you simply aren't up to it, in my opinion.'

'Well, who cares tuppence for your opinion?' said Pam, roused to a rare show of temper by this. 'Keep it to yourself, Olive, for no one else wants to hear what you have to say.'

There were murmurs of agreement from some of the listening girls, and Olive flushed angrily. But she turned away and said no more. Things might have calmed down, if June and Freddie had not walked in at that precise moment. Sensing an atmosphere, June asked at once, 'What's the matter?'

'It's nothing,' said Nora quickly, for she had no wish to prolong the argument and just wanted to forget all about it. But Amy, who disliked Olive intensely, had other ideas, and said in her haughty way, 'Just our dear Olive causing trouble again – as usual.'

Olive turned on Amy at once, crying, 'How dare you accuse *me* of causing trouble, you horrid little snob! Nora was the one at fault, for she stood on my foot – and I wouldn't be the least bit surprised if it was deliberate!'

'Don't be ridiculous!' said Bonnie, entering the fray. 'I saw the whole thing, and it was quite obvious that it was an accident.'

'Well, you would stick up for Nora, wouldn't you?' scoffed Olive, towering over little Bonnie. 'For you are both exactly alike! Spoilt, silly, pretty little dolls!'

Then Olive folded her arms and stood with a smirk on her face, waiting for the foolish little Bonnie to burst into tears.

But she was disappointed, for Bonnie, very angry indeed, stood up to Olive, saying, 'Well, I would rather be a spoilt, silly little doll than a plain, jealous sneak! For that is what you are, Olive. And I know why you are so jealous of Nora and me, for I spoke to Annabel at half-term.'

The colour drained from Olive's face, and she hissed, 'You had no right to speak to her! No right at all!'

'I have the right to speak to anyone I please,' retorted Bonnie defiantly. 'I understand why you dislike your step-sister, Olive, I really do. I understand why you needed to cut her out of your family photograph, as though she didn't exist. But please don't take your loathing of her out on Nora and me, for it is nothing to do with us, we don't deserve it, and we don't appreciate it!'

'One up to Bonnie!' murmured June, who had been watching the scene with enjoyment. So had the others, and how they relished seeing Olive look so taken aback. There was a great deal more to Bonnie than met the eye, and Olive had found out the hard way!

Now June decided to take a hand, and she stepped forward, saying smoothly, 'Do you have any other relatives that you don't want us to know about, Olive? An aunt, for instance?'

Olive looked extremely puzzled, and said, 'I don't know what you mean.'

'Oh, I think you do,' said June. 'You see, we know all about you and Miss Tallant. We know that you have been sneaking to her, and letting her in on our secrets. What do you have to say about that, Olive?'

Olive had nothing at all to say, for she was completely speechless. But guilt was written all over her face, and she was quite unable to look any of the others in the eye. At last she opened her mouth to speak, but the only sound that came out was a little sob, and the girl ran from the room.

Olive almost knocked over Felicity and Susan, who were outside, and when Susan called out, 'Hi, Olive! Whatever is the matter?' she didn't even look round, but ran up the stairs to the dormitory.

'Well!' said Susan to Felicity, in astonishment. 'What do you suppose that was about?'

Felicity, who had glanced through the open door of the common-room and seen the grim faces of the fourth formers, thought, with a sinking heart, that she knew. She turned to Susan, and said gravely, 'I have a horrible feeling that we are too late.'

Susan gave a groan and went into the common-room, Felicity behind her.

At once June, aided by Bonnie, Nora, Pam and Amy, launched into an account of what had happened.

When they had finished, Susan groaned again, and said, 'June, I do wish that you had waited!'

'Why?' asked June, surprised and none too pleased. 'Olive was never going to own up, and as a row had already started I thought that this was the best time to tackle her.'

'But it wasn't, June,' said Felicity, looking very troubled. 'Because, you see, we have discovered that Olive is *not* Miss Tallant's niece. Sylvia is!'

There was a shocked silence, then everyone began to speak at once.

'Surely not!'

'That's impossible! I can't see Sylvia as a sneak.'

'Olive looked so guilty – it simply *must* be her.'

'And she didn't make any attempt to defend herself.'

'Well, perhaps she felt too shocked and upset to retaliate,' said Susan. 'But there is no doubt at all that Sylvia is the culprit.'

And, quickly, she told the fourth formers what she and Felicity had learned.

'I suppose it *must* be Sylvia, then,' said Pam. 'Though I'm very surprised, I must say.'

'Blow Sylvia!' said June, angrily. She felt very guilty indeed for having accused Olive unjustly, and was wishing that she had held her tongue. 'If only you had come back a few minutes earlier and told us this, Susan and Felicity, everything would have been all right.'

'Well, you can hardly blame us!' said Susan crossly, for she felt very angry with June herself. 'The fact is, that you had no right to say anything at all to Olive. As head of the form it was my duty, but, as usual, you had to take the lead, and go in all guns blazing, without thinking things through.'

June flushed angrily. She felt annoyed with herself, and annoyed with Susan. And the reason she was annoyed with Susan was because everything she said was perfectly true.

June was honest enough to admit that to herself. She *did* always have to take the lead in things. And this wasn't the first time she had caused an awkward situation by accusing someone unjustly.

Nora spoke up for her, though, saying, 'To be fair, Susan, all of us thought the same as June. We were all absolutely convinced that she was the mysterious niece, and had been sneaking to Miss Tallant. And the chances are, if June hadn't accused her to her face, one of us others would have.'

'That's very true,' said Bonnie, nodding solemnly.

'Yes, we were all feeling sore with Olive, because of the row she had started,' said Julie.

'So really we are all to blame.'

'No,' said June suddenly. 'I am to blame. Susan is quite right. I shouldn't have tackled Olive as I did. Speaking out of turn seems to be one of my biggest faults! Each time it happens I tell myself that I will think twice before doing it again, and then I go and jump in with both feet!'

'Well, at least you have the courage to own up to it,' said Felicity, admiring June for being honest enough to admit to a fault.

'Yes, but owning up to it isn't enough,' said June, ruefully. 'I need to do something to make amends. I shall go and apologise to Olive, and I will tell her that we know now that she isn't the sneak.'

Susan was a little doubtful about this, for, while she appreciated June's efforts to make it up to Olive, she wasn't sure whether the girl would accept the apology. And if Olive gave June the cold shoulder, June might flare up again, and then another quarrel would break out!

Felicity, seeing the doubt in Susan's face, said, 'I know! Why don't we all go and speak to Olive? Although she isn't the sneak, she hasn't done very much to make us think well of her, so really it's no wonder that we suspected her. But we can go to her now and tell her that we want to wipe the slate clean and give her a chance to become one of us.'

'Jolly good idea, Felicity!' cried Pam. 'Come along, everyone, let's go up to Olive now.'

So the fourth formers trooped upstairs and into the dormitory, all of them feeling rather virtuous about their decision to try and befriend Olive.

Alas for such good intentions! When Susan opened the door and the fourth formers filed in, Olive was nowhere to be seen.

'Oh!' said Susan, rather disappointed. 'She's not here. She must have come downstairs while we were talking in the common-room.'

'Perhaps she has gone for a walk in the grounds, to clear her head,' suggested Lucy.

'Yes, that's probably it,' said Julie. 'Oh well, we shall just have to wait until later to make amends to Olive.'

'There's something else,' said Freddie, looking rather serious. 'We shall have to tackle Sylvia about her behaviour.'

'Yes, I had already thought of that,' said Susan, looking rather gloomy. Bother, now there would be yet another row, and another girl sent to Coventry. She had just been getting to like Sylvia, too.

'Well, Matron said that she will probably be back in class tomorrow, so we will deal with her then. And June . . .'

June held her hands up, and said at once, 'I know, Susan! I shall leave it all to you.'

Where is Olive?

Olive did not turn up for rehearsal that afternoon, and the girls didn't see hide nor hair of her. When she failed to turn up for tea, Susan grew rather alarmed.

'I say!' she said to Felicity. 'You don't think that Olive's done anything silly, do you?'

'Whatever do you mean?' asked Felicity, startled.

'Well, it just occurred to me that she might have run away or something,' said Susan.

'Surely she wouldn't do such a thing?' said Felicity, shocked. 'Besides, where would she go? We know that she is not happy at home, so it's very unlikely that she would have gone there.'

'That makes it all the more worrying,' said Susan, with a frown. 'If she had gone home, at least we would know that she is safe.'

Pam, who had overheard this, said, 'Steady on, Susan! We don't *know* that Olive has run away. Why, for all we know she may have come back and be up in the dormitory now.'

So, after tea, Felicity and Susan, along with Pam and Nora, went up to the dormitory once more. But there was no sign of Olive.

Looking very worried indeed, Susan marched across to Olive's locker and pulled it open.

Some of her personal belongings were gone, and when Felicity took a look inside the girl's wardrobe she could see that some of her clothes were missing too.

'Oh, my word!' gasped Nora. 'It didn't seriously enter my head that she really *had* gone. Now what do we do?'

'We must report it to Miss Williams,' said Susan gravely. 'At once, for there is no time to lose!'

But Miss Williams was out, so the girls went to find Miss Potts, the head of North Tower.

She listened to their story with a very serious expression indeed, then said, 'I must inform Miss Grayling immediately. You girls had better come too, in case she needs to question you.'

So, all feeling rather nervous, the four girls followed Miss Potts to Miss Grayling's study.

The Head called to them to come in, in answer to the mistress's sharp knock, and saw at once that something was wrong.

Quickly, Miss Potts told Miss Grayling what had happened and the Head listened, her expression grave. Then she said, 'Do you girls have any idea at all where Olive may have gone?'

'None at all, Miss Grayling,' answered Susan. 'I only wish that we did.'

'Then do you know of any reason why she might have run away?' asked Miss Grayling.

The four girls looked at one another, and Miss Grayling

said, 'If you know something, it is important that you tell me, for it might help us in finding Olive.'

So Susan told the story of how the fourth formers had discovered that Miss Tallant had a niece at Malory Towers, and of how she had been sneaking to her aunt.

'We all thought it was Olive,' said Susan, rather miserably. 'And one of the girls accused her to her face. But now we know that we were wrong, and that Sylvia is Miss Tallant's niece.'

'Yes, she is,' said the Head. 'I was aware of it from the first, but at the request of both Sylvia and Miss Tallant, I kept it to myself. Both of them felt that they would be able to settle in better if no one was aware of their relationship. But we shall come back to that in a minute, for I must telephone the police at once, so that they can search for Olive.'

Miss Grayling dialled the police station and held a hurried conversation with the person at the other end of the telephone, before replacing the receiver and turning back to Miss Potts.

'Could you organise a search party of any available staff to search the grounds, please, Miss Potts?' she asked. 'The police will be here shortly, but I really don't feel that we should waste any time.'

Miss Potts nodded and left the Head's study, and Miss Grayling looked at the girls in front of her.

'Now that I know the search for Olive is in hand, let us go back to the question of Miss Tallant,' she said. 'Am I to understand that Miss Tallant has been using her position of authority to find out what you fourth formers have been up to?'

The girls looked at one another a little uncomfortably. For some of the things they had been up to were things that they did not want Miss Grayling to know about. The midnight feast, for example, and some of the tricks that June had played.

Miss Grayling saw the doubt in their faces, and smiled to herself, for she had been Head mistress at Malory Towers for many years, and guessed a little of what was going through their minds.

'I am not asking you to reveal any of your secrets to me,' she said. 'I merely want to know how Miss Tallant has been conducting herself, so that I can deal with her accordingly.'

Felicity spoke up, saying, 'Miss Grayling, it is true that Miss Tallant has found out things about the fourth form that she could not possibly have known unless she had someone spying on us. And some of us have been punished because of the things that she has found out.'

'I see,' said the Head, her face very serious. 'And yet, I find it very hard to believe that Sylvia is a sneak, for she has always struck me as a rather honest, forthright girl.'

'Yes, that is what we thought, too,' said Susan. 'We were most awfully disappointed in her when we discovered the truth.'

'But can you be sure that you know the whole story?' asked Miss Grayling. 'Just because Sylvia is Miss Tallant's niece, it does not necessarily follow that she is the one who has been giving away your secrets. In fact, the impression I received was that Sylvia and her aunt were not close at all.'

The girls looked at one another in surprise. They had been so certain that Miss Tallant's niece and the sneak were one and the same!

'Miss Grayling,' said Pam. 'Do you think it is possible that Olive *could* have been the sneak, after all? She looked awfully guilty when she was tackled, and didn't attempt to deny it.'

'It is possible,' said the Head. 'But I think the first thing to do is speak to Sylvia, so that you can be certain it is not her.'

'Will you go to her now, Miss Grayling?' asked Susan.

'Certainly not,' replied the Head. 'The police will be here at any minute, and my immediate concern is to find Olive. I am going to leave it to you, Susan, as head of the fourth form to speak to Sylvia. And I trust that you will use all the tact and wisdom that I know you possess.'

'Of course, Miss Grayling,' said Susan, feeling awfully proud that the Head thought she was tactful and wise.

Suddenly Nora, who had remained silent up until now, said, 'Miss Grayling, I think that there is something else you should know. Bonnie spoke to Olive's step-sister at half-term, and it turns out that the two of them dislike one another awfully, and there have been dreadful problems between them. I don't suppose that that has anything to do with Olive running away, but I thought I would mention it.'

'Thank you, Nora,' said Miss Grayling. 'That could prove very useful.'

Just then there came a tap at the door, and a maid announced that the police had arrived, so the fourth formers left the Head's study and went to join the others in the common-room.

There was great consternation when Susan announced that Olive had run away.

'How dreadful! I wonder where she has gone?'

'It's an awfully cold night! I do hope that she will be all right.'

'The police will find her and bring her back.'

'Well, let's hope so.'

The only person who remained silent was June. How terribly, terribly guilty she felt! If only she had held her tongue, Olive might be here now, safe and warm. Instead, she was out goodness knows where, alone in the dark and the bitter cold. If only she, June, could make amends somehow! But perhaps she could! The others were all pre-occupied discussing Olive's disappearance and, unseen by them, June slipped from the room.

'I wonder if Matron would let me speak to Sylvia tonight?' said Susan. 'It is quite early, and I bet she is still awake.'

'Why don't you ask her?' suggested Felicity. 'I'll come with you if you like.'

So the two girls went along to the San, where Matron greeted them by saying, 'You two here again? I had no idea that you were such close friends with Sylvia.'

'Matron, we need to speak to her quite urgently,' said Felicity. 'It really is terribly important.'

Matron looked at the watch that was pinned to her crisp, white apron, and said, 'Very well. You may have twenty minutes, no more.'

Sylvia looked surprised, but very pleased, to receive a second visit from Felicity and Susan, saying, 'Hallo, there! This is a pleasant surprise.'

'Well, I hope you will think so when you hear what we have come to say, Sylvia,' said Susan. 'You see, we know that you are Miss Tallant's niece.'

'Oh,' said Sylvia, turning red. 'Well, I suppose I should have known that it would be impossible to keep it secret forever. Perhaps I should have told you all myself, at the start, but I didn't want anyone to know that I was related to her.'

Felicity and Susan noticed the distaste in Sylvia's tone, and Felicity said, 'Don't you like her, then?'

'Of course not!' said Sylvia, in surprise. 'Do you?'

'No, but she's not my aunt,' said Felicity.

'Just because you are related to someone doesn't mean that you have to like them, you know,' retorted Sylvia. 'Aunt Aggie has always been spiteful and vindictive. Even my father dislikes her, and he is her brother! They haven't spoken to one another for years. I half-expected him to take me away when I wrote and told him that Aunt Aggie was a mistress here, but he knew how much I liked it at Malory Towers, so he said that I could stay. My aunt and I bumped into each other on our first day, and – as she dislikes me every bit as much as I like her – we agreed that we would both keep quiet about being related. I told Miss Grayling, of course, for it didn't seem quite right to keep it from her.'

Felicity and Susan exchanged glances. Sylvia was being so frank and open about things, that it was harder than ever to believe that she was the sneak. Susan cleared her throat, and said, 'Sylvia, there is something I must ask you, and I do hope that you won't take offence.'

'Heavens, whatever can it be?' asked Sylvia, looking rather alarmed.

'You see, we found out some time ago that Miss Tallant had a niece in the fourth form,' explained Susan. 'And we knew that it had to be either you or Olive. And then we realised that Miss Tallant had someone in the form spying on us and reporting back to her. So we put two and two together . . .'

'And decided that the niece was also the spy,' said Sylvia, looking rather hurt. 'Well, Susan, I can assure you that I am no sneak! And even if I was, Aunt Aggie is the last person I should tell tales to!'

There was such conviction in Sylvia's voice that both girls believed her at once.

'Well,' said Felicity heavily. 'It looks as if Olive must be the culprit after all, and that is why she has run away.'

'Olive has run away!' cried Sylvia. 'My goodness, do tell me what happened.'

While Felicity and Susan were talking to Sylvia, June had slipped out into the grounds to look for Olive. She couldn't join the official search party, for Miss Potts would certainly send her back indoors, so she avoided them and hunted for Olive alone. Where *could* she be? June went to the stables, the gardener's shed, and even the changing cubicles by the swimming-pool, but there was no sign of Olive. June shivered. It really was a bitterly cold night and, in her haste to find Olive, June had not stopped to put her coat on.

Perhaps she should try searching *inside* the school, in the store-rooms or attics perhaps. It would certainly be a great deal warmer!

She heard voices – the search party approaching – and hid behind the trunk of a large tree.

'It looks as though Olive has ventured outside the school grounds,' she heard Miss Potts say heavily. 'I'm afraid we shall have to leave it to the police to search for her now. I must go and tell Miss Grayling, so that she can telephone Olive's father.'

The search party went towards the school, but June remained where she was for a moment, thinking hard. Her instincts told her that Olive was still here, at Malory Towers somewhere. And if she could be the one to find her, it would go a long way towards assuaging her feelings of guilt. Suddenly June remembered the old boat-house, down the cliff-path. It was the one place she hadn't looked, and she would be willing to bet that the search party hadn't thought of it either.

Swiftly, the girl ran across the lawn, past the swimming pool, and down the path that led to the beach. And there was the boat-house, unused now and looking very dilapidated.

June knocked on the door and called, 'Olive! Olive, are you there?'

There was no answer, and, after a moment, a dejected June was about to walk away. But then her sharp ears caught a sound – a muffled sob!

Cautiously she pushed open the door of the boat-house. A heap of old sacks lay on the floor, and there, on top of them, sat Olive, crying as if her heart would break.

June was not the most sympathetic or compassionate of girls, but she felt a pang of sorrow for poor Olive, who was obviously in great distress. Now was the time, she realised, to let her sympathy and compassion shine through, to offer help and comfort to this poor, wretched girl. So June walked forward and said, in a gentle tone, 'Come on, Olive, old girl. You really can't stay here, you know. Why don't you tell me what's up, then I'll take you back up to the school.'

'You!' cried Olive, sitting bolt upright, an expression of horror on her face. 'Go away, June! You don't care what happens to me, you just want to be the one to take me back to school to face Miss Grayling, so that all the others will say what a heroine you are!'

June felt her temper rising, but she conquered it and, flopping down on to the sacks beside Olive, said, 'You're quite wrong, you know. If you must know, I feel simply terrible about accusing you of sneaking to Miss Tallant earlier, without any real proof. I'm sorry.'

Olive stared at June, a strange expression on her face.

Then she laughed, rather wildly, and said, 'There's no need for you to apologise. You were quite right. I was sneaking to Miss Tallant.'

June stared at the girl in astonishment. 'But it is Sylvia who's the sneak! We know that now. You see, it turns out that she is Miss Tallant's niece. Are you trying to cover up for her, Olive? And, if so, why? It's not even as if the two of you are friends.'

'I'm not covering up for anyone,' said Olive, dabbing at her eyes with a crumpled handkerchief. 'I don't know anything about Sylvia being Miss Tallant's niece, but I *do* know that she wasn't the one who was sneaking to her. I was. So now you can go away and tell all the others that you were right, and that I am every bit as bad as you said I was.'

'I'm not going anywhere until I get to the bottom of this,' said June firmly. 'Olive, *why* did you spy on us for Miss Tallant? Was it just because you dislike us so?'

Olive said nothing, but merely shrugged, refusing to look June in the eye, and June felt her temper rising again. Olive really was one of the most infuriating girls she had ever met, June thought, with her odd tempers and mean, spiteful nature. Perhaps the best thing that June could do was to haul the girl back up to the school and let Miss Grayling deal with her. She looked at Olive in distaste. And, as she did so, June saw something else. She saw the misery and loneliness behind the girl's facade and, hard-hearted as she sometimes was, felt moved by it. June thought about her own behaviour during her years at

Malory Towers, and did not feel proud of some of the things she had done. Yet she had been given chance after chance to change her ways. Perhaps Olive, too, should be given a chance.

Olive, lost in her own unhappy thoughts, was most astonished when she felt an arm come round her shoulders, and heard June say rather gruffly, 'You're awfully sad, aren't you, Olive? I would like to help you, if I can. Won't you tell me what is bothering you?'

This sudden, unexpected kindness was too much for Olive, who burst into tears again, and said between sobs, 'I can't. I'm so terribly ashamed.'

'Well, we have all done things that we are ashamed of, at times,' said June, patting the girl's shoulder. 'I certainly have anyway! But the thing I have always found is that if I've done something bad, it seems to become more serious, and weigh more heavily on me, if I keep it to myself. A trouble shared is a trouble halved, and all that.'

Olive's sobs quietened a little, as she thought over what June had said. Then, at last, she turned towards the girl and said, 'Very well, I will tell you. I don't suppose it matters much if you hate me afterwards, for nobody likes me anyway!'

June said nothing to this and, after a short silence, Olive began, 'It all started with my step-sister, Annabel. From the moment that she and my step-mother moved in with Father and me, she has done nothing but cause trouble. But because she is so pretty and behaves so sweetly in front of the grown-ups, everyone believes her when she says that I am to blame. I suppose I don't help myself by flying into a rage every time I am accused of something, but I simply can't tell you how horrid and hurtful it is to be blamed for things that aren't your fault all the time.'

'I should jolly well think it would be!' exclaimed June. 'Go on, Olive.'

'Well, at first Annabel and I went to the same day school together, though she was in a different form from me, of course,' said Olive. 'And soon she started making trouble for me there too. Taking people's things and hiding them in my desk so that it looked as if I had taken them, and playing petty, mean tricks and blaming them on me.'

'What a nasty little beast she sounds,' said June. 'I'll bet that you flew into some fine rages with her!'

'I did, of course,' said Olive. 'But that only made matters worse, for everyone would leap to the defence of dear, sweet little Annabel and became more convinced than ever that I was the one in the wrong. Eventually, Father decided that I was too troublesome to stay at home, and he sent me to boarding school.'

June's heart went out to Olive as she listened. No wonder that the girl felt bitter.

'Of course, I felt terribly unhappy and terribly angry,' said Olive. 'I hated being away from home, and thinking of Annabel in my place, being spoilt by her mother and my father, and getting all of their love and attention, while I had none. That made me feel mean and spiteful, and I decided that if I was going to be sent away from home for doing horrid things, then I really *would* do them.'

'So you turned into the person that everyone had accused you of being,' said June. 'Poor old Olive!'

'Yes, but it gets much worse,' said Olive, her voice trembling a little. 'Everyone disliked me so much at that school, mistresses and girls alike. And, when I look back at my behaviour, I really can't blame them. Things came to a head when I accidentally knocked another girl, who couldn't swim, into the pool. It really *was* an accident, June, but because I had behaved so badly all year, no one believed me and I was expelled.'

June gave a gasp and Olive said, 'You're shocked. I knew that you would be.'

'I'm shocked that one spoilt, silly little girl could cause so much trouble for you,' said June in her forthright way. 'And she will go on doing so, if we don't think of a way to stop her, Olive.'

Olive felt warmed by the way June had said 'we', and suddenly she felt a little less helpless and more hopeful for the future. With someone as strong and determined as June on her side, perhaps she would find a way to outwit the sly Annabel.

'But you still haven't told me how you came to spy on us for Miss Tallant,' June said now. 'I'm very curious about that.'

'Well, I was just coming to that,' said Olive. 'You see, Miss Tallant used to teach at my old boarding school, so she knows all about the trouble I got into there, and about me being expelled. Miss Grayling knows too, but she must have seen some good in me, for she agreed to let me have a fresh start here at Malory Towers and promised to keep my secret.'

'Well!' said June, looking quite astonished. 'That explains why Miss Tallant seemed so friendly with your people at half-term. That was one of the things that made us suspect that you were her niece. Now I see that we were quite wrong, and she had already met your people at your old school.' June paused, her expression becoming hard, then went on, 'And I suppose she threatened to give your secret away unless you reported to her on all the fourth form's secrets and wrongdoing.'

Olive nodded miserably, and June's eyes flashed angrily as she said, 'Well, Miss Grayling will be very interested to hear that, and I shall take great pleasure in telling her! Olive, you really are silly! If only you had told us this from the very beginning, Miss Tallant's hold over you would have been broken.'

Olive hung her head, and said in a small voice, 'I couldn't. I felt so ashamed of myself, and I simply couldn't bear to see the scorn on everyone's faces. Oh, June, I started this term with such high hopes! I had made up my mind that I was going to settle down, and make friends, and Father would realise that I wasn't so bad after all, and would let me come home. Then the first person I met on the train was Nora, and she reminded me so much of Annabel that I simply couldn't help being rude to her. And then I found out that Miss Tallant was teaching here, and I realised that there was no point in trying to change.'

'Oh, Olive!' sighed June. 'I daresay one or two of the girls might have been a little shocked when they heard that you had been expelled, but once you had explained everything, they would have understood. And as for Miss Tallant, I feel quite certain that the Head will dismiss her immediately once she finds out what she has been up to.'

'Do you really think so?' said Olive, brightening.

'I do,' said June, getting to her feet. 'And now we had better get you back to the school, for the police are out looking for you, and I expect that Miss Grayling has telephoned your father by now.'

Olive turned pale at this, and gave a groan. 'And he will think that I have caused yet more trouble.'

'Yes, but no doubt he will be so glad that you have been found that you might not get into a row,' said June. 'In fact, I rather think that the only person who is going to get into a row is our dear Miss Tallant.'

Bonnie puts things right

Miss Grayling was most astonished, a few minutes later, when someone knocked on the door of her study, and June entered, followed by a very scared-looking Olive.

After the Head had telephoned the police to tell them that the missing girl had been found, she turned to Olive and said, 'My dear, what on earth made you run away like that? The school has been in an uproar, and your father is dreadfully worried. He is on his way here this very minute.'

'Olive, you must tell Miss Grayling everything, at once,' urged June.

So, haltingly at first, and with much prompting from June, Olive poured out the whole sorry tale.

Miss Grayling listened intently, her brow furrowing as the girl told of the spiteful way her step-sister had behaved. And when Olive spoke of the part Miss Tallant had played in her unhappiness, June noticed with satisfaction that the Head's serene blue eyes grew cold and steely.

'Well, this is a most extraordinary tale!' said Miss Grayling at last. 'Olive, you really should have come to me, or one of the other mistresses, and told us about Miss Tallant's conduct.'

'I know,' said Olive. 'But I thought that you would be certain to believe Miss Tallant's word over mine. Especially as you knew that I had been expelled from my other school for making trouble.'

'Miss Grayling, what is puzzling me is *why* Miss Tallant was so intent on finding out all our secrets,' said June, who had been looking thoughtful. 'Was it just out of spite, or did she have some other motive?'

'I rather think that Miss Tallant wanted to be offered a permanent post at Malory Towers,' said the Head. 'As you know, she is only here temporarily, whilst Miss Hibbert is ill. She has lost no opportunity to point out to me, and the other mistresses, that she thinks Miss Hibbert is a poor teacher and a poor disciplinarian. It must have been a great stroke of luck for her to discover that Olive was here. She was able to use her to find out what you fourth formers were up to, punish you, and earn herself a reputation for being strict and able to keep order.'

'Well!' cried June. 'Of all the nerve! Miss Hibbert is a splendid teacher, a million times better than Miss Tallant. She is just, and fair, her lessons are always interesting, and –'

'Quite so, June,' interrupted Miss Grayling firmly, though there was the hint of a twinkle in her eyes. 'Fortunately I have known Miss Hibbert for very many years, so a few words from a new mistress was certainly not going to change my excellent opinion of her. In fact, I will be telephoning her shortly, to see if she is well enough to come back to Malory Towers before the end of term.'

June and Olive exchanged excited glances. This was good news, and could mean only one thing – the Head was going to dismiss Miss Tallant!

'Now,' said Miss Grayling. 'Your father will be here very shortly, Olive, so I suggest you go and wash your face and hands, and brush your hair before he arrives. Then we need to talk to him about your step-sister's behaviour towards you.'

Olive's shoulders slumped, and she said glumly, 'He won't believe me. Annabel has been very convincing, you see, Miss Grayling.'

'Yes, he will!' cried June suddenly. 'I have an idea! Miss Grayling, may I be excused, please?'

'Of course,' said the Head, looking rather startled. 'Olive, you go as well, and tidy yourself up, then come straight back here.'

Both girls left the Head's study, Olive to go to the nearest bathroom, and June to go to the common-room, where the others were sitting around looking rather gloomy, as they discussed Olive's disappearance.

June burst in and Freddie cried, 'Where on earth have you been, June? We were beginning to think that you had run away too!'

'I went to look for Olive,' said June a little breathlessly, for she had run all the way to the common-room. 'And I found her. She is with the Head now.'

At once the fourth formers besieged June with questions and, as quickly as possible, she told them what had happened. The girls listened in open-mouthed silence, but they had plenty to say when June told them about Miss Tallant.

'Well, I always knew she was a horrid woman, but I had no idea she was that beastly! If only we had known, we might have been able to help poor Olive.'

'And she was scheming to take Miss Hibbert's job from her too! Lucky that the Head is so shrewd, and saw through her.'

'Thank goodness that Miss Grayling is going to dismiss her. Good riddance, I say!'

'Listen, everyone!' broke in June. 'There is another way that we can help Olive. Bonnie, you spoke to Annabel at half-term, didn't you?'

'Yes, you know that I did, for I told you so,' said Bonnie.

'And she told you, quite plainly, that she had deliberately set out to get Olive into trouble, didn't she?' said June.

'That's right,' said Bonnie, nodding.

'Good,' said June. 'Now, Bonnie, I want you to come to Miss Grayling's study with me, and tell Olive's father that. You see, Olive is afraid that he won't believe her, but you are a stranger, and what's more, you don't even *like* Olive, so you have no possible reason to lie!'

Bonnie, looking rather bewildered at the speed with which June rattled all this off, blinked and said, 'Yes, of course I shall. It's very true, I didn't like Olive at all, but as soon as I saw that Annabel was to blame for everything I began to realise that she might not be so bad underneath it all. I shall enjoy telling Olive's father what a mean little beast his step-daughter is.'

And with that, June and Bonnie left the room together. As the door closed behind them, Nora said, 'My goodness, *how* I wish that I could be a fly on the wall in Miss Grayling's study when Bonnie tells Olive's father about Annabel.'

'I'd like to be there when the Head gives Miss Tallant her marching orders,' said Felicity.

'How nice it will be to have good old Miss Hibbert back!'

Miss Grayling was seated behind her desk when June and Bonnie returned to her study, a grim-faced Mr Witherspoon and a tearful Olive sitting opposite her. The interview had not gone well, and Olive's father had brushed aside her explanation that Annabel had been to blame for everything that had gone wrong. Miss Grayling had spoken up for Olive too, but Mr Witherspoon had said gruffly, 'I accept that this Miss Tallant of yours is badly at fault, and I leave you to deal with her as I see fit. But little Annabel is a good girl, and she would never do the things that Olive is accusing her of.'

June and Bonnie arrived outside Miss Grayling's door in time to hear this, for Mr Witherspoon had a booming voice, and, as June knocked at the door, Bonnie pursed her lips.

'Come in,' called the Head, in answer to June's knock.

The two girls went in, and June said politely, 'Please, Miss Grayling, Bonnie has something that she would like to say to Mr Witherspoon.'

Mr Witherspoon looked at Bonnie and frowned. He

was a big, rather serious-looking man, and he said, 'I don't mean to be rude, young lady, but I am here on a very serious matter and I am in no mood for pleasantries.'

Bonnie smiled sweetly at him, and said in her soft voice, 'That's quite all right, Mr Witherspoon. I didn't come here to be pleasant.'

The two grown-ups and Olive looked so taken aback that it was all June could do not to burst out laughing. Mr Witherspoon opened his mouth to retort, but Bonnie spoke first, saying, 'I don't know why you should believe Annabel over your own daughter, but I am here to tell you that Olive is speaking the truth. You see, I spoke to your step-daughter Annabel at half-term, and she boasted to me that she has been doing mean tricks to get Olive into trouble.'

There was a note of doubt in Mr Witherspoon's voice now, as he said, 'Are you sure that you're not saying this to get your friend out of trouble?'

'Olive isn't my friend,' said Bonnie. 'She has been mean and horrible to me since the day we met, because I remind her of Annabel. But I'm not like Annabel at all inside, for I don't lie. And, now that you can see that I have no reason at all to be nice to Olive, I hope that you will believe me.'

Mr Witherspoon looked completely dumbfounded by this, and Miss Grayling said, 'Thank you for coming and telling us this, Bonnie. The two of you may go now.'

June and Bonnie turned, but Mr Witherspoon got to his feet and said, 'Just a minute! I'd like to thank you as well, Bonnie. You're a very outspoken and courageous young lady. And my Olive may not have been very nice to you, but you have been a good friend to her today. And you jolly well put me in my place too! Now I can see that I'm going to have to make things up to Olive, otherwise I shall have you after me again!'

'Bonnie, you were simply splendid!' said June, once they were outside in the corridor. 'Olive should be very grateful to you, and if she isn't, then I, for one, will wash my hands of her!'

But Olive was grateful. Very grateful indeed! She came into the common-room an hour later, her face glowing with pleasure, looking so happy that the others could hardly believe she was the same girl.

She stood on the threshold for a moment, smiling shyly round, then, spotting Bonnie, she made straight for her, and gave the surprised girl a great big hug.

'Bonnie, I simply can't thank you enough!' she cried. 'Everything has come right, and it's all thanks to you.'

Bonnie smiled and said slyly, 'I didn't do too badly for a silly little doll, did I?'

Olive flushed and said, 'I could kick myself for calling you that. I take it back, and I apologise. Please say that you forgive me!'

'You're forgiven,' said Bonnie. 'But only if you tell us what happened with your father.'

'He was quite overcome with remorse,' said Olive. 'And simply couldn't apologise enough for doubting my word and believing Annabel all the time. He is going to talk to my step-mother when he gets home, and Annabel is in for the scolding of her life tomorrow.'

'Well, she certainly deserves it,' said Susan. 'I just hope that she learns something from it, and changes her ways.'

'She had better, for Father said that he isn't going to stand any nonsense from her,' said Olive with a grin. 'And the best of it is, that I am to go home when term ends, and go back to my old day school.'

'Well, I like that!' said Pam, in dismay. 'You've just changed for the better, and gone all friendly and jolly, and now you tell us that you're leaving!'

'I daresay you will all be glad to see the back of me,' said Olive rather gruffly. 'I can't blame you, for I've been quite unbearable.'

'Yes, you have,' said June in her usual blunt manner. 'But at least we know that there was a reason for it. And we don't want you becoming unbearable again, for this new, happy Olive is much more likeable than the old one, and she is the one we want to spend the rest of the term with.'

'Hear, hear!' cried Felicity.

'Thanks awfully,' said Olive, looking quite pretty now that she was smiling and her eyes were shining with happiness. 'I promise that I shan't go back to my old ways.'

'Well, we're jolly glad to hear it,' said Nora, who had also suffered badly from Olive's rudeness.

Olive remembered this now, and said, 'I owe you an apology too, Nora, and you, Felicity, and ... oh, it will probably take me the whole night if I apologise to everyone one by one, so I'll just say a great big SORRY to you all!'

The others laughed at this, and Olive said, 'I say, Miss Tallant was walking towards Miss Grayling's study when I left. I shouldn't be a bit surprised if she's packing her bags this very minute.'

A great cheer went up at this, and Felicity said, 'What a day it's been! But Miss Tallant leaving will just round it off perfectly.'

The Christmas concert

'Come along, everyone! Places, please!' called Susan.

It was the afternoon before the end-of-term concert, and the fourth formers were having a dress rehearsal for their play.

'Doesn't everything look splendid?' said Felicity happily.

'Yes, the scenery looks absolutely super,' said Sylvia.

'And Bonnie has done a marvellous job with the costumes,' said Susan. 'I don't see how our play can fail to be a hit.'

'It's going to be a wonderful ending to the term,' said Felicity. 'At last everything seems to be going right for us. Olive has changed her ways and become one of us now, Miss Tallant has gone, Miss Hibbert is back and everything is working out perfectly!'

Miss Tallant had left Malory Towers the morning after Olive had run away, and the fourth formers had watched her go from their common-room window.

'Good riddance!' Freddie had said with satisfaction.

'Yes, she is undoubtedly the most unpopular mistress Malory Towers has ever had,' Felicity had said. 'I, for one, won't miss her.'

Sylvia, released from the San by Matron, had added,

'Now perhaps you can understand why I didn't want to admit that she is my aunt. I feel quite ashamed to be related to her. Especially now that I know how she treated poor Olive.'

Olive had clapped Sylvia on the back and said, 'There's no need for *you* to be ashamed, Sylvia, old girl. It wasn't your fault.'

Miss Hibbert had taken a keen interest in the fourth formers' play, but unlike Miss Tallant she had not pushed herself forward or tried to take over. Instead, she had let it be known that she was willing to help if she was needed, and had remained in the background.

'Because Miss Hibbert is a jolly good teacher,' Susan had said. 'And she understands that we are going to learn far more if we do this for ourselves.'

Now the actors trooped on to the stage, and the three producers felt a thrill of pride.

There was Lucy in her teddy-bear costume and Julie, dressed as the toy soldier. Little Molly looked very sweet in her white nightdress, while Pam, wearing a grey wig and an apron, made a very convincing old lady. As for Nora, she looked very pretty indeed in her fairy costume, and Bonnie fussed round her, arranging the skirt and making sure that the wings were in position.

At last everyone was ready, and Susan called out, 'Righto, we are going to do the whole play from beginning to end, so I hope that everyone is word perfect. Olive, are you ready, just in case anyone forgets her lines?'

Olive – a cheerful, friendly Olive – had volunteered to

act as prompter, and was sitting in the wings now with her script at the ready.

'I'm here, Susan!' she called cheerily.

And the rehearsal began. It wasn't *quite* perfect, for Julie tripped over during the dance, Pam forgot one of her lines and Mary, at the piano, dropped her music on the floor and lost her place. But the most worrying thing was Molly. She knew all her lines perfectly, and didn't make any mistakes, but she had been suffering from a sore throat and her voice was little more than a croak.

'Oh dear!' said Felicity, sounding very worried. 'I wouldn't be surprised if Molly lost her voice altogether by tomorrow.'

'Don't say that!' begged Susan. 'Why, if that happens we shan't be able to perform our play, for no one could possibly learn all of Molly's lines and take her place at such short notice.'

'I'm sure that she will be perfectly fine,' said Sylvia, trying her hardest to sound optimistic. 'Why, I had a sore throat myself just recently, but after a couple of days in the San I was as right as rain.'

'But we don't have a couple of days,' said Felicity. 'Our play is tomorrow!'

But, as the day wore on, poor Molly's throat became steadily worse, until she could hardly speak at all, and after tea Miss Williams came to the common-room, with bad news.

'Girls, I'm awfully sorry, but I have just heard that Molly has been taken to the San. Miss Grayling has telephoned her parents and, as it is the last day of term tomorrow, they are coming to take her home in the morning.'

There was consternation at this, of course. Everyone felt terribly sorry for Molly, for they knew how much she had wanted her mother and father to see her perform. But they were also very concerned about their play.

'June, you must do it!' said Felicity. 'You have a better memory than anyone in the form, and if anyone can learn the lines in time you can.'

'I might have a good memory, but I couldn't possibly learn all those lines in time,' said June, quite horrified. 'What about asking Molly's friend Harriet? I know that she helped Molly to learn her lines, so she must know them very well.'

'Yes, but Harriet can't act for toffee,' said Sylvia. 'And she's far too tall to play a little girl.'

'Yes, the costume would never fit her,' said Bonnie. 'And I don't have time to make another.'

'Then what is to be done?' asked Felicity in despair. 'We have all worked so hard on this play. We simply can't abandon it now.'

'There's no question of abandoning it,' said Susan, a determined note in her voice. 'Olive, you will have to play the part of Amelia.'

'Me?' squeaked Olive. 'Oh, Susan, I couldn't possibly!'

'You must,' said Susan. 'You know the part, for you have been acting as prompter. And you're only slightly taller than Molly, so the costume should fit you.'

'But we don't even know if Olive can act,' pointed out Sylvia.

'Well, we'll soon find out,' said Susan. 'Olive, stand up and do the scene where the fairy doll comes to life, with Nora.'

Rather reluctantly, Olive got to her feet, and she and Nora acted out the scene. Olive was very hesitant at first, and her voice shook. But gradually she became more confident, and proved to the others that she wasn't a bad little actress at all.

'We're saved!' cried Felicity joyously, as the little scene came to an end and the others clapped. 'Olive, you'll be marvellous.'

'I don't know that I will,' said Olive, turning pink at the applause. 'I mean to say, it's one thing to act out a little scene in here, in front of you others, but it will be quite different standing up on stage in front of an audience full of parents and mistresses and doing a whole play.'

'The whole form will be in your debt if you do it, Olive,' said Susan.

'Yes, and think how pleased and proud your father and step-mother will be when they watch you playing one of the leading roles,' said Pam.

'And it will be one in the eye for that nasty little Annabel,' said Bonnie. 'She won't like the fact that you are the centre of attention, for once, and not her.'

Olive laughed at this, and said, 'Well, it seems as if I have three very good reasons for doing it. And, apart from my nerves, I can't think of a single reason to refuse.'

Of course, the fourth formers were thrilled to hear this, and everyone gathered round Olive, patting her on the back.

'Good show, Olive! You've really saved our bacon.'

'You'll be absolutely super, you'll see.'

'Yes, you'll bring the house down.'

'And perhaps we can fit an extra rehearsal in tomorrow morning,' said Felicity. 'Just so that you feel more confident.'

Just then the bell went for bedtime and Susan said, 'Come along, everyone. We all need to get a good night's sleep, for we have a very busy day tomorrow.'

And it certainly was a busy day! There were no proper lessons, for the three top forms were busy with preparations for the show. The lower forms felt very happy to have a free day, and spent their time peeping into the hall to watch last-minute rehearsals, and getting under everyone's feet.

'Silly kids,' said Susan rather loftily, after she had sent two giggling first formers packing for laughing at Lucy in her teddy-bear costume. 'Righto, let's try that scene once more.'

Lunch and tea that day were very makeshift affairs, for the kitchen staff were fully occupied with the sumptuous supper that they were preparing for the parents that evening.

'Bread and jam,' said Nora in disgust, at the tea-table. 'I say, Bonnie, where did you get that cake from? No one else has a piece!'

'I slipped into the kitchen and Cook gave it to me,' said Bonnie, with her angelic smile. 'I told her that I was simply *starving* and felt quite faint.'

'Trust you to get your own way, Bonnie!' said Olive. But she was laughing, and there was no bitterness in her voice, as there would have been a short while ago. Once again, the girls marvelled at how much she had changed.

'I feel quite sorry that Olive will be leaving tomorrow,' said Felicity to Susan. 'She really is a good sort now that she has settled down.'

'Yes,' said Susan. 'It seems funny now to think that none of us were keen on the two new girls when they first started. But both of them have turned out fine.'

'Yes, Sylvia even seems to have found her sense of humour now that her aunt has gone,' said Felicity. 'Do you know, she actually told me a joke yesterday!'

Susan laughed, and said, 'She'll be playing tricks on Mam'zelle Dupont before we know where we are.'

At last it was seven o'clock and time for the concert to begin. The parents had already arrived and taken their seats in the big hall, along with the mistresses and the lower school. The fourth formers sat with them for the first part of the concert, for they were on last, and they watched the sixth formers perform their Christmas readings.

'Awfully boring,' murmured Amy to Bonnie. 'I'm surprised the parents haven't fallen asleep!'

The fourth formers clapped politely as the reading drew to a close, then, as the fifth formers walked on to the stage, they slipped quietly from their seats and went backstage, to prepare for their play.

Bonnie darted about all over the place, making sure that everyone looked as perfect as possible, while Amy had graciously agreed to help with the hair and make-up. The three producers dealt ably with attacks of last-minute nerves, keeping everyone's spirits up, while the actors themselves muttered their lines under their breath, quite determined that they were not going to forget a single word.

At last the last bars of 'Silent Night' faded away, the sound of clapping could be heard, and it was time for their play to begin. The scenery was already in place, and the actors walked on to the stage.

There were gasps of delight from the first and second formers as they stared at Nora, dressed as a fairy, Lucy sitting on the floor in her teddy-bear costume, and Julie, standing to attention as the toy soldier.

Then Olive, as Amelia, appeared, looking rather shy and scared, but when she spoke the play's opening lines, her nerves seemed to disappear.

Miss Grayling, in the front row, glanced across at Mr and Mrs Witherspoon, smiling to herself when she saw the proud looks on their faces. Mr Witherspoon looked as if he was about to burst! Beside them sat a scowling Annabel, who didn't seem to be enjoying the little play at all!

But Annabel was the only one, for the rest of the audience enjoyed it enormously, and agreed among themselves that it was the best part of the concert.

'Everything is going marvellously,' said Felicity to Susan, as the two of them, with Sylvia, watched from the wings. 'Olive is giving a splendid performance.'

'I knew that she would,' said Susan happily. 'And Nora looks lovely.'

'I say, look at Mam'zelle, in the second row,' whispered Sylvia. 'She's thoroughly enjoying herself!'

Nora and Olive were acting out one of the humorous moments in the play that June and Freddie had written, and the audience were laughing very loudly. But no one laughed louder than Mam'zelle, whose cries of mirth made heads turn in her direction.

'Dear old Mam'zelle!' said Felicity fondly.

Then came the song and dance routine, which almost brought the house down, and at last the play was over. There was silence for a moment, then clapping and cheering broke out from the audience, and, thrilled, Susan said, 'They liked it! They didn't cheer like that for the fifth and sixth formers.'

'They more than liked it – they loved it!' said Felicity happily.

'Yes, I think we've done a jolly good job as producers,' said Sylvia. 'If I do –'

'IF YOU DO SAY SO YOURSELF!' chorused Felicity and Susan, then the three girls burst into laughter.

The cast took another bow, then the curtain came down and everyone ran off-stage, as the applause died away.

'We had better help them get changed, then we can go and join our people for supper,' said Susan. 'I'm jolly hungry, for lunch and tea were pretty poor.'

June and Freddie were also backstage, helping to hang up the costumes as the girls who had acted in the play got changed.

'I think that we can count that as a success,' said Freddie happily.

'Yes, and that is largely due to you and June,' said Felicity. 'The jokes that you wrote made everyone laugh.'

June seemed unusually quiet and pensive, and Susan asked, 'Anything wrong, June?'

'No, I'm just rather sorry that this term is almost at an end,' said June with a sigh. 'It hasn't all been good, but on the whole it has been fun. Next term won't be, for we shall all be studying for School Cert. And after that, we go up into the fifth. No tricks, no jokes, and no feasts then! We shall have to go all serious and dignified.'

'Well, we have a couple more terms in which to learn to be serious and dignified,' said Felicity with a laugh. 'And I daresay we shall find other ways of having fun. My sister Darrell and your cousin Alicia certainly did.'

'Yes, that's true,' said June, brightening a little. 'Alicia was as bold and bad as I am when she was younger. Yet she turned into a good, responsible top former. But she kept her sense of fun too, and that is what I want to do.'

'You will,' Felicity assured her. 'I can't imagine a serious, sober June!'

'Home for the hols tomorrow!' said Susan happily. 'What fun it will be, and the concert was a simply super way to end the term.'

'Yes,' said Felicity, with a contented sigh. 'A marvellous way to say goodbye to Malory Towers.'

And now we must say goodbye to Malory Towers too, for the moment, but we will come back when Felicity and her friends are in the fifth form.

Don't miss the next Malory Towers story ...

Enid Blyton

Malory Towers

Fun and Games

Written by Pamela Cox

There's tension in the fifth form – Millicent
keeps arranging orchestra rehearsals to clash
with June's tennis matches. But the girls
soon find there's more to worry about when
belongings start disappearing from dorms.

Don't miss the next Malory Towers story ...

Enid Blyton®

Malory Towers

Secrets

Written by Pamela Cox

Malory Towers is full of secrets this term.
How did Daffy pull off her latest prank?
What did Mam'zelle find in her handbag?
And why is the girls' new form-mate
so familiar?

Look out for more classic school stories from

ST CLARE'S

Schooldays at St Clare's are never dull
for twins Pat and Isabel O'Sullivan
and their friends.

There's mischief at St Clare's!

More classic stories from the world of

Enid Blyton

The Naughtiest Girl

Elizabeth Allen is spoilt and selfish. When she's
sent away to boarding school she makes up her mind
to be the naughtiest pupil there's ever been! But
Elizabeth soon finds out that being bad isn't as
simple as it seems. Thre are ten brilliant books
about the Naughtiest Girl to enjoy.

How to Read a Paper

The basics of evidence-based medicine

FOURTH EDITION

In November 1995, my friend Ruth Holland, book reviews editor of the British Medical Journal, suggested that I write a book to demystify the important but often inaccessible subject of evidence-based medicine. She provided invaluable comments on earlier drafts of the manuscript, but was tragically killed in a train crash on 8th August 1996. This book is dedicated to her memory.